Praise for *The Ice House*

"*The Ice House* is a tour de force that sweeps readers into a symphony of powerfully drawn characters, all of whom have been wounded in ways that both cripple and embolden them. This novel is an intercontinental family saga and an exploration of blue-collar life, but at its core it's a very good novel that asks us to consider the lengths we'll go to in order to save the things that matter most: a company, a loved one, ourselves."

—Wiley Cash, author of *The Last Ballad* and
A Land More Kind Than Home

"The kind of novel that makes you sad when it's over because you know you won't be able to be in that world any longer."

—*Advance Reading Copy*

"A beautiful character-driven novel . . . vividly realized."

—*Indie Picks Magazine*

"*The Ice House* offers all the pleasures of the novel—robust characters we worry about and root for, a story that deepens and intrigues, language that charms and surprises, and even some rare and welcome humor. It does all this in a setting unusual to a novel—the world of work, in this case, a family ice making business in Florida. How does Laura Lee Smith keep that small, cold world so large and ardent hearted? *The Ice House* is a marvel of a novel."

—Beth Ann Fennelly, Poet Laureate of Mississippi
and author of *Heating & Cooling*

"Insight, good humor, and generous hearts abound in this . . . saga of starting afresh." —*Kirkus Reviews*

THE ICE HOUSE

Also by Laura Lee Smith

Heart of Palm

THE ICE HOUSE

A NOVEL BY

LAURA LEE SMITH

Grove Press
New York

Published simultaneously in Canada
Printed in the United States of America

First Grove Atlantic hardcover edition: December 2017
First Grove Atlantic paperback edition: December 2018

ISBN 978-0-8021-2864-5
eISBN 978-0-8021-8931-8

Library of Congress Cataloging-in-Publication data is available for this title.

Grove Press
an imprint of Grove Atlantic
154 West 14th Street
New York, NY 10011

Distributed by Publishers Group West

groveatlantic.com

18 19 20 21   10 9 8 7 6 5 4 3 2 1

For Ken and Judy, who gave me yesterday.
And for Iain and Gemma, who give me tomorrow.

Between melting and freezing
The soul's sap quivers.
—T.S. Eliot, "Little Gidding"

THE ICE HOUSE

ONE

Johnny MacKinnon developed a fierce headache just before dawn. He'd slept poorly: spells of fitful dreaming and heart-skittering wakefulness. Now he lay still and chilled, watching through half-opened eyes as gray October light pushed into the bedroom. In his head: jackhammers. Pile drivers. My God.

He looked to his right and found the bed empty. Pauline had already risen. He closed his eyes and listened; she was moving around the kitchen downstairs. There was the soft thunk of the refrigerator door and Pauline's voice, indistinct but lilting, speaking to the dog. There was the music of spoons and ceramic mugs on tile. There was the faint rushing of a compressor. The air-conditioning temperature was set too low. Johnny found it all immeasurably irksome. He was hurting, and he was cold.

The only way out of it is through it. He'd read that somewhere. He willed himself out of bed and made for the bathroom, where he swallowed three ibuprofen tablets with handfuls of water from the tap and took a shower while waiting impatiently for relief. It arrived tentatively. The pounding in his head resolved slowly to a dull echo. He dressed and descended the stairs. Then, standing at the kitchen sink with a cup of coffee, he immediately found himself caught in a nettlesome conversation with Pauline, who thought they ought to give Johnny's son Corran a call today. It was Corran's thirtieth birthday, she reminded him. But Johnny wasn't keen.

"I have a headache," he said. "And I need to get to the factory."

"Well, maybe later then. Did you take something? Ibuprofen? Maybe you need to eat." Pauline was standing next to the kitchen table, rigging an iPod to the waistband of her shorts in preparation for a run. "Eat and feel better. And then we could call him. Or you could call him on the drive in."

"I took something. I'm not hungry."

"Just to say happy birthday. Try to get past this thing."

Johnny regarded his reflection in the kitchen window and didn't answer immediately. The air conditioner finally sighed to rest, and in the sudden silence he could hear the indistinct bickering of fractious gulls, the faint thumping of waves on sand. Two blocks away, the Atlantic Ocean advanced, retreated, advanced.

"I don't think so, Pauline."

"But there's the baby now," Pauline said. "You're a grandfather. Don't you want to mend the fence?"

"There's no fence to mend," Johnny said. "Corran's seen to that." An exaggeration, perhaps, but metaphorically sound.

"He's clean now. It's what we wanted. You could just swallow your pride and give him a call," Pauline said.

"He needs to apologize to us. He could give *me* a call."

Pauline always said stubbornness was the same as stupidity. "One day you'll be sorry," she told Johnny. "Your only child. One day you'll regret this."

"One day *he'll* regret it," Johnny said. Pauline threw up her hands.

"He's your son. And if *I* can forgive him, *you* ought to be able to."

"Pauline," Johnny said. "I can't. Tough love. You wouldn't understand."

That stopped her. She hated that, to be reminded that she wasn't Corran's *real* mother, that she wasn't anybody's real mother, and therefore couldn't possibly understand how any parent could turn his back on his own child. Johnny didn't mean to hurt her. But he couldn't discuss it anymore.

"Lord have mercy," she said, her injury quickly turning to annoyance. She moved to the center of the kitchen and started to do toe raises. "I swear to heaven, Johnny, you could piss off the Pope." Sometimes—like when Pauline was irritated with him, for example—the North Florida argot he always found so arousing became even more pronounced. When he'd first arrived in Jacksonville from Scotland at twenty-seven, he'd been astounded at the local dialect—it was *real!*—and to meet someone of Pauline's beauty and grace and hear the tangy drawl of her voice had been almost too much. The first time he'd ever heard her say "y'all" he'd immediately developed an erection. There were moments even now, all these years later, when the sound of Pauline's voice still had this effect on him, though this morning, with her insistence that he reopen this barrel of emotional monkeys with Corran, was admittedly not one of them. An *apology.* He'd made the point to Pauline a thousand times. He'd wait for an apology from Corran before taking a single step back from the line.

"I'm sorry," he said to her now, "I only meant—"

"Oh, quit," she said. She raised up on her toes again. "I know what you meant. Anyway, *I'm* going to call him."

"I'd rather you didn't."

Pauline put her hands on her hips and stared at him as she bobbed up and down, flexing her calves. He watched a flicker of resistance pass over her face—God forbid he try to tell her what to do!—but he kept his gaze neutral and added "please," and it seemed to work. Her face softened a bit. She settled flat on her feet. She bent one knee, drew a leg up behind her, and clasped her foot to her backside in a move that she'd explained to him as a quad stretch but that always looked to him like an awkward but slightly erotic jackknife.

Pauline had become a runner only a few years ago. She ran on the beach at low tide, when the sand was wide and flat. She was usually in training for some race or other, and she maintained a meticulous log of times and dates and pace rates in her iPhone. At fifty, she was three years younger than Johnny, a point she rarely allowed him to forget, but even with this advantage she was still, in his opinion, aging past the athletic ability to which she now aspired. When she was in her thirties and forties, she was softer and more pliable (*fat,* she would correct him), but since she'd started running her muscles were steely, unyielding. He had very mixed feelings about all this.

"You don't need to train at all," he told her one afternoon recently, when she came in from a long run red-faced and limping. "We own an ice factory. Just come out on the shop floor and throw ice with me for a few weeks, you'll be fit as a fiddle."

"Throwing ice is not the same as athletic training," Pauline said.

"Let me see you throw two bags up onto a pallet. One. Let me see you throw one bag." Pauline narrowed her eyes and didn't answer.

"Fine," she said now. "Don't call your son, and I won't, either." She stretched the opposite quadriceps and then stood still and regarded Johnny somberly. "But I just think it's sad."

"It's sad," Johnny agreed. Though really, "sad" didn't even begin to describe it. Over the past decade, Johnny had paid for his son to attend three different private programs for heroin rehabilitation: two in Scotland and one—the real doozy—a stay at an exorbitant inpatient facility in Jacksonville that was paid for with a second mortgage on the MacKinnons' house. Corran had relapsed within a few months of each treatment. It wasn't that Johnny blamed his son for falling victim to addiction. But last Christmas, Corran came from Glasgow to Florida for a holiday visit and went on a bender that culminated in a violent row upon the discovery that he'd stolen Pauline's wedding ring for drug money. Oh, God, wasn't *that* quite the circus? Denial. Defensiveness. Rage and accusations. *Enough.* Johnny put Corran on the first flight back to Scotland and hadn't spoken with him since. Now, word from Glasgow via Johnny's ex-wife was that their son, inspired by the birth of a child, had recently cold-turkeyed at a public clinic. Which was a lovely thing, if it was true. Even more if it was permanent. But Johnny was afraid to hope.

"All right. I'm going down to the beach to run," Pauline said. She'd stopped stretching and was pulling her blond hair up into a tight ponytail. "Can you feed the General?" General San Jose was the geriatric dachshund who had lived in their house for fourteen years. The old dog slept in the bed with Johnny and Pauline, though Johnny had been trying to insist for years that he should at least be relegated to the foot of the mattress and not be allowed to burrow directly between them, which he usually ended up doing in the middle of the night anyway. The General came downstairs once every morning to eat a bowl of kibble and poke around the backyard for a few minutes, and then he bumped back up the stairs and spent the rest of the day in bed. In cooler months Pauline left a heating pad under the duvet. It was an out-of-control situation. Johnny had given up. The General was now gazing at him skeptically.

"I'll feed you, you fat old thing," Johnny said. "Quit worrying."

"Obdurate," Pauline said. She'd stopped near the back door. "What?"

"That was a word I got this morning in my game. That's what you are, Johnny. Obdurate."

"Well, that sounds a wee bit ugly, Pauline," Johnny said.

"And do you want to know another word I got the other day that reminded me of you?" she said.

"I don't think so."

"Truculent."

"I don't know what that means," he said, though he did.

"I'll leave it to you to look it up, then."

"I've got a word for *you*, Pauline," he said.

"Oh?" she tipped her head to one side and raised an eyebrow.

"Grand."

"Grand?" She scowled.

"Yes, grand."

"That makes me sound huge. And old."

"I mean *grand,* like we use it in Scotland. As in brilliant. And stately. Queenly."

"Those are even worse! What am I, a cruise ship? A cathedral?"

He rolled his eyes. "I can't win," he said.

"Word to the wise, Johnny," she said. "Ain't a woman on God's green earth wants to be called grand. You know they named a canyon for that word, don't you?"

"You're not grand, Pauline," he said. "You're nongrand. Antigrand." She suffered a reluctant grin. "I'll be gone by the time you get back," he added.

"Fine. Grand. I'll see you at the factory later," Pauline said. She waggled her fingers at him. Then she wedged in a pair of earbuds and banged out the back door. Johnny turned back to the kitchen window and watched her run away: shoulders hunched, head down, flesh pressing tight against overpriced Lycra. She *was* grand. If he could see her face he knew she'd be scowling fiercely against the pain of her own exertion. Such a serious business. She reached the beach access and disappeared beyond a dune. Oh, Pauline. It was a mystery beyond reason; he'd never understand how he'd won her.

Johnny fed the General and took him to the backyard. While waiting for the dog to do his business, he checked his phone and found a text from Pauline that she'd evidently sent while running. How did she do that? *Don't forget atty coming to factory this week,* it said. *Want to see work logs. For OSHA. Remember?*

Well, now, there was one more thing to add to what was becoming a thoroughly discomforting morning. Johnny had been rather proud of himself for successfully beating back thoughts of the United States Occupational Safety and Health

Administration throughout the entire weekend. Leave it to Pauline to bring it back to mind on Monday morning. The Bold City Ice Plant, which they'd owned for nearly twenty years, was in the process of preparing an appeal against federal citations levied following a harrowing ammonia tank rupture that had occurred over the summer. There'd been no injuries, miraculously, though clearly the potential for harm or even loss of life had been significant. OSHA didn't like it one bit. The investigation was quick, the safety citations were hefty, and the associated fines, if they stuck, were hovering near three-quarters of a million dollars. Unfathomable! Bold City Ice would never survive a financial hit of that magnitude; the success of the looming appeal was critical. OSHA claimed negligent maintenance on the ammonia tank; Johnny MacKinnon claimed bullshit. And while the expensive attorneys Pauline had signed up were attempting reassurances (throwing around phrases Johnny found intentionally vague, like "nonculpable confidence" and "derivative innocence"), the whole calamity was not something that he was in danger of forgetting about anytime soon. He felt a moment's pique at Pauline for assuming he would.

He texted back a terse *Yep* and went to put the phone in his pocket, but before he did his eye fell on the date depicted on the phone's welcome screen: October 25. Yes, there it was: Corran's birthday indeed.

Don't you want to mend the fence?

It was hot in the backyard, must have been already pushing ninety, and here it was not quite seven in the morning. General San Jose was nosing in the Mexican bluebell. The gulls on the beach were still squabbling, their cries distant but clear through the pines. Johnny pocketed the phone and sat down on the back step while something like an aura washed over him, not quite dizziness, but the opposite: a startling clarity, as though everything was suddenly rendering itself at a higher resolution. His headache clanged with renewed fervor for a moment, then almost as quickly subsided to a mild pulse. He waited until the General was pushing at the kitchen door, then he went inside, gathered his keys, locked up the house, and headed for ice.

For almost a year, Johnny had asked only one thing of Corran: an apology. He was willing to wait as long as it took.

One day you'll regret this.

Johnny knew, of course, that Pauline was rarely wrong. But this time was an exception. Tough love. It's what Corran needed.

Thirty minutes later, Johnny was gaining slowly on the approach to the Acosta Bridge, pushing stubbornly through the familiar traffic-stoppered I-95 bottleneck that was his daily commute from the house on Watchers Island to the ice factory in downtown Jacksonville. The forecast had promised rain, but the morning thus far was searingly, frustratingly bright. In the distance, the city's northern skyline, a loose half dozen high-rises, hugged the St. Johns like corset bones. Jacksonville, Bold New City of the South—city of bridges and Baptists, of Navy bases and nor'easters, of breweries and boats and the hot, holy temple of the fifty-yard line at EverBank Field. Engine rumbling. Radio chattering. Thumping of bass somewhere behind. And through it all, the faint smell of coffee, borne on a hot wind from the Maxwell House factory two miles up the river. Winter, spring, summer, now fall—always, in Jacksonville, the stubborn tinge of burned coffee. It was not something you could get used to.

Johnny crested an overpass and looked south, where the narrow funnel of the river opened wide and the banks winked with the reflections of stately white homes fronting the water in San Marco and Ortega. Where the rich people lived, Pauline always said. A relative statement, Johnny maintained; after all, it wasn't as if Pauline herself had ever known want. No, *rich*-rich, she would clarify. Old South rich. Not *working* rich. Different thing entirely. Johnny had to take her word for it. Johnny had spent the first half of his life in the biting poverty of a cold Scottish slum, so richness of any type was not a world he knew well. Well, fine. Better than working poor, he told Pauline. Johnny had seen the other side.

The ice factory was located in Little Silver, one of the oldest and coarsest neighborhoods in the sprawling city of Jacksonville. Bold City Ice was the biggest player on the Little Silver tax roll, and sometimes Johnny wondered if he and Pauline were keeping afloat not just the factory but the whole community, such as it was: a tight basket weave of avenues crowded with historic but decaying houses that were nothing but termites holding hands, really. Back in the '90s there'd been talk of revitalization for Little Silver. New streets, for example, or at least repairs to the potholes in the old ones. More incentives for business owners to set up shop. Maybe replumb the drainage system so the residents didn't have to wade through standing water and mosquito larvae every time it rained. But it hadn't happened. The money went to other things: crape myrtle giveaways for the Riverside districts, a new library downtown, even a new jaguar exhibit at the zoo (*Go Jags!*). Money attracted money. And Little Silver continued to molder.

Johnny drove down King Street and had to negotiate a narrow passage between a rusted-out Impala and a slow-moving

street sweeper before he could pull into the Bold City Ice lot.
He parked and entered the admin wing. The factory lobby was
quiet, and at first glance it appeared there was no one stationed
at the reception desk, which wasn't particularly unusual. They'd
been having trouble keeping the position filled, and Johnny had
almost grown used to the vacant chair and the irksome sight of
the desk cluttered with the day's rubber-banded packets of mail,
stranded overnight packages, and the marooned calling cards of
thwarted equipment reps who'd been hoping for a sales entrée
and who had gotten, instead, a lobby barren as Gobi.

Then last spring they hired Rosa Kaplan, the eighteen-year-
old daughter of Pauline's assistant Claire, to man the reception
desk. Rosa, sweet kid but a little dim, if anybody was being
honest about it, had graduated from the arts high school last
spring with an impressive sculptor's hand but with a less-than-
impressive GPA or attendant college outlook. Claire had been in
a near-panic over what to do with the girl until Pauline stepped
in and suggested that Rosa take on the receptionist's role, at
least for the summer, until the junior college started sessions.
That it was now October and Rosa had yet to make any move
toward higher education was not a topic that anyone had been
motivated to broach. And really, Rosa was doing a suitable job
in reception—not counting the time she wasted batting her eyes
at the boys on the ice crew, and with one in particular: Owen
Vickers, a feckless delivery driver and a garden-variety jackass,
if you asked Johnny. Every time Johnny came through the lobby
and found Vickers slouched over the reception desk, leering at
Rosa, he wanted to puke. "You're not busy enough?" he'd bark
at Vickers. "You need more to do?" Rosa would bite her lip and
Vickers would slink back off toward the loading bays.

But now the receptionist's station was empty again. Johnny was about to proceed through the lobby to the factory floor when he heard a string of obscenities and approached reception to find Rosa—or Rosa's blue-jeaned backside, rather—emerging from underneath the desk. She sat back on her heels and dangled a dusty wireless router in front of her.

"Damn router!" she said. "I hate this freaking thing!" Her face was red with exertion, and her hair was coated with dust. She'd been putting on weight since getting out of high school, and Johnny was a little sad to see that the first glimpses of harried womanhood had begun to stake a claim on a face he'd always thought of as nothing short of cherubic.

"Settle down there, kidda, you'll hurt yourself," Johnny said.

"I'm going to hurt this bleeping router, is what I'm going to do." Rosa struggled to her feet and pitched the router onto the desk. "Or the people who made this router, that's who. Who makes a router that won't—that won't even *route*?" She wiped the sweat from her brow and spit a strand of hair out of her mouth. "Do you know where Pauline is?" she said. "She needs to sign these I-9's on the new hires."

"Running. She'll be in later. Here. I'll sign the forms."

Rosa shook her head. "They need Pauline's signature."

Now this was irritating. Years ago, when he and Pauline first bought the ice plant from her father, they'd drawn up an elaborately detailed business plan which included an organizational chart that presumably gave each of them equal leadership. It wasn't as if Johnny—a self-taught journeyman with a high school degree—had been to business school. How did he know what all the terminology meant? But there it was in the business plan:

At Bold City Ice, Pauline was CEO, and Johnny was COO. His understanding, at the time, was that the "C"-level titles implied parallel authority. Not that it really mattered, of course. It was just that over the years it became apparent to Johnny that some of the administrative staff seemed to assume that Pauline was the actual boss of the ice venture, while he was more like the lead roustabout in a stationary circus.

Once, out of curiosity, Johnny googled the titles and was surprised to discover that a chief executive officer was widely considered to have greater authority than a chief operating officer. Well, bollocks. He wondered if Pauline knew that when they wrote the business plan. Ah, not that it made a real difference. To his own operations staff, to the workers making the ice, there was no issue. Out on the factory floor, he was the boss. He was "Ice," as the crew called him. But these folks inside. Now *they* were another story.

"I'll sign Pauline's name, then," he said to Rosa, reaching for the forms.

"Forge them? That's dishonest."

"It's fine. I'm half-owner of the company. Hasn't Pauline ever signed something for me?"

"No. She always wants things done right."

"And I don't?"

"Well, you're suggesting we forge government documents. That's dishonest."

"Honesty is overrated, Rosa," Johnny said, just as Roy Grassi, the factory's lead operations engineer, banged into the lobby, shouldering a ladder. "And if anybody ever asks you where you heard that," Johnny continued, "you lie and tell them it was Roy Grassi."

"Roy Grassi told her what?" Roy said.

"Told her she's under the mistaken impression that my wife is the boss of me," Johnny said. "Now give me those papers," he said to Rosa.

Rosa rolled her eyes. "Oh, fine," she said. She handed him the forms. "I'll just tell Mrs. MacKinnon you pressured me to commit a felony."

"Now it's 'Mrs. MacKinnon'?"

Rosa sighed. "My mother tells me I have to behave more professionally."

Johnny signed the forms and handed them back to Rosa, who accepted them grudgingly.

"Pffft," she said. "Anyway, you had two calls. One from Southeastern Distribution. And one from a lady named Sharon. She sounded Scottish." Rosa exaggerated an accent on the word "Scottish," dropping the t's in the middle so it came out *"Scaw-ish."* She handed Johnny two slips of paper with phone numbers written on them. "Like, maybe a relative?" He looked at the numbers, which were fuzzy and out of focus. He rubbed his eyes.

"My ex-wife," he said.

But Rosa had lost interest in Johnny. She picked up the router and called across the lobby to where Roy was now struggling out the front door with the ladder. "Roy," she said. "This router's broke."

"Take it up with your mom, Rosa," Roy said. "I'm busy." He paused and looked back at Johnny. "I know why Southeastern's calling, by the way," he said. "They got a bug up their backside about pallet heights. Ed's gonna come pester you about it."

"Brilliant," Johnny said. "Looking forward to it."

"Oh, and Pauline texted me. She told me to remind you that the OSHA lawyers want to come this week about working on the appeal."

"I know," Johnny said. "*Och,* I know."

Roy grunted and bumbled out the door.

"What did she want, Rosa?" Johnny said.

"Who?"

"Sharon."

"Oh," Rosa said, squinting at him while she tried to retrieve it from her memory. "She didn't say. Just that you should call her back. Oh, and the Southeastern guy? *Rude.*"

Johnny made his way to his office. He dialed the number at Southeastern Distribution but got voicemail. He left a message. Then he dialed Sharon's number but reached voicemail there, too. Didn't anyone answer phones anymore? He listened to the familiar cadence of Sharon's voice on the recording. "I'm not here right now," she said. "But leave me a message. I'll ring you back."

"Returning your call," he said simply. "Hope all's well." *Don't overthink,* he told himself. *If it had been an emergency, she would have called your cell.*

It wasn't just the headache. He was feeling decidedly punk, he realized. He left his office and stopped in the men's room, where he chugged a few gritty nips of Pepto and swallowed three more ibuprofen tablets. Then he donned a parka and headed for the ice floor, the music of Sharon's voice still ringing in his ears.

Johnny's first wife was a survivor. That's what Sharon called herself, and it was true. She had survived a number of seemingly insurmountable obstacles in her lifetime: abuse, poverty, breast cancer, and even—as she often reminded him—marriage to Johnny. But it was funny how things worked out. He and Sharon had loved each other, but they had been terrible together. Far too young, for one thing. Hopelessly poor, constantly overwhelmed, scrapping like cats at every turn. They'd been living in a moldy flat in the housing schemes of Easterhouse, just outside Glasgow, when Sharon discovered she was pregnant. Easterhouse was a place filled with fear and despair, governed by a ring of territorial gangs: the Drummies and Barlanarks, the Monks and the Provies, all of whom had been hacking each other with machetes and Buckfast bottles for close to a century and who showed little sign of slowing down anytime soon. When the baby was born, they called him Corran and gave him the middle name of Boniface, a name Johnny had heard once in a movie and never forgotten. "Good fate," it meant. They laid their hands on the baby's downy head and wished it so.

Johnny and Sharon stayed together for a few years after that, which seemed a miracle now, looking back. There had been no doubt in either one's mind that they should split. The only real surprise was how much more they liked each other after they separated. After a few rueful, stiff meetings with legal aid about custody arrangements, they realized with great relief that they could chuck the lawyers, get the divorce, and still be friends. They even still lived together for a spell. "Just my ex-husband," Sharon would say to the new boyfriends who came calling, pointing to where Johnny sat in the lounge watching telly or in the kitchen making Marmite toast for Corran. "Pay no mind." Sometimes Johnny would fetch them a beer, have a chat about the Rangers while Sharon finished getting ready.

The only problem was money. It was moderately miraculous that they both had jobs: Johnny as a packer in a frozen food
warehouse and Sharon as a night-shift orderly in an elder care
hospital so she could be home days with Corran. They worked
as hard as they could. *Out of Easterhouse,* they said. *We're getting
Corran out of Easterhouse.* They swore on it. They drank on it.
Sharon wept over it and Johnny made grim-faced promises in
the night, hands clenched, watching Corran's thin chest rise and
fall as he slept in the little cot in the lounge. They cut back on
cigarettes and quit going to the pub. They put the extra pound
notes in a biscuit tin and hid it in the oven.

But then the warehouse cut the hours on Johnny's shift
nearly in half, and the Drummies busted into the flat and stole
the stash, and the tenuously balanced scale of solvency they'd
worked so hard to stabilize went plummeting toward paucity
again. Sharon took on extra hours. Johnny spent every afternoon
and evening with Corran and even looked after a little girl from
the other end of the housing schemes to try to pull in a little
extra cash. It wasn't enough. *Out of Easterhouse,* they whispered,
voices growing fainter and more hopeless. The flat was cold,
and icy water dripped from a spongy area in the bedroom ceiling. One day three-year-old Corran stumbled and cut his hand
on a broken Buckfast bottle tossed just outside their back door.
Another day he stood transfixed at the front window, watching
two teenage girls beat each other senseless while a gang of young
men urged them on. Sharon pulled him away from the window,
gave him a zwieback.

Then she met Toole, a physical therapist at the hospital
where she worked. "This is the one," she told Johnny. "You might

be looking for another roommate." She was right. Toole was a good man. And he wanted to marry Sharon, wanted her and Corran to move with him down to Dunedin. Out of the schemes. "He said he'd pay for nursing school," Sharon told Johnny. Toole was on the front steps, goofing with little Corran.

Johnny looked around at the horrid little flat and then back at Sharon again.

"He'll be good to ye?"

"Yes."

"Well, then." He walked over and kissed the top of her head. And then he told her about the lead he'd gotten from a mate on a job in America. An ice factory in Florida. A real salary. Promotions, even. He could send money home. They could save for Corran's education.

"But won't ye miss us?" Sharon said. Toole walked in holding Corran upside down by his ankles. Corran was screaming with laughter, his fat soft belly rolling out of his shirt.

"Ah, no," Johnny said. "I'll make so much money I'll never think of ye again." He looked out the window, at the cold dirty streets of the schemes, and he cleared his throat. Then cleared it again.

"Ye cold basturt," she said, sniffing.

Johnny pulled three Tennent's from the icebox and passed them around. He gave Corran a cup of chocolate milk. They went out to the front steps and stood freezing in the gray haze. "Fuck you, Easterhouse," he said. He raised his beer.

"Fuck you," Sharon said. "Pack a' numpties."

"Fuck you," Toole said.

"Fuck you," Corran said, banging his cup against the rusted metal porch rail.

"Your mouth!" Sharon said. They laughed and went in, then spent the night drinking and talking of schools, airplanes, and America. And about the sweet salvation of money.

The next morning, they were hungover. Sharon left Toole snoring in the bedroom and came out to drink tea with Johnny. "Florida. It's what you want?" she said.

"It's good money," he said. "It's money I'll never make here. It's for Corran, aye?"

"Well, then."

"I'll come visit," he said. "And Corran can come see me." She nodded.

"We're getting him out of Easterhouse, Sharon," he said. And they did.

The frigid operations wing of the old ice factory was a cavernous rectangle, somber as a basilica, three stories high with column-like fenestration that lent the place the look of an art deco Parthenon. The manufacturing gallery was surrounded by its supporting departments: water purifying, drying, storage, shipping. In the center, six twenty-foot-tall cylindrical ice machines stood in formation, and when the light was right, the effect of the looming silhouette of the barrels against the tall windows was like a Gotham City skyline, Johnny often thought. The ice machines were ancient, stubborn as pachyderms, a sextet of cantankerous old beasts that Johnny had been nursing, cursing, and cajoling for nearly three decades.

They had long ago outlived their manufacturer, and Johnny had found it so difficult to find replacement parts when he needed them that he had begun machining them himself in his garage at home: a containment valve, a mounting bracket, a conveyor screw. The old tube machines could lose parts like rotted teeth, and sometimes Johnny felt like an antediluvian dentist, trying to fashion custom teeth for a passel of cranky old hippos that were only going to turn around and bite him once he got the choppers fitted.

Ah, but he loved the old brutes. Who was he kidding? He regarded them. The most problematic of the six was Dumbo, a wholly erratic lunk of a machine that had been rebuilt so many times Johnny was surprised every day to come in and find the old hog still wheezing and clanking away. Then there were the others, which over the years the crew had christened according to reliability, productivity, and personality: Tut, Popeye, GoGo, Samson, and Proud Mary. He wondered how much longer he could conceivably keep this old fleet of rust buckets going. But he'd work them until they were dead. What else could you do?

As if on cue, Dumbo started acting up, clattering like a washing machine with an off-kilter bushing. *Damn* it. Johnny knew what was happening. Lately there'd been a pesky tendency for short-outs on Dumbo's electronic expansion valve, a new-fangled add-on that had been installed on all the old icemakers a few years ago. Before some of these newer technologies had been integrated into operations, a step that Johnny grudgingly accepted as a conduit to more efficient production, the icemakers had been completely mechanical. But increasingly, the old machines were being retrofitted with electronic and even computerized parts, which might have meant gains in efficiency but also meant losses in bloody *fixability*. Johnny could fix a mechanical part. He could even retool one, if necessary. But these computerized valves? They were like highly complex parasites on a bunch of simple old dinosaurs. The only thing he really wanted to do with them was pull them off. He shut Dumbo down and waited for her to stop thrashing. Then he shimmied under the base of the icemaker. If he could reach up and jiggle one of the hoses to the expansion valve, it might help trip the connection back to life.

He'd been at it for only a couple of minutes when a pair of leather loafers appeared next to Dumbo, pivoted once, then stopped. Johnny wondered if it was possible to crawl all the way under the machine to avoid detection, but it was too late.

"Compression valve again, eh, Ice?" The voice belonged to Ed from Sales, who was now squatting on the opposite side of the old icemaker, peering underneath toward Johnny. "A bitch, ain't it?" Ed from Sales, Johnny thought, wouldn't know the difference between a compression valve and an expansion valve if said valve were attached to his own undersized pecker. It had often struck Johnny as gratingly miraculous that Ed could so successfully peddle a product about which he had so little concrete understanding. Johnny had lost track of the number of times he'd tried to tutor the man in the physics of refrigeration and the mechanics of fulfillment, with the idea that perhaps with a bit of background Ed would have a little more respect for what went on out here on the ops floor. But it was no use. To Ed, the ice just magically appeared. He was a good salesman; Johnny would give him that. Head of the department, and top seller, every month. But annoying as hell in the process.

"Expansion valve, Ed," Johnny said.

"Have you read your email, Ice?" Ed said.

"I don't read email, Ed," Johnny said, which was not entirely true. He did read email; just not email from Ed.

Ed suffered a smile. "Well, that must be nice," he said, in an ingratiating *just kidding!* tone. "Some of us *have* to read email."

"What do you want, Ed?"

"I want to request a meeting."

"This is a meeting." Johnny was still on his back underneath the ice machine, one arm snaked up toward the expansion valve and the other shaking a series of hoses in succession, trying to locate the short.

"I mean, a *meeting*. Like, where we sit down and talk."

"We're talking right now."

"Yes, but you're not giving me your full attention. That's why I want to schedule a meeting."

Johnny closed his eyes. Being on his back like this seemed to be causing a troubling sense of vertigo. He dropped his arm and took a deep breath, then slid out from underneath Dumbo and stood up, wiping his hands on his parka. He was dizzy, but he fought off a stumble. He looked at Ed, who was beginning to rub his hands together and bobble up and down on his toes, standard choreography for anyone from admin who came out onto the ice floor without a parka and remained for more than a couple of minutes.

"Shit, it's freezing out here," Ed said.

"What do you *want*, Ed?" Johnny repeated.

"It's not what I want, Ice. It's what my *customers* want. Shorter pallets."

This again. For months, Ed had been fixated on the bone-headed idea of having the packing crew stack the pallets with fewer bags of ice. Set procedure, which Johnny and Roy supervised with an aviator's precision, was to have the crew create eight-foot-high cross-hatching towers of ice bags that were solid as a bunker and that fitted squarely with the dimensions of the trucks, thus maximizing shipping efficiency. The pallet towers were a point of pride with the packing crew, in fact. Only the most skilled could throw an ice bag up to the top of a nearly filled pallet and have it land in the proper position before the entire pallet was forklifted over to be stretch-wrapped and stored for shipment.

But Ed was on a campaign. The pallets were too tall for his distributors' comfort, he said. They were forced to use step-ladders to reach the tops of the pallets in order to break up the shipments for individual orders. Stepladders! Imagine the hard-ship! So Ed's genius solution was to reduce the stacked pallets by a foot or more, thus decreasing the number of bags on each pallet and making it easier for his pansy-ass distributors to fill their orders without having to strain their fragile arms.

"That's asinine," Johnny had told Ed, more than once. "That blows our shipping numbers. That costs more money."

"We gain market share through customer service," Ed argued. "Distributors think we're hard to work with. We've got to make it easier on them. Then we *make* more money."

And on like that.

"Can we at least talk about it?" Ed was saying now.

"No."

Ed sighed. He pulled a folded piece of paper from his pocket and extended it to Johnny. "I knew you wouldn't read the email. So I printed it out for you." Johnny took the paper and put it into his own pocket, then watched the flicker of frustration cross Ed's face.

"Aren't you going to read it?" Ed said.

"I'm pretty sure you're going to tell me what it says."

"It's a *complaint*. From Southeastern Distribution. They say the high pallets are dangerous. And that they slow down their operations."

"And you're slowing down mine right now, Ed."

Johnny moved around Ed and kicked at Dumbo from the other side.

"I want shorter pallets, Ice."

"No, Ed."

Ed actually stamped his loafered foot in impatience, and Johnny had to work to suppress a smile. It was almost too easy to get Ed's goat.

"Well, what am I supposed to do with this complaint, then?" Ed said.

"You'll figure something out."

"You don't respect me, Ice."

"I respect what you do, Ed."

"That's not the same thing."

"Look, what do you want, Ed? You want a fucking hug, or what? I don't hug, Ed. I make ice. And you sell it."

Ed looked away, furious. "And you're lucky I do," he muttered.

"I'm not deaf, asshole," Johnny said.

Ed put his hands in his pockets. "You should treat people better, Ice," he said.

"Oh, for Christ's sake, Ed. You're breaking my heart."

Johnny's phone rang. He pulled it from his pocket and answered it.

"Where you at?" Roy said.

"I'm beating up Dumbo," Johnny said. "And bonding with Ed."

"Can you come out front?" Roy said. "To the parking lot? I need to show you something."

"I'll be there in a minute," Johnny said. "I'll bring Ed. He needs a hug."

"I ain't hugging his ass," Roy said.

Johnny placed a hand over the phone's mouthpiece and turned to Ed. "Sorry, Ed," he said. "Roy says he ain't hugging your ass either."

Johnny restarted Dumbo and waited; the wracking imbalance seemed to have subsided, and the old machine clattered back into operation. Ed shook his head and walked away. His lips were moving, but with the machinery racket, Johnny couldn't hear what he was saying. Though he had some idea.

Out in the parking lot, Johnny had a moment to look up at the hoary old ice factory, and to wonder how it could be that more than twenty-five years had elapsed since he'd first laid eyes on it, yet *only* a moment. Then the bespectacled countenance of Roy Grassi appeared at the top of the building's roofline and pivoted like a bobblehead before drawing a bead on Johnny in the parking lot below.

"The security lights," Roy yelled. "One was out."

Well, of course it was. The security lights were a fancy and expensive system of façade fixtures that Pauline, skittish about the decline of the surrounding neighborhood, had insisted on installing last year. At the time, Johnny had proclaimed it a waste of money and a concession to the fearmongering of the local news outlets. But now, given the recent increase in drug activity in Little Silver, he had to concede that perhaps the lighting system was a pretty good idea. If only the damn bulbs—at eighty dollars a pop!—would quit blowing.

"I found the bad one," Roy hollered from the top of the building. "One dead bulb was shorting out the whole system."

Even from this distance, Johnny could see that Roy was sweltering on the rooftop. And no wonder. It was at least ninety degrees here in the parking lot, Johnny realized, which at least had the benefit of a bit of shade from the few moss-draped live oaks that stretched their roots under the railroad tracks to the west and cast long afternoon shadows to the east. He could only imagine the heat up on the blackened roof of the ice plant. Sure enough, Roy looked to be in a hurry to get down. "Let me toss this to you," he called, holding up a lightbulb the size of a small punch bowl.

Johnny squinted up at him. Roy had become a blurry silhouette against the sun's rays, which were so intense they were beginning to play tricks on Johnny's vision. In fact, there now appeared to be more than one Roy—there were two up there . . . and now *three?* Johnny couldn't get oriented; a formation of green floaters danced across his sight line. He knew he wouldn't be able to see the bulb if Roy threw it, so he held up his hands in a gesture of refusal.

"You ready?" Roy said.

"Yes," Johnny said.

The bulb sailed down from the roof and smashed on the blacktop three feet to Johnny's left, sending razors of glass across two empty parking spaces and clinging to the legs of Johnny's pants. He rubbed his eyes.

"Oh, man," Roy said.

Johnny looked up. "You numpty," he said. "What the hell did you think was going to happen?"

"Well, I thought you were going to catch it, Johnny."

"I told you not to throw it."

"You did not! You said throw it."

"Bullshit."

"I said are you ready, and you said yes."

Johnny squinted at Roy, feeling as he did a fat drop of sweat tracking down his back. Had he said yes? He meant to say no. He searched for an echo in his audio memory. Damn. Maybe he *had* said yes. Why did he say yes? Everything, today, was short-circuiting. Even his brain.

Up on the roofline, Roy was shaking his head. "I'll be right down," Roy said.

Johnny kicked at a few of the larger shards of glass and bent to pick up the broken base of the bulb. Then he brushed his hands across his pants, realizing too late that he'd just embedded tiny slivers of glass into his hands. A few minutes later Roy appeared, sweating and carrying a push broom.

"You should have caught that, Ice," Roy said. "It was right in front of you." He looked at Johnny curiously. "You all right?" Roy said.

"Yeh," Johnny said, though suddenly he wasn't sure this was true. He walked back into the factory and paused near one of the catch bins to cool off. He peered into the bin and watched the cubes of ice fall, bright and clean.

Johnny had come to know many things about ice. He and Pauline once attended a talk at the community center at the Watchers Island town hall. The talk was given by an artist; he was some sort of crystal craftsman, or he worked in glass; Johnny couldn't remember. But he said the reason people are drawn to glass, and to crystals of any sort, is that the reflectiveness reminds them of where they came from, of some bright nascent place, and Johnny thought it was the same with ice. It was an astonishing substance that most people rarely stopped to contemplate. He considered a simple cube of ice—the outer ridge clear as a diamond, and within, a swirling, smoky core. Ice can vanish in a moment and endure for thousands of years. It can freeze metal and burn human flesh. It can sink a tanker and soothe a baby's gums. It can crawl. It can rise from the earth. It can fall from the sky. It can preserve a beating human heart in a flimsy Styrofoam cooler.

At the factory, most men saw it as nothing but a chore. It was the enemy, to them, something to be made, packed, stacked, loaded, shipped. But Johnny never tired of it. Think of it! Water turned to ice. Liquid turned to solid. Who but Christ could take one element and turn it into another? He told Pauline all the time, *We are miracle workers.* Have you ever seen a frozen waterfall? he asked her. It's a violation of everything we know: the space-time continuum, the basic laws of physics. Motion is arrested, energy is suspended, the laws of nature are confounded. *It's magic,* he told her. *It's the fifth dimension.*

It's just ice, she said.

Johnny looked up from the ice in the catch bin. Roy was back inside the factory. He was shouting. Dumbo was convulsing again. Johnny was seized with nausea. He bolted for the men's room and made it to a stall in time to vomit, but as he straightened up and made for the sink to wash up, the room became a kaleidoscope. The ceiling tiles fell around his head, and the floor buckled and wrapped itself around his knees. The light became liquid. He heard his own voice moaning. And then all was dark.

He woke to the sound of Roy's voice.

Ice, you fell.

Ice, you hit your head.

Ice, man, are you with us?

Two

Johnny's father used to have a saying: *And as soon you're oot one load o' shite, there's another.* Johnny could still picture him, face swollen with alcohol, eyes kind but beaten, drinking Buckfast on the cold stoop of that old east Glasgow flat and waiting patiently for the ascites to set in. From time to time, Charlie MacKinnon's expression came back to Johnny, and right now was one of those times. It was early afternoon. Johnny was lying on his back in a wickedly cold MRI machine, his head immobilized in a donut-shaped coil. Pauline was waiting outside the scan room, and a radiology tech named Kevin was talking to him through a set of headphones. It had been an uncomfortable day, to say the least: a trip to the ER at St. Vincent's following the spell in the factory. Then fast-tracked by the attending physician for both a brain scan and a neurological consult. The ER doctor had prattled on about hypoglycemia and stress and sleep deprivation and then ordered up an MRI.

"Just to take a look inside there," he said, tapping on Johnny's forehead. "Just to see."

"You good, my man?" Kevin was saying now. "There's a microphone. You can talk. I can hear you."

"I'm good," Johnny said, though of course he wasn't. Good? Define "good," he wanted to say. If "good" meant submitting to this silly medical fire drill, which was sucking up an entire day's work, just to appease his overanxious wife, then yes, he was great! So he took a header in the men's room! So what? A little dizzy spell was all it was. But Pauline had pushed him to agree to a *brain scan,* for the love of God. At first Johnny refused. There was nothing wrong with him. In fact, he told her, she was probably right that he should have eaten something this morning, so if they could just stop on the way back to work, let him get some food into him, maybe a sandwich or a burger, something solid, he'd be just fine. When she threatened to get hysterical he finally agreed, but not before sending Roy back to the factory to get on production. The damned ice wasn't going to make itself.

He was *fine.* Surely he was. So couldn't they just get this nonsense over with?

"About fifteen more minutes," Kevin said. "I need you to keep real still. We're going to try to get these scans in one take. But you tell me if you're not good."

"All right," Johnny said.

The machine was pinging like a submarine and Johnny had a wicked itch on the side of his face, but he'd be damned if he was going to make a move and risk screwing up this stupid procedure. Screw it up, he'd only have to do it again. He squared his jaw against the itch and counted pings.

"I want you to be all good," Kevin said.

"I'm good, Kevin."

"Don't be nervous."

"I'm really not nervous, Kevin." Johnny imagined the itch as a sharp, invasive sliver of ice poking annoyingly into his cheekbone. He willed it to melt.

"Eleven minutes, Johnny," Kevin said.

"Okay."

"Your wife said they call you Ice."

"The boys at my factory do."

"I bet you feel like ice right now. I know it's cold in there."

"It ain't warm."

"Ten minutes. Be good, my man, be good."

The forced stillness was introducing an unwelcome opportunity to think, and now the result was a creeping unease. Pauline's overreactions aside, Johnny had to admit there'd been something decidedly squirrelly about the way the morning's little swooning fit—or whatever you'd call it—came on so fast and so effectively laid him out. He hadn't been feeling right all morning, no doubt about it. And if he was totally honest with himself he guessed he'd admit to a certain disquietude brought on by uninvited ruminations over Corran's welfare on this, his son's thirtieth birthday. And all right, sure, there was also the ongoing worry over the pending OSHA appeal, a sourly insistent anxiety which had been bubbling since the summer. But those things did not seem like they could have been responsible— either singly or in concert—for the frighteningly psychedelic experience that had leveled him out in the men's room a couple of hours ago. Could they? He'd always heard stress could take an unexpected physical toll. But fainting? Johnny was not a fainter. Something was amiss.

"Think of something else," Kevin said, as if reading his mind. "Just peace out. Take a little nap, even. Go someplace you like, right? Like, the prettiest place you've ever been." Johnny steadied his breathing. He *was* actually tired, in fact. A nap didn't sound half-bad. A little mental vacation. All righty. He imagined Pauline out in the waiting room, probably playing a word game on her phone and trying to tune out Fox News on the television. The pings became more rhythmic. The drone of the MRI leveled out. And then damned if he could help it, but when he started to drift into the gauzy fog of a light doze, the first place Johnny went was to a high, rocky hilltop on a tiny island in the Hebrides. With Corran.

The week before Johnny left Scotland all those years ago, Sharon had got the idea they should all take a farewell day trip. The seaside, she said. Corran needs to have a look at the sea. They borrowed a Datsun Sunny from Sharon's aunt—red; Johnny could remember it clearly—and they all headed out at dawn, even Toole, driving up toward the coast, looking for the ocean. They passed Loch Lomond and pushed on, northwest, with little Corran jumping all over Sharon in the backseat; this was before car seats—what did they know? They reached the town of Oban, saw the crystal blue of the Hebrides and the seals slipstreaming in the current, but still they kept on—took an auto-ferry over to Mull, then pushed on even farther, a full hour across the rocky backbone of the island to its most western point. There they left the Datsun in a car park in Fionnphort and took a pedestrian ferry to a tiny little island in the Inner Hebrides: Iona. And there, finally, Johnny had the feeling they'd reached the end of the line—had gone as far as they could. There was nothing farther beyond but the wide cold sea.

It was spring, and the island of Iona was a chaos of greens and blues. The waters shone so clear and silver it hurt Johnny's eyes to look, and the machair grasslands spread along the coastline and up the hills before giving way to great thickets of smoky rocks, riotous patches of pennywort and roseroot. They walked the beach at Martyrs Bay and fed Corran bread and cheese, and an apple Johnny had brought in his jacket pocket. Toole produced a Yorkie bar, and they split it into four. They went into the abbey of St. Columba and Sharon said a prayer—for fate, she said. For good fate.

Then Sharon and Toole didn't want to climb, but Johnny took Corran and they hiked their way up, up, up, across a rough, scraping hill toward a high plateau from which they could see almost the entire island of Iona and great rocky Mull to the east. Johnny pointed west, out across the sea.

"Florida," he said to Corran. "America. It's right over there."

"I can't see it," Corran said.

"It's a bit of a ways," Johnny admitted. "But it's there. It's where I'll be for a bit, aye? And I'll come to see you soon. And you'll come over there, too."

"On a boat?"

"On an airplane."

"With Mum?"

"Sure," Johnny said.

Corran looked at him somberly. "I don't want you to go," he said.

"*Och*, now," Johnny said. He felt his throat closing. He put his hand on Corran's head.

"Will you come back?" Corran said.

"I will," Johnny said.

"Back to stay?"

"Aye, lad."

Corran's face was flushed pink and damp with sweat, though the winds atop the hill were bitter cold. He'd worked so hard to get to the top, that little bairn, so stubborn, his little legs so sturdy. He wouldn't let Johnny carry him. He made it all the way—*I can do it by myself*—then stood on the tallest rock and shouted, and Johnny had never seen anything as beautiful as that sovereign little boy. Nobody else had a boy like that.

On the way back down Corran finally relented, and Johnny picked him up and carried him as they descended the steep rocks. But of course, the descent was the easy part, not like the breathless climbing on the way up. That was always the way with Corran. Mr. Independent. He'd never give you the satisfaction of helping him when he most needed it.

The other part of it, though, was that he'd always been such a *sensitive* kid. Emotional. Easy to rattle. And more and more distant as he moved from the sloppy, clinging affection of young childhood into a standoffish and awkward adolescence. Once, when Corran came to Florida for a visit and it was time for him to go back to Glasgow, Johnny brought him to the airport to put him on the plane. How old was the boy that time? Early teens, somewhere in there. Not too long after 9/11; the airport was a somber scene. They were early for the flight, so they were killing time in the terminal, eating ice cream and looking at the gadgets in the mezzanine shops. They called to check in with Sharon, who would be there to pick Corran up when the flight landed. After a while, bored, they sat down in a row of rocking chairs and watched the passengers lining up to be checked in.

"Did ye have a good time?" Johnny said.

"Aye," Corran said.

"When ye coming back, Christmas?"

"Nah," Corran said. "Mum's for Christmas."

"Spring break, then."

"I guess."

There was a piano in the center of the mezzanine, a lovely old grand. Corran went over and plinked at a couple of the keys. An old man in a black suit arrived. He smiled at Corran, set a tip jar on the piano, and sat down at the bench. Corran came back and sat with Johnny to listen. The old man played a few standards; he was going for smiles: "The Girl from Ipanema," "Heart and Soul." Corran watched his hands. A few travelers dropped money into the tip jar. Then the pianist paused and sat up straighter. He rested his fingers on the keys and began something slow, mournful. Johnny thought he knew the song, but it took him a few seconds to place it.

"The *Moonlight Sonata*," he said. "Beethoven." Corran nodded. Johnny tried to recall what he knew about Beethoven: deaf, alcoholic, tormented. Quite a résumé. Sold his soul to the devil at the crossroads, maybe. But what a bargain that was for the rest of us, he thought. He wished he could tell Beethoven. You lost your soul, but you gave us this music, this heartbreaking masterpiece. Thanks, mate. We owe you one. Johnny closed his eyes for a moment, and when he opened them he was surprised to see his son was crying.

"What is it, Corry?" he said, alarmed.

Corran pointed to the piano. "This song," he said.

"Is it too sad, kidda? Do you want to go walk around now?"

Corran shook his head. He was trying to stop crying, and he was failing. He turned away so Johnny couldn't see his face. Johnny put his hand lightly on his son's shoulder, but Corran shrugged it off, and Johnny didn't touch him again. They sat until the piano player finished the sonata. Then Corran wiped his eyes and stood up.

"God damn it," he said. "I wish I could play piano like that."

"That's terrible language, lad," Johnny said. He stifled a smile. "Don't let your mum hear that kind of mouth."

"I better go," Corran said. Johnny put a five in the pianist's tip jar, and they walked over to the security checkpoint. This was new. No more walking the lad to the gate. Johnny handed Corran his boarding pass.

"Keep it safe now," he said.

"I know."

"Mum will be there when you land."

"I know."

Johnny felt an impulse to hug him, but just then Corran moved toward the checkpoint. "I'm going, then," Corran said. He looked up at Johnny. "Don't tell Mum I cried."

"I won't."

"Ta."

Corran hitched his backpack up on one thin shoulder. Johnny stood at the barricade and watched until Corran had cleared security and rounded the corner to the gate, but the boy didn't look back. That afternoon Johnny sent Sharon a check. "For piano lessons," he wrote on the card, "if he wants them."

Ah, Corran. Beautiful lad. The best you could ever want. Just, well . . . unfocused. Clattering. Loose around the edges.

Got to be a teenager, turned into a bit of a drinker, got caught a few times with quid-bags of weed, and ended up with a blot on his record. But it was typical stuff, nothing half the kids in Glesga hadn't done. Maybe they all should have come down harder on him—Johnny and Sharon and Toole and Pauline. Or, God, maybe they should have gone *easier* on him. Who knew? Corran blew off college after one semester, even though Johnny was standing by with the checkbook. And although he stuck with the piano lessons for several years, he eventually quit those too and started knocking around the city ska scene; he played keyboards in a couple of bands but never made any money at it. Then he worked as a phone monkey in a call center for a while, then a stint as a bin lorry driver and another as a line cook in a chip shop. Ah, Corran. A bit of a disappointment, but nothing to break your heart over, in retrospect. Nothing to complain about, come to think of it.

Until he found heroin.

Johnny had to work hard not to think too much about the past decade of Corran's life, but every time he made a payment on the equity loan that had paid for the bulk of Corran's third rehab, a ball of fury surfaced in his throat. He knew Sharon and Toole lost money, too. Corran had nearly bankrupted them all. And for what? Subhuman flophouses and poison-filled syringes and the company of jitter-eyed junkies breathing death from every pore. Measured suicide, that's what Corran was committing. A year, and then another year. And then ten years. The whole thing was a horror show of epic proportions, and there came a time when Johnny—who had initially tuned in to the broadcast freighted with adrenaline and hope ("We'll get you well! We'll beat this, Corry!") but who, as time went by, had felt his resolve gradually transmuted to the impotence and lung-crushing despair peculiar to parents of drug addicts—simply couldn't watch it anymore.

Last Christmas had been the straw that broke the camel's back. Johnny paid for his son to come over for the holiday, but when Corran arrived he was in a bad way: edgy and sullen, back on the junk, no doubt about it. Most days he slept until noon and woke up cagey, brittle. He went for long walks and came back smelling of weed. He borrowed Pauline's Prius and ran it out of gas in two days. Ran it out of gas! How do you run a Prius out of gas? Johnny could not fathom where he was going.

Pauline was patient. Johnny thought she was being intentionally naïve. "He's just at odds," she said. "He'll settle in. Don't *ride* him, Johnny. The poor kid. Give him a break."

"He's not a kid, Pauline. He's a badly behaved adult. He's an addict, and he's using again, I can feel it." Pauline bit her lip and went to Publix. She dropped a near-mint on groceries and spent hours in the kitchen making everything Corran liked best: baked Brie, chicken parmigiana, Caesar salad, sun tea, Toll House cookies. "We'll just love him up and he'll bounce right back," she said brightly. They set the table and waited. Johnny texted Corran. *U hre for dinner?* Two hours later, when the food was put away and the table cleared, a text came back: *Don't wait for me.*

"Why is he like this?" Johnny said.

"I don't know," Pauline said.

"What does he need?"

"I don't know."

Then an iPad went missing. Then a silver vase that had been sitting on the mantel for years. They might not have noticed it was gone but for the empty circle left in the dust. Then Johnny thought he noticed twenties disappearing from his wallet. On Christmas Eve, Pauline returned from running on the beach and couldn't find her wedding ring, an antique art deco band with a cluster of sapphires encircling a single diamond. As a young man, Johnny had saved for more than a year to buy it. He remembered the first time she put it on, how her hand shook, how she looked at him, astounded at the weight not just of the ring but of the gesture. When she started running she developed the habit of leaving the ring in a Spode ramekin on her bedside table. To save it from the sweat and sunscreen, she said. That afternoon, Pauline turned the bedroom and the house upside down, but the ring was gone, and Corran was nowhere to be found. He didn't come back to the house until the next morning, in fact. Christmas. His eyes were red and darting. His limbs shook. He denied taking the ring.

"I wouldn't do that," he said to Johnny. "I'm not an *asshole*, you asshole."

Johnny said something back; he couldn't even remember what, and then within seconds they were shouting, following each other through the house and dragging the argument with them until it was nothing but tattered, raw despair. Before the row was over, Corran threw a punch, and Johnny returned it. To this day, his hand ached with the memory. Corran's lip bled a bright rose on the Berber hall runner. Johnny's cheek throbbed. General San Jose was yapping hysterically from under the dining room table, and Pauline was weeping. "Stop it," she was saying. "Please stop."

Corran was kneeling awkwardly on the floor in the hallway. He got up and went to the kitchen. Johnny followed. He watched Corran fill a plastic bag with ice and press it against his mouth with a trembling hand. He wouldn't look at Johnny. He was mumbling something into the plastic bag.

"Speak up," Johnny said. "I can't hear you."

Corran lowered the bag and looked at his father.

"I said I didn't take Pauline's ring, and if you don't believe me, you're a shitty excuse for a father."

"You're a drug addict. And a liar. And I don't believe you."

"Fuck you." Corran put the ice back up to his lip and turned to exit the kitchen, but Johnny stepped in front of him.

"I want you on the next flight out," Johnny said to his son. "I want you gone." He called a taxi and then spent a fortune to have Corran's reservation changed, getting him a seat on an afternoon departure to Glasgow. Christmas Day. The last he'd seen of his son had been the back of Corran's disheveled head disappearing into a dented Bold City Taxi.

Clean, Pauline kept telling him. Sharon had sent an email. Corran is clean. And Johnny was supposed to believe this, evidently, and believe that even if it was true today, right this minute, it would be true an hour from now, or a day from now, or a week from now. And there was more news: Corran had taken up with an old girlfriend, who'd appeared on his doorstep one day with a baby that she claimed was his. Johnny thought this was something that happened only in movies. And what does Corran do? He marries the girl! The baby's name was Lucy, a detail Johnny wished he didn't know. And Corran had a job evidently, steady work on an oil rig off Aberdeenshire. For weeks at a time, he left his wife and the baby in a little shore-side flat and became a cog in a cold metal machine tethered to a well in the North Sea, halfway to Norway, a helicopter ride from the mainland. Top of the list of the most dangerous jobs in the world, where every day was a day closer to sure injury. Or disappearance. Or death.

Cleaned up his act for real, Pauline said. Well, Johnny hoped it was true. It was now late October. Johnny hadn't spoken to Corran in nearly a year. *I want you gone,* he'd said to his son. And *poof.* Corran disappeared.

The silence brought Johnny back. The MRI pings had stopped, and he found himself shivering uncontrollably in the cold radiology room, the flimsy gown mere gauze against his skin. Kevin came in to release him from the coil. Johnny dressed and rejoined Pauline.

"How was that?" she said.

"Delightful," he said. "Even had a little nap in there." He was surprised to see that she looked like she'd been crying.

"You all right?" he said. She nodded.

"I'm fine, Pauline," he said. "Stop worrying."

Kevin came out to the waiting room with a chart. "Go on up to Dr. Tosh's office," he said. "He can access the scans in our system."

"What did you see?" Johnny said.

"I'm not qualified to read the scans, my man," Kevin was scrawling something on the front of the chart. "Dr. Tosh will talk to you. He's the boss. He is the brain *master.*" He handed Johnny the chart and smiled.

They took the elevator to the fifth floor and were escorted back to the office of one Dr. Russell Tosh. When they walked into the office Johnny discovered that his new neurologist was a paraplegic. It was startling. The doctor beetled out from behind his desk in a motorized wheelchair with his hand extended.

"The MacKinnons!" he exclaimed. "Come in, come in, come in. Have a seat. You been down getting your pictures made, right? I'll pull them on up here in the system in just a minute. Come in, have a seat."

Johnny and Pauline shook his hand. There was a leather sofa against one wall and, with the way Tosh was moving the wheelchair back and forth in front of them, Johnny felt they were being herded toward it, so they sat. Tosh dragged a laptop on a stand over toward the sofa and sat fiddling with it. "Gonna pull up these scans here, folks. Just take a minute," he said.

Johnny couldn't help feeling there was something unsettling about a doctor who couldn't walk, some erosion of authenticity, like a singing teacher who couldn't sing or a chef who couldn't eat. To correct for his own ridiculous prejudice, he allowed himself to instead imagine the cause of Tosh's confinement: a spinal cord injury, perhaps. Car crash, a Mercedes, no doubt. Or a mishap on the steeplechase, a thoroughbred horse balking at the fence and throwing Tosh over the rails.

But after a few moments, Johnny found himself growing comfortable with Dr. Tosh—with his strident cheerfulness and his outsized drawl. (Texas, was it? Yes. Definitely Texas.) The doctor hadn't stopped chattering since they'd walked into the room. He was fussing at the computer still, something about the scans not showing up in the system yet.

"You know," Tosh was saying. "The old days, you just had somebody walk up the stairs and hand you the films, you hear me? Now it's all this email and server crap and what-all. And here we sit. Waiting for pictures." He rolled his eyes and looked at Pauline. "You know?"

"I know," Pauline said.

Johnny got up and paced around the office, which, it was beginning to dawn on him, looked more like a shrine to the Rolling Stones than a physician's office. Framed Stones albums adorned the walls, along with a collage of what looked to be hundreds of concert ticket stubs. A lip-and-tongue paperweight rested atop a stack of medical journals. There was even a guitar signed by Keith Richards mounted on one wall.

"So, you're not yourself, is that right, Mr. MacKinnon?" Tosh said. "I hear you had a seizure this morning. That's not too good, is it?"

"Not a seizure," Johnny said. "I just passed out for a minute."

Tosh tipped his head to the side. "You pass out often?"

"No," Johnny answered.

"I think he eats too many bananas," Pauline offered.

"Beg pardon?" Tosh said.

"Bananas. He eats them all the time. I read somewhere that you can build up too much potassium. Every time I look at him, he's standing there eating a banana."

"It's not the bananas," Johnny said. "Bananas are healthy."

"Not the way you eat them." Pauline looked at Tosh. "I mean, you should see it," she said. "Constantly. Bananas."

Tosh took a cell phone from his pocket and called down to radiology. "No scans up here yet, friend," he said into the phone. "Mr. MacKinnon. Can you put a hustle on those? I got these nice people sitting here waiting." He hung up and sighed. "Not like the old days, Mr. MacKinnon," he said.

"Call me Johnny," Johnny said. No reason not to be friendly. "You play?" he said, pointing to the Keith Richards guitar on the wall.

"Nah," Tosh said.

"This looks like an expensive hobby," Johnny said. He gestured around the room.

"You have no idea," Tosh said. "My wife is ready to leave me. Do you know that last year alone I spent nearly fifteen thousand dollars following the Stones? I keep thinking each tour will be their last, you know? I did the entire West Coast with them, from Seattle to San Diego. Every bit of my vacation time." He said this proudly, then paused as though waiting for Johnny's response.

"Wow," Johnny said. And after a moment: "What are you getting out of that?"

Tosh's eyes narrowed. "Have you ever been to a Stones concert, friend?" he said incredulously.

"No," Johnny lied. He actually had been to see the Stones, with Corran ages ago in Edinburgh—'97, maybe; '98?—but he felt like being contrary. Pauline raised her eyebrows at him.

"Then I'm sorry," Tosh said. "But you wouldn't understand." The doctor sighed, and now Johnny was sorry to have annoyed him. But a tone pinged on the laptop, and Tosh bounced back quickly. "Well!" he said. "Pictures! And it's about time!" He picked at the keyboard and then studied the screen intently. He was making small grunting sounds. Pauline tapped her fingernails on the arm of the sofa. On an end table next to her sat a framed photo of a somewhat younger Tosh alongside Mick Jagger. It looked like it might have been taken after a show; Jagger was wearing a tank top and tight red pants. He held a towel in one hand and a bottle of water in the other, and he was looking the other way, across the room. He'd retracted his elbow and shoulder in what looked like an attempt to elude Tosh's touch. Tosh was seated in his wheelchair, beaming at the camera, his arm outstretched around Mick in a hug that ended up awkwardly encircling the singer's thighs. The photo made Johnny sad. He looked away. Tosh was talking. He needed to pay attention.

"So, he's acting up," Tosh was saying.

"Who?"

"Your tenant. Mr. Meningioma. He's probably been there for years, and you never knew it. I just met him on the MRI. Left temporal lobe. You want to see?" He pivoted the laptop on its cart and pointed the situation out to Johnny and Pauline—the situation being a cloudy white blob floating in a lima bean of gray aspic. In Johnny's *brain*. Pauline gasped.

"A tumor," Johnny said flatly. His chest tightened.

"Weelllll . . ." Tosh said, drawing out the word. "More likely a benign cyst, from the looks of it. We see them quite frequently. People can walk around with them for a long time and never even know they are there, which is what you've been doing. But now . . ." He clicked his tongue. "He's been misbehaving. I think it's time your little stowaway was evicted."

"What do you mean?" Pauline said.

"The fact that Johnny had a seizure indicates the cyst might be growing, pushing its limits. Creating symptoms. Not a malignancy, necessarily. But definitely a nuisance. And that means it needs to come on out."

"Surgery?" Johnny said.

"That's the only way I know of, friend."

"Christ," Johnny said. Brain surgery! A vision of the procedure—or at least what he imagined the procedure to be—appeared in his mind, and he reflexively touched his forehead. "Christ," he said again.

"Oh, Johnny," Pauline said. She reached for his hand.

Johnny was mildly impressed, he had to admit, with his body's capacity to surprise itself. Sneak attack! Here he'd been walking around in the old beast for fifty-three years, keeping reasonably fit, wearing his seat belt, watching his cholesterol, cutting the cigs down to just one or two a day, and though Pauline would tell him that right there was senseless, Johnny actually felt rather accomplished in curtailing the two-pack-a-day habit he'd practiced in his youth.

He was far from perfect, but until today, he thought he knew everything there was to know about his own body's weaknesses: bum hip, remnant of a car accident back in Glasgow; nagging tinnitus that got worse after too much time on the factory's clanging shop floor; stubborn insomnia. But *this*! A brain tumor! It caught him broadside. Nobody in his family had ever had a brain tumor. His memory was still sharp. His wit was quick. He could think on his feet. He could no more have predicted an invading tumor in his left temporal lobe than he could have predicted he'd give birth to a litter of Angolan meerkats. But there it was, a fat white egg on a brain scan with his name on it. *Brain surgery.*

"When?" he said to Tosh.

"We'll get some steroids going, get the swelling down. I'd say two weeks of that, then *bam* . . . in and out, no big deal. We'll get you a consult with the neurosurgeon. Dr. Vogel. He's the best. He'll explain the drill. Ha. Pardon the pun!"

"Can't it wait?" Johnny said. "This isn't really a good time. Our factory—we've got an OSHA mess going on."

"Negative," Tosh said. "Seizures are no joke. Watch-and-wait works for some people. Not for you. You're what we call hit-and-run." He mimed a handgun and pointed it at Johnny's chart. "Ka-pow," he said. Pauline stared at him.

"I wouldn't call it a seizure," Johnny said.

"Yes, but you haven't been to medical school, friend," Tosh said. "I have. And it was a seizure." He looked over the top of his glasses at Johnny.

The next hour was a bit of a blur. Prescriptions, instructions, and a raft of paperwork. An uncomfortable screening of an educational video: "Meningioma and You." One horrific pamphlet depicting the actual steps involved in a craniotomy. Johnny caught the word "auger" in a photo caption. He closed the brochure and put it at the bottom of the pile of papers. When Tosh motored out to the hallway at one point to fetch a plastic brain model, Pauline grabbed Johnny's arm and announced they would be getting a second opinion.

"How do we know he's right?" she demanded.

Johnny looked back at the white blob on the brain scan and didn't answer. He was no neurologist, but there was something in his brain that sure as shit wasn't supposed to be there. That much was clear. He didn't like it any more than Pauline did, but his instinct was that Tosh was right. They'd get a second opinion. But Johnny had a feeling they'd be back here.

By the time they finished going over all the details, the shadows outside Tosh's office window were growing long and the footsteps of the staff outside his doorway had quickened, the unmistakable sound of a shift of workers looking to shut down the day's duties and go home. Johnny knew it well.

"And now your lovely wife will take you home," Tosh said. "And you will take your medications. And you will not *work*. And you will not *drive*. And you will not *stress*. For two weeks. Until we get the swelling down and get that bad boy out of there. *Capisce?*"

Johnny looked at Pauline. Her eyebrows were knitted and she was staring back at him intently. They shook Tosh's hand and walked, a little dazed, through the hospital.

"Lord, honey," Pauline said in the elevator. "This beats all."

The doors closed with a vacuuming shush. She pushed the button for the lobby, and they waited in silence for the lurch downward.

"I didn't see it coming," Johnny conceded. "But then I don't know how you would."

She leaned to the right until their shoulders touched, and she let her weight sink into his. When the elevator bumped against the ground floor, she lost her balance and stumbled a bit, until Johnny righted her.

Johnny let Pauline take care of the details. She was good at it. And she was fast. She spent the next morning on the phone. By afternoon, Johnny had visited two more neurologists for a second—and then a third—opinion. Sure enough, all roads were leading back to the same "most likely benign" meningioma, so in the end they returned to the hospital and consulted again with Tosh, who put the ball into play. They met with Dr. Vogel, the surgeon. They met with the pre-op nurse. They met with the insurance coordinator. They met with the anesthesiologist. Then they met again with the surgeon, who said he wasn't crazy about the quality of the MRI, said he wanted another done, this one with a contrast dye injection to better clarify the images. Could Johnny please submit to another MRI? He could. He did. Another visit to radiology, another gown, another awkward climb onto the sliding platform of the MRI table to submit to the immobilizing head coil again. This time, a nurse came over and injected a contrast solution into his arm. And then there was Kevin's voice in his ear.

"You already know the ropes," Kevin said. "I need you to stay real still, all right, my man?"

"All right."

"You good, Ice?"

The machine began to ping, drone, lull.

"I been better, Kevin."

On the ride home from the hospital, the skies finally opened up, and the rain arrived with a vengeance, rattling so hard on the roof of the Suburban that it was hard to talk. Which was okay by Johnny. Then the rain surprised them by turning to hail, and Pauline pulled the Suburban under an overhang at a defunct Waffle House, where they waited for the storm to pass.

"Funny," Johnny said. "Ice. We have to work so hard to make it. And here it is falling from the sky."

"Hope it didn't dent the car," Pauline said. She touched his shoulder. "Are you okay?" she said.

"Sure," he said.

Johnny looked at his phone and saw he'd missed another call from Sharon. He'd nearly forgotten she called yesterday. She hadn't left a message. It was nearly midnight in Scotland now, too late to call. He sent her a text: *I'll call you tomorrow.* He turned the phone off and sat with Pauline in the dark car. She took his hand. They watched the pavement beyond the overhang, where the ice pellets bounced like popcorn in the glow of a nearby streetlamp. Johnny took stock of the moment: It was raining ice on an eighty-degree evening in Northeast Florida. He had a bruise the size of a baseball on his forearm, left over from the fall in the men's room. The factory was in an unsettling limbo. His name was the latest entry on a neurosurgeon's schedule: craniotomy with resection, two weeks from today. And under all of this: *Corran.*

One of the few passions that incline men to peace is fear of death. Thomas Hobbes said that; Johnny had read it somewhere. It's a pity, he realized now, that we don't think of it sooner.

THREE

Of all the many wonderful and terrible things that had happened to Pauline MacKinnon during her fifty years on this planet, this was the one that seemed to come back to her most frequently in dreams. In the dream-memory, she was fourteen, and an immature fourteen at that, still a child at a time when many of her peers—taut, angular girls with shimmering hair and tanned skin—were honing a craft of coy bewitchery that left Pauline puzzled and cowed. She was awkward among the sophisticates, shy around boys. She could still be convinced, very easily, to run after the ice cream truck, to play with her sister's Barbie dolls, to watch cartoons.

It was summer. She'd gone with her father to the ice factory, where Packy Knight had a meeting, some distributor or other. She liked going out with Packy; his big wide car smelled of leather and smoke, and the clatter of tools in the trunk made a simple song. Sometimes Packy was in a low mood, and she knew to keep quiet and small. But sometimes he was like a party—playing Johnny Cash on the eight-track and banging his knuckles against the dash in time to the music. That day, he'd promised a stop at the Dreamette for ice cream after they left the factory. Pauline had brought her roller skates to pass the time, but the meeting was taking forever, and she was becoming impatient. She rolled up and down the ramp of the loading bay for a while. The sun was blistering hot, the white sizzle of a Florida August, with no shade in the factory yard. Across the street, a breeze stirred the trees over the tight, shaded streets of Little Silver.

She skated into the neighborhood, past crumbling wooden cottages, broken curbing, a dilapidated concrete-block house collapsing upon itself. An overturned grocery cart rusted on an empty lot. An old woman sat on a porch, humming, rocking a baby, and she raised her hand at Pauline as if benediction. Pauline dropped her eyes and skated on. If Packy saw her here, he'd make her come back. *Brown town,* he'd say. *You stay out of Little Silver.* She turned a corner to break the line of sight to the factory and found a long stretch of smooth enough roadway with a wooden fence running along one side. The sun was low behind the oaks, and the hanging tongues of Spanish moss made lacy shadows on the ground. They were mesmerizing. She skated into the shadow web, threading needles. Around. Through. Back. She imagined red bugs in the Spanish moss, watching her.

Four men came up behind her on bicycles. Two were black and two were white. They were shouting to one another, laughing, and they carried tall cans of beer inside sweating paper bags. They rode quietly behind her until one whistled and the others laughed. Pauline pulled over near the fence to let them by, but they hovered behind and one came up alongside her on his bicycle. She shrank away, but he pulled her hair, and she stumbled on her skates, had to grab the man's bicycle to keep from falling. He smelled like sweat and beer. He kept his hand in her hair and she was forced to stand still. She was wearing a black polka-dot halter top that tied at the neck. The man pulled at the string and untied the halter, and Pauline struggled to hold up her top with one hand and grope for the fence with the other. She tried to scream but the effort came out a piteous whimper. Two of the other men whistled, but the fourth, a wide-faced black man with hair graying at the temples, didn't. "Leave her, Billy, she's a baby," he said.

"Baby doll," Billy said. He still had one hand in her hair. "She's Packy Knight's baby, that's who she is. You want a ride, ice baby?" he said. He put his other hand on his crotch and made a pumping motion with it. The men hooted.

"Billy, leave her," the older man said. He was angry. He rammed Billy's bicycle with his own. Billy laughed and pushed Pauline away. The force of Billy's shove knocked her off balance again, and she scraped her hands against the wooden fence, feeling the splinters pierce like fire before she fell to her knees. The older man got off his bike and tried to help her up, but she recoiled from his touch. The rest rode off, and the older man looked at her sadly, then gazed up at the sky and shook his head.

"Come now, Jesus, where you at?" he said. "Wasn't nothing right about that." It was such an odd phrase—*Come now, Jesus, where you at?*—that Pauline remembered that even in her terror she'd felt a bit envious that the man seemed to enjoy so casually companionable a relationship with Jesus that he could even chide Him for negligence. The man rode away. Pauline retied her top, took the roller skates off, and ran in her socks back to the factory.

She locked herself in the women's washroom and stayed there until she stopped shaking and crying. She said nothing to her father about what had happened. In the car, she told him she had a headache and wasn't in the mood for the Dreamette after all. She closed her eyes and rode in silence until they arrived home, where she went to her room and pitched the roller skates into the back of her closet. She spent the evening picking wooden slivers out of her palms with her mother's eyebrow tweezers.

"What happened?" her sister Caroline said.

"I fell," Pauline said.

Why that memory came back to her so frequently in dreams she'd never know. She had the dream again last night, and the memory of it lingered under her skin this morning, even after a decently paced run at low tide and a long, hot shower. She should have been feeling pretty good after the run, but any valiant endorphins that might have been trying to elevate her mood were being summarily crushed by two competing distractions: one, a throbbing right knee; and two, the heart-stopping terror of Johnny's impending brain surgery.

The knee pain, at least, was nothing new. After one meniscus surgery, one ACL repair, one eroded kneecap, and enough osteoarthritis to sink a ship, it was a wonder she could still walk, let alone run. "You runners are what keep me in business," the orthopedist, shaking his head, said after the first ACL post-op visit, when she asked how long it would be before she could run a 5K. "Why don't you take up swimming?"

But Pauline didn't want to swim. She didn't want to go to a spin class or dance Zumba or strike a downward dog. She wanted to run, and she'd been secretly thrilled when the knee doctor had called her a "runner," enjoying his unquestioning appraisal of her as an athlete. An athlete! She, Pauline, who hadn't even started running until she was in her mid-forties, who hadn't even exercised regularly since the collapse of the aerobics madness in the 1980s! She'd grinned stupidly at the doctor and lumbered awkwardly out of the exam room, her leg encased in a brace the size of a small cannon. "Four months," the doctor called after her. "Don't even think of it before that." She'd waited two and a half, then pulled out her Nikes.

No, the knee pain was bearable. She could live with *that*. It was rather the dream of Billy and its attendant lack of sleep, plus the memory of the near-hysterical tone of some of the posters on MeningiomaMeetUp.com, that was going to get to her today. She'd spent an hour on the site last night, reading about brain tumors, until Johnny looked over her shoulder, saw what she was doing, and told her she was going to make herself a nervous wreck, and him by extension. *Don't believe what you read on the Internet,* he'd said. *Half of it's rubbish. The other half's trash.*

Brain tumors. Her stomach swiveled again like it had been doing since the other day, when Dr. Tosh pulled up the brain scan on the laptop. In the twenty-five years of their marriage, she'd never seen Johnny so clearly frightened. And the fact that *he* was afraid was rendering *her* nothing short of terrified. The anxiety was coming in waves—thick marmalades of fear. She'd just get one wave stilled when another would come blobbing in, slow and wicked. Because maybe the doctors were wrong! What did they know, really? Maybe the cyst wasn't benign. Maybe it wasn't a cyst at all, but rather a ravenous malignancy, spreading right this minute through the most tender crevices of Johnny's brain. Maybe it had already spread beyond his brain. Maybe it was creeping down his spinal cord by now, a cancerous kudzu, reaching long tentacles around his vertebrae and into the trembling chambers of his heart. Maybe it had infiltrated his bones. Maybe his blood. Maybe, maybe, maybe.

She'd been hovering over Johnny for two days now, trying to bring him tea and convince him to nap. Nap! As if he was a nap-and-tea kind of guy. She couldn't get Johnny MacKinnon to keep still if she sat on him. Already this morning he'd spent two hours in the garage machining a new part for one of the ice machines. With a tumor in his skull! She finally went out to check on him.

"Shouldn't you be resting?" she asked him.

"This is resting," he said. He was hunched over a vise, trying to wrench loose a stubborn bolt. A sheen of sweat glossed his face and arms.

"I'm worried you're exerting yourself."

"Uph," he said, leaning into the wrench. "Didn't you say you were going to the factory?"

"I am. But I'd feel better if you'd come in the house and watch TV or something. It's too hot out here."

"Uph."

"Or can't you just sit and read a book or something?"

"Uph."

She threw up her hands. She went to the kitchen and filled up a glass with ice water, which she took to the garage and left on the workbench. He'd broken the seal on the bolt and had moved on to adjusting a lathe.

"Please don't have a seizure while I'm gone," she said.

"I'll try not to, Pauline."

Fine. There was little else she could do for Johnny now except keep the proverbial boat afloat, which meant getting to the factory and taking care of business. Plus, it would get her mind off things. She drove away from the house, feeling a satisfying ache in her calf as she stepped on the accelerator. She'd done five miles this morning. Not bad at all, though the last mile had been a struggle and more than once she'd almost caved in to the desire to cut her stride and just walk for a stretch. But she'd pushed through, and she was glad. Five miles without stopping meant she was right on schedule for the training plan she'd mapped out: incremental mileage increases for the next two months, plus interval and incline training every three days. Then the nine-mile Gate River Run in March. The race was an intimidating prospect—an unforgiving course including two bridges—but she was pretty sure she could finish it. Maybe. If she stayed the course with the training.

She shook her head. *Listen to yourself, Pauline!* "If," and "pretty sure" and "maybe"? What kind of weak thinking was that? She spent so much time reading runners' magazines and blogs that she had a full repertoire of motivational quotes she could summon at times like this. So let 'em fly:

Never give up.
Dream it, dare it, do it.
Attitude is everything.

She thought of Rohan Bergonia. He was something of a celebrity in runners' circles, known as much for his split times as for his enormously popular "Get Runspired" podcast, which Pauline listened to when she needed a little extra motivation. He was rather ridiculous, she had to admit—a breathy and overly earnest little guy of absolutely indiscernible ethnicity—but he was good for serving up an extra dose of drive in the form of inspirational clichés when the tank was really running low. *Go hard or go home,* he said. *Forget "can't."*

And her favorite: *Failure is not an option.*

Failure. Oh, Rohan, easy for you to say! Sometimes she felt marked for failure, even when she catalogued the many clear successes of her lifetime. College-educated. Happily married. Successful in business. Financially stable. What else was there? And yet, she was dogged with a silly, niggling idea that she was fundamentally predisposed to fail in some significant way, given that she'd been raised in a place that had borne failure as a cross since its inception: Laudonnière—just east of Jacksonville, on the south bank of the St. Johns River's final winding course before it spit itself outward into the Atlantic.

The neighborhood had been named by a city manager in the 1950s, somebody who'd fished around to name the new development and had settled on Laudonnière, charmed by the French name but ignorant of its namesake. Pauline had looked it up. Turns out her childhood neighborhood was named after the failed sixteenth-century French Huguenot René Laudonnière, who had royally bunged up the one job he was charged with: to lead a small group of intrepid colonists setting up camp at Fort Caroline. The fort was the first French settlement in the newly discovered Florida, and Laudonnière was placed in charge and told to keep the peace while awaiting the arrival of his boss, Jean Ribault, from France.

By the time Ribault arrived, the settlement was in disarray— hungry colonists mounting a revolt and pissed-off Timucuan natives demanding repayment for the food they'd advanced Laudonnière. Fiscal mismanagement, in a nutshell, and poor

internal communications to boot. Ribault promptly sent Laudonnière packing back to France in humiliation. And what does the
city of Jacksonville do? It names an entire neighborhood after
this clown. What a cluster. What a celebration of failure. Unreal.

Pauline piloted the Prius across the bridge out of Watchers
Island, where a young woman in a bright yellow shirt was running up the incline. Pauline slowed to watch her. The girl was
fast. A steely stride, unwavering. Back straight, arms pumping.
Very impressive. The last time Pauline had tried this bridge she
was hunched and panting on the incline, her stride so short
she was nearly shuffling, and she had to stop and walk the last
hundred yards to the top. Which didn't bode well. If she couldn't
take the wimpy Watchers Island span, how did she think she'd
manage the Hart Bridge—epic finale of the Gate River Run?

Just over the bridge she stopped at Starbucks. She'd made
a deal with herself a long time ago that if she had to put up with
a fifty-minute commute each day to get from Watchers Island to
the factory in Little Silver, then she darn well deserved a decent
cup of coffee for the ride. In the Starbucks parking lot, the rain
had left deep puddles, and a layer of steam carpeted the blacktop.
As Pauline approached the building, a portly old woman in a
capacious denim dress was struggling to step off a steep curb
while balancing two cups of coffee and a mound of pastries on
a cardboard drink carrier. Pauline approached her and took the
tray while the woman made it down the curb.

"Thank you, darlin'," the woman said. "Very kind." She
was out of breath.

"Let me walk you to your car," Pauline said.

They crossed the parking lot to a frost-colored Buick, where
an elderly man sat in the driver's seat, reading a magazine.

"My husband does not walk as well as I do," the woman said. "Which isn't so damn good! Ha!"

Pauline smiled. The woman opened her car door, sat down heavily, and regarded Pauline. "Oh, honey. I wish I had your youth," she said.

Youth? Pauline supposed everything was relative. She tried to think of something deferential to say. "I wish—I wish I had your knowledge," she managed.

The old woman laughed, tickled. "Oh, sweetie. That doesn't mean anything," she said. She took the tray from Pauline. The old man leaned across from the driver's seat.

"I know you," he said. "You're Packy Knight's daughter."

Pauline's stomach contracted.

"I owned a distributorship on the Westside for years," the man said. "Logan's? You remember us? I'm Bob Logan. We used to get our ice from Packy."

"Oh, yes," Pauline said. It was steaming in the parking lot. She could feel her makeup beginning to melt. She glanced toward Starbucks, where the air-conditioning inside the building had created rivulets of condensation on every window. She smiled wanly at the old man.

"We closed up shop a long time ago," Bob Logan was saying. "But I remember Packy! He was a piece of work! He still around?"

Pauline started to shake her head, then caught herself— Lord, what was wrong with her? Her father wasn't dead. He was all but incapacitated with Alzheimer's and had been for some years, but he wasn't *dead*. She ought to be more sensitive to the distinction. "Yes," she said. "He's around. He's not too well these days, though. He's . . ." She searched for the right word. "He's diminished." *Diminished*. It sounded so feminine. It didn't seem the right word for her father at all. Destroyed, she might have said. Vanquished. And by his own bungled neurons, of all things! Bob Logan looked pained to hear it; not everyone, Pauline knew, would have shared his sentiment.

"Aw, nuts," Logan said. "Dementia?"

She nodded.

"He still know anybody?"

"He recognizes my sister and me," she said. "But he's slipping up on everybody else. Sometimes he remembers stuff from years back but can't remember what happened yesterday."

"And your mother? Jo?"

"She died twenty years ago. Ovarian cancer." Though she'd had long years of practice in making this report, it still sometimes took Pauline by surprise to say it. *Mama.* Scent of lavender and talc. Van Cliburn on the eight-track. Lipton tea bags by the gross. Ah, Mama. Pauline clenched a fist and let her fingernails dig into the heel of her hand. Sometimes that helped.

"Oh, I read about your factory in the paper," Logan's wife said. "You had a big accident there, didn't you?"

"Blew the hell out of the neighborhood, was what I heard," Logan said.

"Not really," Pauline said. She felt a familiar defensiveness flaring up. "It wasn't as bad as the news was making it out to be. Nobody was hurt."

"Coulda been, though," Logan added helpfully. "Coulda been folks killed, matter of fact, don't you think?"

Matter of fact. Fact! What did Bob Logan know about fact? Pauline was getting a little tired of people in town—from the *Times-Union* editors to her busybody neighbors on Watchers Island to this old fart before her—thinking they knew the facts about what happened at Bold City Ice last summer. Please. She was there. She knew what happened.

The *facts* of the accident were these: At 4:07 on a stultifying afternoon, a rotting branch fell from an oak tree in the factory yard and hit a tank filled with nine hundred gallons of pressurized anhydrous ammonia. The vessel ruptured in a blast that shook the building, sent a chill down Pauline's spine, and sent a long white plume of ammonia snaking through the streets of Little Silver. Johnny and Roy knew what to do, of course: shelter in place, keep everyone inside, call the police and the first responders to secure the neighborhood, and pray that the residents of Little Silver would have the sense to heed the warnings and stay indoors, until the wicked ammonia vapors dissipated, which, thank God, they did.

Then came the aftermath—those oppressive weeks of fending off news reporters, absorbing community ire, and trying to address factory morale. The OSHA investigation was swift and damning: The investigator found two gaps in the maintenance logs on the ammonia tank—minor gaps!—and that was all it took. A few weeks after the accident, certified mail delivered a devastating document: a Citation and Notice of Penalty from the United States Occupational Safety and Health Administration to the tune of $750,000 for violations of safety standards. Those were the facts.

And yet—it was maddening. Johnny insisted that the tank was properly maintained and always had been. Somebody had been a shitty record-keeper, he admitted, but he and Roy maintained those tanks to a T. He said he'd stake his life on it. Then *why* did it rupture? Johnny and Pauline had a theory: The drug activity in Little Silver was reaching a tipping point, and every junkie in the world knew that anhydrous ammonia was a critical ingredient in making meth. If someone in the neighborhood decided to scale the fence and tap into the ice factory's ready supply of meth-making ammonia, you could bet good and damn well he wasn't going to follow safety procedures to do it. A loosened bleeder valve, a break in a seal, even abrasions on the feeder hose—any one of these factors could have contributed to the rupture, Johnny said, and any one of them could have been caused by an overzealous meth dealer tapping ammonia in the middle of the night. Criminal tampering—it was a perfectly reasonable conclusion.

But OSHA needed proof. Johnny and Pauline met with the OSHA area director to present their theory. The man was sympathetic, but immovable. "We've identified path of failure," he said. "Your factory is liable."

"We want to appeal," Pauline said.

"Well, that's certainly your right," the director said. "File a notice of intent. We'll get you in the pipeline to have a hearing scheduled." They lawyered up and hunkered down. And now they were waiting.

Not that any of this was Bob Logan's business, of course. Facts. *I'll give you facts,* she wanted tell him. *You're getting on my last nerve, as Claire would say. That's a fact.* Pauline looked at the old man in the Starbucks parking lot and bit her tongue in forbearance.

"Shame about your daddy," Logan was saying now. "I'm sorry, honey. Packy Knight—we go way back." How far back? Pauline wondered. The image of Bob Logan swinging an ax handle alongside her father on a steaming summer night suddenly presented itself. *That* far back? She looked at the man: old white guy, probably in his late seventies. Fat with prosperity.

Expensive golf shirt. Cushy Buick. He fit the bill. She watched as Logan pulled a brown paper napkin off the tray of pastries on his wife's lap. He plucked a pen from the glove box and wrote his name and phone number in a spidery hand on the napkin, then handed it to Pauline.

"If your daddy comes to himself at any point, you ask him to give me a call," he said. "He might remember me. I'd like to say hello to old Packy. He was a force to be reckoned with, wasn't he?" She took the napkin and told him she would. Bob Logan finally eased himself over toward the driver's seat and backed the Buick out of the space, leaving Pauline standing in the damp lot. Logan's wife rolled down the window and waved as they drove off. "Don't get old!" she called out.

Pauline tucked the napkin into her purse and walked into the Starbucks. *A force to be reckoned with*. Well, that was one way to put it. And maybe Bob Logan knew better than most. As a young man, Packy had been one of a mob of whites who marauded in the streets of downtown Jacksonville on a summer day in 1960, wielding ax handles to beat bloody a group of blacks who had staged a sit-in at the lunch counter at W. T. Grant to protest seg-regation. Some of the white men wore Confederate uniforms. Some carried nooses, lest anyone miss the message. The brutal day went down in history as Ax Handle Saturday. A handful of whites were arrested, though most withdrew unchecked into the safe web of local cronyism.

But even Packy and his companions couldn't hold back the tide of civil rights. By spring the next year, the same blacks who had led the initial protest were eating their hamburgers and drinking their malts alongside wide-eyed whites at the lunch counters of Woolworth's, Cohen's, Grant, Kress, and McCrory's.

Packy never spoke of Ax Handle Saturday, but Pauline had read accounts of the beatings, and one night when she was a senior in high school, she heard her mother whispering into the phone to a woman from the Junior League. Jo twisted the phone cord as she spoke. "I don't think he *meant* to hurt anyone," she said. "He was just—I don't know—caught up in something, you know what I mean? It was the *times*, is what I mean."

Pauline retreated to her bedroom that night and lay awake for a long time, staring into the darkness, her chest clenched in shame and confusion. In the morning, Packy was in the kitchen, making bacon. She watched him turning the meat through roiling grease. She told him she was thinking of becoming a vegetarian, and oh, he *laughed*. "You playin' like one of those hippie-dippy types now?" he said. "Shee-ut. Eat some bacon. You want that this little piggy died in vain?" She watched his thick white hands until she felt nauseated, and then she went to school hungry.

Pauline hadn't even been alive on Ax Handle Saturday. She reminded herself of this regularly. She could hardly be held accountable today for the decades-old actions of her father, despicable though they might have been. Still, old-timers in Jacksonville knew the score, knew Packy had been one of the Ax Handle whites, and some were proud of him for it, even today. Others were angry, nursing grudges. Pauline had lived under this shadow all her life, had tried to distance herself any way she could, even while running the same business on which Packy had built his name and his fortune. Fifteen years ago, she changed the name of the ice plant from Knight's Ice to Bold City Ice, telling Packy it was an effort to give the company a hipper brand, appeal to the younger generation of distributors and consumers. But the real reason was that she didn't want to be associated with Packy Knight.

The White Knight. She'd been thrilled to change her own name to MacKinnon when she married Johnny.

Packy still lived out in Laudonnière, in the big house on the river, but he was quelled with dementia and medication now; he was physically fit enough to shuffle around the house but he spoke little and rarely went out, preferring to spend his days staring blank-faced at what seemed a never-ending marathon of *Judge Judy* and *Ellen* episodes while his live-in caregivers cycled through their shifts.

But it was true, what she'd told Bob Logan—Packy still recognized his two daughters. She almost wished he didn't, and she'd made the mistake of voicing that sentiment once to her sister Caroline, with whom she was familiarly cordial but not exactly *close*, a fact which took years for Pauline to admit to herself, but which was strangely freeing when she did. "Then it wouldn't make any difference if we visited or not," she'd told Caroline. "I mean, it's not like he *enjoys* seeing us. I don't think he enjoys much, at this point. Maybe he'd be just as happy to forget he even has daughters." Caroline, who primly kept up weekly visits with their father (though Pauline was sure these were executed more out of a self-righteous ambition to impress the caregivers than out of any genuine filial sentiment), scolded her for it. "He's not going to be here forever, Pauline," Caroline said. "You'll feel rotten if you just ignore him and then he ups and dies. Selfish and rotten." Pauline wasn't so sure.

Did she love her father? She'd stumbled into a debate with Johnny once over this. They'd been sitting on the porch with a bottle of cabernet, and she'd been tipsily chiding him about his estrangement from Corran. "You can love a person and not love his behavior," she'd said. "He's your son. He's your family."

"I do love him," Johnny said. "Don't tell me I don't love him."

"Then make peace with him."

"It's not that easy."

"Family's family."

"But you've got to draw the line somewhere, aye?" Johnny said. "Family can do bad shite, Pauline. You can't just march along as if nothing happened." She'd been ready to press the point further when she realized Corran wasn't the only member of the family Johnny was referring to. She bit her lip and swatted at a mosquito on her wrist. "Forgiving is one thing. Forgetting is something else," Johnny said. He drained his glass of wine and got up to go inside.

"I haven't forgotten about what my father did, if that's what you mean," she said.

"I don't mean anything," Johnny said. "I'm just saying."

"You're avoiding the issue of your son by making this about my father."

"I'm not."

"Let's not forget we wouldn't even have a business if it weren't for my father," she said. "Not everything he did was terrible. I know he's not a saint, Johnny. But . . ." she started to say "Family's family" again, but it was hard to form the words this time. "It's complicated," she said. "I don't know why you had to bring this up."

"You brought it up."

"I didn't," she said. She was making no sense now, and she knew it. "I'm going to bed," she said. She stood up, too quickly, and had to steady herself on the porch railing. Johnny held the screen door open for her, and they went to bed in a strange mood, the two of them, morose and grieving and a little bit drunk.

But that was weeks ago. This morning she was briskly sober, and Starbucks was like a song she'd heard a thousand times before:

Grande Sumatra blend, please, half a Splenda, room for cream.
Try a delicious blueberry scone?
No thank you. I wish!
Love your hair. Highlights?
Low-lights. Salon Belleza. Ask for Pepper. And thank you.

Pauline got her coffee, pulled out of the Starbucks lot, and then immediately had to swerve to avoid a jackass in a pickup truck drifting into her lane. She leaned on the horn and watched a tanned arm extend out of the truck's driver's-side window and shoot her the bird. You are a horrible person, she told him silently. My husband has a tumor and my business may be shut down, and I hope you drive your stupid ugly truck into the next ravine and stay there. Then she decided her mental indictment was hardly an adequate reproach. She rolled down her window and shot him the bird right back, but he was well ahead and it was doubtful he even saw it.

Good Lord, what was she doing?

Deep breath, Pauline: Focus. Control. Power. You've got this.

Failure is not an option.

At the factory, Pauline entered the building through the back door and walked past a narrow staircase leading to the second floor. Though the factory had been built as an ice plant more

than a hundred years ago, at one point in its history parts of the
admin wing's second floor had been repurposed and rented out
to an orphanage, of all things. Longtime ice staffers liked to scare
the newbies, telling them that at certain moments, when the ice
machines were quiet, you could hear the ghosts of abandoned
babies crying in the rafters. Pauline didn't admit it to anyone,
but she hated that story. Awful! Why did people come up with
such terrible things?

When she passed the staircase leading to the second floor,
she always quickened her step. Now she walked past the first-
floor's rows of cubicles to the lobby. Vickers, one of the ice drivers, was hanging over the reception desk talking to Rosa, but
when he saw Pauline he feigned hurry and scuttled down the
long hallway that connected the staff offices to the factory itself.
What did Rosa see in that lout? Pauline looked at Rosa and shook
her head, then felt self-conscious. Oh, what do I care who flirts
with who? she thought. Who am I, the church lady? When she
reached her office, she pulled out her phone and texted Johnny.
You okay?

Fine, the text came back. *Not dead yet.*

Not funny, she typed. She put the phone back into her purse
and hung the purse on the back of her desk chair. She'd just
turned on her computer when her desk phone buzzed. "You
there, Pauline?" Rosa said.

"Yes."

"Roy's looking for you. He said he wants to talk staffing,
about how they're going to make do out there without Johnny.
He wants to know if you can come to his office."

"Tell him I'll be there in a few minutes," Pauline said.
She walked to the window to open the blinds, then felt a catch

in her throat. Rosa's phrasing was unsettling. *Make do without Johnny?* Unimaginable. Pauline didn't even know who she was without Johnny. She tried to picture herself before she met him: so young and lonely, coming off those four foggy years of college that had been nothing but studying and tests and riding around the steaming streets of Gainesville, smoking weed with boys dumber than chimpanzees. Before Johnny, she'd never even had a boyfriend who'd lasted more than a month.

And then, the day after graduating from UF, she came back to Jacksonville, settled in for a career in ice, and met Johnny MacKinnon. There was a lot of talk, in the beginning, about Johnny hitting pay dirt, coming over a poor young Scot and within a few years married to the boss's daughter with his eye on a series of promotions that would bring him right up to the top of the ranks, but he'd earned it. She was proud of him.

When they first started getting serious she'd made a bold proclamation that he could marry her if he wanted, but that she had no intention of having children. He was already a father, anyway, and for her part Pauline had seen enough of her sister Caroline's life by then—of the jars of putrid pureed carrots, the screaming tantrums, and the frightening fatigue of those first shell-shocked years of motherhood. Caroline had her girls eighteen months apart and stayed home with them full-time while her husband Donny worked as an executive in research technology (what the heck *was* that?) in a huge office on the top floor of the Modis Building.

When Pauline's nieces were tiny, Caroline told her she was so debilitated with sleep deprivation and baby-brain that she once left the house in two different shoes, once left an entire chicken in the oven for three days. Once, exhausted, she lost her temper

and slapped her shirtless, screaming older daughter on the back
so hard that the blow left a splotched red handprint that lasted
all day, and then she spent the afternoon weeping, applying cold
packs to the girl's skin, and considering turning herself in to
Child Protective Services. Pauline was horrified, not so much at
her sister's confession, but at the pure chaos her life had fallen
into. Caroline, it seemed, had very little control over *anything*.
How could she stand it?

No thank you, Pauline decided. Motherhood was not in the
cards for her. Besides, Johnny had Corran, who was just a little
thing when Pauline first met him. Five years old, and a beautiful boy, too, curly brown hair and a mouth always twisted into a
smile. Pauline loved Corran. *Still* loved him, for heaven's sake,
missed him terribly, what with this awful falling-out he'd had
with his father. When Corran was a child, they'd brought him
over for Christmases and summers, took him to the beach, to the
movies, to the zoo. It was lovely. And it had been just enough for
Pauline—part-time mothering, just a little bit here and there and
then send the darling boy back on over the pond until next time.

She thought it was all she needed.

"What an *idiot*." She startled herself now, saying that out
loud. She looked around quickly, but she was still alone in her
office. A tide of self-loathing had risen. Stupid, stupid, stupid.
That sweet little boy's hand in her own, leading her across the
dune to dig for mole crabs or out into the crashing waves, laughing at her as she cringed at the cold. "Pauline!" he yelled. "Come
on, Pauline! Come *with* me!" What a lovely thing, a child. What
a gift. And to think she'd contented herself all those years with
being a vacation-mother to Corran and then watching cheerfully
as he was packed onto an airplane to go back to Scotland to his

real mother. To think she could have had a child of her own. Two. Three! And to think that she hadn't. Wouldn't.

Now Johnny didn't want her calling or emailing Corran, and she'd acquiesced to his wishes. But Johnny didn't know that she and her stepson played iPhone Scrabble together. It was just a phone app, but it was wonderful—she and Corran could share coded messages whenever they got lucky enough to find the letters to do it. LOVE, she'd sent him recently. And then a two-turn combo: MISS YOU. He was clever with it, too. She'd laughed out loud at his most recent effort: YOU ROCK. It was a brilliant trick! They never discussed the wedding ring, or the rotten estrangement, and she didn't have to lie to Johnny. I won't text Corran, she'd promised. Or email. Or call. But she never said she wouldn't keep up with her stepson somehow.

"That's just wrong."

Pauline turned from the window toward the voice, which belonged to Claire Kaplan, who was standing in the office doorway with a piece of coffee cake on a paper napkin.

"What is?" Pauline said.

"That cake in the kitchen. Somebody brought it in and I've had two pieces already. It's just wrong. It's evil, I'm telling you." She put the napkin and the cake on Pauline's desk and pulled a plastic fork from the back pocket of her jeans. *"Pour vous."*

Claire was like something out of *Easy Rider*, with a wardrobe that could have been hijacked from Dennis Hopper. She had a smoker's voice, clear brown eyes, and long strawlike hair she wore either loose and wavy or pulled back into a hectic ponytail, depending on the occasion, the weather, and her general mood, which as Pauline well knew, could swing from bad to worse in a New York minute. Last Halloween, Claire had come in wearing a beaded vest and a floral headband and carrying a flask of Jack Daniel's. "I'm Janis Joplin," she told everyone who asked, and Pauline had to admit the likeness was quite believable, or at least it *would* have been if Janis Joplin had made it to her late forties, was single-parenting three kids, and had maneuvered a contentious divorce from a philanderer who had then unceremoniously died (heart attack, jogging) just before the split was made final, leaving Claire a resentful widow with a mountain of debt.

Claire had been hired years ago as a receptionist and quickly moved up through accounting and human resources to her current position of Vice President of Everything, as Pauline called her. She knew more about some of the distributors' contracts than most of the sales team, had negotiated a darn good deal on the group insurance policies, and was the only one in the factory who knew both the password for the ISP *and* the trick to resetting the flapper on that one toilet in the women's room that kept running. She even kept up on truck maintenance calendars, far better than the series of surly fleet managers they'd been through over the past twenty years. She was, in short, a miracle of competence.

Pauline looked at the coffee cake Claire had just deposited on her desk and imagined how much distance she would have to add to her run to burn off the calories in that small square of flour and sugar. She took a tiny bite, then pushed it away.

"I told you. It's evil," Claire said.

"I don't believe in evil," Pauline said.

"Oh, I'm just kidding," Claire said. "Take it. It's just cake." She waited a beat, and when Pauline made no move toward the cake, Claire flicked out a wiry wrist and plucked the plastic fork back. "Well, if you're not going to eat it," she said. Now, why was it that Claire could eat anything she wanted, and drink like a fish, for that matter, but still have the physique of a ten-year-old boy?

"So, how's Ice this morning?" Claire said between bites.

"He's all right," Pauline said. "Hates staying home, but he's supposed to just rest up before the surgery. I don't know how this is going to work. He's going to be climbing the walls if he has to sit in the house for two weeks." She sighed. "I gotta go talk to Roy. Come with me?"

"Sure," Claire said. They stopped at the kitchen, and Claire cut another piece of coffee cake. ("For *Roy*," she said, when Pauline looked at her.) They walked down the hallway leading to the shop floor, stopping before the heavy metal door to take two parkas from a wide rack of coats. They donned the coats and stepped through the factory entry, where the cold always took Pauline's breath away, made her lungs actually ache with the chill. Fifty years she'd been breathing this ice. Fifty years it had never stopped hurting.

They found Roy in his little office just inside the loading bay. He was staring at an Excel spreadsheet on his computer, scratching his head, and he looked up when they came in.

"Oh, Lord," he said. "I am being invaded."

Pauline was relieved to see that while Roy looked slightly ruffled, he was nowhere near complete panic—not yet—over the prospect of Johnny's indefinite absence from the shop floor. Roy had been their operations engineer for more than a decade, and before that he'd been packing supervisor, and before that water feed tech, and before that—well, Pauline couldn't even remember all the things that Roy had done at the factory. He'd been here a long time, that's all she knew. And he did a lot.

She regarded him—of late he'd put on a few pounds, she thought, but interestingly, he wore it well. He had a shag of dust-colored hair and a full beard a shade or two darker that he sometimes kept trimmed but often let grow to an alarming length—the beard length, Pauline knew, corresponding to the current state of his love life. A trimmed beard meant a new woman was in the picture; creeping growth meant the ship had sailed and he was back in his own lonesome port again. He wore glasses with thick black frames, and the effect of all that facial hair topped off with the concealing spectacles was one of a person trying very hard to hide from something, or perhaps hide from everything. Roy was like a yeti, Pauline thought. A furry, loyal yeti.

As a young man, Roy had worked for the *Times-Union* as a typesetter, a job he dearly loved both for the technical prowess it required and for the pranking capital it offered. He took liberties with the editorials—usually the dry "in-depth" articles on state politics that you could bet a dollar nobody was reading—sometimes changing a word or two to see if anybody noticed: "public" to "pubic," "election" to "erection," and so on.

He was married young; it didn't take, but Ally, the daughter who had come from that union, was Roy's pride and joy—"My best girl," he often said. Ally called or texted her father at least once a day, and, under the terms of the more-or-less-amicable divorce, had come to stay with him every other weekend and every summer since she was a tiny kid. She was now in her first semester at UF, and Pauline didn't think she'd ever seen a father who was crazier for his child than Roy. His desk was covered in photos of Ally: Ally going to her prom, Ally clutching her first driver's license, Ally at her high school graduation. If you got him talking about Ally, you had to make sure you had some time on your hands. It was sweet, though. Pauline admired the bond he had with that kid. Envied it, really.

But Roy had his share of troubles, too, and the biggest among them started on Christmas Eve in 1989, when a freak snowfall that had hit Jacksonville bunged up the driving conditions pretty good; nobody in town had any idea how to pilot an automobile on an icy road, and cars were sliding around the city like pucks on an air hockey table. Most of the accidents were minor, but not Roy's. He'd been out with his buddy Nathan, driving around in Roy's Nissan to look at the snow. They'd smoked a joint and then parked for a little while at the Treaty Oak on the south bank of the St. Johns, marveling at the ice crystals hanging like diamonds from the great tree's limbs. They'd never seen anything like it.

On the way home, the pot made Roy sleepy, and the unaccustomed whiteness of the snow-covered world blinded him. The next thing Roy knew, his Nissan had clipped the back of the car in front of them, spun around, hit the curb, and rolled down a sixty-foot embankment. Roy took a shard of glass in his left eye, but he walked away. Nathan survived, but he never walked again.

Staggered with remorse, Roy had been—for almost thirty years now—carrying his accountability like a fat, rotting albatross. He devoted himself to doing everything in his power to care for Nathan, even after Blue Cross did the heavy financial lifting and got Nathan set up with a power chair, a motorized car lift, and top-quality physical therapy. It wasn't enough, as far as Roy was concerned. Nothing would ever be enough.

In the early years after the accident, Roy visited Nathan almost every day at his parents' home, bought him a Sega

Genesis and a raft of game cartridges, even sneaked some fat doobies into Nathan's nightstand when nobody was looking. "A little visit from Aunt Mary," he told Nathan. "Gainesville Green. I drove down to get it." Later, when Nathan wanted more independence, Roy helped him get settled in his own apartment, and since Nathan was by then taking classes at FCCJ and was even dating a bit (raucous girls—drinky types, adventure seekers, not the least daunted by the wheelchair), all of which left him little time for the occupational therapy he'd need to prepare for joining the workforce from a wheelchair, Roy paid half the rent.

His own negligence behind the wheel had left his friend with half a body, he reasoned, so it was the least he could do, and never mind the fact that Roy had plenty of his own bills to pay, and child support for Ally. When the cable station started offering premium access for an additional thirty dollars a month, Roy signed Nathan up, and he paid for half. When the Internet took hold, Roy hooked Nathan up with an IBM tower and a CompuServe subscription, and he paid for half. When cell phones came out, he took Nathan to AT&T and told him to pick out his favorite. And Roy paid for half of that, too.

It's true that Nathan's spinal injury had been a horrific blow—had left him maimed and limited in a way that Roy could never hope to understand, though God knew he tried. But it was also true that Nathan was a resolutely adaptable guy, stubborn and opportunistic, able to make the most acerbic but satisfying lemonade out of life's lemons in the same way a cockroach can lose several of its legs and still drag itself quite smartly along the stovetop to raid the Fig Newtons you so foolishly left on the counter.

So while Roy—who had lost 75 percent of the vision in his left eye from the accident, had trouble reading or studying, and had to give up his typesetting job to find work which required less close-up scrutiny—was working his way up the blue-collar ladder of Bold City Ice, Nathan transferred to UNF, earned a degree in communications, was never wanting for female companionship, and now worked in New Media Services at Citibank. And still Roy paid for half of Nathan's rent, half of Nathan's phone bill, and half of Nathan's cable. It never occurred to Nathan to cut Roy loose, and it never seemed acceptable to Roy to ask for release. Had Nathan offered, Roy would have accepted. But until that day came, Roy kept paying. It was his penance, he said.

Claire had fits over it. "He's taking advantage of you, Roy," she told him, over and over. And to Pauline: "Why does he let himself get used like that?" Pauline looked at Claire's hands, and at the wedding ring, given to her by her philandering dead husband, that still encircled her finger. Why indeed, Pauline thought.

But Roy was a stayer, just like Claire. Roy had outlasted a raft of useless foremen, a boatload of shipping coordinators, a small army of inept packers. Roy could do it all, and he, like Claire, had become such an integral part of the whole ice concern that it was difficult to envision the plant without him in it. After all, there were four sets, and *only* four sets, of keys to Bold City Ice: one each for Pauline, Johnny, Claire, and Roy. When Pauline thought about the operations of the factory, it seemed to her that it came down to four corners, like the four legs of a table. Take any one of them away, and the table would tip. Take two, it would fall. And here they were, one down.

"We're coming to check on you," Claire said to Roy now. She put down the coffee cake. "You surviving out here?"

"Sort of," Roy said. "For now." He pointed through his office window to the shop floor beyond. "But going forward? This is going to be a problem." He was referring to Johnny's imposed hiatus. "I mean, Pauline," Roy continued, "usually when he's out, I have time to plan for it. Like when y'all go on vacation and such. This came on me so fast. I can do all his shit. But who's going to do all my shit?" He gestured around his desk, picked up a shipping order, and let it flutter dramatically back down to the blotter.

Then he raised one eyebrow the way he did when he was worried, and the movement called attention to Roy's damaged left eye, the murky blur of the iris that should have been the same clear green as the right eye. Roy told her once that, despite his thick glasses, everything he saw out of his left eye was blurred nearly beyond recognition. He could see shapes and colors, Roy said, but no defining lines or details. So, you're seeing only half the world? Pauline had asked him. I'm seeing all the world, Roy said, but it's only half as good. Now he cocked his bushy eyebrow over the top of the glasses.

"All right," she said. "We'll get it covered out here. You want Ed from Sales?"

"Pauline," he said, putting his hands to his heart. "Please don't do that to me. That boy's so dumb he has to get naked to count to twenty-one."

"I disagree," Claire said. "He's quite sharp."

"Sharp as a bag of kittens," Roy said.

Pauline held up her hands. "Okay," she said. "I'll figure it out. I'll get you some more help out here, all right?"

Roy finished chewing and looked at Claire. "There any more of that cake in there?" he said. He walked back to the admin wing with Pauline and Claire and dealt a deathblow to the dwindling coffee cake in the kitchen before retreating once again to the shop floor.

If she had been in a decent frame of mind, the situation that unfolded at lunchtime might have struck Pauline as mildly amusing, or at least *interesting*. She'd sneaked out of her office just after noon with an idea to run a few errands, but just as she put the Prius in reverse to back out of the factory parking lot, Ford, the neighborhood drunk (well, *one* of them), appeared behind her car and promptly took a crocked header off his bicycle, no doubt because he was trying to ride with a recycling bin full of lemons propped on his handlebars.

Ford had, for years, cornered the market on pilfering from Little Silver's straggling but stubbornly productive fruit trees. Word was that he lived on the fruit, which Pauline always found implausible at best (how could you live on *lemons?*), and he certainly appeared robust enough this afternoon, thrashing around as he was behind Pauline's car in a pile of dusty citrus, now effectively blocking her escape. She got out and went around to help him gather his spoils.

"Don't touch my lemons," Ford said. He was an ungainly old man, gnarled as a cypress knee and prone to outbursts of either giddiness or fury, in equal measure and with no predictable pattern. Pauline was dismayed to see he was edging toward the latter of his two moods now. He righted his bicycle and scowled at her with the passionate indignation of the perpetually drunk.

"I'm trying to help you, Ford," Pauline said.

"You're trying to take my lemons."

"I'm not." She bent over to pick up some of the fruit.

"Don't be stealing my lemons, baby!"

For God's sake! She straightened up and tossed the two lemons she was holding into his recycling bin, then glared at him. Baby! Who did he think he was? He righted the bicycle and stumbled around in a tight circle, gathering lemons and muttering. *Baby*. For real? A street sweeper rumbled past, and Pauline noted the irony while waiting for the noise of the mechanized brooms to subside. She couldn't remember the last time the city had indulged Little Silver with a sweeper. It was only a shame the contraption couldn't sweep up the sotted geezer before her, and his stupid lemons too.

"You stealing my lemons," he burbled. "You need to get your own lemons."

"I don't want your lemons," she snapped. "I just want to get out of here, and you're in my way."

"Damn ice plant people. Damn Packy Knight," Ford was muttering now. He was standing next to the bicycle, peering up at the factory. He seemed to have forgotten *she* was one of the ice plant people, and she set her jaw and didn't answer. Did he know he was talking to Packy Knight's daughter? Hard to tell, though Pauline certainly felt no need to clarify her identity. "This place, these people, they think they own Little Silver, you know what I'm saying?" Ford was saying. He shook his head. "I am *telling* you." Pauline stooped to pick up the remaining lemons and pitched them back into the recycling bin. Sometimes, she decided, this neighborhood made her crazy; these kinds of battles were always springing up.

She got back in her car wordlessly and waited for Ford to wobble his way out from behind it. She watched in her rearview mirror as he moved slowly down King Street. She was hot, and she was frustrated, but she felt strangely transfixed, watching the old man on his bicycle. There was something about him, something . . . reassuring? Yes, reassuring, she decided. Maybe it was his predictable righteousness; she found it comforting.

She waited until he'd rounded a corner a few blocks to the south before she pulled out of the parking lot and headed for a route that would allow her to make a stop at the Publix on Baymeadows Road. Sometimes, if she was lucky, this particular Publix stocked Maynard's Wine Gums. What made her think she should be lucky today she had no idea, because the last couple of months had proved that she was on anything *but* a lucky streak. Not that *she* was responsible for any of the recent disasters that seemed to be vying for top position lately. She could have neither caused nor prevented any of them. Still. Calling it bad luck seemed to help. Bad luck was a temporary thing. It could pass. It *would* pass.

The wine gums. They had to be Maynard's, imported from the UK—other brands, according to Johnny, were gastronomically inferior, though Pauline didn't know how something so awful in the first place as a wine gum could have epicurean degrees of superiority. She couldn't stand the things, ever since the first time she'd gone to Scotland with Johnny and he'd pressed her into eating one, and the darn thing was so chewy and gummy that it actually pulled a silver filling out of one of her back teeth. This actually worked to her advantage in the long run, because when she got back home and visited the dentist she was able to have the old silver filling replaced with a much more attractive white composite, which was a silly vanity, admittedly, though one she could not help appreciating. But wine gums!

She renamed them "filling pullers" and never ate another one, but the same could not be said for Johnny, who, she believed, could happily exist entirely on bananas, beer, and wine gums, and probably *would* had he not married her and been forced to recognize common sense, at least some of the time.

In Publix, she located the wine gums and felt through the bag to determine their consistency. Not too hard. Good. Sometimes, probably owing to delayed shipping or lazy stocking, the candies aged to the consistency of a pink eraser, rendering them even less edible than they already were. Johnny was particular about his wine gums. They should be soft enough for teeth to sink into, tough enough to offer a satisfying fight. That's why he loved Pauline, he often told her. She was like a wine gum. She never knew quite how to respond to this particular endearment. She brought the candies to the checkout line, and while she was waiting, she texted him. *All good?* She held her breath and waited. She pictured him out in the garage on Watchers Island, probably still banging at that piston situation. The reply came right away: *Yep.* Man of few words. She checked Scrabble on her phone; it was still Corran's turn. She couldn't move. She looked at the last few words they'd played: BUSY. FINE. GOOD. That's it, Corran. One day at a time.

The checkout lane was moving slowly. She catalogued the list of tasks still waiting for her attention at the factory today, then worried that maybe she didn't have her priorities straight. Her husband was dealing with a brain tumor, and here she was preoccupied with shipping receipts. Maybe she should just stay home with Johnny for the two weeks prior to the surgery. What if he had another seizure and nobody was there to help him? Tosh had said the possibility of that was remote, as long as he took the medication. But still. Pauline should reassign some of the ops crew and free Roy up a little bit to help with fleet management. And maybe Claire could get Ed from Sales to take over payroll for a couple of weeks so that Claire could then deal with the distributor correspondence that was no doubt piling up in Pauline's email in-box. And maybe Rosa would have intuited a need by now to get focused, stop flirting with the drivers, and do something useful—*It's all hands on deck now, Rosa! Four-alarm emergency, can't you see that?* And now here Pauline went with the maybes again.

Or maybe OSHA would just shut the whole factory down. There! Problem solved.

The Publix line finally moved. Pauline rummaged in her purse to find her wallet and saw the crumpled brown napkin with Bob Logan's phone number. She smoothed it flat and slipped it into her billfold; she'd indeed be a dutiful daughter and talk to Packy about it the next time she went to see him, which—note to self—should probably be soon. Wait; she'd forget it for sure if it was stuffed out of sight in the wallet. She dug for it, paid for the wine gums, and got back into the Prius. She tucked the brown napkin into a clip on the passenger-side visor and headed back to the factory.

The rest of the afternoon was a headache. Ed from Sales was having a panic attack because the roll-up booth graphics he'd ordered for the trade show on Friday had come back from the printer looking like "fried poop," or so he said. The colors were off, he complained, and the Bold City logo was out of register. And he was right, Pauline thought, the darn thing was a mess, but there was little they could do about it now, with less than two days to correct it. Except fire the printer. Which she made a note to do. Then the Wi-Fi went down for nearly an hour and Claire had everyone on edge with the language she was using—*loudly*—as she battled it out with some poor help desk tech who was probably in Mumbai working the graveyard shift. By three o'clock, when the second customer service rep they'd hired this month quit abruptly, claiming a child-care issue, Pauline had had enough. She was thinking she should get back to the house, check on Johnny. Plus, the tantalizing thought of a second run began to wage a battle in her mind with the prickling of guilt she felt over the amount of work still piled on her desk.

Ah, but why shouldn't she? One of the few—*very* few—benefits that came with aging, Pauline decided, was the slightly devil-may-care attitude she found herself taking more and more in matters of propriety, responsibility, or even morality, for that matter. Do what you want! she told herself. Life's too short! After all, she'd hit *fifty*, which meant that more than likely she was well past the halfway point in this particular rodeo. When she was forty-nine, she could still convince herself that it was possible, if unlikely, that she would one day be a ninety-eight-year-old woman. But a centenarian? Not so likely. She'd googled it. She had a 17 percent chance of living to a hundred. But my God. Did she even *want* to live to a hundred? Shriveled up and dried out and dribbling down the front of her Velcro-close duster? Of course not. Then what did she want?

"I want to get the hell out of here and go run," she said out loud. She texted Johnny, told him she'd be home soon. She buzzed Rosa out front and told her she'd be gone for the rest of the day. She drank a bottle of water in ten quick gulps. Hydrate, hydrate, hydrate. Then she plugged her iPod into her computer and quickly arranged a new playlist in iTunes. Time to turn it up. Three miles, thirty-four minutes, allowing for warm-up and cool-down. Put the Kanye and Eminem up closer to the beginning, stack the middle with Beastie Boys and Green Day, round it out with AC/DC and Aerosmith. There. She was going to dream until her dreams came true.

She stopped by Claire's cubicle on the way out. "You good?" Pauline said. "I'm taking off early." Claire glanced at her watch and said nothing, but Pauline saw a flicker of annoyance pass over her assistant's face. And there it was—that old tension, palpable as twine. At Bold City Ice, Pauline was the owner; she could arrive when she wanted, leave when she wanted, do what she wanted. She'd take her Prius back over the bridge to sunny Watchers Island, complete her run, maybe hit the grocery store. She and Johnny would open a bottle of wine while cooking dinner, then they'd watch some television and she'd do a little stretching before climbing into bed with her iPad.

Claire would be stuck at her desk until five, then would fight the worst of the traffic back home to Baymeadows, rush her kids through homework and pizza, and fall asleep in front of the television with a basket of unfolded laundry at her feet. Funny how this worked. Claire was the closest thing Pauline had ever had to a best friend, and yet there was this—this—*thing* they could never quite get around, this obstacle they could never surmount. Pauline was the boss. Claire was not. Well, text her tonight, Pauline told herself. It was just like everything else. Pretend it's all fine, and it will be.

The phone on Claire's desk buzzed.

"Can you catch Pauline, Mama, when she goes past you?" came Rosa's voice.

"She's right here," Claire said.

"There's a lawyer up here, Pauline," Rosa said. "He wants to see you."

Shoot! Of course. Knowles & Frusciante, the firm they'd hired in the wake of the accident. She should have remembered this appointment. Claire raised her eyebrows.

"I forgot about this," Pauline said. "They said they were going to start auditing our records today. I guess somebody needs to get all the work logs out and get this guy set up in the conference room or something." She paused, hoping that Claire might offer to meet with the lawyer in her stead. Claire kept her face expressionless. "That sounds like a big job," Claire said; then she turned to her computer and started typing.

Great. There went the second run. Pauline sighed, hitched up her purse, and went out to the lobby to meet the lawyer, whom she found sitting on a sofa adjacent to the reception desk, jiggling his knee. He looked like he was twenty years old.

"Are you Mrs. MacKinnon?" he said. He stood up.

"Yes," Pauline said.

He opened his wallet and pulled out a Knowles & Frusciante business card, which he handed to her. "I'm Sam Tulley. They sent me over to start a review of your work logs? For your appeal?" Pauline looked at the card, and then back up at him. He was tall, with clear green eyes and a dark boyish haircut. "For OSHA?" he added, as if she didn't know.

"Yep," she said. She tried to hide the impatience in her voice. How old was this kid? What was that overpriced law firm doing, anyway, sending over the junior guy? Or was this the intern? The *temp*? She looked again at his card. The initials J. D. were clearly printed after Sam Tulley's name. Well, fine. He was a lawyer, then. The youngest lawyer on the face of the earth.

"I was just about to head out," she said. "I'm sorry, but I blanked on our meeting."

He looked a little dejected. "They said it was important that I begin today. That it might take a while? And we want to be ready? You know?"

Oh, Lord have *mercy*. "I can get you started," she said. "There's the conference room." She gestured to the room just off the lobby. "We can work in there. Let me get my notes." Sam Tulley nodded appreciatively and headed for the conference room.

"Pauline!" Rosa whispered, as soon as he was out of earshot. "He's hot!" She was watching the young lawyer through the conference room's open door.

"Mind yourself, Rosa," Pauline said. "Don't make me go get your mother." She went back to her office and picked up a notebook and one of the stacks of operations logs she'd been poring over since the accident. By the time she made it back to the conference room, Tulley had a laptop booted up and had resumed his knee jiggling.

"This is quite a building here," he said, attempting pleasantries, it seemed. "It's old?"

"Nineteen twelve," she said. She decided to follow his lead. Friendly, okay. Fine. None of this was *his* fault, after all. "It started as an ice factory but for a while before our company took it over, it was used as an orphanage."

"Really?"

"Yup. Sometimes we hear ghost babies crying."

He looked at her intently, and it appeared as though he was trying to make out whether she really believed what she was saying.

"Boo," she said. He gave a funny sniffing laugh, a sound, it seemed to Pauline, of admiration. He was cute, wasn't he? Reminded her of Johnny when she first met him. She deposited the work logs and sat down at the table, but as she did she felt a tightening in her uterus and then the unmistakable release of fluid. She jumped back up again. "Oh!" she said.

"You okay?" Sam Tulley said.

"I forgot one of the files," Pauline said. "I'll be right back." She made it to the bathroom in time to avoid a complete mess. Thank God Claire kept the ladies' room stocked. The bleeding was copious. She couldn't remember it being this heavy since she was a teenager, and the last time she'd been to the doctor she'd been proclaimed "perimenopausal," which pissed her off pretty good. God! Period doesn't come for four months and now this? What kind of cosmic comedy was going on here, anyway? She got herself together and was washing up when, ridiculously, her throat closed and a prick of tears appeared. Because this wasn't fair. It wasn't. This stupid OSHA *crap*, and all the work she hadn't touched yet today, and Claire mad at her, and—most horrible—Johnny, sitting home with a tumor in his brain. *Don't worry,* Dr. Tosh had said. *Trust me,* he'd said.

Impossible, Pauline should have answered; *we don't even know you.*

She dabbed her eyes with a paper towel and tossed it into the trash, remembering another time she'd been in this bathroom crying, the day of the roller skates, the day of Billy. *Come now, Jesus, where you at?* The aching cramp tightened in her belly, and just then she really *did* hear the orphan babies weeping, somewhere up in the ceiling. Or maybe it was just the catbirds, gotten into the rafters again.

FOUR

The MacKinnons' house, in which they'd lived for twenty-five years and whose stairs Johnny descended in the weak, wet light of a Florida dawn the next morning, had a story, as some houses do. From every room, Johnny could hear the pounding Atlantic surf, a sound so ingrained now in his consciousness he was hardly aware of it anymore, though when he thought about it in the darkness of a sleepless night, he was amazed at the unerring violence of the sound track of his life: by day the gnashing machines of the ice factory, by night the battering hammer of frothing water on sand: *Whump, shhhhh. Whump, shhhhh.*

The house was built more than a hundred years ago; it was the first house on Watchers Island, in fact, which back at the turn of the twentieth century was just a big, nameless pancake of sand wedged between the ocean and a wide swath of the Intracoastal Waterway. Back then, the island was accessible only by way of a rickety one-lane bridge, and the house was little more than an outpost built by a resourceful pioneer who had one hand in the shrimp trade of Mayport and the other in the palm trade of Palm Valley, and who found that the remote island offered convenient proximity to both enterprises.

In the twenties, an enterprising recluse named Donald Stone bought the house. Johnny pieced Stone's story together from a few articles curling in smudged glass display cases at the Watchers Island library. Stone took a perverse enjoyment in being the easternmost resident of a thousand-acre island that was home to only a few dozen intrepid homesteaders and no end of mosquitoes, languorous snakebirds, and puddle-headed armadillos. But after a couple of years, he found he was tired of having to row out and haul drunken boaters—usually moneyed tourist types on their way to drop cash in the restaurants of St. Augustine—off the vessels that ran aground just offshore on foggy nights. The currents surrounding the island created continually shifting sandbars, and without a solid reference point, many captains piloted too close to shore and quickly got stuck.

So Stone got smart. He converted his home into a lighthouse by means of a sturdy windowed cupola added onto the east dormer. He added a three-foot Fresnel lens to fashion a powerful beacon visible four miles offshore, thus signaling shallow waters and significantly reducing the number of pesky wrecks that interrupted his pleasantly lonesome cocktail hours. But the lighthouse design had proved untenable in the long run, given its relatively diminutive tower and the tendency of a rowdy buttonwood tree behind the house to sprout new branches and obscure the light. When the island's population began to grow, thanks to the construction of a new bascule bridge linking it to the mainland, the Coast Guard decided something had to be done and built a proper lighthouse at the north end of Watchers Island.

By the time Johnny and Pauline bought the old lighthouse, it had been renovated and updated through a series of owners, all of whom did their part in bringing the old beast up to comfortably elegant standing. It had been shingled, painted, insulated, scrubbed, weather-stripped, air-conditioned, plumbed, and enlarged. The old Fresnel lens had been sold to a collector, and its housing in the cupola had been dismantled and removed, leaving only a round, rusty imprint in the wood floor, like the ring under a coffee cup.

But none of that was the story for which the house was known. The *story*, as Johnny had heard it, was grisly enough to have made Pauline hesitate before they'd signed the sales contract all those years ago. It happened back in the thirties, when old Stone still kept the light. One day the Coast Guard was summoned to a terrible scene. A luxury yacht had run aground just off the island. The five passengers—a family, including three young children—had been shot through the head, the yacht plundered for cash and jewelry.

When the tug came to pull the yacht off the sandbar and take the bodies to the coroner, somebody mentioned that Stone's light was out, that it had been out for quite some time, in fact, which probably explained the reason the yacht ran aground in the first place. The police rowed over to the island and searched, but found no sign of Donald Stone. The old lighthouse was empty save for a hungry, mewling tomcat. A half-pack of cigarettes lay damply in the kitchen sink. One kitchen chair was overturned. The Fresnel lens was cool. And Stone was never heard from again.

It was not until three years later, when the house came out of receivership and a new buyer started renovations, that Stone's body, now a skeleton, was found under the floorboards of the front room, its skull cracked wickedly across the brow. A pirate's trusted strategy: kill the lightkeeper, snuff the light, rob the ships that subsequently ran aground.

The house story had never bothered Johnny before, but lately he'd been thinking more about old Donald Stone and his unfortunate end here at 15 Beacon Street, and lately the vision of the rotted corpse beneath the foundation was becoming increasingly unsettling. Johnny wondered if Stone was still alive when the boards were nailed down over his head. He used to tease Pauline, saying that he heard knocking on the floorboards in the middle of the night, but lately he was sorry he'd come up with that, because there were times when he actually *did* hear an odd rhythmic tapping coming from the front room, and he had to concentrate hard on the sound before convincing himself it was only a branch from the pecan tree off the porch, rattling against the gutter. The poor tree was now looking nearly bald on one side for all the limbs he'd cut back in an effort to curtail the rattling and settle his own nerves.

Still and all, it was a wonderful old house. Johnny had always loved it. He and Pauline had bought it for a song during a time of cruelly depressed home values, and though Johnny felt a little guilty about it, they had walked away with quite a deal from the previous owner, a recently divorced, hard-drinking fellow who was clearly losing his shirt. They bought it with the original intention of restoring it and selling it to turn a profit, but the island's quiet and the smell of salt air outside their bedroom windows had seduced them, even in the early days when the road was still rutted and sandy, when they still had to drive across the old bridge and up to Ponte Vedra to get to Publix.

Now, steady development had done a lot for Watchers Island, which was today populated by a few thousand residents, mostly Jacksonville commuters, young families, pothead beach urchins, and the independent sort of seniors who rejected the gated communities and "active retirement" neighborhoods of some of their contemporaries. Johnny liked to think he and Pauline fit squarely in the first category, but as the years went by he could see that perhaps they were destined for the last, which was not an unpleasant thought. As long as Watchers Island didn't wash away anytime too soon. What with algae blooms and sea-level rise and all the rest of it, some scientists were already announcing that the entire Florida peninsula would be underwater by the end of the century, and though Johnny himself believed this could be true, he also knew he wouldn't be around to have to worry about it. Let the waters rise.

The cupola that once housed the light was today accessible only by means of a pull-down staircase, and the little room the stairs led to was cramped and low-ceilinged, with barely enough space for even a man of Johnny's small stature to stand up straight. Pauline only occasionally ventured up anymore; it made her claustrophobic, she said. But the windows opened nicely to a view of the Atlantic to the east, the Intracoastal to the west, the green canopy of trees to the north and south. Johnny kept a chair and a little table in the cupola, and he went up to look at the ocean and have a smoke now and then, a habit of which Pauline disapproved and for which he feigned subterfuge and the sense of guilt it implied, out of respect. As if there could be a secret between them. As if after all these years there could be something they didn't know about each other.

Outside, the air was thick with moisture, and on the front walkway, Johnny noted that now, on top of everything else, there was a problem with frogs. Thousands of them. Cuban tree frogs, nonindigenous invaders, brought by the night's rains. He wasn't entirely surprised. A number of frogs usually appeared on Watchers Island each year around this time, when the barometric pressure was low and the humidity was high.

But this year's influx was more intense than any Johnny had witnessed before. It seemed to be a multigenerational invasion: thick-bodied adult frogs the size of golf balls and spindly insect-like youth, all hurling themselves, lost, through the sawgrass. Frogs dotted the driveway and clung to the windowpanes, drawn by insects and the glow of lamps. They piled in muddy layers on the porch and suctioned their wet way up the front door. They shat in the grass and clogged the drain return. With the break of dawn, it looked like many of the frogs had begun a flopping, jerky retreat to the standing puddles and sodden gullies around the house. Many had died, and some lay stricken, wounded, on the driveway and on the walkway leading to the house. It was Frog Normandy, Johnny decided. Frog Leipzig. Frog Armageddon.

He went for a broom and started to sweep the driveway, but the frogs were resisting. The effect was a little horrifying— they flattened themselves against the concrete and let the straw bristles of the broom scrape across their backs. When he nudged one into a fleshy ball and swept at it quickly and perhaps a little too forcefully, it pitched across the driveway and panked against the trunk of a pine, leaving a bright silvery spot. Oh, God.

"All right!"

He turned toward the voice to see his neighbor Jerry coming down to the end of his own drive, where their two bricked-in mailboxes stood side by side.

"Six-pointer!" Jerry called. "Nice!"

Jerry was an interesting specimen. He was once a competitive bowler, taking a Florida championship and competing seriously in a Southeastern conference before he suffered a stroke at the age of fifty that partially paralyzed the right side of his body, and thus his bowling arm. So he started over as a lefty. He was at first lauded for his spirit and his determination, but he confessed to Johnny one day, when he'd cornered him at the dustbins, that the left-handed bowling wasn't going so well. No more trophies, put it that way.

Things tended not to go well for Jerry. He'd been a bachelor for years, desperately lonely, given to lingering like a remora in Johnny's driveway and around his mailbox, hoping for a confab. Then a few years ago, he'd married a woman named Tina. He met her online and she moved down from Detroit. She was Hispanic, quite attractive, and hardworking (a dental hygienist, if Johnny recalled correctly), but it turned out that the Tina package included a teenage son who was something of a train wreck. Pauline was friendly with Tina, had her over for a glass of wine now and then, and had gotten the whole story. It seems the kid had gotten into some trouble for shoplifting and vandalism. Then he failed his junior year and refused to go back to school. *And* he'd evidently called the principal a cunt on the way out the door, so Johnny couldn't imagine he was entirely welcome anyway. "He just needs direction," Johnny overheard Tina sighing to Pauline one day. "He just needs to get *inspired* by something, you know? I mean, don't we all need to be *inspired?*"

Johnny saw the boy almost every day, walking barefoot to the beach, shag-haired and slow-moving and indeed, by all appearances, bereft of inspiration. Usually he was dressed in a military jacket of some sort, insignia across the back and down the sleeves. But sometimes he went shirtless, and his arms and belly wobbled with stubborn remnants of baby fat. Last Christmas he'd gone back to Detroit to live with his father and had gotten a job busing tables at an upscale steakhouse. Jerry was thrilled. Tina told Pauline the kid was doing great up there, really thriving, just *soaring,* and that they were so proud of him.

But then there was more trouble—a skirmish with a mouthy customer at the steakhouse followed by a dustup with the heavy-handed dad, Pauline said—and next thing they knew the kid was back with Tina and Jerry on Watchers Island. "Can you imagine?" Pauline said. "They just don't know what to do with him." Johnny could imagine.

Now he stopped sweeping at the frogs—he was beginning to think they were suicidal—and steeled himself for his neighbor's approach. Jerry was wearing rubber Crocs that made his feet look like large hooves, and he walked with a sliding shuffle, not so much sidestepping the frogs in his driveway as plowing them out of the way as he advanced.

"You believe this?" he said. He spread his arms wide. "Frogs!" he said, as if Johnny had not noticed. Johnny seldom made a habit of stopping to chat with Jerry, and that morning he was less inclined than ever. But Jerry was marching over, resolute. He was a dark, wiry man, very big on Bible studies and men's fellowship groups, for which he was incessantly trying to recruit Johnny's membership, and that effort notwithstanding, Johnny had a reluctant fondness for the little fellow. He'd noted with amusement since Tina's arrival that Jerry's bristly hair had taken on an unnaturally uniform ebony wash. Johnny suspected he was having it dyed. But what was that to him? He decided to be friendly.

"Hiya, Jerry," he said.

Jerry approached, shaking his head and gesturing at the frogs.

"Eh?" he demanded.

"Aye," Johnny said. "Ah dinnae ken." Americans in general, and Jerry in particular, seemed to like it when Johnny laid on the brogue, though it was really a bit of a put-on at this point, considering how long he'd lived in Florida. But it was an easy matter to slide back, and he could do it to be entertaining. "It seems we have a pestilence," he added.

"The Bible says they will come," Jerry said. "I looked it up: 'Their land swarmed with frogs, even in the chambers of their kings.'"

"We're not kings, Jerry," Johnny said.

"Sure we are," Jerry said. "Look at us. You're king of ice. And I'm king of fire." Jerry was the PR guy for the Jacksonville fire marshal's office. He grinned at Johnny, pleased with his metaphor.

"I just want the sons of bitches off my driveway," Johnny said.

"True that," Jerry said. "Anyway." He crossed his arms, then uncrossed them again and stuffed his hands into the pockets of his cargo pants. He was wearing a pink shirt, and though normally Johnny had no patience for this, on Jerry it was darkly touching. Jerry shifted his weight and looked at Johnny, waiting for conversation.

"How's the family, Jerry?" Johnny said finally.

Jerry looked over at his house and furrowed his brow.

"Well," he said. "It's hard, I guess, to be seventeen these days. I can hardly remember. The kid's a waste. And Tina won't do anything about it."

"Is he working?" Johnny said.

"Who's going to hire him?" Jerry said gloomily. "One, he's a dropout. And two, he's a freak."

"Little harsh, Jerry," Johnny said.

"Call it like I see it, Johnny." Jerry sighed. "Maybe you can hire him at the factory?"

"Didn't you just tell me he was a freak? Not exactly a glowing recommendation."

Jerry nodded sadly.

"Anyway," Johnny said. "He has to be eighteen to work at the factory. Liability."

Jerry looked at him sadly. "Oh, boy," he said. "Frogs."

Jerry walked back to his house and went into the garage. He came out with a rake, which he took to the frogs rather viciously.

Johnny's phone buzzed in his pocket. It was Sharon.

"Phone tag," she said. "I've finally got you."

"Sorry," he said. "It's been a little weird around here."

"Well, it must be contagious," she said. "It's pretty weird here, too."

"What's going on?"

"Anna's been arrested," she said flatly. Johnny had to think for a second. Anna? And then he remembered: Corran's *wife*.

He sometimes forgot that Corran was a married man. "She was trying to smuggle heroin back from Tenerife; that's where her parents live. She put it in Lucy's *diaper*. It's horrible. Makes me sick."

"So, they're using again," Johnny said. His stomach clenched.

"Not Corran. Just Anna."

"How do you know that?"

"I *know*, Johnny. Been through this enough times, I can tell when he's on and when he's off, can't I? Yes, I can."

"When did this happen?"

"Little bit ago. Six weeks? No. Two months."

"Christ. Why didn't you tell me?"

"Well," Sharon said. Her voice took on an edge of irritation. "You took yourself out of the loop, now didn't you? Talk to your son yourself sometime, why don't you?"

"I didn't take myself out of the loop. Corran kicked me out."

"That's your interpretation."

"Anyway, he wouldn't talk to me even if I did call him."

"That's not the issue. The issue is that Anna's going to prison. For a long time, and to tell you the truth, I'm relieved. I'm sorry, but she's somebody else's worry, not mine, and Corry has a far better chance of staying clean without her around. But here's the next thing: Corran's on his own with the baby now. And I don't know about that."

"What do you mean?"

"He's fragile, is what I mean. I really believe he's cleaned himself up this time, but that doesn't mean I consider him exactly fit to raise a child."

"I thought he was out on a rig?"

"Well, he had to take leave of that. You can't take care of a baby from the middle of the North Sea. He's got himself up in Port Readie in some mate's little cottage, trying to make a go. Got Lucy in day care, and he's working on the ferry at Loch Linnhe. I'm proud of him, on the one hand. But on the other, I'm worried. How's he going to manage, Johnny? I mean, how is he going to *do this*?" She paused. "Ah, but she's the sweetest little thing, Johnny. You should see what a sweet thing she is."

Johnny tried to envision it: Corran on his own, taking care of a baby. It was impossible to summon the mental picture. And while he agreed with Sharon—it was a good thing, in the long run, to have Anna out of the picture—it was hard to reckon how Corran, who for the last decade had been hardly able to care for himself, was going to care for a baby.

"Anyway," she said, "I just thought you should be up to speed. I know you and Corran are not getting on. But still. You never call me, so I decided to call you."

"I'm bad with communication."

"Among other things." Funny how Sharon could pick up right where she left off—that same kindly acidic tone, that same disarming directness. When Johnny first met her, he had mistaken her asperity for aggression, and he was both aroused and intimidated by it. But he came to understand that was not it at all. She was simply tough in her loving, as impatient and demanding as a lioness. Being loved by Sharon was a like an assault of affection, a contact sport.

"How are *you* doing, Sharon?"

"I'm all right."

"Yeh?"

"Sure. We're getting along. I'm finished with chemo, thank God. Remind me never to get breast cancer again, aye? Now just working all the time. You know, same as ever. I tell you, I think every day about bringing little Lucy down here with us, but we just can't. Toole had his knees replaced, did I tell you that? *Och,* what a pain in the ass he's been in the recovery. He wouldn't do what the doctor advised and do one at a time. Had to bang them both out in one go. What a numpty. Who opts to disable both of his legs at the same time? My husband, that's who, Johnny. Why do I marry daft men, can you tell me that? I thought I'd go mad with the fetching-tea business. Hell of a road back. But getting better, day by day."

Johnny told her to hang tight. He thanked her for the update. He hung up. A vision of Corran holding a baby on a cold Argyll hillside appeared, and he took a deep breath and pushed the vision back. He felt a chill and looked down, then kicked reflexively to dislodge a pale frog, nearly translucent, that had landed on his ankle and clung, desperate, trying to move up the leg of his trousers.

Christ. He was being invaded. Everywhere, breached.

Inside the garage, the air was hot and stale. Johnny turned on a window air conditioner—a secondhand junker that had been holding on through the last few summers, keeping the garage bearable, if not comfortable. The unit wheezed once, then died.

"Bag of shite," he said to it. The *heat.* It was the only problem with this garage—it got so damn hot out here. Other than that, it was perfect—a full three cars wide, with space for both commuting vehicles plus a project car. It was more of a machine shop than a garage, really, and Johnny was proud of the accumulation of tools he'd acquired through the years. Welders, grinders, shears, and a press brake, even a lathe and a full-sized milling machine hulking next to the water heater. It could get a little cramped at times, but he didn't mind. On weekends, he could pull cars out to the driveway for the day to make more room for working.

Johnny pushed the button to open the garage door. It clanked up the tracks, hell of a racket, and in came the wet smell of salt air, the clatter of cicadas, and a shrieking gull, not far. He maneuvered around the VW Beetle parked in the garage, thinking, as he did every day, about how much he'd like to banish *that* damn time-waster so he could fit in his *real* project car: a gorgeous 1972 Chevelle with a throaty V-8, close to mint! All it needed was a bit of bodywork to the right front quarter-panel and some attention paid to the interior, which ought to be doable enough, if he could ever get to it. And getting to it was exactly the problem, in terms of both time and access, because for the last two months the Chevelle had been criminally parked along the side of the house and relegated to a car cover, thanks to the bloody 1977 VW Beetle taking up prime garage space.

What a disaster this Beetle was proving to be. An albatross. It was a project car he'd taken on with Corran years ago. The idea was that they'd work on it together during summers and that Corran would have it to run around Watchers Island in when he came for visits. Johnny *never* liked the idea of the Beetle, but he gave it a go after seeing Corran's teenage eyes light up when they'd stumbled on the banty little car in a used car lot behind the ice plant. Ah, let him have it, he thought at the time. It would be good for them—something to work on together. He bought it and had it towed out to the house. The problem was that Corran had scarcely begun to learn his way around the engine compartment when he discovered heroin, and that was that.

Johnny'd hung on to the car for years, waiting for Corran to come around and show a renewed interest, but no more; he'd had enough of looking at it. Only thing to do was sell it. Both instinct and the Internet VW message boards told him the wisest step was to just unload the car for parts—quick and simple. But something else, some niggling perfectionism, perhaps, was telling him to pull the heap back from decay just enough to tease some adventurous buyer with the idea of restoration. He'd get it running first, then sell it. Just because *he* hated Beetles didn't mean *everybody* did. No sense giving the wretched thing a death sentence.

He went back into the garage and moved around, turning on lights and tools. He liked this part of the day. Normally he was the first one to get up, having developed in his youth a peculiar feeling of urgency in the mornings, a restlessness to *get stuff done* that often sent him out to the garage in the early dawn to fiddle away an hour or two on a project or to work on tooling a part for one of the icemakers before heading to the factory for the day.

This morning, though, he'd been slower to rise. After Pauline's alarm jarred him out of sleep, he remained in bed for a while, staring at the ceiling and stubbornly *not* thinking about his brain cyst by turning over possible solutions for the latest problem on the VW—how to unfreeze a pigheaded piston that was locked up in a cylinder. He'd been struggling with it for nearly a week now, but it was thus far intractable. A few days ago, in a near-rage, he'd spent hours pulling the engine. He then propped it on its side and left a forty-pound battery parked atop the frozen piston, hoping that the weight of the battery would eventually press the damn thing loose in its housing, but he didn't have high hopes.

Now Johnny pulled the battery off the piston, then gave the piston a diagnostic thunk with a ball-peen hammer. Still stuck, immovable as granite inside the cylinder. This thing was going to total the engine if he didn't get it loose. He'd seen the likes of it before. That time back home in Glasgow, the piston immobilized in his Triumph motorbike. He'd beaten on the cylinder for more than an hour before dousing it in oil, tying a thick rope around the cylinder head, and suspending the entire bike from a blackthorn tree in the back garden to let gravity do the work. It was still hanging there when Sharon and Corran had come back from the shops, and Corran—what was he then, two? three?—had laughed so hard at the sight of a motorcycle hanging in a tree that Johnny was afraid the boy would wet himself. But that was many years ago. And there was no hanging a Volkswagen from a tree.

However, Johnny was nothing if not tenacious. In fact, Pauline accused him of being stubborn past the point of clear thinking, but he admired a little intransigence in a person. He respected it; it bespoke temerity. There was a famous wrestler in sixth-century Greece, Milo of Croton. He was said to have lifted a calf every day from the calf's birth. Once the animal was grown, Milo was lifting a full-sized ox. This was the kind of tenacity Johnny admired. This was what the world was lacking today. It was nearly the end of October. By Christmas, he would finish this fucking Beetle.

He leaned over the engine, placed a block of wood on the piston head, and hit the wood with the hammer. Then hit it harder. Harder. Harder. On the fourth swing, he hammered the tip of his index finger and let out a grunt of pain before the hammer clattered down into the engine block. He straightened up. This stupid car. He didn't know if he hated anything as much as this stupid car.

"Why are you fussing with it, then?" Pauline had asked him, more than once. "Just sell it as it is. Let someone else fix it."

Johnny fetched the hammer, leaned back under the hood, and continued banging at the piston.

An hour later, Johnny had made no progress on the VW. He retreated to the house and cooled off with a shower. He washed the coffeepot and unloaded the dishwasher, then checked on the frogs. Fewer, but still a crowd. General San Jose didn't want to come down for his breakfast, so Johnny brought the bowl of kibble up to the bedroom and left it on the bed atop a bath towel. Pauline had created a monster. He wandered through the house and tried to decide what to do. He felt like a child, confined to the house. He tidied the bathroom and folded a load of laundry, mostly runners' singlets and sports bras. He took his steroid medication and peed on a sugar test strip, which he had to do twice a day to make sure the steroids weren't causing diabetes. Good times. He tried to read but couldn't concentrate, and then he spent a fretful period wondering if the reason he couldn't concentrate was the parasitic cyst on his brain. My God, couldn't it have been anywhere else? He thought about other parts of his body that could more comfortably host a tumor. A finger, he decided. Or a toe.

This was abysmal, Johnny thought then. What a waste of a day. He should be at the factory, shouting at the loading crew to hurry up, kicking at the conveyor motor on Dumbo to get her working again, comparing distribution logs with Roy in the break room. How was he supposed to do this for two weeks? There was nothing to do but *think*, and that was going to get him nowhere. He went upstairs and fetched the General to take him out back for a pee. Then he locked up the house, turned toward the beach, and started to walk.

I want you gone. The sentence was becoming a refrain, insistent and unwelcome. Johnny's ears began to ring with the incantation. He breached the dune and headed south along the waterline, listening to the crash of surf, willing it to drown out the words.

FIVE

Vic's House of Crabs was dead. This was not unexpected, given that it was three o'clock on a weekday afternoon. Not a time Johnny would normally have found himself stopping in at Vic's for a cold one. But thanks to his intracranial tenant, as he'd come to think of it, things these days were decidedly nonnormal. The notion of visiting Vic's had come to him while he was strolling along the beach, and he'd slapped his pocket reflexively to see if he'd brought his wallet, which, thankfully, he had. He'd reached the pier and ascended the dunes toward Vic's, reasoning that if he couldn't drive to his factory and make ice, he might as well make the most of a sunny afternoon with a quick pint before Pauline got home. Meds be damned. Besides, Dr. Tosh hadn't said anything about not drinking a beer or two while taking steroids. And Johnny—well, Johnny hadn't asked.

The crab shack was a curmudgeonly little building, all bleached white cinder blocks and salt-rotted trim. It was parked on a concrete boardwalk pointing east toward the ocean, so that while its patrons parked in back, in the pier parking lot, they had to walk around to the front of the building and face, Zen-like, the saline spray of the Atlantic before entering. Vic's had a roof that slanted upward in the front like the brim of a baseball cap, and this brim formed an overhang under which, later on, the beachgoers would queue at the walk-up window for quick-serve crab sandwiches and hush puppies, while the eat-in and take-out set crowded the small interior of the little restaurant, if it could be called that, with only its six wooden stools along a counter under the beach-facing windows.

But that would be later. For now, the surfers were still in the ocean wresting the final rides from a dwindling nor'easter. The toddlers were home for their naps. The Jacksonville commuters had not yet returned to the island, and the seniors were still at home, holding out impatiently for Vic's five o'clock early-bird specials. In fact, at the moment, only one of the six stools at the window counter in Vic's House of Crabs was occupied, and it was by Johnny himself, who was nursing a beer and watching a thunderhead track south.

The crab shack's front door banged open, and in came an argument. Johnny turned on his stool and saw the group of old men he'd come to think of as the Bocce Quartet: Sid, Tony, Errol, and Bill. They came to the beach every day to play bocce on the courts just behind Vic's. Or at least, ostensibly to play bocce. What they really came to do was drink sangria from a plastic jug, ogle bikinis, and goad each other into a series of overblown debates that served little purpose, as far as Johnny could see, other than to pass the time and keep the old men away from their wives for a while. But the debates were generally quite entertaining, and for lack of anything better to do, Johnny was feeling inclined today to order a second pint and settle in, even though the old geezers *could* get carried away. The last time Johnny had seen them in Vic's they were so worked up over Social Security he thought he'd have to physically intervene.

Sid Hoying was his favorite. He was ancient—had to be in his nineties, Johnny would guess—but was the most energetic of the bunch, badgering and haranguing the others long after a debate had died a slow death, long after the other men had thrown up their hands, refilled their paper cups with sangria, and returned balefully to the bocce court. Sid had been retired for years from a long career as an attorney for the City of Jacksonville, though he still kept his generously proportioned nose in every bit of city business he could. He'd been a progressive back in the day, had raised the ire of many of his contemporaries by taking a hard line on the small group of white thugs—Packy Knight cleverly not among them—who'd been arrested after Ax Handle Saturday, though despite Sid's efforts most of the culprits still got off light.

He was around during Jacksonville's 1968 consolidation with Duval County, too, and the city's subsequent effort to minimize some of the pains of its recent past through a more positive branding campaign. There was a famous photo of Jacksonville mayor Hans Tanzler posing with a new sign at the county line after the big consolidation brouhaha. In the photo, Tanzler is standing on a high ladder with the actress Lee Meredith, who'd been enlisted by a PR firm with a connection to Hollywood to bring a little sex appeal to the moment. Meredith strikes a wildly seductive pose at the mayor's side—chest thrust into Tanzler's face, one long tanned leg extended out at her side. "Jacksonville," the sign proclaims, "Bold New City of the South." On the ground, a man holding the ladder has the good fortune of the best view in the Bold City that day: the underside of Lee Meredith's microscopic miniskirt. And that was Sid. "Finest day of my career," he often said. He had a framed enlargement of the photo hanging above the television set in his living room.

The topic today appeared to be reverse mortgages.

"You're letting the bank eat your equity!" Sid was saying to Tony. "Don't you want to have money to leave your kids?"

"Not particularly," Tony replied. "Have you *met* my kids?"

"You're using the most expensive credit there is!" Sid said.

"Equity-rich equals cash-poor. This just reverses the equation."

"What if you have to go into a home?"

"I'm not going into a home. Shoot me first," Tony said.

And so on. Sid looked over and saw Johnny.

"Johnny!" Sid said. "Tell him. He's getting raped!"

"You're getting raped, Tony," Johnny said mildly.

"You don't know what you're talking about," Tony shot back. "This is about *money*. We gotta make our own way here, you know. You're used to that socialism over there in England."

"I'm not from England."

"What, then. Scotland, then."

"Even socialists like money, Tony," Johnny said.

"Ah, bullshit," Tony said.

Sid peered at Johnny. "It's Wednesday," he said. "What are you doing here on a Wednesday afternoon?"

"Took the day off."

"Well, that's a first," Sid said. He patted the leather case of bocce balls he'd laid on the counter. "Play a round with us."

"No thanks," Johnny said. "That's an old fart's game."

"Of which you are one," Sid said. Most days Johnny would have let this slide. But today it got his goat. He was only fifty-three!

"Sid, you've got forty years on me," he said.

"You think so?" Sid said, genuinely surprised.

"I do."

"It's funny," Sid said. "I don't remember getting this old."

"You're old, Sid."

"I guess you're right, Johnny." Sid pulled out an empty stool and climbed atop it like a spider monkey. "Then I suppose I better get moving," Sid said. "I still got drinking to do." Bill, Errol, and Tony took stools at the end of the row and continued their quarrel. Johnny's phone buzzed in his pocket, and he fished it out to see Pauline's name on the screen. He answered.

"I'm about to head back," she told him. "You good?"

"Brilliant," he said. "How's the ice industry today?"

"Fair to middling. Roy's crying about missing you."

"Aw. Sweet."

"You home?"

"Just out for a walk," Johnny said. Sid snickered.

"Back in a bit," Pauline said.

"Drive safe, kidda."

"You should just tell her you're drinking with sweaty old farts in a filthy dive at the beach," Sid said after Johnny hung up. "Why hide it?"

"Is that what you tell your wife?" Johnny said.

"I tell her I'm going to play bocce. That's the truth. And she tells me to take my balls and get the hell out. We have an understanding."

Johnny looked at his watch. It was nearly five. Pauline would be met with the first swell of evening traffic and it would likely be six o'clock before she reached the house. He had a fifteen-minute walk ahead of him. Time for another beer? He couldn't see why not. He raised a hand and motioned to Vic.

"So, how's the ice business out there?" Sid said. "Making it?"

"So far," Johnny said. "But we're still waiting on the OSHA appeal to be scheduled." He accepted his second beer from Vic and touched it to Sid's paper cup of sangria. "Here's hoping we stay alive, Sid. You, me, and the ice plant."

"Salud," Sid said. "And how's Knowles treating you?" Knowles. The name was becoming quite the thorn in Johnny's side. Knowles & Frusciante (*"We're on Your Side"*) was one of the biggest law firms in Jacksonville, and the firm's labor law specialists were supposed to be the superheroes who were going to pull Bold City Ice back from the precipice. "We feel your *pain*," Knowles had told Johnny and Pauline solicitously in a boardroom at the top of the Riverplace Tower. "And we can *help* you."

"Christ," Johnny said. "Don't get me started. Are lawyers always this pompous?"

"Of course we are. That's what makes us so lovable. But are they making progress on the appeal?"

Johnny shrugged. "They sent in the big guns for two days back in the beginning. Knowles himself was at the factory for maybe an hour, tops. Now they say they're in the 'research' phase. Which makes me laugh. I haven't seen anything solid from them yet. It's piss. We're no better prepared to appeal the citations than we were before we started writing checks to Knowles. OSHA says negligent tank maintenance. Our boys were sloppy with the logs. How are we going to argue against this?"

Sid positioned his sangria cup in front of him and peered into it like he was reading tea leaves. After a moment, he shook his head and looked at Johnny. "It's a tough nut, friend."

"Sid," Johnny said. "You used to deal with the Jacksonville Sheriff's Office, right?"

"In city cases. Sure. All the time."

"Answer me this: Why can't we get more police presence in Little Silver? We're beating our heads against the wall. We've got a house right across the street from the factory that I'd bet my bollocks is part of a drug operation, and the cops aren't doing a thing about it. If there was a bust there, it could have a bearing on our OSHA appeal—I think the druggies tampered with the ammonia tank."

"Oh, I know about that house," Sid said.

"You do?"

"Big gray Victorian?"

"That's the one."

Sid nodded. "That's Leonard's house. You've seen him? Snaky-looking guy, rides a bike around?" Johnny had seen him, all right. He'd noticed him right away when he showed up in the neighborhood last spring. Always whistling. Looked weird around the eyes, something a little unbalanced there. There was a strung-out-looking blond woman living there with him for a while, and the way Leonard would shout at her—*You heard what I said, you dumb bitch*—would make your hair stand on end. Johnny was relieved when she beat a path. Even the shiftless bunch of old guys that hung out down the block, drinking and cupping hands around their fat-rolled joints all day, seemed to want little to do with Leonard. "That dude scary," one of them, old Ford, had said to Johnny once. "That dude ain't *right*."

"Leonard's well-known to JSO," Sid was saying. "He's dealing, all right."

Johnny slapped the countertop. "Well, you see? What if he's cooking meth in there? And what if he's using our ammonia to do it? Sid, if we had evidence of meth-making, like a drug bust and a police report, I'd sure like to share it with OSHA."

"Sherriff thinks he's doing more than cooking meth," Sid said. "Trust me, Johnny: They're paying attention to that house. They think Leonard's connected to a pretty big operation. Heroin, guns, all of it. I'd steer clear."

Johnny shook his head in frustration. "Why don't they bust it, for God's sake?"

Sid raised one eyebrow. "Because they're being strategic. You know how these things go. They gotta get it right. Probable cause. They can't get a warrant without the right evidence. Plus, they want to catch them in the act so they get the whole caboodle, not just some dime-bag transaction."

"I want that house busted. I want to have evidence of a nearby meth lab entered into my OSHA appeal."

"You think it will help?"

"It can't hurt. It's across the street, for God's sake. I wouldn't be surprised to find a Bold City Ice hand truck over there. Probably half our missing bleeder valves sitting on Leonard's kitchen counter. He's helping himself. I can feel it. He's getting in."

"Let me guess. You talked to the lawyers about this idea?"

"Pauline and I both did."

"And let me guess. They're not interested?"

"Right."

"That's because they're lawyers, Johnny! Take it from me—they want a paper trail, not a half-assed theory."

"A bust at Leonard's house. A meth lab bust would produce a paper trail."

"Probable cause, Johnny. Repeat after me: JSO needs probable cause. And they're willing to wait for it. You can bring your theory to the OSHA hearing. But my guess is it's not going to get you where you want. Evidence, John. *Evidence*." Sid climbed down off his stool. "I better get back to my posse over there," he said, nodding toward the Bocce Quartet.

"How do you stay so informed, Sid?" Johnny asked.

"Johnny, I'm a pushy old man with not enough to do. City of Jax is my beat. They see me coming, they start talking, hoping it will make me leave faster. Ha!" He clapped Johnny on the shoulder affectionately. "Hang tight, Johnny. Let your pompous lawyers do their jobs. Maybe it will all work out," Sid said. "You never know." He didn't sound very convincing.

Johnny texted Pauline and Roy an abbreviated version of Sid's report on Leonard and the Little Silver drug scene. *Doesn't really help us,* Roy replied immediately. *Unless/until they bust him.* Johnny waited, but Pauline didn't reply. He pictured her—hunched over the steering wheel, locked in traffic on the Acosta Bridge; she'd surely have glanced at her phone and seen his message, but she wouldn't text back until she pulled the Prius into the garage on Watchers Island, knowing full well that by then Johnny would be in the kitchen waiting for her. *Don't text and drive,* she told him all the time, earnest and righteous. Ah, Pauline. So sweetly prim. So moral. She really would have made a good mother.

Johnny paid his bill. He exited the crab shack and felt the heat wrap around him like a wet towel. He made his way to the waterline and headed toward home, carrying his shoes and sloshing through the surf while a shrimper moved north along the horizon, bound for Mayport. The beer was buzzing pleasantly in his chest and the water on his calves was soothing, familiar. He stopped and looked east, where four thousand miles away, the great crashing waves of the Atlantic were calming in the coves of the Caledonian firths, lapping at the pebbled shores, then fingering up into green machair, just beyond.

Having grown up on one side of the North Atlantic and having made his life on the other, Johnny felt an affinity to the coastline so strong he sometimes wondered if it betrayed a latent phobia of landlock. Back in Glasgow, he could ride his bicycle three miles to the south and put his hands into the cold current of the tiny North Calder Water river. There he could set a leaf afloat and know that it would progress down into the River Clyde and out through the firths, past the tip of Ireland and into the great wide sea. Here in Florida, he could pitch a buffed green piece of sea glass out toward the breakers and imagine it tumbling deeper, deeper, into the tidal tumult for days and then weeks and then months, scuttling along the seafloor until it washed up again, smoother now, lighter, on the bright cold beach at Iona.

When Corran was little, Johnny told him he'd pitch a stone every day, and that if Corran could get over to the sea, maybe he'd find one of the very same stones that Johnny had once fingered in America, on tiny Watchers Island. Johnny hadn't thought of that in a long time. He bent now and ran his fingers through a trough of shells until he found a piece of glass. He stood, grunted, and threw.

After a while he started walking again. He could see the top of his house, the old lighthouse cupola, from the beach. He headed up the dune.

Johnny was still standing at the back door, beating the sand from the bottoms of his shoes, when the home phone rang. He jogged to the kitchen, expecting Roy or Pauline. It was Dr. Tosh.

"Good afternoon," Tosh said. "Still with us?"

"Yes, sorry to say," Johnny said.

Tosh chuckled. "Johnny," he said. "You are a pisser. When all this surgery business is over you and I should go play golf."

"You play golf?"

"Sure!"

"In a wheelchair?"

"You'd be surprised, friend," Tosh said. "All right, now listen. Johnny. I need to talk to you about the repeat MRI. The second one, that you had done yesterday."

"Yes?"

"Well, the contrast brought some new details out. When Vogel and I looked at it together, we saw some concerns."

"What do you mean, concerns?"

"In the tumor," Tosh said.

"The cyst?" Johnny said.

"Yes," Tosh said. "We're seeing some fingerlike extensions, something we don't usually see with benign meningiomas. And it's a bit larger than the first MRI revealed."

"What does this mean?"

"It means I'm really glad we have you scheduled for surgery," Tosh said. "But I'm afraid it also means the surgery is going to be more complex than we had anticipated. And we can't be as confident about the outcome."

"Are you saying I have cancer?"

"Well, no."

"Then what do I have?"

"You have the potential to have cancer."

"Don't we all have that?"

"Yes," Tosh said. "You just have more of it, friend."

Johnny looked out the kitchen window, where a half-dead frog was clinging to the screen. "Brilliant," he said.

"Now listen. Talk to your wife, let her know about this, okay?" Tosh said. "We're still going ahead as planned. I want to keep you on the prednisone to get the swelling down before we let Vogel in there. Surgeons, you know," he said. "They're a little high-maintenance. They like to have everything just so."

"I think that's probably a good thing," Johnny said.

"Keep up your steroids. Take it easy. Don't panic," Tosh said. "You'll be on the other side of this in no time. It will be fine. You just have to trust us. Okay?"

Trust him? Why should he trust Tosh? Why should he trust anyone?

"Hey, Doc," Johnny said. "What happened to you?"

"What?"

"Your legs," Johnny said. "Why are you in that wheelchair?"

"Fell off a stage," Tosh said. "I used to perform musical theater off Broadway."

"You did?"

"Yep. We were doing *The Pajama Game*," Tosh said. "And I took a header off stage left. You didn't see that coming, did you?"

"Must have been rough."

"Oh, yeah. One minute you're a dancer—a goddamned *tap* dancer, okay?—and the next minute you're waking up in a hospital and they're telling you you'll never walk again? Bam!" Tosh chuckled. "I gotta tell you. I thought about killing myself. Glad I never got around to it. Turns out you can get all the way through medical school sitting on your ass. Johnny—listen to me. It may not be cancer. And if it is? You can fight it."

Johnny didn't answer right away. Through the phone, he could hear the Rolling Stones' "Gimme Shelter" playing in the background.

"All right?" Tosh said. "Tell me you're all right, Johnny."

"I forgot something," Johnny said. "I did see the Stones in Edinburgh. It was a long time ago. I think I was pretty drunk at the time. But they were incredible."

"Well, then!" Tosh seemed to think this settled it. "We all keep going, Johnny. We just keep going until we can't."

After Johnny hung up, he stared at the phone. An electric current erupted in his stomach and surged outward, toward the tips of his fingers. Something was changing.

That night, when Pauline came home from the factory, the rains returned. Johnny fried some tilapia with onions and made a salad. He said nothing to Pauline about Tosh's phone call. Because what good would that have done? Why should they both be worried sick? It wouldn't change anything. He was having the surgery in two weeks, fingerlike extensions or no fingerlike extensions. Give her this, he thought. You can't give her everything, but you can give her this. If he was going to metastasize, he'd do so alone.

Pauline had brought wine gums. Bless her. They settled on the couch and watched an episode of *Top Gear*—the one where the boys tour around Vietnam and visit the fishing villages of Ha Long Bay off the east coast. Johnny had read about the place. The villages are made up of floating houses. They are painted bright blues and greens and they are lashed together, tucked against storms into limestone coves. There are hundreds of people in these villages, and there are some who live their entire lives on the bay, buoyant, never walking on dry land. Birth to death, rising and falling with the tides, praying for soft winds.

Oh, Pauline. This was the way of things. Johnny thought of his workers, shivering in a man-made wind, turning water into ice and breathing air so cold it burns. He thought of his son, alone on a highland hillside with a baby daughter Johnny had never seen. He thought of Pauline, running from something that he hoped was not him. He thought of gray fingers reaching into his brain.

When the show was over, Pauline went upstairs and Johnny went to the file cabinet in the study. He found his passport and checked the expiration date—still good. If he wanted to go see Corran, he could fly to Scotland and be back within a couple of days—well in advance of his surgery. Not that he *did* want to go see Corran. But just *in case* he wanted to go see Corran. He tucked the passport under the blotter on the desk. He'd look at it again in the morning, when he was thinking more clearly.

They went to bed. Late in the night, the General was terrified when a thunderstorm blew through with the last of the rains. He couldn't settle down. He paced circles across the top of the quilt, dug his way underneath, dug himself back out. Johnny was awake anyway, and he could feel the dog's legs quaking through the duvet. He sat up; the whites of the General's eyes shone like ivory in the dim light. Pauline was fast asleep.

"It's all right, wee matey," Johnny said to the General. He put his hand out and covered the dachshund's trembling little head with it. "It's just fear, that's all. You'll get through it." He pulled the dog up onto his chest, and together they watched the lighting shatter the darkness, heard the thunder crash.

We are the houses of Ha Long Bay, Johnny thought. We cling together, we try to survive. If we are very careful and very lucky, we float.

SIX

Pauline had learned a few things about Sam Tulley, the young research attorney from Knowles & Frusciante who seemed to be taking up residence at the Bold City Ice Plant. More than just a few things. God, what a talker. Sam Tulley had been picking the place apart backward and forward, going over every square inch of the factory and poring through every file in the admin wing, and he'd chattered glibly the whole way, even while making self-important marks in his notebook and snapping photos of the compressors, the water purification system, the nurse tanks.

He talked to Roy about an iPhone app that would warm your hands when they got too cold. ("Hell on the battery, though," he said.) He talked to Claire about a new restaurant in San Marco that sold nothing but ice pops. Yes, *ice pops*. He talked to Ed from Sales about the new iPad ("Not enough storage!") and to a googly-eyed Rosa about something called the "flame of thrones." (Or was it the "game of drones"? Who knew?)

But mostly, he talked to Pauline. He told her that his father was a podiatrist, that his mother was born in Venezuela, and that his whole family was bilingual. That he was new to Jacksonville. That he wasn't married, not that she'd asked, of course. He told her he was training for the Gate River Run, which got her attention, and when she asked him how it was going he told her he trained on the Hart Bridge in the early mornings. That she should do it sometime. Then he told her he was from Ann Arbor but had gone to law school at New York University in Manhattan. As an undergraduate he majored in industrial psychology. He told her that was not as abstruse as it sounded. She said she didn't think it sounded abstruse. She thought it sounded pretentious, but she didn't tell him that. Did he think she wouldn't understand what industrial psychology was? Did he think she wouldn't understand what "abstruse" meant?

At first, she was brusque. It was still annoying the bejesus out of her that this overpriced law firm had sent the low man on the totem pole over to the factory to work on Bold City's appeal. What happened to Knowles? What happened to Frusciante, that seasoned, power-suited woman they'd met on the first day they contacted the firm, the lady who'd grasped Pauline's hand firmly, looked her in the eye, and said confidently, "We'll beat this, Mrs. MacKinnon. We're on your side." Where was *she?* Instead the firm had sent over Sam Tulley, an overgrown man-child who brought little packets of Cheetos in his bagged lunches and fidgeted like a fourth-grader anytime he was seated more than a half hour.

But then a funny thing happened—Sam Tulley started to grow on Pauline. His affect was so buoyant and his chatter was so . . . well, so *charming,* that after a while she got tired of cultivating her annoyance. He was a pleasant enough fellow, really. Handsome, to be honest; she had to agree with Rosa on this point—that sweepy bit of hair that kept falling over his eyes, those bright green eyes. Who had green eyes like that? She'd never seen anything like it. Be nice to him, Pauline. *Be nice.*

Now Tulley was reviewing yet another set of work logs from a chair pulled up to the front of Pauline's desk. He'd been at it since just after nine and had kept going through the sandwiches they'd brought in for lunch, yammering a blue streak all the way.

"City that never sleeps," he was saying. He was telling her about his time in New York. "Center of everything."

"So, you liked it there?" she asked.

"Oh, yeah," he said. "Nothing like it in the world. Don't you think?"

"I've only been there once," she said. "I didn't exactly fall in love with it."

"Seriously? I would have stayed there forever, but it was just too expensive. After college, I went back to Ann Arbor for a while, but I started to want to live somewhere warmer. My college roommate's dad is a partner at Knowles & Frusciante. That's how I ended up here in Jacksonville."

She tried to imagine Sam Tulley in college, and she realized he probably didn't look much different back then from the way he did right now: tanned, clothes a bit rumpled, hair disheveled and longish in a way only a young man can pull off. Older men with long hair may think they're looking rakish or jaunty, but God—nine times out of ten, didn't they just look like vagrants? Johnny nowadays kept his hair short. She glanced at a photo on her desk: she and Johnny beaming and a little buzzed in a Glasgow pub. Years ago, before things got so bad with Corran.

Who took that picture? Sharon, maybe? Toole? The barmaid? Johnny's hair was thick and dark and curled gently over the fold of his collar. It had gone a bit grayer since then. She wondered how long it had been since she had thought about Johnny's hair.

"How old are you?" she said to Tulley, and then was immediately embarrassed. "I mean, if you don't mind my asking."

He smiled. "I'm thirty-one," he said. "I know I look younger. I get that all the time. Believe me, I've been fighting it my whole career."

"You shouldn't fight it. Do you know how hard some people work to look younger? Do you know how much money they spend on it?" Do you know how much money *I* spend on it? she wanted to ask. She stopped herself. What was she doing? She sounded like an idiot. Shut up, Pauline. Shut *up*.

He looked at her and paused before speaking. "Well, *you* don't need to do that," he said.

"Ha!" she said.

He closed one work log and opened another. He coughed.

"Yeah," he said. "So. You know what they say about New York. It's a place for the very rich or the very young. I was one of those things when I lived there. That's probably why I liked it."

Pauline was neither of those things now, and hadn't been for quite a while. Maybe that's why she failed at New York. That's how she looked at it—she *failed* at it. She simply could not manage the Big Apple. She'd tried it, and she'd failed at it in spectacular fashion. (Failure! Thanks, Laudonnière!) The one and only time she had been there was five years ago, the summer she turned forty-five, and she must have been dealing with some sort of midlife bug up her backside, because when Johnny started making plans for a trip to Scotland, she announced that she wasn't going to Glasgow, that she was going to New York City. For a week. Alone.

"You go on over to Scotland," she said. "Spend time with Corran. You don't need me hanging around every minute."

"Why New York?" he asked. "What's up there?"

"Johnny," she said, a little condescendingly, "what *isn't* up there?" In truth, Pauline had no idea what was or was not in New York City, other than what she'd read in books and seen in movies. But that had been enough to convince her that she was missing some large and important thing in the world, something intangible and electric and a little bit dangerous that she'd never find in Jacksonville or Watchers Island or inside the walls of the everlasting ice factory. But she had a feeling she'd find it in New York City. And she was going to go have a look. Plus, she'd done some research and discovered there was an industrial marketing conference happening in the city the same week. "Marketing Performance Now!" it was called. Bold City's marketing could certainly use a boost. And if she made it a business trip, she could write it off on the taxes. She'd never traveled alone. A wick of daring ignited, and she let it burn.

She found a listing on HomeAway from a woman who was going to be gone the same days the marketing conference was held. The woman was offering an affordable rate on a very upscale Brooklyn apartment in exchange for keeping company with her two cats, who "would need someone to talk to." Pauline thought the woman sounded batty, but it sounded like a sweet deal. She booked the apartment and went to T.J.Maxx, where she bought a Jackie Kennedy gray suit and a pair of knockoff Ferragamos to wear to the conference. At the last minute, she threw in a gigantic orange tote to make the outfit.

Pop of color! So what if it was $69.99 and not even real leather? Just—just—*so what?*

In New York, she landed at LaGuardia and took a cab directly to the Brooklyn apartment, which was indeed very nice and very clean, thank God. There were two cats to greet her: a fat black pudding named Percy and a string bean of a Siamese named Vera that Pauline soon learned was sociopathic in a way only a cat can be. While Percy was content to sleep nearly constantly, to the extent that Pauline once went over and nudged him to make sure he was still alive, Vera was as strung out as a crack addict, and equally criminal. The first day, after Vera had executed three different aerial assaults from the backs of the living room chairs that left Pauline with raised pink welts across her shoulders, she learned to hug the walls when walking through the apartment. Vera stole a hoop earring off the nightstand, gazed at Pauline for a beat, and then batted it casually into the air-conditioning vent before Pauline could save it. Vera ate every packet of Splenda from a brand-new box Pauline had picked up at the corner store and then barfed yellow paper all over the apartment for two days. She even got hold of the new orange tote bag and chewed right through the handle, rendering it completely unusable. Pauline had an urge to phone up General San Jose, who was vacationing at Pet Paradise on Watchers Island, and tell him what was going on. "Sweetheart," she'd say. "You were right. It *is* an inferior species."

But Vera was hardly the worst of it, as Pauline found out as soon as she ventured out into the streets the next day. Pauline was a square peg in New York City. She did everything wrong. She was intimidated by the crowds on the streets, shocked by the poverty of some of the people camped around the subway stops. The first day, she lost five dollars to a guy in a coffee shop who approached holding a five-dollar bill and asked her if she could break it; after she'd fished the five singles out of her purse and handed them to him, he walked away without handing her the fiver in return, and her face burned with anger and embarrassment. Then she didn't know how to use the MetroCard in the subway, and she made a dummy of herself by running the card through a jammed turnstile reader over and over, trying to get the damn thing to work, before an aggressively kind old man shouted at her that she was draining all the funds from the card—*Jesus!* he said. *Don't give the goddamned MTA all your money!*—and directed her to the ticket booth to straighten it out. That done, she waited forty minutes for the B train from Brooklyn to Midtown before realizing that she could have ridden any of the dozen Q trains that she'd watched pass. When she finally got on the right train, she missed her stop in Midtown and had to walk twelve blocks back down Fifth Avenue in high heels that rubbed blisters on her toes and wreaked havoc with the plantar fasciitis she'd been trying to manage since starting to run.

The marketing conference was even worse. She was the only person wearing a suit. All the other attendees were decked out in the trimmest jeans she'd ever seen, paired with skintight shirts in various shades of black and ironic faux-nerd glasses. Most of the women had edgy pixie haircuts, waifish physiques, and skin so white it was nearly translucent. The men were marginally androgynous—metrosexually impeccable young fellows with supple leather man-bags and smartphones suggestively peeking from tight back pockets. Every single person carried either a Starbucks cup or a bottle of something labeled "Organic Water." (Organic *water?*) Pauline had the feeling she was the only person in the entire conference center over the age of forty.

They all talked about things she'd never heard of: deliverables and messaging. Target markets and netiquette. Paradigm shifts, core competencies, learnings—*learnings*? What the hell were learnings? She pictured herself back home in a meeting with Claire and Roy, trying to implement some of the tactics being expounded at Marketing Performance Now! She amused herself for a little while, mentally writing the screenplay:

> INT: Bold City Ice Plant. Conference room. Day.
> *Pauline: Okay, great meeting, team. So, what are our next-step deliverables here?*
> *Roy: Same as always. We haven't changed our delivery routes (looks at Claire). Have we?*
> *Pauline: Claire, what learnings can we take away from this SWOT analysis? What core competencies should we focus on?*
> *Roy: Claire, you gonna finish that bagel? (reaches toward bagel)*
> *Pauline: I mean, we need to close the loop, team. We've got an event horizon coming up. We might need to consider some knowledge process outsourcing.*
> *Claire: It's raisin, Roy. You don't like raisin. (slaps Roy's hand)*
> *Pauline (with note of frustration): Team! Our sustainability is at stake here!*
> *Claire: Pauline, what in the name of sweet little baby Jesus are you smoking?*
> *Roy: I like raisin. Sometimes.*

When the conference presenters got to talking about how important it is for marketers to develop a "BHAG"—a Big! Hairy!

Audacious! Goal!—Pauline stood up. The hipster project manager she was sitting next to didn't want to adjust himself to let
her out of the row of seats.

"Would you move your big hairy ass, please?" she said. She
watched his mouth fall open, and then she pushed past him
and clicked in her stupid fake Ferragamos out to the lobby. The
next day, she was relieved to fly home to the happy little ten-gate
Jacksonville Airport, overjoyed to glide the Prius unchallenged
onto the wide lanes of I-95 south, thrilled to smell the burned
coffee drifting upriver as she crossed the Dames Point Bridge.
Big sky! And heat! And palm trees! She nearly wept with the
joy of familiarity. Well, there you have it, ladies and gentlemen!
Pauline MacKinnon in New York City . . . *fail!*

"I'd like to go back sometime," Sam Tulley was saying now.
He closed a fat binder of work logs and opened another. "To
New York. Maybe when I'm rich. Maybe when I win the lottery."

"Sounds about right," Pauline said.

"Question," Tulley said. He was tapping his pencil on the
edge of her desk. "I'm thinking about your theory—about the
tank tampering. What about your security cameras?"

"We already checked. There was nothing recorded."

Tulley frowned.

"And what about the gates?"

"They're closed and locked every night."

He stared at her, still frowning.

"What?" she said.

"Mrs. MacKinnon . . . let me be candid with you here. I
keep looking for something I can bring back to Knowles. I'm
not finding much."

"Yes, I know that," she said. *That's why we hired you suits!* she wanted to scream. *Come up with something! Get us out of this!* "I guess we were hoping you'd come up with a strategy. Look—here's what my husband and I think happened: Someone came into the yard and tried to tap into the tank to get ammonia. They screwed up the pressure in the tank, and it blew."

"How can we prove someone entered the yard?"

"Can't we claim, like, circumstantial evidence or something? There are drug deals happening all over this neighborhood. In fact, my husband thinks it's related to a meth operation. Can't we get JSO more involved in this?"

"I don't know how much that's going to help. We have no evidence of outside tampering. Meanwhile, OSHA is pointing at gaps in your maintenance logs. We need to be ready to defend against that."

Pauline shook her head. "Clerical oversight," she said. "We do all our maintenance like clockwork."

"We can't prove that. OSHA wants evidence. They're not in the business of taking people's word on things. I mean, I'm doing everything I can to help you. I *want* to help you. It's just . . ." He threw up his hands hopelessly and let his voice trail off. He raised his eyebrows and gazed at her.

Call it a sixth sense. Call it woman's intuition. Pauline could tell when a man found her attractive. A slight softness in voice register. An intensity around the eyes. Side glances and double takes. Once she walked into a room late during a quarterly meeting with a bunch of distributors and the guy who was talking stumbled in his speech when she crossed his line of vision to find her seat. It was subtle, almost imperceptible. She sat down and looked up at him. He caught her eye and then looked back at his notes to remember what he was saying. She could do that. She knew she could do that. Although lately those moments of recognition, those surprising but not unwelcome realizations that she had attracted a man's desire, had felt fewer and farther between. But she was having one now.

"We need a convincing piece of new evidence that helps make the argument that there was tampering," Tulley was saying. "Otherwise, path of failure is still on you. You won't win the appeal."

Path of failure. Now, that had a ring to it, didn't it? Pauline wondered if Rohan Bergonia had ever considered *that* for a slogan for "Get Runspired." Tulley handed the work logs back to her, and when he did, the tips of his fingers brushed her wrist.

"But now listen," he said then. He must have seen the despair in her face. "We'll keep digging. We'll play around with some other arguments. We won't give up. I'm on your side, Mrs. MacKinnon," he said.

"They make you say that, don't they?"

He looked a little hurt. "No, I really am," he said. "I believe what you're saying is true. I want to see you win, Mrs. MacKinnon."

Pauline looked up at him. "It's Pauline," she said. Really. Why had she been letting him call her "Mrs. MacKinnon" all this time? What was she, an old schoolmarm? He grinned. Lord. Those eyes. Were they contact lenses? Couldn't be.

"Failure is not an option, Sam."

"Okay, then," he said. "I guess I'll get back to work, Pauline."

She returned to her computer and started pecking away at emails. But it was so distracting, having him sitting right there across her desk. God, did he have to be working on that stuff right here in her office? Couldn't he take it back to the conference room? She should ask him to relocate, she told herself. Just ask him if he'd mind. She started to gather the words. She edged her eyes over and caught sight of his profile. And then—*Oh, for heaven's sakes, Pauline, leave him be. He's all spread out here, comfortable. He's not hurting you. Let him work.* She returned to the monitor and leaned in tight, hoping to give the appearance of being deeply engrossed in reading something. Though actually what she was doing, she realized after a moment, was listening to the sound of him turning pages, and beyond that, to the rhythm of his deep, warm breathing.

SEVEN

After Pauline left for the factory, Johnny called next door. He knew Jerry wasn't home, but it wasn't Jerry he wanted to talk to. The teenage son answered.

"Yo," he said.

"Yes," Johnny said. "It's your neighbor, next door. Is this Jerry's son?" He realized he did not know the kid's name.

The boy snorted. *"No,"* he said. A television chattered somewhere behind him. Johnny walked through the house to the dining room window, from which he could see across the two yards into Jerry's house. The kid was standing in his living room, on the phone, talking to Johnny.

"No?" Johnny said.

"He's not my father."

"Oh. Sorry."

"Happens." Johnny watched him through the window. "He's my *step*father." Why was he talking so loudly? Johnny held the phone a few inches out from his ear. The kid aimed a remote at the television and clicked rapid-fire through the stations.

"Right. Also, I'm sorry," Johnny said, "but I've forgotten your name."

"Chemal."

"Chemal." Shuh-*mall*. He didn't recall Jerry ever saying this name. "Chemal, are you doing anything today?"

"Why?" Chemal said. He sounded suspicious.

"I need a ride," Johnny said. "I have this medical thing. I'm not supposed to drive, and my wife's not home."

"Oh," Chemal said. "Wow."

Through the window, Johnny could see that he'd stopped changing channels. The TV was stuck on a motorcycle race. Dirt bikes. They jetted up dirt ramps and flew in great wide arcs across jumps.

"I'll pay you," Johnny said. "I have a few places I need to go. It shouldn't take too long. Fifty dollars?"

The TV screen went black.

"Yeah, man," Chemal said. "No prob."

Johnny told him to come over when he was ready, told him they could take his car. He had a moment's hesitation over the idea of the kid behind the wheel of his Suburban, but what could he do? Desperate times. He dragged the General out of bed and made him go for a pee. The dog took two steps off the deck, lifted his leg, then trudged back into the house and back to bed. Johnny locked up and went outside to wait for Chemal. The sun was warming the street, and what puddles lingered from the rains were turning slowly to steam. A few frogs remained on the driveway, some dead, some dying. He went around to the side of the house and got the hose to clear them off.

When Johnny saw Chemal shuffling over across the driveways, he did a double take. The kid was wearing gray cargo shorts that hung almost to his ankles, a pair of rubber flip-flops that he slap-dragged along the concrete as he walked, and a tattered military jacket covered in patches. The whole effect was one of a child wearing clothing at least six sizes too large. Chemal had made it almost across to Johnny's driveway when one of the lingering frogs bounded in front of him.

"Whoa!" Chemal said. He stopped in his tracks and looked over at Johnny. "You see that?" he said. "There was a *frog* right there!" He looked at his feet and then turned a slow circle. "There's another one!" he said. "Two frogs!" By the time he reached Johnny he was up to five frogs. Johnny extended a hand to him.

"I'm Johnny," he said. Chemal took his hand and pumped it. "Chemal," he said. He was friendlier than Johnny had expected. "Wait—should I call you Johnny?" the boy said.

"It's my name," Johnny said.

"Yes, but should I call you that? Or should I call you 'Mister' something? I mean, I just feel it's best to ask this right up front." This kid was weird. Johnny was starting to regret calling him.

"I mean, yo. I've had folks give me issues with this in the past," Chemal said. "I feel I have a right to ask. Self-preservation, yo."

"Some people just call me Ice," Johnny told Chemal.

"They do?"

"Yeah."

"Oh, my God. They call you *Ice*. That is *awesome*." Chemal was nearly shouting. He seemed to have trouble with volume modulation.

"It's fine," Johnny said quietly, looking around. He wondered how many of the stay-at-homers on Watchers Island were taking in this little one-act. He could imagine the Meehans across the street, for example. "Look out this window here, Diane," Jim Meehan was probably intoning to his wife right now. "What's Johnny doing home on a Thursday? And what's he doing with that little criminal?"

"No, it's awesome," Chemal was saying. "*Ice,* baby." He threw his shoulders back and cocked his head. He extended his arms in front of him and pointed his index fingers toward the ground. "You so hot, you *cold.* You so chill, you *ice.*"

"I own an ice factory," Johnny explained.

"Oh." Chemal looked disappointed. He dropped his arms and looked around. "Okay, so, this frog shit is whack," Chemal said. "Five frogs. I've never seen so many in one place. Like, *five* frogs. Crazy, dude." Still yelling.

"They've been here since yesterday," Johnny said. "Haven't you seen them?" Chemal looked at him blankly. Johnny let it drop.

"Thanks for helping me out, mate," Johnny said.

"You from Australia?"

"Scotland."

Chemal nodded but looked at Johnny skeptically. "Huh," he said.

"Shall we go?" Johnny said.

"We shall," Chemal said, bowing.

Johnny backed his Suburban out of the garage, then got out, took a deep breath, and handed the keys to Chemal, who bumped happily into the driver's seat. Johnny got in on the passenger's side and buckled his seat belt. "Nothing crazy," he said.

Chemal laughed as though this was hilarious. "Oh, dude," he said—and now that they were closed in the car Johnny cringed at the volume of Chemal's voice—"worry not." And, in fact, Johnny was surprised to find that Chemal could actually drive quite well; he backed out of the driveway attentively and maneuvered through the neighborhood at a reasonable twenty-seven miles per hour. One of the mysteries of the automobile that Johnny had long noted was the fact that some people were naturally just good drivers—confident, alert, nimble. Others were not. He wouldn't have anticipated this—God, the kid was so lunky and loud on his own feet—but within just a few minutes, it was clear to Johnny that Chemal had an instinct for how to handle a vehicle. However, in light of the kid's affect, which was registering on the weirdo scale somewhere between Gomer Pyle and Marilyn Manson, Johnny found his prowess behind the wheel only mildly reassuring.

"Where are we going?" Chemal said.

"A few stops," Johnny said. "You don't mind? Errands. Drugstore and stuff. And if you have time I wanted to see if you could take me out to a junkyard I know. I'm looking for some parts for a car."

"A junkyard? Awesome," Chemal said. "Parts for the Chevelle?"

Johnny was surprised. "You've seen the Chevelle?"

"Peeked under the car cover one day, dude. Sorry, couldn't resist it. Seventy-three?"

"Seventy-two." Johnny glanced at Chemal. "I don't think many kids your age would know anything about that car," he said. "You almost got the year."

"I dig cars," Chemal said. "Cars with power. I read *Car and Driver*. I watch *Top Gear*. You watch *Top Gear*?"

Johnny nodded.

"And do you know why we do this?" Chemal said. "I bet you don't know why we do this."

Johnny looked at him.

"It's a coping mechanism. Males who like cars, and particularly muscle cars, like your Chevelle—they are attaching themselves to representations of power because they have trouble reconciling feelings of helplessness or vulnerability. They—well, we, I guess—can't manage emotion well." He shrugged. "Makes sense, I guess."

"That's daft," Johnny said. "Who tells you this?"

"I read it," Chemal said. "I think it's plausible," he added, a little defensively.

"I think it's rubbish."

Chemal shrugged. They approached the bridge out of Watchers Island.

"Well, anyway, I'm looking for parts for a Beetle. For someone else's car," Johnny said.

Chemal grimaced. "A Beetle? No horsepower there, dude."

"Tell me about it."

"What do you call a VW bus at the top of a hill?" Chemal said.

"You're talking really loudly."

"Sorry. I do that. What do you call a VW bus at the top of a hill?"

"I don't know."

"A miracle." Chemal drummed on the steering wheel. "Ba-dump-bump," he said. "And what do you call two VW buses at the top of a hill?"

"I don't know."

"A mirage."

Johnny allowed himself a smile. "That's pretty good," he said.

"But that Chevelle," Chemal said. "Sweet car."

"Yes," Johnny said. "I think so, too."

Chemal reached for the stereo. "You mind if we do some tunage?" he said. He pushed the button and the car filled with the sounds of classical music from the CD Johnny usually kept in the player. Beethoven's *Moonlight Sonata*. "Quasi una Fantasia": "Almost a fantasy." Chemal nodded approvingly.

"You like?" Johnny said.

"Well, I'm really a rock guy," Chemal said. "I'm in the KISS Army, see?" He pointed at the patches on his jacket, which Johnny now saw all bore the same logo—the KISS graphic accompanied by a retro military insignia. "I'm a field marshal, in fact. Defending the cause, right?" He positioned his fingers in the thumb-and-pinkie heavy metal sign and pumped it toward the car roof. "But classical's all right, too," he added.

"You seem a little young to be a KISS fan," Johnny said.

"I was just born at the wrong time," Chemal said. He shook his head sadly. "I missed everything. KISS. Zeppelin. Ozzy. AC/DC. It breaks my heart, let me tell you." He drove west, through the center of Watchers Island's little business district.

"Over the bridge," Johnny said. "Discount Auto."

"You got it, Iceman," Chemal said. "So, anyway, how come you can't drive?"

"I have a thing," Johnny said. "I'm on medication."

Chemal glanced at him. "Are you contagious?" he said.

"No."

"I'm sorry to have to ask that. I just feel I have a right to know."

"Turn right," Johnny said. Chemal turned to the north, up US 1 toward Jacksonville. Johnny looked at him. "What's your name about?" he said. "Is that a family name?"

"Are you saying is it a black name?" Chemal said.

"No." God! What was *with* this fella? "I'm saying it sounds exotic. Your mom's from Puerto Rico, right?"

"Oh, yeah. Well," Chemal said. He fiddled with the air conditioner until the fan came on nearly full blast. "I think my mom wanted me to be black," he said. "She was in love with this black dude? Only she was married to my dad? Not Jerry, my ass-wipe stepdad, but my *dad*. My *real* dad. So my mom says that when she was pregnant with me she didn't really know if it was the black dude's or my dad's. I mean, if *I* was the black dude's or my dad's. And then she had me." He held out his arm. "Whitey," he said. "Tough break."

Johnny had no idea how to respond to this. He realized he was freezing. "Mind if I turn this down a little bit?" he said. Then he remembered it was his own Suburban, and he felt annoyed for asking. He cut the AC down to mid-blast.

"My mom tells me shit," Chemal continued. "She tells me all kinds of shit. She tells me stuff she probably shouldn't tell me, you know? Like about Jerry and his limp dick."

Johnny was pretty sure Chemal was making this up—at least the part regarding his mother's disclosures, though not necessarily the part regarding Jerry's reluctant johnson, about which Johnny had no opinion—but he took the bait. "That's lovely," he said. "It sounds like you and your mom are very close."

"That sounds a little bit sarcastic there, Mr. Freeze."

"Only a little bit?" Johnny said.

Chemal laughed gleefully. Johnny decided to stop the small talk.

They stopped at the auto parts store, where Johnny bought three quarts of Marvel Mystery Oil. They stopped at Staples to buy an ink cartridge for Pauline's printer. At Target, Johnny stocked up on his prescriptions and on sugar pee strips and dropped a small fortune on an iPhone power converter and charger that would work with the outlets in Scotland. Then they were hungry, so Johnny directed Chemal to Shakey's Fish Camp on Doctors Lake, a fan-cooled shanty of a place where Johnny sometimes took some of the factory boys for shrimp and grits. The place was nearly empty save for a couple of tables of retirees and a group of women in scrubs. The waitress, Betsy, approached, and she looked from Johnny to Chemal and back again. She raised an eyebrow.

"New friend?" she said. Johnny nodded.

"My word, the editorials in the newspaper lately. On the ice plant. You seen 'em?" she said.

"No."

"Probably best. You got a ruling on your OSHA thing then?"

"No," he said. And he looked at her levelly, offering nothing else. God, what a busybody Betsy was.

"None of my business," she said, offended. "Iced tea?"

"Belhaven," Johnny said, and she raised her eyebrow again but said nothing.

"And something for my friend here," Johnny said. "What do you want, a Coke?"

Chemal made a dramatic show of scanning the menu. "I might need a moment or two," he said. Betsy walked back toward the bar to pick up a tray of drinks for another table.

"Buy me a beer," Chemal muttered. "Iceman. Do it. Do it. *Do it.*" He kept his eyes on Betsy and spoke out of the side of his mouth.

"Piss off," Johnny said. "He'll have a Coke," he called to Betsy.

Chemal looked stung.

"*God,*" he said. But he recovered quickly when he saw the television behind the bar.

"Check this dude," he said to Johnny.

Johnny watched the television. It was a talk show, one of those daytime TV chaos scenarios in which the host and the audience members hurl insults at the guests. In this case the guest appeared to be a teen dad who was not living up to his paternal responsibilities. Every time the camera cut to the young father, a superimposed caption flashed on the screen. "Baby-Daddy Won't Step Up!" it said.

"You need to grow *up,* son," the host was saying. Chemal smiled. The camera cut to the crowd and zoomed in on an angry woman on her feet, pointing a finger at the slouching young dad on the stage.

"You need to keep your *pants* zipped up, slick," the woman said. Chemal snorted. "And get a *job,*" she added. The superimposed caption on the screen changed. "Lives with Girlfriend, Plays Video Games All Day!" it said.

"That girl needs to kick your butt to the *curb,* son," the host said. "You are a father, and you need to start acting like one or find the door, one or the other."

"This dude reminds me of my cousin," Chemal said. Betsy brought the drinks and set them on the table.

"That host guy?" Johnny said.

"No, the kid there. I've got a cousin like that. He got this girl pregnant and then didn't do a thing about it. She had the baby, and she named him Braden Morgan Warner. Some name, huh? Like an investment firm or something. He was a cute kid, too, like, I would have taken care of a kid like that. My cousin's a total loser. The baby's two now, I think. I haven't seen him in a while."

"This was in Detroit?"

"Yeah. Motor City." Chemal looked a little wistful.

Johnny felt a twinge of sympathy. How old was this kid? Seventeen? He was a lonesome kind of fellow, for seventeen. "Tell me about the baby," Johnny said.

"Oh, dude. Well, my cousin's girlfriend, her name was Misty. She worked at Rite Aid and took care of the kid just fine. The family was helping her out, right? Because my cousin was in prison by this time for possession. So Misty decides she's going to get a tattoo of her baby's initials. Kind of sweet. When she gets to the tattoo parlor and they get going on it, the tattoo guy points out that the baby has the same initials as the car company: BMW. Misty's like, *No shit?* She's not superbright, okay? So in addition to the baby's initials, she goes ahead and gets the BMW *logo* as well."

"She got a BMW logo tattoo," Johnny said.

"Yep."

"Dare I ask where?"

"Across her chest," Chemal said.

"Lovely," Johnny said.

"Well, not on her *boobs*," Chemal said. He leveled his hands in front of his chest and moved them up toward his neck. "Like, above her boobs." Johnny found it slightly endearing that

Chemal, whose repertoire surely included more colorful terms for a woman's breasts, chose "boobs" to reference Misty's. It was respectful, somehow.

"You don't have brothers or sisters?" Johnny said.

"No. Well, I used to. I had a brother." Chemal looked back at the television again. "He died."

"Oh," Johnny said. "Of what?"

"He jumped out of the back of a moving school bus and hit his head. He got bullied a lot. Because of a lisp."

"When was this?"

Chemal shrugged. "I was six. He was eleven."

"I'm sorry," Johnny said. And then, because it somehow, ridiculously, seemed like it might make the kid feel better, he disclosed to Chemal what he had yet to tell anyone else: "I might have cancer," he said.

Chemal's eyes widened. *"Dude,"* he said.

"Yeah."

"Might?"

"Yeah, might."

"When will you know?"

"Couple of weeks."

"Is that the medical thing?"

"Yeah."

"Are you going to die?"

Johnny stared at him, struck by the baldness of the question.

"Was that rude?" Chemal said.

"I don't know."

"I'm sorry if it was. I have issues with that. I don't follow social cues. That's what they tell me, anyway. You've probably noticed. I'm smart, but my social skills are very bad. I saw my chart one time at the shrink's office. 'Marked verbosity.' 'Poor prosody.'"

"It wasn't rude."

"Like, my volume control can be bad. You've probably noticed. I talk too loud."

"I would like to think I'm not going to die."

"I'm pulling for you, Iceman."

"Thank you."

Johnny pushed his half-empty glass of beer over to Chemal and stood up. "Don't get drunk on that," he said. "I still need you to drive me around."

"*Duuuuudde,*" Chemal breathed.

"I'm going to the loo," Johnny said.

In the bathroom, he regarded himself in the mirror. Fingerlike extensions, huh? He ran a hand along the left side of his skull, picturing the tumor just beneath the bone.

"You're letting me down, old man," he said. "Cut the crap now, okay?" He pulled out his cell phone and called Sharon but reached voicemail; he left a message telling her he was thinking of coming over, told her he'd email the specifics. There. Done. The first step out onto any limb, Johnny had learned, was telling somebody else about it. Once that was done, it was harder to go back.

At the table, Chemal was sipping his Coke. The beer glass was empty. The topic on the talk show had changed to Internet addiction. Now the host was chastising a young married couple who spent all their time on their computers in separate rooms, hardly interacting with each other. They even had cybersex. With *each other.* "Do you not see the depravity of this?" the host was saying. The people in the audience were booing and shaking their heads in disgust.

Chemal shook his head.

"Going about it all wrong," he said.

"What do you mean?" Johnny said.

"He's damning them for using technology to enhance reality. You see that all the time. People are afraid of tech."

"It *is* a little weird," Johnny said.

"Dude, to you, maybe," Chemal said. "But maybe it's working just fine for them. Who are we to judge? This dude on the show is assuming that the technology is taking something away from them. He doesn't see it's adding new layers. It's, like, hyper-experiential. Those two still have the opportunity to get busy in person anytime they want. But they know they have more options, so they experiment. A new reality. It's very creative. It's, like, pioneering."

"Chemal," Johnny said. "Why aren't you in school?"

"School sucks." Chemal knocked back the rest of his Coke. "You ready to go?"

"I think you should be in school," Johnny said. "You should be thinking about college."

"Dude, you're, like, lecturing me."

"Well, I think you need to hear it."

"I want this, I can go hang out with Jerry."

"I have a question for you, Chemal."

"Go."

"And I happen to have a son, so I think I can speak with some authority here."

"We'll see."

"Have you considered the fact that Jerry might be thinking of your best interests?"

"Absolutely not," Chemal said. "The only thing Jerry is thinking of is my mother's ass." It was hard to know exactly what to say to that. "And now, I have a question for *you*, Chilly Willy," Chemal continued.

"What's that?"

"It's important."

"Then ask it."

Chemal leaned forward and peered earnestly into Johnny's face. "Friend," he said. "Have you accepted Jesus Christ as your personal Lord and savior?" Johnny looked down and massaged his temples. Then he sat back in his chair and stared at Chemal, who was waiting, face expectant, eyes wide. Great. A proselytizing KISS Army field marshal.

"Listen," Johnny began, "I don't—"

Chemal slapped the table, exploded into laughter. "I'm kidding, Iceman!!" He leaned back and rocked his chair up onto two legs, gleeful. "Bam!! Nailed your ass, dude!"

Johnny stared at him, then picked the car keys up off the table and tossed them at him. They hit Chemal in the belly and tumbled into his lap. Johnny left a twenty on the table and they walked out of Shakey's Fish Camp into the blinding sun.

"Do me a favor," Johnny said. "Don't tell my wife what I told you."

"She doesn't know?"

"No."

"That you have cancer, or that you have a kid?"

Jesus. "She knows about the kid. And he's not a kid. He's an adult. About the cancer. It's not even cancer. Maybe precancer, or something. I don't know. Just don't say anything to anybody."

"Ice," Chemal said. "You have my word. And anyway." He jerked his head to the side to clear the bangs from his forehead. "I don't really hang out with your wife. I mean, no offense—she's a pretty lady. All the running." Chemal looked away then, embarrassed, it seemed, to be talking about Pauline. To be talking about lying to Pauline.

Johnny nodded. "Yes, she is," he said. "A pretty lady." Not the kind of lady to lie to.

They drove west, then south along the river, across Julington Creek and down State Road 13 through Fruit Cove and Switzerland. The road was lined with loblolly pines burned brown from the late autumn sun, and as they drove, the houses and businesses along the roadway began to drop away until they were deep into a deserted quiet stretch, nothing to see but blacktop, trees, the canvas of blue sky above.

"Where is this place?" Chemal said.

"We're almost there."

Johnny rolled his window down and listened to the tires skimming over the road. At an isolated four-way stop, they idled for a moment.

"Listen," Johnny said. "Quiet."

Chemal opened his window.

"You hear it?" Johnny said.

"Hear what?"

Johnny often thought that if he was abducted by aliens, transported through space, then blindfolded and dropped back to Earth in either his native Scotland or his adopted Florida, he would be able to discern his location based solely on the quality of the silences. He compared the silences often—both from memory and from the many trips he'd taken back to Glasgow. The city was always noisy, sure—loud with cars, people, the jarring business of living. But you could go out a bit into the Scottish countryside to find the heavy silences.

In Florida, silence was a porous thing, damp and fragile, never quite solidified. Always there was sound, somewhere. Cicadas whirring, rustle of palmettos, rumble of afternoon thunderheads. Pecans dropping through the canopy. Mosquitoes buzzing at earlobes. In Scotland, out in the country, the silence was dry, hardened, complete. It was a silence so absolute it was almost deafening, softened only now and again by a cold wind cutting through wide yellow fields of oilseed rape. Johnny always felt that the silence in Scotland was older, perhaps wiser. Florida quiet was restless, wild, as unrestrained and lightsome as a bobcat cub.

"La Florida," Johnny said. "I'll never get over it."

Chemal looked at him, skeptically at first, but then he closed his eyes, listened, and nodded.

"Dude," he said. "You speak the truth."

After a few more miles, Johnny directed Chemal to pull down a long driveway toward a large property shielded from the road by a row of live oaks. Behind the trees, Chemal let out a low whistle. Before them lay five acres of junk: oxidized appliances, mildewed lumber, a small massif of carburetors, engines, alternators, flywheels, and manifolds. The debris was arranged in an intricate labyrinth, with worn footpaths meandering in and among the piles as if this were a botanic garden. In the near-distance was a series of formations of stacked cars, like Stonehenge. In the middle of it all was a low cinder-block house. It looked like a bunker. A hand-painted sign was nailed to a television antenna: "Pellum's 'You Pull 'Em' Salvage."

"Cool," Chemal breathed.

"You like?"

"I like."

A gigantic black dog came racing around the side of the building, baying like Cerberus.

"Damn, Ice, check this dog," Chemal said.

"He's fine," Johnny said. "That's Cujo."

The dog circled the Suburban, barking and growling. He jumped up on the driver's-side door and bared his teeth at Chemal through the window.

"He ain't joking, Ice."

"He's fine. Just don't let him smell fear," Johnny said. "Come on."

He reached into the backseat for a canvas tote bag of tools, then he opened the door and climbed out, noting with some relief that Cujo seemed to recognize him; the dog gave him a cursory sniff and barreled back around the Suburban to wait for Chemal, who still sat in the driver's seat.

"Let's go!" Johnny said.

Inside the truck, Chemal shook his head.

Johnny sighed and walked around to Chemal's door. Chemal rolled the window down. Cujo growled.

"He's gonna bite my nuts off, Ice."

"He won't. He'll see you're with me. He knows me."

Cujo barked. A line of saliva worked its way loose from the dog's lower lip and dangled under his chin. Chemal shook his head again.

"Oh, come on, lad." Johnny opened the door. Cujo pushed his way in front of Johnny and sniffed at Chemal's legs, growling and making oafish grunting sounds.

"Holy shit," Chemal said.

Johnny pushed Cujo away with his knee. Chemal grabbed Johnny's arm and slowly climbed down from the driver's seat. Cujo growled again. Chemal pushed himself up against Johnny like they were dancing.

"Oh, geez, Ice," he said. "He hates me."

"Get off me, ya poof," Johnny said. He pushed Chemal away and tried to walk toward the house. Chemal edged his way around behind Johnny but still held on to his arm. "Come on. Now quit," Johnny said. "If he thinks you're scared he'll react to that."

"I *am* scared."

"Cujo!" Johnny said. "Git now!"

Cujo stopped barking. He gave Johnny an injured look, then fell back to a slow walk behind them.

"God," Chemal said. He let go of Johnny's arm but still walked uncomfortably close to him all the way up to the house. Johnny knocked. After a moment, the door was yanked open and a short, heavy man with curly gray hair appeared. He wore a blue T-shirt, voluminous blue jeans, and enormous glasses with lenses the size of drink coasters. He was beaming.

"Hiya, James," Johnny said.

"Johnny!" he yelled. "Where you been, son?" He turned around and yelled into the house. "Fayette! It's Johnny!" He turned back to Johnny and clapped him on the shoulder, and then he was joined by a woman who looked almost exactly like him: same curly gray hair, same ballooning jeans, same oversized glasses.

"Johnny!" she said. "Where you been hiding? You don't never come see us no more."

James and Fayette stepped out into the sunshine, and Johnny was struck by their appearance. Did these two ever age? They had to be nearing eighty, both of them, but they looked exactly as they did when he met them thirty years ago. Back then, Johnny had just signed on as a loader at the factory, James was the drying room foreman, and Fayette worked at a travel agency on the Southside. By the time Travelocity and Priceline pushed her out of a job, James was sniffing around retirement anyway, so they bought the salvage yard. James got to fiddle around to his heart's content with cars. Fayette got to bake, read, and visit with her grandbabies. They were all set, they told Johnny. Just all set.

"Doing all right, son?" James asked.

"All right. Pretty all right," Johnny said. James nodded.

"This is Chemal," Johnny said.

Fayette immediately hugged Chemal, who looked around awkwardly in her grasp. She let him go and he stood there, blinking. "You in luck, young'un," she said. "I just made me a Tootsie Pie."

"What in the world is that?" Johnny said.

"You never had that?" she said. "That's 'cause you're from that overseas there. Tootsie Pie—it's got the butter and the Tootsie Rolls in it and so forth? Oh, you'll see."

James was looking over Chemal—not unkindly, Johnny thought, just curiously. He watched James take in the baggy shorts, the chains, the military jacket. Good grief.

"You work at the factory, son?" James said.

"He's my neighbor," Johnny said quickly. "He's helping me with some driving. I've got a little medical thing going on. Not supposed to drive."

"What do you mean, a little medical thing?" Fayette demanded.

"I don't want to get into it," Johnny said. "It's fine. Not a big deal. I'm just not supposed to drive for a bit."

James and Fayette both stared at him. Hard.

"Please," Johnny said. "I just came by to say hi. And to see if you have some parts I need."

"All right, Johnny," James said quietly. He and Fayette exchanged a look but didn't say anything else.

"I need a steering wheel," Johnny said.

"For the Chevelle?"

"No. For a Beetle."

James raised his eyebrows. "A Beetle?"

"Yes. I know," Johnny said, holding up his hands. "It's not mine. It's Corran's."

James shook his head.

"I was gonna say," he said.

"I know, James. I know."

"All right. Let's head out there, then. You know I don't like them German cars. But I sure enough got me one Beetle out there. Way out the back. It's got a steering wheel. And if you can pull it you can have the damn thing."

"Now listen," Fayette said. "You come back when you're done, hear? My Tootsie Pie's cooling."

"Wait here," James said. "I'll get our ride."

He disappeared around the back of the house and reappeared a moment later in a stripped-out Dodge minivan that looked more like a large piece of shrapnel than a vehicle. It had once been white, Johnny reckoned. Or silver? Hard to tell. The windshield was held together with electrician's tape, with only a small window of visibility in front of the driver's seat. All the doors were missing, as was all the seating. James was driving while perched on an overturned five-gallon bucket.

"Awesome," Chemal breathed.

"This here is my yard transport," James said. "All aboard." Johnny and Chemal climbed in and knelt down awkwardly on the metal flooring. Chemal looked around the gaping, empty interior for something to hang on to, but not seeing anything, he leaned forward and put his palms flat on the floorboard for balance. Johnny was straddling an eight-inch rust hole between his knees. James took off like a rocket and Johnny watched the ground rushing by underneath the van. They careened down the center aisle of the salvage yard, past a half dozen thirty-foot metal mountains, each one a study in automotive archaeology. Toward the bottom of each mountain Johnny could make out the gutted carcasses of cars from the eighties, the seventies, maybe even a few older than that. As the scrap heaps rose higher, the cars got newer. And every time Johnny came out to this old yard, there was something novel—some new treasure or find that James had happened upon. Johnny and Chemal bumped uncomfortably in the back of the van and Johnny tried to listen to James, who was talking about some of his latest discoveries.

"Look at that," James was saying. "Cadillac XLR roadster. Body shot but engine good. And look at that one." He pointed at a late model car, shiny and spiffy, under a metal carport toward the edge of the property. "Brand-new Kia Sedona."

"That's a horrid thing," Johnny said.

"I know it. But I got it for twelve grand, and only five hundred miles on it, can you believe that? Old guy bought it and then died. Wife unloaded it. Like new. Hasn't even been farted in. I'm going to eBay the shit out of that thing. Make enough for me and Fayette to go up to Cherokee for a week, still have some left to take the grandbabies to Universal. You know they got that Blue Man Group down there? Those boys is something else, Johnny. No joke. And you too, son—Chamile, is it? It's an all-ages show. Shit!" James braked, and Johnny and Chemal jolted forward. "Almost passed the gee-dee Beetle, I'm talking so much!"

They had reached a pile of cars toward the rear of the yard. It was thirty-five feet high if it was a foot, Johnny figured. He counted six layers of cars working themselves up toward the top like a pyramid. At the top sat a rusted red Volkswagen Beetle.

"There you go," James said.

"Up there?" Chemal said. "How is he going to get up there?"

"He's gonna climb," James said. "It ain't gonna come down to you, Johnny."

Johnny got out of the minivan. He knew the drill. He'd been out to the salvage yard enough times to know that it was a do-it-yourself endeavor: said so right on the sign out front. James would get you to the right car, or the right pile, as the case may be. After that, you were on your own. Johnny picked up his bag of tools and got out of the minivan.

"Where's Cujo?" Chemal said to James.

"Aw, he stays up there at the house with Fayette," James said. "Specially when she's cooking."

Chemal got out of the minivan.

"I'm going to help you, Iceman."

"Not necessary," Johnny said.

Chemal looked a little hurt, but the last thing Johnny needed was for this kid to get injured climbing up a heap of rusted cars

in a junkyard. Not on my watch, Johnny thought. I've got enough
to worry about. He hitched the bag of tools up on his shoulder
and started to climb. If Pauline and Tosh saw this, they'd have
a conniption. No exertion, they said. Take it easy, they said. And
here he was climbing Mount Tetanus, toting a bag of tools, in a
heat wave. Johnny said a little prayer to the meningioma gods.
Deliver me from evil. Amen. He kept going. His foot slipped once
on the flattened quarter-panel of a rusted Pontiac, but he regained
his stance and kept going. The metal was hot under his hands.
He touched the broad surface of a black roof (what was that, an
El Camino?) and it burned his fingers.

By the time he reached the top of the car mountain he was
wet with sweat and out of breath. He opened the door of the
Beetle and started to climb inside, but his bag of tools caught
on the chrome wing mirror. He wobbled frantically and grabbed
at the door frame to steady himself, which he finally did, but
not before dropping his tools. The bag cartwheeled twice, then
burst open and sent the tools clattering to the ground. Johnny
watched them fall. He sat back in the driver's seat of the Volkswagen, breathing hard and noting with irony that the steering
wheel was in perfect shape. Exactly what he needed. If only he
had the tools to pull it.

"Hang on, Mr. Freeze!" Chemal yelled from below. "I've
got 'em!"

Johnny looked down. James was leaning against the Dodge,
laughing. Chemal was gathering up the tools.

"Don't worry about it!" Johnny yelled. "I'll come back
down!"

But Chemal was already scrambling up the side of the scrap
heap like an orangutan, the tool tote slung over his shoulder.

Well, all right, Johnny admitted to himself. So *that* was what a forty-year advantage could do for you. In less than a minute, Chemal was up the heap and crouched, balancing on the trunk of a Pontiac like a yoga instructor, at the Beetle's door. He handed the bag of tools through the window.

"Thanks, mate," Johnny said. Chemal grinned.

Johnny disassembled the horn and loosened the nut on the steering wheel. He pulled on the wheel but found it immovable, probably some corrosion on the shaft cementing the whole damn thing together. He pulled again, but the wheel wouldn't budge. He took a hammer and beat against the back side of the steering wheel. No luck. He was sweating like a rhinoceros at this point, fat dollops of sweat slipping into his vision and running down his nose.

"Let me try," Chemal said.

They executed an awkward position change across the front seat of the Beetle—Johnny shifting over to the passenger side and Chemal shimmying around the open door and into the driver's seat, where he started to pull on the steering wheel.

"It won't move just with you pulling. I need to beat on it from the back side at the same time," Johnny said. Chemal slid the seat as far back as it would go and then got up on his knees to get his weight behind the pull. Johnny crouched down to assume an angle that would allow him to hammer the back side of the steering wheel.

"On the count of three," he said to Chemal. "One. Two. Three!"

He gave the back side of the wheel a terrific bash, and at the same time Chemal leaned forward and jerked the wheel off the shaft. The force of its release sent the two of them pitching toward the backseat, and with the shift in their weight, Johnny felt the car begin to rock backward on the pile. They both instinctively lurched forward to compensate. The Beetle teetered like a seesaw.

"Hot shit!" James shouted from below. "Hold on!"

It happened so fast Johnny barely had time to think. With the shift in weight, the Beetle tipped precipitously forward on the pile of cars, then started a descent. The noise was deafening. In the time it took Johnny to pray that the whole thing wouldn't go end-over-end, the Beetle executed a flawless slalom down the side of the thirty-foot scrap heap, coming to a grinding but miraculously intact stop just a few feet from James's stripped-out Dodge.

"Hellfire!" James yelled. "That's a new one!"

Johnny looked over at Chemal, who had bloodied his bottom lip on the edge of the steering shaft.

"Are you okay?" he said. Chemal turned to him, grinning like the Cheshire cat, covered in sweat and rust and with a thick stream of blood dripping down his peach-fuzzed chin.

"Dude!" Chemal said. "That was awesome!"

"Jesus," Johnny said. He put his head in his hands and steadied his breathing. No exertion. No stress. Steady, fella.

"Rock and roll!" Chemal said.

They fiddled with the Beetle for a while longer and then rode around the salvage yard for another half hour, and by the time they were finished Johnny had pulled the steering wheel, a VW fuel pump, a replacement headlight housing for his Suburban, and a brand-spankin'-new brake line for the Chevelle. The total came to forty-seven dollars. Johnny rolled his eyes and protested that it was too little, but James wouldn't take a penny more, so when he wasn't looking Johnny sneaked back to the Kia Sedona and put a fifty on the dashboard. He took a pen out of his bag and wrote on the bill: "Blue Men." Afterward, they went back to the house for Tootsie Pie and sweet tea. Fayette set them up at a picnic table in the side yard. Chemal fed a bite of pie to Cujo, who then curled up at his feet and went to sleep. Then Chemal told them all about some of his inventions.

"Well, not inventions yet," he said. "I haven't produced them. But I'm conceptualizing them."

"Why you yelling, child?" Fayette said.

"Sorry." Chemal lowered his voice. "I have a book of ideas at home. Like here's one," he said. He pointed at Cujo. "Big dogs equal big poop, right?"

"Lord have mercy," Fayette said. "You got that right."

"So, my invention is that you put something in the dog's food," Chemal said. "Like, a luminescent substance. Maybe heat-activated phosphors. And then when the poop comes out it glows in the dark."

"Seriously?" James said.

"That way you'll never step in shit. You'll see it before you step in it."

Johnny laughed. He couldn't help it. Where did this kid *come* from?

"I'm serious, Iceman. I'm going to market it. You can get in on this with me if you want. Be, like, my venture capitalist or something." Chemal took an ice cube out of his cup and held it against his fat lip. "I'm going to call it 'Go-n-Glo.'"

"I think that's a damn good idea, son," James said, nodding.

"And then I've got this other idea," Chemal continued. "Shark repellent. For people going to the beach. You put it in sunscreen. Double duty. Only problem is that it smells like dead shark. I need to work on that."

"Do people really need shark repellent?" Johnny said. "I mean, what are the honest odds you're going to be attacked by a shark?"

"Don't matter if they need it. Only matters that they'll buy it," James said. "I think it's a great idea, Chamile. Think of it: Are people afraid of sharks? Yes. Will they buy shark repellent? Damn straight. They'd probably buy gator repellent, come to think of it. Don't matter that all they really gotta do is stay out the swamp. People get scared. They buy shit. It's the American way, Ice."

Chemal nodded. "Gator repellent," he said thoughtfully.

"You credit me for that one, son," James said. "When you get rich, you remember me on that one."

On the ride home Johnny started to worry that Chemal's mother might have a word to say about her son coming home with bloodstains on his pants and a busted-open lip.

"I'm sorry about the lip, mate," he said. "Your mum going to be mad?"

Chemal snorted. He eased into a throng of traffic on Butler Boulevard and shook his head. "She won't even notice it," he said.

They rode silently back to Watchers Island. Johnny was bone-tired. He closed his eyes and leaned back. In the passenger seat. Of his own Suburban. He was a little surprised that he was able to relinquish control of the driving situation as completely as he was doing right now. Ah, but what the hell? This kid knew how to drive. Let him get them home. He squeezed his eyes shut tighter, then watched a kaleidoscope of shapes pass along the insides of his eyelids. He tried to remember if he'd ever seen these particular shapes before. Or was this the fingerlike extensions in action? How could he ever be sure, these days, that what he was seeing, feeling, hearing, tasting—any of it—was real?

He opened his eyes. They were on the bridge to Watchers Island. At the top of the span, the ocean was visible, stretching cold and deep. The CD came around to the *Moonlight Sonata* again. Johnny pulled out his phone and checked Travelocity for flights. Today was Thursday. He could be in Scotland by the weekend: fly into Glasgow, rent a car, zip down to see Sharon and then up to Port Readie to see Corran. Then he remembered: He couldn't *drive*. Shit.

Johnny looked over at the KISS Army field marshal sitting next to him. The KISS Army field marshal who didn't have enough to do. "So, listen," he said. "Why are you having such a hard time? In school and such?"

"You mean in life?" Chemal said.

"Yes. In life."

"Because I'm poorly socialized. And I don't sense boundaries. And I don't do well with authority. Haven't you noticed?"

"You're doing fine with me."

"You're not authority."

"I could be."

"Nah," Chemal said. "I can smell authority a mile away."

Johnny didn't know whether to be annoyed or pleased. "Well, a lot of people I work with see me as an authority figure. I'm the boss, in fact. Did you know that?"

"Authority is a relative attribute," Chemal said. "Depends on the relationship between the two parties. Their degree of investment in reward and acceptance—"

"Oh, Christ. Whatever. Enough with the psychobabble."

"You asked."

"Chemal," Johnny said, "do you have a passport?"

"A passport? Yeah. I went to the Bahamas with my mom last year. Why?"

"Just wondering if you want to go on a trip with me. To Scotland. Just for a few days." He watched Chemal's face, which went slack with delight.

"Seriously?" Chemal said. "Like, when?"

"Tomorrow. I know it's sudden, but I need to go. And I'll need help driving when I get there."

"Dude!" Chemal said. "I'm on board."

"It's tricky now," Johnny said. "Other side of the road and all."

"No fear, Iceman. I am nothing if not adaptable."

"What will your mum say?"

"She'll say have a good trip. And don't hurry back." They pulled down Beacon Street. Johnny hit the button on the garage door opener, and Chemal pulled the Suburban in, parking it perfectly.

"Seriously," Chemal said. "Scotland? Really?"

"If your parents say it's okay."

"Not parents. Mother and *step*father."

"I'm sorry. I forgot. I'll call them."

"They'll be thrilled. Believe me," Chemal said. He handed Johnny the keys and gave him the peace sign. Then he started to walk across the driveways back to his house before stopping abruptly and turning around.

"Wait—you're not, like, a pervert or anything, are you?" he called.

"Not the last time I checked."

"Good enough," Chemal said. He grinned. "I'll go pack. Sweet!"

Johnny went inside and took a shower. He called Jerry and Tina, who were, as Chemal predicted, thrilled with the idea. Then he got online and bought two tickets: Jacksonville to Glasgow, tomorrow, connect in Charlotte. The price was astronomical. He put it on a credit card.

It was almost five o'clock. Pauline would be home before too long. He'd have to tell her he was booked on a flight to Scotland tomorrow. She wasn't going to be happy about it. He fell asleep on the couch. He dreamed he was walking with Pauline in a field covered with snow, and it was back in Scotland, cold and windy but everything bright and blue. They were walking toward a shoreline, and across a narrow channel was a small rocky island. The sun was preparing to set over the water. They came to the edge of the snowy field and walked into a meadow of roses. "Why are they all burned?" Pauline said. Johnny looked across the water and could see Corran on the little island, Corran as a child, throwing stones into the water. An air-raid siren screamed, and then a bomber appeared and dropped a bomb, and the explosion rocked Corran off the shoreline, sent him plunging into the water. Pauline screamed and Johnny ran into the cold channel and slipped under the water. Frogs swam all around him. He held his breath and swam and swam, then finally he saw Corran under the water and moved toward him, but the boy remained just out of his grasp. The water went from cold to hot, then began to boil, then turned into fire, the flames licking through the current. Above, Pauline had turned into Sharon, who was throwing the charred roses into the burning water. Johnny reached for Corran. Corran shook his head sadly. *No,* he said. *No.*

EIGHT

The second cup of coffee was proving as impotent as the first. Roy Grassi yawned, pulled on his parka, and drained the last of the coffee anyway, thepping a few rogue grounds off his tongue and back into the cup before leaving his office and heading out onto the ice floor. It was just after lunch, with still the whole long afternoon to go, and here he was, weary as a sharecropper. Well, it was his own fault. He knew he shouldn't have opened that letter last night. He'd found it in the mailbox when he got home from the factory, and what he *should* have done was left it on the counter next to his keys, where he'd find it in the morning and could safely open it once he was suitably distracted by the impending mental commotion of the workday ahead. But no, he'd opened it during his standing-at-the-counter dinner of a Marie Callendar potpie and a bottle of Rolling Rock, thus violating his own long-standing rule of never opening a missive of potentially bad news late in the day, when it had the very real potential of annihilating any chances of a decent night's sleep. And in this case, he certainly should have known better. The letter was clearly marked as being from the University of Florida's Bursar's Office, which meant that it wasn't a letter at all, but rather a bill.

Ah, God! Why did he open it? If he'd only waited, maybe he would have gotten more than a few minutes of fitful dozing before the alarm went off this morning. As it was, the sight of the overdue balance—more than two thousand dollars—had him queasy with worry all night, especially combined as it was with an ominous asterisked disclaimer: "Failure to meet this financial obligation in full within thirty days of receipt will result in forfeiture of Study Abroad enrollment." Which meant the forfeiture of his daughter Ally's heart's desire: a second-semester freshman year Study Abroad program in fashion design in Florence, Italy.

Admission to the program hadn't come easy. Ally had worked her butt off, creating an impressive portfolio of sketches and essays and even producing a specialized video presentation as part of her application. The competition, the program literature had warned, was fierce, with only a dozen students selected from a national pool of talent that included applicants from elite private schools and big-city academies who had every advantage and lorded it over a scrappy little Jacksonville kid from a Title I school on the Westside. Roy had distractedly approved Ally's application effort, dubious of its potential in light of the odds, and had made a foolish and far-reaching promise that if she was admitted, he'd "find a way" to pay for it.

But Ally had gotten in! His initial astonished pride had quickly given way to a creeping sense of panic as he started to assess the reality of the program's costs. Thanks to his ex-wife's contribution, plus the Florida Prepaid College Plan, a Bright Futures scholarship, and a generous textbook grant from the local Kiwanis Club, Roy had been fairly certain that the basic costs of Ally's on-campus college education would be doable. But Florence was an expensive add-on program. His ex-wife, Bonnie, a good woman but irritatingly practical to the core, had told Ally there was no way she could afford to contribute, and that if her father wanted to make Study Abroad promises that was up to him, but that they could count Bonnie out for any money toward it. So Florence, basically, was down to Roy. How could he possibly do it? Then again, how could he possibly not?

Roy walked around the ops floor, checking fluid levels and temperature readings on the icemakers and compressors. He threaded the bag handler with the long sheets of serrated plastic that would become thousands of pillow-sized sachets of ice by the end of the afternoon. He glanced at the clock. Was anyone else planning to come back from lunch today? The crew in the water treatment room was already at it, he'd credit them with that, but where was everyone else? No doubt in the break room still sucking down coffee, or taking their sweet time smoking out in the loading yard before clocking back in. The cat was away, they had obviously heard. With Johnny out of the picture for the next several weeks, at least, it was going to fall to Roy to whip some of these lard-asses into gear. Well, fine. Given the mood he was in, he was more than up for the job.

He pictured Ally, who was probably walking into her UF dorm about now, back from her morning classes. She'd open the dorm room door and what would be the first thing she'd see? That poster of Florence, the one she'd toted with her from where it hung on her bedroom door all summer at home and that had been the first thing she'd installed in her college room. His fingers twitched with the urge to text her. Just to say hi. But he'd been forcefully limiting himself, lately, to one text a day, just to give the kid some space. He'd rather save today's exchange for later in the evening, the time of day when she was most likely to be chatty. Afternoons were okay, but evenings were best. He never called or texted early in the morning, not wanting to burn his one daily opportunity to connect with her. He knew that in the first few sleepy moments of Ally's day, she didn't like to talk, though whenever she was home with him, she would often pad down the stairs in a T-shirt and oversized pajama pants and quietly put her head on his shoulder for a second before pulling out the Rice Chex and folding herself over her iPhone at the kitchen table.

Ally. God, he missed the kid.

And if he missed her this badly when she was only two hours away, he could hardly imagine what it would feel like to put her on a plane to Italy in just a few short months. What a rotten catch-22 this was. He didn't *want* her to go to Florence. But he didn't want her to be denied anything, ever. She'd earned the opportunity, and she should take it. She was supposed to be in Florence in January—touring the great fashion houses and taking classes with famous designers and eating pasta in quaint cafés, or whatever the hell it was that they did over there. But unless he made the next payment of two thousand dollars, and did so soon, Florence wasn't going to happen.

There were two voices competing for attention inside Roy's head.

Charge it, said the first.

Your credit card is maxed, said the second.

How 'bout open another card?

How 'bout just tell her no?

Well, that was certainly a reasonable suggestion, he admitted to himself. Just tell her they couldn't afford it. *I'm sorry, Ally, we can't do it. No.*

Claire's voice came over the intercom. "Roy!" she said. "Call Claire please!" Why did Claire always seem to be yelling? He didn't know whether to be chagrined at her tone or simply grateful that she wanted him for something, whatever it might be. He pulled his cell phone out of his pocket and called her extension. She picked up right away.

"Did I leave my keys out there?" she said. "In your office, maybe?"

"I didn't see them," he said. "But I can go look." Claire had stopped in his office on her way back from lunch to pick up a pile of shipping receipts. He'd cleared a spot on his sofa, hopeful that she'd sit for a few minutes, but she'd been characteristically frazzled and hadn't seemed to notice his effort. She'd breezed through in a hurry, complaining about the chill, ponytail swinging, leaving a faint scent of something citrusy in her wake. Now Roy moved across the ice floor back toward his office, trying to think of something interesting to say while he had her on the line. That was the problem, he decided. He just wasn't very interesting.

"I'm walking back there," he said. She didn't answer. "To look for the keys," he added lamely.

She sighed. "I'm always leaving things," she said. "I can't keep my head on straight."

"You're working too hard," he offered. He reached the office and glanced around. The keys were nowhere in sight, but he was reluctant to say so just yet. "You need to decompress sometime," he said.

"Ha," Claire said.

"I mean, you got a lot on your plate, Claire."

"True that," Claire said. "Hang on." He heard her put a hand over the phone and say something to someone else in the admin wing. It sounded like she was annoyed. She uncovered the mouthpiece and her voice came back on the line, conspiratorial this time. "My God, Ed from Sales!" she whispered to Roy. "He's getting on my last damn nerve in here!"

"I told you he's an idiot."

"Yes, you did," she said. "And I have to concede you are correct, Roy. He's driving me crazy. And another thing—this OSHA stuff has me a nervous wreck. The little lawyer-boy is making a mess all over the place. Research. For what? I feel like we could all lose our jobs, Roy. Pauline keeps saying a bust at Leonard's house would break the case. I don't know. That seems like a long shot if you ask me. Should I go over there myself and buy some meth? Would that give us enough evidence? God. I got three kids. I don't know how much more of all this I can take."

"You need a break, Claire." He'd given up the pretense of looking for her keys. They weren't in the office. He stood in his doorway and looked out onto the empty ice floor. Still no crew. "We should go have a beer sometime," he said. He chewed on his lip, surprised by his own moxie. Claire didn't answer right away. He laughed a little bit. Like it was a joke. Was it a joke?

"Ed!" she barked. "I invoice Southeastern every two weeks, not weekly! Stop pestering me!" She sighed into the phone. "I gotta go, Roy," she said. "Oh, and listen. I just found my keys. They were in the bottom of my purse. I'll talk to you later, Roy."

Roy put the phone into his pocket. He shivered and zipped his parka up a little higher.

All right, so Florence. Maybe he *could* open another credit card. He'd look into that.

Owen Vickers was waiting on the loading bay with a bill of lading. Roy signed it. "That the only one?" he said. Vickers shrugged. He was wearing Oakley snow-ski sunglasses (in *Florida*) and had the most annoying hair arrangement Roy had ever seen, some sort of gel making it stand up in a ridge along the top of his head. He looked like an overgrown Kewpie doll.

"I think not," Roy said. He motioned for Vickers to follow him back to his office, where he checked the delivery schedule and printed out three more bills of lading. "Get the loaders to fill you up," he said. "Don't be pulling out of here with a half-empty truck."

"Wasn't my fault," Vickers said. "They're the ones loaded the truck." Roy squinted at Vickers.

"And you can't take it upon yourself to tell them to load up more?" he said. "Can we not work together here, Owen? Maybe take a little initiative?" This was maddening. Bold City Ice had had a perfectly good foreman's position open for months, yet Roy had yet to find anybody on the ice floor who displayed enough potential to be promoted into the job. And wouldn't you think they'd *try to* prove themselves? Everybody knew the position was sitting open. Here was Owen Vickers, for example: The guy certainly had enough brainpower in his head to do the job if he'd just apply himself to it, but the little turd was so lacking in the motivation department it was appalling. In fact, the only thing he appeared to be motivated to do lately was shark around the reception lobby, eyes trained on Rosa.

Which was another thing. Last week Roy had spotted the two of them out together at lunchtime, sharing a cigarette at the picnic tables outside Deb's Deli. A cigarette! Claire would serve Rosa her own head on a platter if she knew her daughter was smoking cigarettes and tramping around with Owen Vickers, and Roy told Rosa as much later that afternoon when he caught her alone in the lobby. Rosa begged him not to tell Claire, and so far, Roy had complied, but he didn't like it. We're just *friends*, Rosa had insisted. Please, Roy. *Please?*

"Hey, Owen," Roy said now. "Why don't you lay off Rosa Kaplan?"

"What?" Vickers said. "I'm not doing anything to her."

"Yes, but you *want* to," Roy said. Vickers snickered. "I'm serious," Roy said. "Back off. That one's off-limits."

"Why, you got plans?" Vickers said. Roy looked at him. He extended the bills of lading, but when Vickers reached out to take them, Roy pulled them back. He extended them again. Vickers reached out. Roy pulled them back. Then he leaned in a bit closer.

"Keep your hands off that girl," he said quietly. Vickers blinked. "You got me?" Roy said.

"God, settle down, Grassi," Vickers said. He reached forward and took the bills of lading. "Let me go run my route before it melts." He saluted and walked out of the office and over to the loading bay, where he started shouting at the loaders about more product. "Come on, come on!" he said. "Grandpa Grassi says to fill me up!"

One of these days, Roy thought. *Pow.* Right in the kisser. The pair of guys loading the truck looked at Roy and grinned, and

Vickers laughed and said something else, but a street-cleaning vehicle scuttled past on the road beyond the loading bay at that moment and drowned him out, which was just as well. But what was it with the goddamned street sweepers lately? City of Jax must have a maintenance budget surplus this year, for crying out loud. Maybe he should put in an application for city work. Couldn't hurt.

Roy walked back to the surge bin and raked away the ice that had melted during the lunch break and was now sticking together, which made it unsuitable for packing. The cubes had to be perfectly shaped and bone-dry to keep the quality of each bag pristine. The tiniest bit of melting meant that misshapen bricks of ice arrived at the distributors' receiving docks instead of the rattling sacks of crystalline cubes they should have been; the guys on the floor called it "boner ice" when it hardened like that, a phrase which Pauline and Claire disapproved of but which Roy himself found pretty accurate. In any case, Johnny wouldn't have it. Chunked-up boner ice was a no-no. Keep it dry, keep it loose, keep it cold. Roy raked the clumps toward an open drain in the floor and let them sit there to melt. What a waste. He hated to see fresh product not being used, but so far, they hadn't come up with a profitable way to repurpose misshapen ice. One of these days he would figure it out, Roy told himself. Just not today.

He made his way back to his office and as he crossed the threshold, the toe of his boot caught something in the corner of the doorjamb and sent it spinning. What was that? He leaned over and picked up a Bud Light bottle cap. All right, now *this* pissed him off. Somebody had brought beer out to the shop floor, which was absolutely verboten in safety procedures and which everybody knew was intolerable to both Roy and Johnny. He pitched the bottle cap into the trash. It was the fucking second-shift pallet loaders, no doubt, a near-useless lot to a one. If he caught them with beer on the ops floor—if he caught them with the *idea* of beer on the ops floor, even—they were going to wish he hadn't. No wonder Bold City Ice was dealing with an OSHA mess! Didn't anyone pay any attention to safety around here?

Dumbo was wobbling again. Roy left his office and went over to kick at her and then, on second thought, he shut her down completely. He wasn't going to play the Dumbo game today. They'd have to get by with five icemakers for the afternoon, not six. With Johnny out, it would be all they could do to keep up with ice yield in the coming weeks anyway. No sense letting Dumbo beat the whole factory apart for a few extra spits of ice. The production reports this month were going to look like pure ass, that was for sure. But Roy didn't see how that really mattered, not while they were in this state of arrested development, prepping for an OSHA appeal hearing that hadn't even been scheduled yet. Not that he was in a hurry for it. If the appeal failed, the odds of Bold City Ice remaining in operation were slim indeed. And then where would Roy be? And Ally? Goodbye, ice. Goodbye, paycheck. Goodbye, Florence.

Fifteen minutes later Roy still hadn't seen anyone come back from lunch. He went to his office and used the intercom to talk into the break room.

"Hey, team," he said sarcastically, "how 'bout we make some ice today?"

No one answered, but he kept the intercom open and heard the scrape of chairs against the floor, followed by the reluctant shuffling of steel-toed boots against worn linoleum.

"Thank you, ladies," he said. "Oh, and Dumbo's down."

"Good," someone said. "Just shoot her and let's be done with it."

Roy clicked the intercom off. His phone buzzed and he looked at it: a text from Ally.

DadDadDadDadDad . . . 96 on my Italian quiz! Ready for Florence! ☺ ☺ *<3 <3*

Roy got up and paced. He took the maintenance manual for Dumbo down from its dusty home atop a steel file cabinet and flipped through it, trying to put his finger on the cause of the imbalance. It was no use. The machine was such a hodge-podge of old and new at this point, such a jimmied-up claptrap of home-tooled replacement parts and ancient rusting mechanisms that there was no telling where the problem could be originating. Plus, he was distracted with trying to mentally compose a suitably positive but noncommittal answer to Ally's text. Ah, God, Dumbo. He closed the book. He was beginning to feel like a handicapped icemaker himself, beginning to feel that there would be something quite satisfying, in fact, about having a full-on tantrum and flinging himself against the walls of the office to mimic the thrashing of Dumbo in her housing. He took a breath and texted Ally back.

Go, girl! <3 you. Proud of you. Mwah.

All right. Now focus, Roy. Dumbo. She was going to knock herself to pieces if they couldn't resolve this. Roy was reminded, then, of something Johnny's son Corran once talked about when he was over for a visit. Corran was a good guy. A little misguided, yeah, but so what? Who wasn't? He was sweet-hearted and quietly smart, a scrappy little dude, still built like a teenager even now, with a ready grin and the same charming Scots affect as his father. Ally was head over heels with a schoolgirl crush on him for a while when she hit about fourteen and Corran came over for a summer, but Corran, who had more than a decade on Ally, never gave her a look, and Roy couldn't say he was sorry about that.

Things had taken a sad turn in recent years, though, and he knew Corran and his father had been at a standoff for quite a while now. Roy didn't know why Johnny was so hard on the kid. Well, yes, he did know why. Corran got messed up with heroin, which was some scary shit, no joke, and then he blew through the MacKinnons' retirement fund trying to get clean, only to fall right back off the wagon after the last rehab. It sucked, for sure. But still—it was hard to imagine just cutting your kid off the way Johnny had done. Just the thought of it made Roy a little short of breath.

At any rate, the last time Corran visited, he told Roy something interesting, about a phenomenon called "ground resonance," an aviation term describing what can happen if a grounded, running helicopter's blades slip into an unbalanced, asymmetrical rotation, like a washing machine that slips its bushings during the spin cycle and begins to wobble uncontrollably. In ground resonance, the result to the helicopter can be catastrophic—once off-kilter, the craft can't regain its balance. In mechanical terms, the center of gravity disconnects from the axis of rotation, and the resulting untethered energy creates violent oscillations that can destroy the aircraft—the rotors collapse and begin striking the helicopter's body until the entire machine self-destructs. Basically, Corran said, the chopper will beat itself to death right there on the landing pad, before it ever gains even a foot of altitude.

Roy was pretty sure he knew the feeling. He squinted to look out of his good right eye and catch sight through his office window of the afternoon shift finally taking up their places at the icemakers and catch bins and loading zones. That's it, boys, he thought. Let's make some fucking ice before we all go down the drain.

NINE

The rigs were easier, Corran MacKinnon concluded. Easier than this. Waterlogged isolation, diesel fumes, bone-chilling cold, even the sickening pitches of North Sea swells—all of it was easier than what he was doing right now, which was walking around in the moonlight outside a tiny crofter's cottage on a highland hillside above Port Readie, trying to get his nine-month-old daughter to stop crying.

It was biting and damp, but Lucy had herself worked into such a lather of exertion that Corran doubted she was feeling the chill. He was walking slow circuits around the cottage, rubbing her back, talking to her, pleading with her. She'd been crying most of the evening. The reason they were outside in the cold was that earlier, when he was trying to console her with a bottle in the cottage's little kitchen, she thrust out a pudgy arm and knocked the bottle to the floor, where the top burst open and sent a spray of formula across the baseboards and under the refrigerator. Corran, clutching the screaming baby to his chest, had felt an impulse to throw the child herself down onto the linoleum.

That spark of rage frightened him so badly he immediately walked her outside, where he policed himself by imagining that the old man and woman who lived in the house at the bottom of the hill were looking out their window at this very moment, taking in the sight of a shadowy figure jiggling a baby around and around the croft grounds. "Look at that daftie from the ferry with the wee bairn, again," they were saying. "No mum, nah, she's a junkie gone to jail, you know. He's got the wee one on his own up there. At least he's patient with her, aye?"

God, she could wail! Corran had tried everything—feeding, diapering, burping, dancing, singing. He'd tried the jumper and the music box, the activity quilt and the stacking cubes, the dummy and the teething ring. He'd tried it all. He called his mother an hour ago, but Sharon just sighed and suggested he try it all again.

"She's inconsolable," he said. "I can't get her to stop."

"What can I really do, Corran?" Sharon said. "I'm nearly three hours away."

"I'm going mad here."

"I'll be up this weekend to help you. Maybe just put her in the crib and let her cry it out," Sharon said.

"I've tried that. She screeches so, it sounds like she's going to pass out."

"Oh, she's a stubborn thing," Sharon said. She sounded almost proud. Lucy arched her back and screamed. "The poor love," Sharon said.

"The poor me, you mean," Corran said. He had to nearly yell to be heard over the baby. "What do I do?"

"Just be patient," she said. "She's an infant. She'll fall asleep soon." Corran doubted it.

"Call me back when she's asleep," Sharon said. "I need to tell you something."

"She'll never be asleep. Never."

Sharon said something else, but he couldn't hear what it was. Then she hung up.

The moon over Loch Linnhe was high and Corran could see, even from here, the distant masthead light atop the Drumscaddle ferry, which he would board in less than ten hours for another mind-numbingly boring day of ushering cars up and down the loading ramp to make the eighty-three-second voyage across Loch Linnhe. He'd timed it. About a million times. Eighty-three seconds! The crossing was that narrow. Why did they not build a fucking bridge? How hard could it be? Some days he wanted to build it himself, put all these poor ferry-crossing Highlanders out of their misery.

Because it was always the same: There was no timetable, just a constant ping-ponging route of the rusted old ferry back and forth from one side of the loch to the other. And no matter how hard you tried, you always ended up driving to the loading ramp just as the boat was departing for the other side. So here you went again—queue up, wait it out, watch the damn ferry puttter its way across the water and execute the laboriously slow process of docking, securing the ramps, ushering the cars off, preparing again for departure. And then eighty-three seconds (that was the quick part!) back across the loch. A bridge, Corran wanted to scream, some days. Build a fucking *bridge*. But then he'd be out of a job.

He squinted until the ferry light blurred, and then he followed a ray of mist-softened luminescence down to the west, where from here in the cottage yard he could imagine, but could not see, the tiny village of Port Readie. A village? If you could even call it that: Really all it consisted of was an off-license shop, a tiny post office, and a pub that thank God put out passable cod and chips; otherwise Corran hardly knew how he'd survive.

There were a handful of cottages there, too, these owned mostly by folks who had jobs across the loch—either up at the shops of Fort William or down in the holiday rentals in Ballachulish. These were the people, Corran had learned, who'd roughed it in the Highlands long enough to know that living on the west side of Loch Linnhe was an affordably inconvenient way (or an inconveniently affordable way, one or the other) to have an unmortgaged, snug enough little home of one's own, nestled in the shadow of the same Ben Nevis that the tourists on the east side of the loch were gaping at from the windows of overpriced HomeAway rentals. A stout, windswept lady named Margaret lived in one of the plucky little Port Readie homes; Corran paid her to watch Lucy during his shifts on the ferry. "What's the difference," Margaret often demanded, "between that what *I'm* lookin' at and that what *they're* lookin' at? Same old mountain, innit?" She'd point at Ben Nevis in the distance, its rocky white top rising stubborn and insistent, like an old man.

"It is," Corran would say, nodding. And though the statement was certainly true enough, he had to admit that these last couple of months on his own with Lucy, he'd learned to agree with pretty much anything Margaret said. She'd raised four children by herself up here in the Highlands after her husband died when the oldest was just five. And, as she often said, they all turned out fine, didn't they? Corran had no idea how they turned out, but as far as he was concerned, if Margaret had done what he was now doing with Lucy *four times,* and if both she and her fatherless progeny were all still alive, then the venture was a smashing success.

She was liberal with her advice, but he didn't mind. *Stop with the carrots, the baby's turning orange,* Margaret said. *Don't let her sleep with you, she needs to know her own space,* Margaret said. *Let her have the bottle, don't rush the cup. You ever see a teenager with a baby bottle?* Corran did everything she told him. She was a godsend. Not long after she started watching Lucy, he stood on the ferry deck one day, looking back toward her house, and he thought he might even be in love with Margaret. Crazy! There she was, thirty years older than Corran, broad as a barn door, coiffed like Prince Valiant, and outfitted day after day in nothing but tracksuits and plimsolls!

That trance, thank goodness, quickly resolved itself into what Corran now knew it was: simple, desperate appreciation for the care and structure the woman was giving his daughter. Every weekday morning, when he fastened Lucy into her seat on the bicycle and rode down to Margaret's house, Corran had one thought on his mind: *Thank God we have Margaret.* But as each weekend drew near and the inevitable void in the day care arrangement loomed, that thought was replaced by another: *How are we going to make it to Monday without Margaret?* So far, there'd been only one reliable answer: Sharon. Corran wasn't proud of how abjectly he'd come to rely on his mother for her weekly three-hour drives up to Port Readie. But he didn't know what else to do.

One of his ferry mates, an older guy with a kind smile, asked Corran every now and then why he was living in Port Readie. "What are you doing all the way up here, anyway?" the man said. "And with no car? Ye daft? Why don't you move back to the city, closer to your mum? Get some help with the baby?" Corran always shrugged, noncommittal. But the answer was simple enough, had he cared to share it: There was no skag in Port Readie. And no way to get any. The ferry salary was just enough to pay for food, for Margaret's services, and for the rent on the tiny crofter's cottage. No extra money. No extra means. No extra mobility. It all translated to one thing—no heroin.

"Shush, Lucy," he said now. It was growing colder outside the cottage. He opened his sweatshirt and held the baby closer to his chest, then wrapped the sweatshirt around her. "Go to sleep, Lucy. Baby. Baby. Shush, now."

She wailed.

"Lucy," he said. "I beg you from the depths of my tortured soul: Stop crying."

She took a breath and screamed. He was then seized with the ridiculous notion that Lucy could have stopped crying any- time she wanted, but that she was simply tormenting him out of boredom and vindictiveness. Never mind that she was nine months old. She was capable. He pulled out his phone and checked the screen, hoping for—for what? A text from his rig- mate Jintzy, he admitted to himself. That's what.

When Anna was busted and Corran gave up the rigs to care for Lucy, he gave up a damn good job. Being a crewman on an offshore oil derrick was cold, hard, dangerous work, sure, and not something just anyone would want to do. But it paid well, and if you had the disposition for it, which Corran did, then the work was fine: solid and satisfying, with good benefits and a rugged wholesomeness (no alcohol, no drugs) that wasn't a bad idea at all for a recovering addict. The positions were in high enough demand that getting back on once you'd stepped out of the rotation wasn't easy. In two months Corran had yet to see any new openings posted on the company job site. His mate Jintzy, who just recently had been promoted from roughneck to motorman, had promised to see what he could do; he'd ask around, he said, feel out the supervisors, put in a good word at the HR office.

But Corran didn't know why he'd even asked Jintzy about it. It was pointless. What did he think he was going to do, tuck Lucy into a duffel bag, haul her out to a freezing oil rig, and leave her stashed on an activity quilt in the crew quarters while he pulled ten-, twelve-, sometimes fourteen-hour shifts on deck? Face it, he told himself, again and again. He wasn't going to be able to work on the rigs *and* take care of his baby. It was one or the other. The screen on the phone was blank. Corran put it back into his pocket.

Lucy leaned her head on his shoulder, momentarily stymied by exhaustion.

"You want your dummy?" he said softly. She looked at him with damp, round eyes. "Come on, love," he said. "Let's find dummy." He walked her back toward the house, a box-shaped cottage in the middle of a wide heath at the top of a steep hill. Inside, the rooms were arranged in perfect symmetry—a small bedroom and bathroom toward the back of the house, a living room and eat-in kitchen toward the front. The furnishings were spare: only a pressboard dinette set in the kitchen plus a frumpy pullout sofa and a rattan table in the living room.

In one corner stood an electronic keyboard on a metal stand. Corran had been carting the old keyboard with him for nearly a decade now, even when he went out on the rigs, and the captains never seemed to mind the extra cargo since it meant a certain measure of entertainment in the form of Corran's ability to play the rock and blues standards that kept the rig workers' spirits up during the long nights at sea with no beer taps to ease the tedium. He was pretty good, too, if he'd say so himself, thanks to the years of piano lessons at the old music studio in Dunedin. God, those days seemed a million years ago.

In the bedroom, Corran's twin bed and Lucy's crib stood side by side, as in barracks. He found the dummy in the crib and paced, rubbing the thick rubber bulb along Lucy's lips and trying to get her to accept it. Well, no wonder the poor baby cried so much, he thought. She had no mum. All she had was a strung-out da with a dwindling bank account and a specter of smack always trailing at his heels. She took the dummy and Corran put her down on the activity quilt. He wanted to cry himself.

No man is an island. So said John Donne. Well, Corran begged to differ. He'd been an island all his life, an unmoored archipelago adrift in the human brine. When he was a child Sharon used to nag him, "Go out and play with someone, Corry! Call up a mate!" And so he would, to appease her, but he always felt better alone. He was just wired that way. Better alone.

The only time he had ever truly craved interaction with others was when he was on heroin. In that situation, the proximity of other people was a built-in safety net—an assurance that the next fix would be somewhere close at hand. That's when he'd gotten involved with Anna, in fact. *Involved*. Was that what it was? On again, off again, hot, cold—*years* of that nonsense, and really, he was pretty sure now that the only reason they gravitated toward each other in the first place was to enable each other to use. Now, see that? He felt like calling up Sharon—all that rehab, and I *did* learn something! *Enabling.* He understood it now.

When he looked at things today, from the sober side of the pipe, he realized that his love affair with Anna was really just a love affair with skag. They were one and the same—having one meant having the other. Not having one meant not having the other. Anna—God, poor dumb Anna. A year and a half ago he thought they were finally through, but she resurfaced last winter. She had a brutal web of tracks on one arm and a baby on the other that she said was Corran's. She swore she'd been clean during the pregnancy. Lucy's *healthy,* she told him, and indeed the baby was lovely—pink-faced and solid and the sweetest little bairn he'd ever seen. Corran felt crushed under a wave of sentiment.

He married Anna. Sharon nearly had a conniption, of course, but in light of Anna's arrest, Corran realized now it was good he *had* married her; it meant custody of Lucy. It was a terrible time, though, when Anna first came back. After they signed the marriage license they went out and picked up a hit. They spent a few wasted days together in Corran's cold, dirty flat, and he cringed now to think of how heinously they must have been neglecting Lucy. On the third day Corran woke to find Anna in nothing but a tattered bra, shooting a needle directly into her groin in order to get a bigger rush. She'd been told it would be *amazing.* Lucy was wailing on the floor. Corran walked over and picked her up.

"If we don't stop, we're going to die," he told Anna. "And strangers will take Lucy away." She looked at him stupidly, a thin line of blood and heroin residue snaking down her thigh. He walked out of the flat with his daughter that day and kept walking until he reached the addiction clinic. This time, Lucy made the difference. He'd tried and failed so many times before, but this time, he *had* to get clean. He begged Anna to clean up with him, actually got down on his knees and begged. Finally, she let him lead her. The weeks of withdrawal weren't fun, but they made it through. A quarter of the people who use heroin even once never walk away from it. But they did. Well, Corran did.

Not that he walked away completely. The skag was still with him—thoughts of it, memories of it, goddamned fantasies about it: every day, every hour, every minute, every second! He'd never felt such desire—before or since. Not for food, not for sleep, not for sex, not for love. Heroin eclipsed it all. Corran marveled, even today, at the perfect beauty of the rush. His father used to get so mad at him. *Why do you do it, Corran?* Johnny would demand over and over, genuinely bewildered. Because it feels wonderful, Corran wanted to tell him. It was the most lovely way to live. Or the most lovely way to die. One or the other.

He got the placement on the rigs not long after the worst of the withdrawal symptoms started to subside. He tested clean and the company gave him a go. They got a little flat in Peterhead near St. Fergus for Anna and Lucy. Corran spent shore breaks in the flat and toughed out long shifts offshore with nothing but the battered keyboard and the pain of hard labor to think about. The rigs saved his life, in fact. Those long days and nights in the first months after withdrawal, when his skin itched and his breathing was ragged with longing for skag. Had he been on the mainland for any length of time he would have buckled. It was better to be offshore, with no way to get to smack other than to swim to it. The rigs kept him an island and kept him alive.

He felt guilty that Anna hadn't had the same chance. Maybe if she, too, had become an island, things could have been different for her. As it was, she stayed in Peterhead, worked at Asda, looked after Lucy, and made friends with some of the local girls: not junkies, no—they'd left those behind in Glesga—just lushy rig birds, crude and wind-battered, but with a brassy, hearty resilience Corran hoped would infect Anna. It was strength she needed, strength she lacked. Those friendships didn't help. Having Lucy didn't help. By summer, the tracks were back on Anna's arms.

Corran didn't love her. Given that at least one of them was almost always high as a kite when they were together, he didn't even *know* her, really, and he was ashamed to say he didn't want to. There seemed little to know. When he heard of the smuggling arrest he got a chopper flight off the rig. He took Lucy and went straight to Sharon's house, where it gradually began to sink in that Anna would not be a part of her daughter's life until Lucy was well into adulthood. If ever. And when the drums started beating in Corran's ears and the sounds of Glasgow turned into the seductive siren calls of skag, he came up here to Port Readie and created a new island where he and Lucy would live. He wangled cheap rent from the uncle of one of his rig-mates on a crofter's cottage three hours away from his heroin supply. He sold his car. From the cottage, he could see only sheep and nettles and a curl of chimney smoke rising from the old couple's house at the bottom of the hill. He made porridge for breakfast and cheese pies for dinner, and he cajoled Sharon into coming up on weekends to help. He tried to divine a plan for getting back on the rigs. He shook himself out of fitful dreams and got up in the night to stand at Lucy's crib and watch the soft rise and fall of her chest.

In this way, hour by hour, he kept himself from dying.

Corran bundled Lucy into the stroller. He pushed the pram out to the edge of the croft and started down the lane in the dark for the long walk to the village below. Two miles each way, but Corran was used to it. The walk down to Port Readie was easy enough. It was the walk back *up* to the croft that could get him sometimes, but Lucy always seemed appeased by the movement and the gentle bumping of the carriage along the stone-grouted lane. "Uh-uh-uh-uh," she said now, appreciating, evidently, the bumping percussion of her voice. "Uh. Uh. Uh." Corran kept one hand on the pram's handle, and with the other he checked his phone, where there was a text from Jintzy.

HUET on Tuesday, it said. *Can you make it?*

Shit! Another training session that Corran would have to miss. HUET—Helicopter Underwater Egress Training—was an annual requirement for anyone working on offshore rigs. Once you took leave or were furloughed, you had to be recertified before you could get back in the rotation for a rig assignment. Tuesday's would be the second HUET session Corran would be missing in as many months, and there was no getting back on the rigs until he took a recertification class. He was sober; he could pass it. If only he could get there to *do* it. He looked at Lucy in the stroller. Now, think about this, pal, he told himself. He was

Mr. Mom these days. It wasn't as if missing HUET training was the only thing standing in the way of rig work.

Still, he imagined the scene on Tuesday—a row of men lining up on the side of a huge, deep training pool, dressed in full work coveralls and flotation vests. Sometimes there'd be a woman or two, but this was rare, and when Corran told Sharon about the dearth of women in the training sessions she always said it was because women had far more sense than to do what these men were about to do. The trainees would board the test helicopter, which was suspended by a winch above the water. They'd clip on safety harnesses and swallow back the rising waves of fear. Then the helicopter would be released from the winch, plunged into the water, and rotated upside down to simulate an offshore crash. The game was to unclip, bash out a window, shimmy out of the chopper's fuselage, inflate your flotation vest, and drift to the surface before panic and lack of oxygen made you gasp in a lungful of pool water.

It wasn't easy. Lots of the newer boys got beaten by HUET. The first time Corran had attempted it, he was thrown off when the bloke next to him panicked on the chopper's impact and inflated his life jacket too early. Then the guy was too big to fit through the exit window and he panicked underwater, blocking Corran's path as well. Corran had to wiggle to the back door of the fuselage, and in the process he'd snagged his foot on his own harness and got stuck, had to be fished out by one of the trainers. He got better at it after that, though, and before he won his certification he actually got to a point where he enjoyed it—the rush of water, the tactical challenges, the heart-stopping scramble for egress. He'd miss it on Tuesday.

He texted Jintzy: *I can't make it, mate. I wish I could.*

It struck Corran as vaguely shameful that he would rather be thrashing about in the fuselage of an upside-down, sinking aircraft than pushing his baby daughter down a moonlit pathway in the Highlands. Ah, but bollocks. It was what it was.

There was a tiny pub in Port Readie, barely larger than a garden shed, and Corran parked the pram at the door and carried Lucy in. He one-armed a wooden high chair over to a table and set her up with a digestive biscuit. Her spirits seemed to have improved with the change of scene.

"Pah," she said.

"That's right," he said. "Biscuit."

He ordered a Belhaven. Though the counselors at the rehab disapproved, he allowed himself one a night, and so far, he'd been staying the course. He sat down opposite Lucy and regarded the pub, which was empty save for him and Lucy and a pair of middle-aged men at a table near the bar. He nodded to them; he knew they were regulars, both workers at the aluminium plant near Inverlochy. He'd caught a pint with them a couple of times, and now he drummed his fingers on the table, waiting for their names to come back to him. *Nick.* That's one. And the other . . . *Angus.* There. Got it.

They waved him over, and he waited until his beer arrived, then gathered up Lucy's things and dragged the high chair across the floor to position it at the other table, where Lucy stared at the men suspiciously.

"Corran," Nick said. "Save me from this sot. He's gone 'round the bend."

"What's on?" Corran said.

"He's sexually perverted," Nick said.

"I'm not," Angus said. "It's just good fun, see? My wife and I. We're trying to spice up the bedroom business, see?"

"He's batty," Nick said. "Tell him what you're doing."

Angus sighed. He gestured toward the table, where a gadget the size of a lighter sat next to a cell phone. "I've got a button here, see?" he said. He picked up the gadget and pressed a button on it. "And it's connected to a little vibrator. Tiny size, like a peanut, see? And when I press the button, it makes the vibrator wiggle. It's got amazing range. Great long distances."

"Ask him where the vibrator is," Nick said. Before Corran could assure them that he had no particular curiosity about where the vibrator was, Nick spared him the trouble.

"It's in his wife's thingy, that's where," he said. He took a long swallow of his beer and looked at Corran wide-eyed, waiting for a response.

"Well," Corran said. He looked at the gadget in Angus's hand. Angus pushed the button, then pushed it again. Corran looked away, embarrassed.

"Can you beat that?" Nick said. He slapped the table. "My wife would never agree to it, I tell you. I can hear her right now. 'Stick it up your own arse,' she'd say. 'Nae mine.'"

Angus frowned. "Well, it's not all it's cracked up to be," he said. He put the buzzer down on the table and picked up the cell phone. "She's supposed to text me when she gets a zap, aye? And she's supposed to tell me something randy. Only she's not been texting me like we planned." He looked at the cell phone sadly.

"Maybe it's out of range," Nick said kindly.

"Supposed to be capable of miles," Angus said. "She's only doing the shopping, isn't she? Across the loch at the co-op."

"Well, then maybe it's out of battery," Nick said. He looked at Corran and raised his eyebrows.

Angus sighed. "I don't understand it," he said.

"D'ye want me to try it?" Nick said. He reached for the buzzer.

"Get yer filthy hands off," Angus said. He picked up the buzzer and put it in his pocket. "Talk about perverted. *You're* the one." He glared at Nick and then turned his attention to Lucy, who was still staring from one man to the next.

"Looka that bairn," Angus said. "At's a good one." He smiled at Lucy and waggled his fingers on the tabletop in front of her. "How'd you get such a good one, mate?"

"Same way as most," Corran said.

"Aye, but at's a *good* one."

"How's the metal factory?" Corran said. Both men shook their heads.

"*Och,*" Nick said. "It's a crippler. Don't get us started. But at least it's Friday night, thank God Almighty."

"Problem with a factory," Angus said, "is that there's no finish line. You're never, ever, ever fucking finished, see? Make fucking metal all day long. What does that get you? A chance to do it again tomorrow. It's a fucking nightmare, innit, Nick?"

"You can't look at it that way," Nick said halfheartedly. "You'll go mad. You see, what I do, is I tell myself I'm making *things*, not just metal. I'm making saucepans and airplane wings, what have you. Puts it more in perspective, aye?"

"Ah, you're making fucking metal, same as the rest of us."

"Watch your dirty mouth in front of the bairn, would you?" Nick said.

Angus looked at Lucy, shamefaced.

"Christ. I'm sorry," he said.

"I don't think she knows what you're saying, Angus," Corran said.

"Anyway," Nick said. "It's a living."

"My da owns a factory," Corran said. He surprised himself by offering this information. "In Florida. Ice factory."

"Well, he's doing it right then, if he *owns* it," Angus said. "Them that own it don't mind it. It's only them that work it that mind it."

"And why are you not over in Florida with the ice factory then?" Nick said.

"I'm not interested in Florida."

"But aren't you interested in the *money*?"

Corran shrugged.

"Was me, I'd be over there. Making ice and staying warm," Nick said.

"Ah, leave 'im," Angus said. "Maybe he doesn't get on with his da."

Lucy knocked her biscuits off the table and watched blandly as they scattered across the floor. Corran took a napkin and swept them up. *Doesn't get on with his da*. Was that how you'd describe it, then? Corran hadn't seen his father since last Christmas, and they'd hardly parted on good terms. He ran his tongue across the inside of his bottom lip, remembering the gash that had lingered there for weeks last winter after he returned from Florida—the gash that resulted from Johnny's hand connecting with Corran's face. The last he'd seen of his father was the disgusted, stone-faced countenance of a man who'd evidently decided he'd been disappointed by his son for the final goddamned time. Johnny had stood at the window in his house on Watchers Island when

Corran shuffled out the front door toward the cab that would bring him back to the airport, back to Scotland. He didn't say goodbye. *Good ole Dad,* Corran thought, articulating in his mind his best Yankee accent. *My old man.*

It wasn't that Corran hadn't had it coming. For God's sake, he understood why Johnny was angry. Corran had been off the chain for a long time by then; he was well aware that much of his behavior—shit, *most* of his behavior—had been horrific for at least a decade. And he understood that Johnny was frustrated, tapped out, pissed off. Completely justifiable. Corran couldn't have expected anything different. He'd put them all through the wringer—Johnny, Pauline, Sharon, and Toole—thanks to the smack, and for ten long years he'd given them little occasion to hope that he'd ever be anything but a junkie. He'd had little hope of that himself. There were days, even today, when he still had little hope.

Except here was the thing: Last Christmas, Johnny had made it very clear, after the fiasco over Pauline's wedding ring, that he wanted Corran out of his life. Forever. "I want you gone," he'd said, and Corran hadn't heard from him since, though surely news of Corran's daughter and his nine-month triumph of sobriety had reached Johnny's ears by now. And all right, Corran thought, maybe it was true that he didn't have a whole lot going for him right now *except* sobriety. No education. No money. A shitty job on the Drumscaddle ferry to try to make ends meet and buy food for his daughter.

But he *did* have a small measure of pride left. And he'd be damned if he was going to be the one to blink, the one to come crawling back to Johnny with a simpering apology in his hands—*again.* Especially for something that—for once!—Corran didn't

do! Johnny had accused him of stealing Pauline's ring, a crime
Corran *didn't commit.* Granted he'd been on quite a bender at the
time, and granted there were heroin-induced gaps in his memory
for much of that Florida visit, but Corran wanted to believe—no,
he *needed* to believe—that he was a decent enough human being
that even in a delirious panic for skag, he would not have stolen
his stepmother's wedding ring off her nightstand and sold it to
buy more drugs. He wanted to believe his father thought that,
too, but alas, such was not the case.

    He wants you to admit to taking Pauline's ring, Sharon told
him.

    I want him to admit he's being an asshole, Corran responded.
Because I didn't take the ring. Even Sharon looked doubtful. Which
made Corran even angrier. After a while, the fact that everyone
wanted him to own up to the theft had become an offense itself.
Johnny said he did. Corran said he didn't. And there they were.
A Mexican standoff. Fine.

    When Corran was growing up, Johnny visited a few times a
year and flew Corran over to Florida whenever the idea seemed
to strike him, but Corran had always gotten the feeling that it
was more out of a sense of obligation to Sharon than anything
else. Fatherhood was easy for Johnny: Show up now and then,
write some checks, and then exit stage left, go back to sit on a
sunny Florida beach and enjoy the spoils of ice. Sure, Johnny
sent money. Plenty of it—all through Corran's childhood and
right on into the financial catastrophe of Corran's drug addiction.
And sure, Corran was grateful. Absolutely. God knew it took a
great deal of pressure off Sharon and Toole, who were always
staring down the voracious working-class maw of credit cards,
home equity loans, and car payments.

But grateful or no, and money or no, Corran had grown up thinking that Johnny might have *loved* him in a very abstract, duty-bound way, but that his father didn't particularly *like* him. Corran couldn't remember—apart from the fisticuffs last Christmas—a single time when he and his father had ever touched each other, except for a formal handshake, even after months spent apart. A single time! It was baffling. There were photos around Sharon's house of Corran as a very young lad—sometimes up on Johnny's shoulders, sometimes standing against his father's knees, Johnny's hand on his head. But Corran couldn't remember any of those instances, and they had certainly ceased to occur by the time Corran reached adolescence. Sharon was the hugger in their family. Not Johnny.

In the months since Corran had gotten to know the blessings of Lucy's soft skin and the saving grace of her fine, sweet-scented hair, the memory of his father's austerity was gradually changing, taking on a hue more akin to resentment than to its familiar bewilderment.

Sharon tried to defend Johnny. "It's hard for him, Corran," she'd say. "He doesn't show affection well, that's all." Which was bullshit. Corran had nothing against Pauline whatsoever—he loved her, in fact, considered her nothing short of a saint—but one look at Johnny going moonstruck over his second wife the way he'd been doing for the past twenty-five years was enough to demonstrate that the old man *did* have a heart. He just didn't open it much.

Johnny had always maintained that he left Scotland to earn a better income, and that this better income (which was indeed forthcoming) was won through great personal sacrifice in order to provide a better life for Corran Boniface. Good fate! Corran had heard that one all his life, and the irony of the moniker these days was not beyond him. But Corran had another theory about Johnny's departure for the States and, more precisely, about Johnny's decision to remain there: His father found two loves in America. One was Pauline. The other was money. And he wasn't about to let Corran get in the way of either of them. In fact, the exact location of Corran on Johnny's list of personal priorities was vague indeed, and as the years went by and Corran's life became more problematic, as he watched his father counting the costs—both personal and financial—of Corran's drug problems, he came to one conclusion: His father didn't particularly want him. If Corran ever had any doubt, last Christmas had erased it.

I want you gone, Johnny said. Corran had agreed. It was probably the best for them both. For ten months now, he'd held the line. And he wasn't going to apologize to Johnny, because he didn't take Pauline's ring. Of this, he was ninety-nine and three-quarters percent certain.

He just *wouldn't* have done that.

It was cold in the pub. Corran pulled Lucy's jacket around her shoulders and fastened it at the neck to keep it in place. It looked like a cape. Superhero Lucy. She was staring at a TV above the bar, which seemed to be airing a cop show of some sort. A police officer was taking a crowbar to somebody's windshield. The program title ticked across the screen: "World's Wildest Police Videos." Brilliant. Corran stared at his daughter, wondering if he should let her watch this.

"I didn't get on with my da," Nick was saying. "Nasty piece of business, he was. Beat the living piss out of you just as soon as look at you. I couldn't be done with him quick enough."

"Mine was all right," Angus said. "Very kind, really. But depressed. He'd been an officer in the war, but when he came back it was nothing but foundry work. That was the only job he could find. A big comedown. I don't think he ever got over it."

"He died?" Corran said.

"Aye, he died. Ten year ago," Angus said. "And the poor thing is still knockin' about purgatory."

"You don't think he made it out of purgatory yet?" Nick said.

"He won't never. On account of the priest didn't give him last rites."

"What are you talking about?"

"My da was on his deathbed," Angus said, "and the priest was called to give him the rites. But when the priest heard who it was, he wouldnae come do it. They'd had a row, see, years before, over one owed the other money. Da and this priest. So my father died without the rites, because that fucking priest wouldnae come."

"They have to come. They're required."

"Well, he wouldnae."

"They should have got another priest."

"There was no other. This was way up Dornoch."

"That doesn't make any sense, even by the standards of the church," Corran said. "Think of all the people who die without last rites. Think of soldiers. Think of car accidents."

"Yes, but if you die on a deathbed, of sickness, you're supposed to have the last rites. Otherwise, why'd they even make them?" Angus protested. "Ah, it's a mess," he sighed. "I just console myself with knowing that fucking priest has my father's soul to answer for now."

Angus looked at his cell phone, then pulled the buzzer gadget out of his trouser pocket. He pushed the button once, then twice, and stared at the phone expectantly. They all sat in silence, waiting, staring at the phone. After a moment, Angus put the buzzer back into his pocket and signaled the barmaid for another beer.

Lucy started to fuss. Corran paid his tab. He said goodbye to Nick and clapped Angus on the shoulder, but now the man was staring at his beer, deep in thought.

"My poor da," he was saying. "My poor, poor da."

Corran picked up Lucy and exited the pub. The wind hit him like a fist. He turned his body to shield Lucy from the chill, but she started to cry again anyway. He went for the stroller. The little shopping district on the other side of the loch was lit up, and he instinctively looked at his watch. Those numpties better get on the last crossing, he thought. Ferry would be shutting down in an hour. Ah, so what? He was off shift. He shouldn't be worried about it. Funny, the useless habits you develop. Then he imagined Angus's wife over at the co-op, and an image presented itself to him: a rejected peanut-sized vibrator, buzzing like a jumping bean and gathering lint at the bottom of an oversized shopping bag. He actually laughed out loud at the notion, just as he was leaning over to put Lucy—who was starting to cry in earnest again—back into the stroller. The baby fell silent. Corran regarded her.

"Hae ye never heard me laugh, Lucy?" he said to her. He did it again. She stared at him, two fat teardrops wobbling on the bottoms of her eyelids. And then her face—ah God, Lucy—broke into a smile.

Corran circled his belt around the stroller handle and then hooked it through a belt loop on the back of his jeans. It was easier to pull the stroller up the hill than to push it. He gave Lucy a bottle and she was content then, lying back in the stroller and staring up at the stars with a bellyful of biscuits. He tucked the blanket tighter around her, fastened the safety harness, and started to walk. He remembered he was supposed to call his mother back. He pulled his phone out of his pocket and checked for text messages. Nothing more from Jintzy, but one from Sharon.

Your da called. He's coming over, be here tomorrow. He'll ride up with me this weekend.

Corran stopped in his tracks and gazed up at the star-sprinkled firmament. Oh. Well, brilliant. Just fabulous. His hands were freezing and it took him a few moments to get his fingers to text accurately.

Tell him no, he typed. He waited. The phone pinged Sharon's response.

He's already en route. Texted from Charlotte.

Johnny! This was beyond annoying. Corran pictured his father arriving at the house on Boscombe Road, bantering with Sharon and working his way through a few pints at the kitchen table with Toole. Then, just like in the old days, lumbering a little unsteadily through the house and up to the second floor to drop his duffel bag on the floor next to one of the single beds in Corran's little room at the top of the stairs. He'd kick off his shoes—work boots they were, the only kind of shoes his father ever wore—and hit the bed, hard. "Made it!" he'd announce to the ceiling. "Jumped the puddle!" Just in case the fact of his arrival had gone unnoticed. *Johnny MacKinnon.* The one and only.

A flash of anger coursed through Corran's veins, and then was replaced by something else he couldn't quite name. Remorse? No, not that. Grief, maybe. Maybe grief. Well, shit.

What are you trying to do to me? he texted his mother. He turned the phone off. Nothing good was coming from it tonight. He took a step forward to take up the slack in the belt and felt the weight of his daughter behind him. Then he and Lucy started back up the hill.

TEN

For Johnny, the first great relief of landing in Glasgow was that the pressurized tumor in his head had not exploded. Bully. The flight had been nightmarish enough—nine hours of Chemal's fidgeting plus an overly talky woman seated behind them and a throbbing headache that Johnny worried indicated an altitude-induced compression on the meningioma in his overtaxed brain. The woman was fixated on the topic of CrossFit. Johnny wanted to slam her head into the side of the beverage cart when it came up the aisle. This was alarming—such vitriol!—but also satisfying. He slipped pleasantly and fully into the fantasy. Then he dozed for a little while, but only in the fitful upright manner of humans on airplanes, and he was jolted awake more than once by the sound of his own wet snoring. Not that he was the only one. Transatlantic air passengers were a motley crew, he decided, looking around at the snoozers and droolers and twitchers. What a weird business this was.

The second great relief, which Johnny experienced after they'd secured the car rental and navigated the spaghetti of airport exits, was that Chemal seemed, as he'd boasted, completely adaptable to Scottish driving. Even jet-lagged and directionally disoriented, he appeared to have simply flipped a switch and reversed his Americanized instincts to effortlessly manage right-hand-drive, left-side-roadways, and even the daunting roundabouts that Johnny had seen completely flummox a good many older and more experienced American drivers who couldn't take the pressure.

Pauline, for example, had refused to drive a car in Scotland at all after her first memorable attempt at a roundabout in Glasgow years ago, when she'd been caught on the inside lane for a half dozen rotations before she could brazen her way out to the perimeter to exit, after which she'd promptly pulled the car over and relinquished the wheel to Johnny. "What the hell?" she'd said, sweating and exasperated. "Could that design be any stupider?" The design was actually quite brilliant, Johnny told her—a roundabout kept the traffic moving and eliminated gridlock on Scotland's already congested roadways, but Pauline was having none of it. "Absurd," she kept saying. "I think it's some sort of national joke to play on Americans." Johnny smiled but held his tongue.

Chemal, on the other hand, had it under control. The rental was a mite-sized four-cylinder Volkswagen Polo, and Johnny at first balked at the wretched irony of *this* state of affairs. Crossed an ocean, and still sentenced to a Volkswagen? But the woman at the rental desk said they were out of everything else, and it was either take the VW or wait two hours for another car to be returned.

"Pick your battles, Iceman," Chemal said. So the Polo it was. Chemal took the wheel, and Johnny was left free to navigate the route out of Glasgow and down the M74, where the village of Dunedin nestled itself against the eastern bank of the Clyde. Johnny had worked it out with Sharon: The plan was to land in Glasgow and drive straight to her house to nap off the jet lag and have a wee visit. Sharon said she'd put in for time off from work so she could join Johnny for a few days in Port Readie to see Corran. And Corran's baby. Johnny was still trying to get used to this idea. He was relieved, actually, to learn that Sharon would come along.

"I don't feel jet-lagged at all," Chemal said now. He yawned. "Just regular tired."

"We gained time," Johnny said. "Get ready to merge here. Going east is a win—you get ahead of it. Going west is a lose."

"What if you just kept flying east?" Chemal said. "You keep flying into earlier time zones. Pretty soon you fly into yesterday. You keep going. Fly into the day before. And the day before that. You're turning back time. Ever think of that, Ice? Like, you can go back and redo stuff you like to do. Or see people who are gone. Or do things differently than you did them the first time. Make new decisions. Reboot. Fuckin' A."

"That's very romantic. I bet you think you're the first person who's ever thought of that."

"Of course not. But I bet *you* never did."

"Turn right."

Though the air was cold and a heavy mist still hung over the city, as they drove the sun began to make an effort, and the thick brown skyline of Glasgow began to give way to the palette of suburban Scotland's autumn foliage: burnt orange, bright yellow, a weak but insistent mossy green, and here and there jolts of bright purple and red. Johnny watched the motorway's lanes whittle themselves down to two, watched the silver birch and alders multiply until they were approaching the city's bedroom villages along the Clyde. Chemal was astounded, and uncharacteristically hushed. "The colors," he kept whispering. "Look at the colors."

Johnny pulled up Google Maps on his iPhone and watched the blue dot shimmy down the little roadway in his palm. It was more satisfying, somehow, than looking out the window at a landscape he remembered as quite beautiful but also quite cruel. But the iPhone began to irritate his headache and Chemal was nagging him about international roaming charges, so he pocketed the phone and instead played a game of putting himself inside Chemal's head—now *that* was scary—and seeing the country with the kid's uninitiated eyes. The chill of the clouds. The burning riot of autumn. The sky was smaller here, Johnny decided, pinched and crowded by mountain ranges that bled terrible stories of uprising and slaughter into lonely glens.

The Polo had a sunroof, and Johnny opened it and tipped his head up to look out at a square of fuzzy blue sky. A wet mist filtered in through the aperture, so he closed the sunroof and contented himself with studying the passing businesses. There were stores and restaurant chains he had nearly forgotten existed: Tesco and Asda, Arnold Clarks and Esso. They passed the exit for the road leading to Easterhouse, and Johnny felt both the familiar gnawing of that hard place and a long-dormant but passionate pride in his little family's exodus from it. *We're getting him out of Easterhouse, Sharon.* The miracle of that old egress was still dazing. The familiar density of the city streets thinned as they moved into the suburbs and through rolling farmlands. They were scarcely out of Glasgow when they saw their first blackface sheep herd, all muddy and gawkish against a straining wire fence, red keel marks like scarlet letters across their haunches.

"Sheep!" Chemal said.

"Get used to them," Johnny said.

Near Bothwell Johnny told Chemal to pull over next to the Clyde Walkway, and they got out of the car to have a look at the river. Johnny had read somewhere that the Clyde was much cleaner than it had been years ago, now that the environmentalists had gotten after the factories in Glasgow about runoff and waste. But it still looked to him as grim and foreboding as ever. Everything felt heavier here, in fact, Johnny decided. The air. The earth. His own tense limbs. A boat was chugging upstream, probably toting buckets of grayling and brown trout. Johnny remembered. And my God, the chill! Johnny had nearly forgotten. They stood on the bank and shivered. Chemal jumped up and down and threw rocks.

"It's cold as shit here. Reminds me of Detroit," he said. Then he pointed. "What's that?" A fat brown otter bigger than General San Jose was darting along the bank just downriver.

"Dog otter," Johnny said. "They're hard to spot. Good eye."

"Sweet."

They watched the otter for a little while. It approached the water's edge and dipped black hands into the water, feeling around in the silt. It looked like a tiny pianist. "He's cute," Chemal said. He was smiling widely. He looked like a little boy. He was seventeen, right? Johnny did the math. Corran would have been around thirteen when Chemal was born. A lifetime ago, but then again nothing at all.

"Should you be calling your mum? Tell her we've arrived?" Johnny said.

"Iceman. Please. I doubt very much she's worried about it."

"You're not giving your mum enough credit."

"Credit for what?"

"For putting up with you, that's what."

"Hey, man," Chemal spread his hands wide. "You take your chances in this life. You get what you get. She didn't get the golden boy. She got me."

"I thought she wanted a black boy."

"You know what I mean."

Johnny handed Chemal his cell phone. "Call your mum, kidda." Chemal rolled his eyes but took the phone and dialed. He walked upriver and after a moment Johnny could hear the defensive cadence of his voice: "Yeah. No. Yeah."

What was it with kids?

Johnny buttoned his jacket. The cold was cutting through him. He walked a bit to try to warm up, and to try to reclaim some life in his limbs after the long, cramped flight. The walkway, paved and tidy, wound tightly along the river, and now and then he passed a jogger or a young woman with a pram. They nodded at him, and he felt dodgy, dishonest. They didn't know about him. He looked like any other middle-of-the-road Glaswegian, he reckoned; there was certainly nothing about his appearance that would brand him an expatriate, an American, a *Floridian*, for heaven's sake.

"Ice! Ice! Bay-bee!" Chemal was shouting through the trees from a long way down the walkway behind Johnny. In a moment, he appeared on the path, jogging toward Johnny, his voluminous jeans and sneakers looking like some sort of space attire. "Where

are you, Ice?" Rather than a sensible winter coat, Chemal had
opted to outfit himself for the trip by layering as many sweat-
shirts and sweaters as he could *under* his KISS Army jacket.
He looked like a heavy metal marshmallow. With a booming
American accent. A woman with a toddler looked at Chemal,
then at Johnny, then back at Chemal. So much for blending in.

"All right," Chemal said when he'd caught up to Johnny.
He didn't seem to have modulated his voice at all from when he
was fifty yards down the path.

"Shhhh," Johnny said. "You're shouting."

"I called my mom," Chemal said.

"Still shouting."

Chemal handed back the cell phone. "I called my mom,"
he stage-whispered. "She said to tell you hello." He walked down
the bank to toss stones into the river.

Johnny looked at his phone. He needed to call Pauline.
He wouldn't say he was *scared* to call her, necessarily. But she'd
been so livid with him over his determination to take this trip
that he was, well, a little *concerned* about calling her. When he
told her his plan, and when he added that he'd already paid
the airfare for himself and Chemal, she'd stared at him silently
for so long that he waved one hand in front her face, trying to
focus her vision.

"I hope you're joking," she finally managed. She'd been
standing next to the kitchen table, and she sat down abruptly.

"Well, no," Johnny said. "I think I need to see Corran."

"You won't even talk to him for all these months, no matter
how much I've begged, and now you're going to drop everything
and *go there*?" she said. "This is the worst possible timing. You're
supposed to be resting up for brain surgery."

"I know. . . ." he began.

"*Brain. Surgery.*"

"I'm aware of that," he said. "But I think I need to settle this thing with Corran. I don't think I should leave it on the hook."

"You're not dying," she said. "The tumor is benign."

"I didn't say I was dying," he said. "I said I wanted to see my son."

"You're panicking."

"I'm making use of my time off."

"And may I remind you," she said, "about OSHA?" She stood up and started to pace. General San Jose waddled into the kitchen and watched her anxiously.

"What about OSHA?"

"About the appeal."

"The appeal that's not even scheduled yet? The appeal we don't have any grounds for? You mean that appeal?" He walked over and put his arms around her. She stiffened. "Come on, Pauline. We're probably weeks out from the appeal. And I'm not even allowed to go to the factory, so what good am I to Sam Thompson or whatever his name is?"

"Tulley."

"Whatever. If anybody needs me they can call me. I'll be back in no time. Less than a week. It's not that big of a deal." Pauline stood frozen in his embrace, and eventually he let go. When she spoke to him again her voice was so low and steely it was alarming.

"Let me get this straight," she said. "You're taking the juvenile delinquent from next door, and you're flying to Glasgow with a seizure-inducing tumor in your head, and you're leaving me to deal with the lawyers and the paperwork and the fact that our livelihood is teetering on the edge of ruin, is that correct?"

"Well," he said. He paused. "Yes, I guess that's pretty accurate." He thought perhaps he could turn the conversation toward a more comic tone. He was wrong.

"I don't even know what to say to you," she said.

Pauline. He hated to see her this angry. *Tell her,* he said to himself. *Tell her about the second MRI. Tell her about the fingerlike growths. Maybe then she'll understand.* But he couldn't. He kept his eyes trained on the General. He was afraid to look in Pauline's eyes. "Don't be mad," he said.

"Too late," she said. She picked up her dog and went upstairs. That was the last time they'd spoken before he left.

Now, standing at the edge of the icy Clyde, he took a deep breath and called her. She was distracted with a household situation.

"A frog got into the house," she said. "The General tried to eat it and now he's throwing up everywhere."

"I think that dog's trying to tell us something."

"Like?"

"Like he's had enough. That's a bold move right there. Dogs know frogs are poisonous."

"Are you saying you think my dog is suicidal?"

"I think he's on the verge."

"Well, that's very nice. I'd like to think he's happy, thank you very much. Oh, no, *General!*" she said. Johnny could hear her moving through the house. "He just barfed again. I really don't need this today, Johnny."

"We landed."

"I gathered."

"You needn't be so pissed at me."

She sighed. "How's Sharon?"

"We haven't gotten there yet." Pauline was quiet. "You okay?" he said.

"I better go, Johnny," she said. "I've got puke up to my eyeballs here."

"I wish you weren't mad," he said. He stomped his feet to try to warm up.

"I wish you weren't in Scotland with a tumor in your brain and our business on the brink," she said. "That's what I wish."

"Cyst."

"Yes," she said. "Cyst."

"I love you," he said. "Let me know if Tupper makes any progress."

"It's 'Tulley,'" she said. "For the tenth time. Good luck with Corran." She hung up.

"That's sweet," Chemal said. He'd returned to stand next to Johnny. "Nice to know the romance is still alive. I mean, at your age."

They went to the car and got back on the road. Twenty minutes later, they pulled into Dunedin, and Johnny directed Chemal to Sharon's house on Boscombe Road, an impeccably neat semidetached just around the corner from the grammar school. Johnny hadn't been here for ages. How many years? He couldn't think. As he knocked on the door he had a clanging bout of regret. To avoid getting into the whole medical thing over the phone, he hadn't told Sharon that he'd be bringing somebody else along, somebody being the bouncing, chattering kid on the doorstep with him right now. But he had no time to consider this. Toole threw open the front door wide and stared at them, shocked, before tugging Johnny into a half-hug and extending a hand to Chemal.

"Come in, come in, why didn't you call, why didn't you tell us?" he said. "And who is this lad? And how is Pauline? And why didn't you *call*?"

"I did call," Johnny said. "Didn't Sharon tell you?" Toole shook his head.

"This is Chemal," Johnny said. "He's my neighbor."

"Howdy-do," Chemal said seriously. Toole pumped his hand.

Toole stood beaming at them. "Well, this is a surprise. My God, Johnny! It's been a long time, mate."

Johnny took off his jacket and ventured a look around the tiny living room. So little had changed since he'd last been here. He remembered nearly all of it: the rust-colored carpeting, the flagstone fireplace, the lace-curtained windows, vinyl roll-up shades lapping against the cold panes. Even Toole's old cigar-store Indian was still here, a four-foot wooden carving of an irritated-looking Native American in a flamboyant headdress, his right hand raised either in formal greeting or, as Sharon maintained, in the universal gesture for "talk to the hand."

Toole had found him at a charity shop in Paisley years ago. He had dragged him home in delight, stood him in the corner, and immediately named him "How." Why someone had gone to the trouble to transport the old statue from America only to abandon it in a thrift store Johnny would never know, but at any rate, How was now a permanent fixture here. Sharon had pointed out more than once that times had changed and that Toole was on increasingly thin ice in terms of the racial sensitivity of his favorite piece of home decor, but Toole maintained that this was no time to be taking the high road; he kept his eye on the resale market and had been watching the prices of similar carvings climb for years. How was going to finance his retirement one day, Toole insisted. And until then, How would remain exactly where he was, standing dour sentry over a tiny, drafty Scottish living room.

The room, though, did appear to exhibit some upgrades that had been made since Johnny's last visit. The spindly TV cart had been replaced with what looked like an electric massage chair, and an enormous flat-screen television was now mounted on the wall opposite the couch. A trendy leather ottoman squatted in the center of the room. A laundry basket filled with bright baby toys was tucked in a corner. *Lucy.* Johnny stared at the toys.

Toole was firing questions at Chemal. You hungry? You want tea? You're *neighbors,* you say? And where's *Pauline?* Johnny decided to head it all off at the pass.

"All good, Toole," he said. "Pauline's fine. I just came over for a couple of days. Hoping to catch Corran. Chemal is helping me out. I've got a medical thing, not supposed to drive."

"A medical thing?"

"His brain," Chemal offered. Johnny glared at him.

"Did I ask you for input?" he said.

"What, you didn't tell me it was a big secret!"

"It's not a big secret."

"Dude, it must be—you're having a conniption over there."

"What the hell?" Toole said.

"Never mind it. We're moving on," Johnny said. Toole raised his eyebrows but agreeably changed the subject.

"I have a mate who can't drive," Toole said. "He has narcolepsy."

"Seriously?" Chemal said.

"Yeh, he falls asleep uncontrollably. Out of the blue."

"That's awesome," Chemal said.

"I don't think he's so chuffed about it."

"You're not at work?" Johnny said to Toole.

Toole didn't answer. Instead, he looked at Chemal. "I write books," he said. "When I'm not enslaved to the man."

"Oh, I hear ya," Chemal said.

"When are you ever enslaved to the man?" Johnny asked Chemal.

"Maybe right now," Chemal said pointedly.

"Tea," Toole said flatly.

"Sweet," Chemal said.

They followed Toole to the little kitchen at the back of the house, and in the light of the garden windows Johnny was surprised by how much Toole had aged—the skin on his neck gone loose and slack, the lines around his eyes drawn a little tighter, a little more weight around the midsection, and, most noticeably, a pronounced limp. Toole, whose first name was Gordon but who went by his middle name, was the last man standing of a set of identical triplets. His brother Glyn had succumbed to lung cancer at age fifty, and his brother Gerald collapsed in a Sainsbury's with a massive heart attack at fifty-three. Toole was left with the tough nut of wondering when his own genetic number—identical, right?—might be up. It rattled him.

For a time, after Gerald died, Toole became obsessed with medical research. He spent hours on health websites, subscribed to *Prevention* and *Men's Health*, even got Sharon to borrow drug manuals from the hospital where she worked so he could brush up on his pharmaceuticals. He gave up drinking, went vegetarian, took up yoga, kept an arsenal of herbal supplements in the dish cupboard. After a while, though, two things happened. One, Toole got thirsty and came to the inevitable conclusion that a life without Tennent's lager might very well be a life not worth living. And two, he developed an interest in crime writing and realized that his new knowledge of physiology came in pretty handy in developing the forensic details to fit his crime scenes. His first novel—a psychological thriller set in the Victorian Orkneys—had been a modest success, garnering some good reviews in the UK press, if Johnny remembered correctly. He'd written a handful since then, all solid sellers but none profitable enough to allow him to give up his day job as a physical therapist, much to Toole's heartbreak.

"I hear you have new knees," Johnny said.

"*Och*," Toole said. He sat down and pulled up both legs of his trousers, revealing two tidy but appallingly large scars.

"Dang," Chemal said.

"It's been a nuisance, to say the least," Toole said. "But I'm told I'll soon be leaping tall buildings in a single bound. Or something."

"So, Sharon's working, I guess?" Johnny said.

"Right." Toole got up, plugged in an electric kettle, and rummaged in a tin for tea bags. For the longest time, Sharon had worked as a labor and delivery nurse at Rottenrow hospital, but several years ago she moved into palliative care and now worked as a visiting hospice nurse. "Went from bringing them in to showing them out," she often said. Johnny wondered how she could do it, be so intimately involved with a patient during those final, gasping days, but she said she liked it. "It's usually quite peaceful," she told him. "You'd be surprised." Johnny didn't want to know.

"What time does she get finished?" he asked Toole.

"Well . . ." Toole seemed confused. He looked up at the ceiling as though he might find the answer there. "I don't know," he said finally.

An orange cat came over and jumped into Johnny's lap. He petted it absently. Toole turned toward them, holding three tea bags. "Do we really want tea?" he asked. "Is that what we want?"

"I'm thinking not," Johnny said. Toole called Sharon and told her to meet them at the pub when she got off work. "Johnny's here," he said into the phone. "And a friend of his." He paused, then lowered his voice. "You did? Well, I don't *remember* you telling me that."

Toole insisted on walking—said it was part of his therapy—so they strolled the frigid five blocks from the house to the Deoch an Doris, a stout old watering hole that had been fortifying the locals for as long as Johnny had been coming to Dunedin and two hundred or so years before that as well. It had changed in some ways—signs advertising Wi-Fi and a smoke-free establishment having taken up residence in one of the street-facing windows, for example, the former widely appreciated and the latter categorically ignored—but in other ways it was exactly the same as it had been every other time Johnny had seen it. Same ancient carpeting. Same dark pine paneling. Same cramped seating and dim lighting. Same curved wooden bar, where baskets of bagged crisps fought for space among pub mats, ashtrays, and menus. The Deoch an Doris—the "drink at the door."

By the time they sat down, Johnny's hands were brittle, his eyes were watering, and he was cursing the impotence of his flimsy Carhartt jacket against the winds channeling down the Clyde and through the crooked streets of Dunedin. "So, how's ice, then?" Toole was saying. He held up three fingers to a pony-tailed young woman behind the bar, who nodded.

"It's okay," Johnny said. He told Toole about the accident and the OSHA case.

"*Och*, sorry, then," Toole said.

"Yeh."

The bartender approached and placed three pints on the table. "How ye, Toole?" she said. "Better now, Janie," he replied. She rolled her eyes and walked away, and Toole nudged Chemal. "Look at that bahoochie, eh?" he said. "See, now if I was a younger man . . ." He let his sentence trail off and glanced at Chemal knowingly. Chemal gazed at Janie's bahoochie as if contemplating some of the things a younger man *might* do with it. Then he turned back to gape at the pint frothing in front of him on the table.

Toole sighed. "If I was a single man, I'd ask that one out," he said.

"Toole, a young girl like that wouldn't go out with an old married sot like you if you were fartin' ten-bob notes," Johnny said.

Toole looked injured. "You're almost as old as I am," he said.

"Which is why I'm not making an ass of myself after young girls," Johnny said. They looked across the room at Janie. She was indeed a lovely girl. With a lovely bahoochie, in fact. As if she felt them watching her, she looked up and shot them the bird.

"Ice," Chemal whispered. He nodded at the beer. "Seriously? I can drink this?"

Toole waved his hand dismissively. "Drink up, lad!" he said. "You're in Caledonia!" Chemal grinned and tipped up the glass.

"And how's physical therapy, then?" Johnny asked Toole.

"Ah," Toole said. "Pffft. I'm so sick of physical therapy. When I'm not on the receiving end myself for these bloody knees, I'm administering it to patients. And it's a day's work, I tell you. Have you ever had to lift a fifteen-stone woman out of a swimming pool?"

"Can't say I have."

"Well, it's hell on the back, I tell you. Some job."

We all, Johnny decided, want to be something other than what we are.

"So, listen, then. I've been reading about your Disney there," Toole said.

Toole had a fascination with Walt Disney World, a fact Johnny could never quite reckon. A grown man, fantasizing about puppet creatures and princesses? It didn't compute. But Toole seemed to think that the most incredible and fortunate result of Johnny's move to Florida was that he and Pauline lived within two hours of the Magic Kingdom. "Do ye go often, then?" he asked Johnny every time he saw him. Johnny had been to Disney exactly once—when Pauline's sister Caroline had strong-armed the entire family to go for a long weekend to entertain her girls. And once was enough. "Not very often," he always told Toole.

"You know what they have at Disney?" Toole said now. "Smellitzers."

"What?"

"Smellitzers. They're these patented contraptions that pump aromas into the parks. Like fresh cookie smells, or oranges, or like that. It's a marketing thing, see. They get you in those shops to buy cookies whether you want to or no."

"Manipulative bastards."

"No, no. They're genius, I tell you! Brilliant. They've extended the bounds of conventional selling."

"Sensory marketing," Chemal piped up.

"Exactly, lad."

"So, what's next?" Johnny said. "Hand jobs to sell condoms?" Chemal snorted.

"Well, now you're being crude," Toole said. "They don't sell condoms at Disney."

"I bet they do," Johnny said.

"Rubbish. It's not that kind of place."

"It's the Happiest Place on Earth, Toole," Johnny said. "How do you think it got that way? They're all shagging in those underground tunnels, that's how. I bet you can pay extra at the gate for a run at Snow White in her castle there."

"That's Cinderella's castle."

"Both of them, then. A threesome."

"You're sick, Johnny," Toole said. "You dinnae ken about Disney."

"Ah, *you've* never even been," Johnny said. In fact, Toole had never been outside the UK. Johnny had long ago laid down a standing invitation to Sharon and Toole to come visit, to stay in the guest room on Watchers Island and enjoy a real Florida vacation, but so far they'd never taken him up on it.

"I've read enough," Toole said. "I bet I ken more about it than you."

"I won't argue with that." The pub was filling up now, and each time the door opened a wave of cold air shuttled in around Johnny's legs. Chemal had reached the bottom of his pint glass with alarming speed and was now looking a little unsteady on his stool.

"Let's get this lad some food," Johnny said to Janie when she passed by.

"Cod and chips?" she said.

"That'll do." She made for the kitchen.

"Toole," Johnny said finally.

"Yeh?"

"How's Corran?"

Toole sighed. "Well," he said. "He's definitely off the junk, if that's what you're asking. Thank God. But he's got his hands full up there with the wee one. Katie."

"Katie?" Johnny said. "I thought her name was Lucy."

Toole stared at him vacantly, then popped himself in the forehead. "Why do I do that?" he said. "Lucy. It's Lucy."

"I told you. You're getting old, Toole."

"Sometimes I think I'm not getting there, Johnny. I *am* there."

Toole looked genuinely downcast, and Johnny was starting to wonder if he was needling his old friend too much, but then a familiar peal of laughter rang across the pub, and Johnny looked up to see Sharon in conversation with a couple who were evidently heading out of the pub just as she was heading in. He watched the way she gripped the man's coat sleeve as she talked to him, the way she folded the woman into an embrace when they said goodbye. Sharon was a toucher, he remembered that. Any interaction with her was a full-body experience: rubbed shoulders, squeezed hands, patted knees.

She took off her coat and hung it on a rack near the door. She had put on a little weight, it seemed, and the effect was quite lovely, making her face softer and her curves fuller. She looked across the pub and caught Johnny's eye. Ah, Sharon. The awareness that he was still half in love with his ex-wife was nothing new to Johnny. But he had come to terms with it, savored it, even. After all, it was nothing like the love he felt for Pauline, which rarely wavered, even during the bouts of ennui and the occasional prickly battles that came with the territory of a long marriage.

Still, the past he shared with Sharon could cast a powerful spell at times, especially times like this one, as he felt the warming effects of the beer, as he watched her move across the pub toward their table, and as he was pulled off his stool into an unreserved hug that left him wobbling, a little off balance. He had a fleeting awareness of her breasts—or were they prostheses? She'd had breast cancer, he knew that. *Sharon.* He held her a moment longer. When they backed away from each other he noticed her eyes were brimming, but she blinked quickly and turned her head. She moved over to Chemal and gave him a hug, too. His eyes were wide over her shoulder.

"Welcome," she said to Chemal. "Whoever you are." She sat down next to Toole.

"This is Chemal," Johnny said.

"He helps with driving," Toole said. He looked at Chemal proudly. Toole was getting lit.

"What, Johnny can't drive?" Sharon said.

Johnny held up his hands. "Long story," he said. "Maybe later." Sharon looked at him quizzically but, thankfully, let it go.

"Well, welcome back, anyway," she said. "Finally." She waved over to Janie at the bar and held up a finger for a pint. "You're like the prodigal father."

"Not as bad as that," he said. "It's not like he was missing me." Sharon didn't disagree. She settled in then, asking for all the latest updates from Florida. *Warm there? Lovely. And the factory? Och, I'm sorry.* She seemed to take to Chemal right away, and Johnny watched with admiration the way she slipped into an easy banter with the kid, telling him flatly to lower his voice when it started climbing but then picking up the conversation again right where they'd left off, sparing him embarrassment and distraction. They went right through the KISS Army, which Sharon somehow knew all about, and continued on into a series of topics that left Johnny baffled: Instagram? Memes? Snapchat? He watched her. He ordered another pint. He felt himself becoming pleasantly inebriated.

By the time they made it back to the house, they'd consumed £87 worth of beer and cod between the four of them and had decided to postpone Port Readie until the morning. It was getting late, Sharon pointed out, and there was no point driving in the dark after a load of lager, especially since Johnny's driver, unaccustomed to the alcohol, was by now blaringly, shufflingly drunk. Chemal had to be pointed immediately to a twin bed in the extra room upstairs—Corran's old room—which, Sharon announced, he'd be sharing with Johnny.

"I'm in, too, then," Toole said, once they'd gotten Chemal dispatched. "I'm knackered. See you in the morn." He kissed Sharon and slapped Johnny on the shoulder, then went to bed.

Sharon waited until he left the kitchen, then turned to Johnny.

"So, what's this about then?" Sharon said.

"What?"

"You not driving."

"My eyes are bad," he offered lamely. "I need new glasses."

She pulled a pack of cigarettes out of her purse and offered him one.

"Aren't you a nurse?" Johnny said. He took the cigarette.

"I'm a nurse who smokes a cigarette now and then, and you're a man who's lying," she said. She put an ashtray on the table between them. "You think I can't tell there's something more to this story?" She arched her eyebrows and looked at him.

"Brain tumor," he said. "Benign. Probably. Maybe. I don't know. I'm having surgery when I get back."

Sharon's eyes were wide and bright in the dim kitchen light. "Oh," she said. They were quiet for several moments. She reached out and took his hand.

"You cut your hair short," he said.

"Don't tell me you just noticed this now."

"Noticed it as soon as I saw you at the pub."

"But you waited until Toole went to bed to comment on it."

"That I did." He reached across the table and touched one of the curls above her ear. "I like it," he said.

Sharon rolled her eyes. "How's Pauline?" she said.

"She's running all the time now," Johnny said. "You should see her." One of the most unexpected circumstances of his second marriage was that Sharon and Pauline seemed to genuinely like each other. Or at least, Pauline seemed to genuinely like Sharon, and Sharon seemed to genuinely . . . well . . . tolerate Pauline. It was nothing personal, she'd once told Johnny. She's a lovely woman, she said. We just come at the world from different angles, you know? Johnny did know. Pauline, for her part, was friendly to Sharon almost to the point of being cloying, which was altogether a shock to Johnny, as he'd never known Pauline to display such obsequiousness to anyone else. *She's the mother of your child,* Pauline had once told him, almost reverently. *She deserves my respect.*

"Oh, don't tell me about Pauline's running," Sharon said now. "I can barely get my fat ass into my pants anymore."

"Your ass looks fine to me."

"Don't be looking at my ass."

"You brought it up." They grinned at each other like high-schoolers. She shook her head. "All right, so. We'll drive up to Port Readie tomorrow. I've taken a couple of days off, but I need to be home by Wednesday."

Johnny nodded. "Wednesday's good. We fly home on Thursday. Thanks for coming along."

She snorted. "I go every weekend. Help with Lucy. But I'm happy to jump in with you two for a change rather than have to drive myself."

"Why doesn't he bring the baby down here?"

"He doesn't like to come to the city. Temptations, he says. Plus, he hasn't a car."

"He's really clean then?"

"Seems to be. I'm hopeful this time. I think that's why he liked the rigs. Kept him away from the smack, you know? But now there's Lucy . . ." Her voice trailed off, and she shrugged. "He's got a lady in the village who keeps Lucy during the week, and then I come up to help on weekends. It's not easy."

Johnny sighed. "I know I haven't been good at keeping in touch."

"I half thought you were dead." She looked at him sternly. "And listen. About this brain tumor business? You can't let it beat you."

"I'm trying not to."

"We're survivors, Johnny. That's all there is to it."

"I know *you* are."

She stubbed out her cigarette and looked at him. "Listen," she said. "I've got scars from here to here." She gestured from one armpit to the other, across her chest. "Total mastectomy. You know that, right? Both of them—gone."

Johnny didn't know how to respond. Of course, he remembered when she was going through treatment some years ago, but the baldness of her statement was startling. Leave it to Sharon to present something so personally tragic with such offhand bluntness. God, she was something. Cast iron, this one. And something else occurred to him then: This was the second time today he'd discussed scars in this kitchen. Wounded people, all of us, he thought.

"Ah, Sharon," he said.

"I know," she said. "It's a shame. They were prize, weren't they?" She started to laugh. "So I've gone without for a while. But now I'm thinking about reconstruction. Is that silly? My age? I don't know. I just sort of miss them. I'm sure Toole does, too, but he's kind enough not to mention it." Johnny wasn't sure what to say to that, and the discomforting lunacy of sitting half-drunk in a dark Scottish kitchen while having a chat with his ex-wife about her lost breasts was beginning to dawn on him. She must have realized it, too. She stopped laughing. She leaned forward and looked at him carefully. "The point, Johnny," she said, "is that you don't take no for an answer. Cancer or no cancer. You just keep going." She got up and hugged him hard. "Now. You're sharing Corran's room with Chemal. So go to bed, you arse, before somebody wakes up and sees us two old farts flirting," she said.

"Is that what we're doing?"

"Well, I don't know about *you*." She smiled at him and left the kitchen. She went upstairs. When she opened her bedroom door he could hear Toole snoring, and then the door closed again and all was quiet in the kitchen on Boscombe Road. Johnny finished his cigarette and made his way up the stairs to the bathroom. He took his steroids and peed on the sugar strip. Then he brushed his teeth and fumbled through the dark hallway to the room at the end, where now, just like long ago, a teenage boy lay sleeping.

ELEVEN

Johnny had developed a theory that insomnia was really a form of misguided self-preservation, an innate revulsion for the deathlike trance of sleep. How else could you explain it? It made no sense. There you were, stretched out in a bed with every comfort, weariness in every limb, but unable to tip your consciousness over the edge to slumber. He could *see* it sometimes, the cool soft fabric of dreams, there in the distance, but so often he just couldn't get there. He tried listening to white-noise recordings through headphones. He tried drinking less than usual. He tried drinking *more* than usual. He tried pestering Pauline for sex, hoping the release would bring sleepiness. He tried full darkness and nightlights, electric blankets and Benadryl, earplugs and early rising. He loathed sheep, having once hit one of the damn things outside Paisley, so he counted Chevelles instead, saw them prowling under an oak canopy on a Florida back road. One hundred Chevelles. Two hundred. Six hundred. Nothing worked.

When he was at home, after a few hours of staring at the ceiling, he'd often tip up on one elbow to watch Pauline sleep, and though this was soothing and restful in its way, he'd usually end up getting up to watch a movie, or to noodle with some little widget in the garage, or to puzzle over one factory issue or another—investing in a new water treatment system, for example. Or automating the shrink-wrap system to save money but having to lay off three good employees in the process. Or surviving an OSHA fine. And this last would keep him up and pacing even longer.

Funny that sleeplessness seemed to be a purely human concern. He'd never seen a dog or cat suffer with it. Perhaps animals were braver than people, he concluded. Feared death less. One of the most frustrating things about being an insomniac was that he'd fall asleep at long last near four or five in the morning, only to have to wake up a couple of hours later, start the day, and assume that the elusive fatigue would inevitably show up like a Mack truck at some point in the afternoon. Take today, for example. He'd just started awake. He was embarking on a journey to Port Readie to attempt a truce with his fragile and long-estranged son. And he was going to attempt this fool's errand under three handicaps: insomniac fatigue, jet lag, and one hell of a hangover.

The bedroom was overwarm. A layer of dampness coated Johnny's chest. He sat up. Across the room sat Corran's old bed, rumpled from Chemal's recent sleep. Through the years, on the occasions when he came to visit Corran on his own, Johnny bunked up here with his son, and in this room, he had always felt like a kid at a slumber party. It wasn't like that when Pauline came with him. Then they would book a room at a little B&B

overlooking the Clyde, make a vacation out of it. The stays in Corran's room had been different when his son was a child. Johnny could lie awake and watch the shadows of alder trees dance across the moonlit ceiling, could listen to the sound of Corran's breathing, and could try to make sense of the words the boy murmured in his sleep. "Electric!" Corran had called out one night. "I'm *not* bleeding," he muttered another time. Johnny would sit up, peer across the dim room, trying to understand it all.

Now, the morning after the pub, the sound of different voices murmured up through the floorboards, and from these— modulated, bright—Johnny gathered that Chemal was still getting on well with Sharon and Toole. Ah, but those two were good at boys, weren't they? Knew how to tend to them, how to love them in that loose, baggy way boys respond to. Nothing too sweet now, nothing cloying. Jokey stuff—farts and burps and lightly barbed insults. Keep 'em laughing. Pocket money and huge meals. Now and then big bear hugs, a kiss on the top of the head when the guard was down. Sharon and Toole made it look so easy.

A magpie cackled from the eaves just outside the window, and Johnny recalled an old superstition his mother used to tell him: A magpie near the window foretells death. Brilliant. He got up, went over to the window, and shook the curtains against the glass pane. The magpie departed. He looked at his watch. Nearly nine! The last he'd looked at the clock it had been three-thirty a.m. He swallowed a couple of ibuprofen, then showered quickly and made it downstairs in time to find Sharon and Chemal already packing the Polo for Port Readie.

They made it as far as the high street before Johnny had to stop at a convenience store and get a cup of coffee for the drive. No sense welcoming in a big headache before they even got started. And then he remembered that he hadn't peed on his sugar strip, so he had to dig through his suitcase to find the damn things and then wait in line to use a men's room that looked like something out of *Trainspotting*. He had the feeling that men had been just standing at the threshold of the doorway and arcing their urine in the general direction of the john. He held his breath and got the procedure over with to satisfactory effect, but then he was so repulsed by the idea that he'd likely been stepping through a thick coating of other people's piss that he went to the counter and bought a tiny bottle of Germ-X (for £3.50!) and stopped by the side of the car to squirt it all over the soles of his shoes.

"Really?" Chemal said. "What, now you're OCD or something?"

"You didn't see that loo, mate."

"You think too much."

"Better too much than not enough."

"Hey, now," Chemal said. "I think just enough. What do you think, Miss Sharon?"

"I think you're both mad," Sharon said. "Let's get going."

By the time they finally got up to speed on the highway, it was nearly ten o'clock, and they had a three-hour drive ahead to Port Readie, the first twenty minutes of which Johnny spent wondering if he'd successfully eradicated the E. coli he'd picked up in the men's room and then wondering if he *was* now OCD. What was wrong with him? Was Mr. Meningioma acting up? It wasn't like him to be so fastidious. Still, that men's room. Oh, God. Let it go, Johnny. Let it go.

He texted Pauline: *Hi kidda.* He waited a moment, but seeing no response, he pulled up a browser on his phone and checked the Jacksonville news. The *Times-Union* had another opinion piece on the Bold City Ice Plant, this one written by a spokesperson for a newfangled environmentalist group Johnny had never heard of: JaxGreenDreamers. Well, all righty. The editorial was refreshing in its stance, he had to admit: Rather than crucify the ice factory's principals over issues of employee safety and human health like most critics had been doing, this writer had, as he stated coyly, written on behalf of a victim unable to speak for itself: the St. Johns River.

Johnny shook his head. The *river*? This was a new one. "Harm to our city's most precious and historic waterway by the Bold City Ice Plant from its negligent release of unidentified toxins is not only inexcusable," the spokesman wrote, "it's also abwhoren't [*sic*]." For the love of Christ. Unidentified toxins? Try pure anhydrous ammonia, jackass. It was right there in the accident report, which was on public record if you cared to check. And harm to the river? The ammonia never came within a quarter-mile of the St. Johns. It dissipated into the atmosphere over Little Silver within an hour of the rupture. The accident at the Bold City Ice Plant, it seemed, was becoming favored fodder for any uninformed hipster who wanted to see his name in the paper.

"Do your homework, you fucking numpty," Johnny said aloud.

"Who are you muttering at?" Sharon said. "You're always making yourself mad for no reason. Why don't you put the phone down and enjoy the scenery?"

"You're using data there, Iceman," Chemal said. "I keep telling you about these overseas roaming charges. Stay off the

Internet, dude. You're going to have a beast of a bill when you get home."

Johnny looked from Sharon to Chemal. Now, how had he managed, for the past fifty-three years, to make his way through the world without these two to tell him what to do? He bit his tongue, checked once more for a text from Pauline, and, seeing none, put the phone back into his pocket. A mail truck bulleted past them on the left.

"I'm glad you're driving, Chemal," Sharon said. "I hate the motorways. Too aggressive."

"No worries, Miss Sharon."

"And I hate the way Johnny drives. Like he's being chased."

"I'm sitting right here," Johnny said. "You could at least wait until I'm out of earshot to insult me."

"But then I wouldn't get to see your reaction," Sharon said.

"I'm sure you could imagine it."

"Yes," she said, absently. "I suppose I could." She dug in her purse and came up with a CD. "Would you two mind if I brushed up on my Spanish while we drive?" she said. "I'm doing an online class. And I'm so far behind. *Dios mio.*" She handed the CD to Johnny. "Put that in the player," she said.

"*Hablo español,*" Chemal said. "*Mi madre es de Puerto Rico.*"

Sharon hesitated. "Help me out a bit," she said.

"I said 'I speak Spanish. My mother is from Puerto Rico.'"

Sharon gasped. "Really? Oh, my God, this is fantastic! Can you help me practice? I never have anyone I can practice with."

"*Sí.*" Chemal grinned.

"Forget the CD, Johnny," she said. "Eject it."

"*¿Por qué estudias español?*" Chemal said.

Sharon hesitated again, then shook her head slowly.

"Nope," she said. "Not there yet. Give it to me."

"Why are you studying Spanish?"

"So she can order people around in another language," Johnny said.

"Ha ha," she said.

"Señor Hielo está de mal humor," Chemal said.

"What does that mean?" Sharon said.

"'Iceman's in a bad mood.'"

Oh, and then they *laughed*. Christ, this was going to be a long ride.

Just outside Crianlarich they passed a sign for a spiritualist camp. Sharon leaned forward from the backseat.

"I've always wanted to go to that place," she said. "Montebella. I drive past it every weekend but have never taken the time to stop. Did you see that sign?" Johnny had seen the sign. And his first thought upon seeing it was that he hoped Sharon hadn't noticed it. He'd never known anyone in his life as enamored of mumbo jumbo as Sharon. She was always on about one new trend or another: Enneagrams, or biorhythms, or meditation, or God knew what all else. He couldn't understand it. She was a perfectly intelligent woman in all other respects. But let her catch one whiff of new age bullshit and she'd fall on it like a dog on a bone.

"No, sorry, I didn't see a sign," he said.

"I saw it," Chemal offered.

"It's a spiritualist camp," Sharon said. "They have psychics and readers. Mediums, you know? Communicate with the dead and see your future, like that. You can just walk right in, don't need an appointment. This girl Maura I work with, she went there. She and her husband had been trying to have a baby, but nothing was happening. So she went there and saw a psychic, who told her she was pregnant right then! She went home and took a pregnancy test. And guess what? He was right."

"No way," Chemal said.

"Sharon," Johnny said. "That's bullshit."

"I don't think so. I think there's something to it."

"Yeh, there's something to it. It's called sex. It makes babies."

Chemal nodded.

"What are you nodding about, smarty?" Johnny said. "Like you know something about it?"

Chemal scowled. "Well, I know how babies are made, if that's what you mean."

"How?"

Chemal stared straight ahead at the road. "I'm not talking about it with *you*. And anyway, just because the people might have been having sex, that doesn't mean the psychic was a fake. He knew she was pregnant before she even did."

"Exactly!" Sharon said.

"I know Chemal's hungry right now, but that doesn't make me a psychic," Johnny said.

Chemal's eyes grew wide. "How did you know I'm hungry?"

"Because you haven't eaten anything in an hour. Easy."

"Well, anyway. Wouldn't it be interesting to stop in Montebella?" Sharon said.

"Yeah!" Chemal said.

"No," Johnny said. "And we've already passed the turn."

"I can yooie," Chemal said.

"Come on, Johnny," Sharon said. "This could be very helpful. Maybe we could even get some advice. On Corran and such. And your accident case, yeah?"

He rolled his eyes. Sharon! The woman was smarter than nearly anyone else he knew. So why was she so attracted to idiocy? Of course, if he'd asked her that, she'd probably respond that it was lucky for him that she was, since without that weakness she'd never have hooked up and had a child with *him*. She could do that—zing off a one-liner that would cut you off at the knees just as you were getting your arguments lined up solid. And come to think of it, it was the same with Pauline. In verbal sparring with both of his wives, he was always slain before he even started. How had he managed to intellectually handicap himself so spectacularly, not once, but twice? Chemal was slowing down. Johnny was about to protest further when his phone rang. He looked at the screen. Dr. Tosh.

"Uh-oh," he said. He hesitated, then answered the call.

"Johnny!" Tosh said. "How are you, friend?"

"Fine," Johnny said. "You're up early."

"Dang straight, rise and shine. I'm calling to check on you."

"I'm good."

"Feeling all right, then?"

"Yeh." Chemal was exiting the road. Sharon was still leaning forward, giving Chemal directions.

"Take the roundabout," she was saying. "We can double back."

"No!" Johnny said.

"You're not good?" Tosh said. "What is it?"

"No. I mean, yes. I'm good. I was talking to someone else. Hang on." He lowered the phone and turned around to look at Sharon. "Sharon, this is daft!" he said. "Psychics?"

"Oh, hush," she said. "It won't take more than a half hour. We've got time." Chemal accelerated back up the road, back in the direction they'd come.

"Johnny," Tosh said. "Are you at home?"

"Well," Johnny said. "No."

"You're supposed to be taking it easy."

"I know. I'm taking it easy."

"You're not driving, are you?"

"No."

"Still taking the steroids?"

"Yeh."

They were now approaching the turn for Montebella, but Chemal was still moving at a pretty good clip.

"Here!" Sharon shouted.

"Whoa!" Chemal said. He curved the Polo sharply to veer around the turn. "Almost missed it!"

"Johnny," Tosh said. "Where are you?"

"Well," Johnny said. "I'm in Scotland."

Tosh didn't answer for a beat. "You're in Scotland," he said finally. "And on what page of your treatment plan did it say to go to Scotland?"

"Don't worry," Johnny said. "I'll be back in time for the big event. I know we've got a date."

"Not with me, friend. With a brain surgeon. A dang cranky brain surgeon who is expecting me to manage my pre-op patients."

"I know, I know. I'm good, okay?"

"Is Pauline with you?"

"No. She didn't want me to come."

"I bet she didn't. In fact, I bet she wants to slap you silly right now. I know that's what I want to do."

"Well," Johnny said. "You can't always get what you want, Dr. Tosh."

Tosh sighed. "It's your rodeo, Johnny."

Johnny hung up with Tosh and looked out the window to find they were parked in front of a crumbling Airey-style duplex painted chalk white on one side, potato brown on the other. On the brown side, a sign over the front door read "Matthew Terry: The Sixth Sense." And beneath that: "Clairvoyant * Medium * Healer."

"Why doesn't it just say 'Con Artist'? That would cover it," he said.

"Come on, Chemal," Sharon said. "Let's leave Prince Charming out here. He'll only stink it up in there. Sit here and wait for us, Johnny."

Johnny was remembering now why he and Sharon were no longer married. He looked at his watch. How long had this realization taken? Around sixteen hours, total. And around six *sober* hours. That seemed about right.

"Ask the psychic if you'll ever stop being so bossy," he said.

Sharon gave him a *look* but climbed out of the car with Chemal. They disappeared into the house. Johnny grabbed his iPhone and found that the wireless network from the psychic's house was named "Truth in All Things." He checked his emails. One from Roy with the week's production report. One from Tosh's office with more insurance forms. And one from Sam Tulley. Johnny clicked on it.

From: stulley@knowlesandfrusciante.com
To: MacKinnon, Pauline
Cc: MacKinnon, Johnny; Kaplan, Claire; Grassi, Roy
Subject: Need Vendor List!

Hi Pauline!

I think we're making good progress! ☺ *We'll find something, I know it! I forgot to ask—could you please forward factory vendor list? Need to document suppliers of equipment, materials, etc.*

Thanks!
Sam

PS, ran Hart this morn. Go early, no traffic!!!

Now wasn't this guy just the shit? Johnny got out of the car and took a walk around the psychic's house, where the sounds of water beckoned him down a small incline. Sure enough, a few minutes' walk revealed a tiny rushing creek, and he crouched by the water and smoked half a cigarette, then put it out and stuffed the butt into his pocket. After the surgery, he was quitting for good, he decided. A bright blue stone, glinting in the shallow waters of the creek, caught his eye. He had a thought to pocket the stone for Pauline, but when he started down the bank to fetch it, his foot slipped on a patch of brown moss and he ended up skidding gracelessly into the creek and muddying up one whole leg of his trousers. His right foot was completely underwater. His right thigh was a filthy mess. But at least, he realized as he heard the ringing, his phone hadn't gotten wet.

"*Och,*" he said. He managed to get up and out of the water before answering the phone. It was Pauline.

"I just fell into a creek trying to get a stone for you," he said.

"Are you drinking already?" she said. "Isn't it still early there?"

"I'm not drinking," he said. "I'm just a klutz."

"I missed you earlier," she said, and he was touched, until he realized she was simply talking about the phone call he'd placed a little while ago. "I was out running," she said. Then she was unexpectedly chatty, telling him about Ed's latest trade show leads, and about her run training, and about the retreat and disappearance, finally, of the Cuban tree frogs.

"I'm glad you're talking to me," he said.

"Obviously I'm talking to you."

"So you're not still mad at me?"

"I'm absolutely mad at you. I'm furious. But I'm not so juvenile that I'm going to have a long-distance snit about it. It can wait until you come home. It can probably even wait until after your surgery. Then I'll let you have it."

He wasn't sure what to say to that, so he said nothing.

"How are you feeling?" she said.

"Fine. Good. Tosh called me a few minutes ago."

"Did you tell him where you are?"

"Yes.

"I bet he was mad."

"He wasn't happy."

She snorted in satisfaction, which was irritating, really. Why did he have to make everyone else happy in regard to this blasted surgery? Wasn't it *his* brain? Wasn't it *his* tumor? He had a moment's fantasy in which he was free to do anything he pleased without a wife, an ex-wife, a teenage delinquent, and a paraplegic doctor having an opinion about it. How old was he, anyway?

"So, what's with this Tulley?" he said.

"What do you mean?"

"Why's he so goofy and happy? I thought he was a lawyer. He writes like a cheerleader."

"You saw that email."

"Is he driving you crazy?"

She hesitated. "A little," she said. "But he's not too bad. He's pleasant enough."

"Is he gay?"

"Why would you think he's gay?"

"I don't know. The smiley face, maybe."

"You're ridiculous. Straight men don't use smiley faces?"

"None that I know."

"He's just friendly. He's really very nice, you want to know the truth."

"Dollars to donuts he's gay," Johnny said. What the hell. He'd begun this asinine debate simply to play with Pauline and enjoy her upward mood swing, but suddenly he found himself hoping Tulley *was* gay. No particular reason. Just because.

"Johnny," she said. "Trust me. He's *not* gay."

"How's your father?" Johnny said. He felt the need to redirect.

"Fine. Same. I guess."

"You been by?"

"No. And Caroline will be having a stroke soon, if the caregivers rat me out and tell her I haven't been over there. Maybe tomorrow. Or the next day. I don't know. It's depressing, going there."

He wasn't sure how to answer that.

"Listen, I was thinking," she said then. "If you and Corran manage to clear the air, why don't you tell him to bring the baby over for a visit, after the surgery? I'd love to meet her."

"I don't know. He's barely speaking to me."

"But you're going to fix that. That's what you're over there to do!"

"I'm going to *try*, Pauline. But he's got to meet me halfway, you know. I'm not sure he's going to be willing to do that." She didn't reply. He thought he heard the rhythmic tapping of her fingernails on the kitchen counter. He had an impulse to change the subject.

"I saw in the news that we're now being hammered about damaging the river," he said.

"Yes, I saw that too," she said, though she didn't sound particularly interested. "Johnny," she said abruptly, "are you happy?"

"Happy? About the river bullshit? No, I'm not happy. Why would I be happy about that?"

"No, not about the river," she said. "I mean happy. Just happy. In life. I mean, before all this awful stuff started happening, with Corran and everything, would you say you were a happy person? Really at *heart*, happy?"

"I'm happily *married*."

"That's not what I mean. I mean you—individually, singly— are you satisfied? Like, are you content? Do you feel like you're doing what you're meant to do?"

"Why on earth are you asking me this?"

"Because I want to know."

Happy? What was she talking about? "I don't even know what happy means," he said. "I'm not a giddy person, Pauline. I don't go around skipping and whistling."

"You're not answering my question."

"I don't understand the question."

"Are you happy?" she said. "I think a toddler would understand that question."

They both fell silent. Johnny was bothered to have to come up with a response. Why was she fussing over such a thing as happiness right now, with all the varied catastrophes they had on their hands competing for their attention? He wasn't in the habit of dissecting joy, for God's sake. *Happy.* He remembered once having a conversation about this same word with Sharon, years and years ago, when they were splitting up. Sharon had told him he deserved to be happy, and he'd looked at her, bewildered, surprised by and doubtful of the veracity of her statement. Was that true? Did anybody *deserve* to be happy? On the basis of what? Didn't happiness have to be earned, fought for, and won, like any other asset? He'd puzzled over the notion for some time and then, somewhere in the catalogue of years and the carnival of living, he'd forgotten all about it.

Happy. Huh. Johnny looked down and saw that the blue stone he'd wanted to fetch for Pauline had been pushed by the creek's current into easier reach. He leaned over and picked it easily out of the water. It was a cool sapphire blue, smooth as an apple. "Yes," he said finally to Pauline. "I would say I am more or less happy. Worried, I suppose. There's a lot of crap going on. So worried." She still didn't answer. He softened his voice. "But happy. Yes. Happy."

He paused. She seemed to be waiting. He knew what for. "Are you happy, Pauline?"

"No," she said promptly. He felt a ripple in his abdomen.

"Pauline," he said. "Come on, now."

"I messed up," she said. "I should have had a baby."

"Pauline."

She was sniffling. "I messed up," she said again.

Well, *this* was a new one. Johnny rose to gaze down the line of the creek. He pocketed Pauline's stone. What in the world was going on? It was starting to seem as if anything that could possibly go wonky these days was just going right on ahead and doing it. He remembered the line from Yeats: *Things fall apart; the centre cannot hold.* Pauline had never talked like this before, about regretting their decision—well, *her* decision—not to have a child. Corran was enough, they'd always said.

"I think you're under a lot of stress," Johnny said carefully. "I think we're going through a very emotional time. And, well, I think you're conjuring up feelings that might not be . . . they might not even be real."

She sniffled again. "Nope. They're real. I was selfish, is what it was. Didn't want to upset the applecart. Didn't want a messy kitchen or sleepless nights or stretch marks, that's what it was. But if I'd done it, Johnny, I mean, if we'd done it, I'd have something else to focus on now, and in the future. Some*body* to focus on, do you know what I mean? If the factory folds. If things change. If . . ." She stopped herself. *If you die on the operating table,* Johnny thought. And then he understood. So *that's* what she was afraid of.

"Two things, kidda," Johnny said. He tried to make his voice light. "No, three things. One: You can have Corran, okay? I'll sign him over. And he's already out of diapers, so there's that.

Two: I'm happy. I'm ecstatic. When I come home, I'm taking up skipping. And three"—here he felt a catch in his throat but choked it back—"I'm not going to die." He repeated the third thing twice in his own head, trying to convince himself.

"Oh, Johnny," Pauline said. She blew her nose. "I'm sorry. I know I'm going batty. It's a midlife crisis. Don't give it a thought. I don't mean to give you more to worry about. I'm fine, okay? I'm fine. My God. I don't need a child. I'm just wallowing around in might-have-beens. I'm happy."

"How about we get you a kitten when I get back?" he said.

"Ha, ha," she said. "Very funny. I hate cats. And anyway, the General would have a conniption. Leave it. Forget I said anything." Johnny ran his fingers across the stone in his pocket and watched the water chug down the little creek.

"But anyway. I almost forgot," Pauline said. "There's some sort of oil dripping in the garage. It's running out from under the Beetle."

Damn! The Marvel Mystery Oil on the frozen piston! He'd forgotten he rigged that contraption up. He pictured the oil drizzling a path across the garage floor. Great.

"Can you just put a pan under it?" he said. "I'll deal with it when I get back." She said she needed to get ready for work. She told him that the General was feeling better. She told him Jerry and Tina seemed to be enjoying their Chemal-free weekend. She told him she had a nightmare about the ghost of Donald Stone knocking at the floorboards, but it turned out to be a pileated woodpecker on the buttonwood tree just off the lighthouse cupola. He told her he'd call her again tomorrow.

"And Pauline, about the Beetle," Johnny said.

"Yes?"

"Just on the remote chance that my brain does explode over here and I don't make it back, be sure and give that Beetle to someone I don't like, okay?"

"Don't joke like that."

"Like maybe Sam Tupper."

A pause. Barely noticeable. "Tulley. I'll do that," she said. "Although I'm expecting you back."

"Hell yes, I'll be back," he said. "It's too damn cold here."

"Give that baby a kiss for me, Grandpa," she said. "And tell her it's from her *step*grandma." She hung up.

It was, in fact, too chilly to keep walking around, especially with a wet foot. Johnny went back to the Polo, fished a wad of paper towels out of the glove box, and put them to rather ineffectual use against the mud stains on his pants. Then Sharon was abruptly pulling open the driver's-side door and dropping into the seat.

"That was quick," Johnny said. "Was that a thirty-minute consult?"

"I'll drive a bit," she said. Johnny looked behind him. Chemal was climbing into the backseat, his face a mask of pain.

"What?" Johnny said, startled. "What happened?"

Sharon pursed her lips. "Psychic guy was a jerk," she said simply. "Told Chemal he couldn't make contact with his brother."

Johnny looked at Chemal again. "You asked about your brother, mate?"

Chemal nodded but then turned to stare out the window. Johnny could tell he was trying to fight back tears, so he faced forward to give the kid a bit of privacy.

Sharon shook her head. "Jackass could have handled that differently," she muttered. She looked over at Johnny's pants. "What in the world have you been up to?" she said.

"Don't ask."

"You look a mess."

"Yes, Sharon," he said. "I'm aware of that." They rode in silence for a few minutes.

"Chemal, what happened to your brother, love?" Sharon said finally, glancing into the rearview mirror.

"He fell out of a bus. Cracked his head open," Chemal said. "So they say."

"What do you mean?" Sharon said.

"Well, *I* never saw it," he replied. "I never got to see him. You know, when he was dead. He was just there one morning for breakfast, and then he wasn't. They *told* me he died. Next thing I knew there was an urnful of ashes." Sharon downshifted as they began a climb up a steep hill.

"So how do I really *know* Davey's dead, if I didn't see him?" Chemal continued. "How do I know they're not all just lying to me?"

"Why would they lie to you?" Sharon said.

"They've lied to me about lots of things. Why not this?"

"Let me ask you something, Chemal," she said gently. "I'm a hospice nurse. I see people die all the time. Did you love your brother?"

"Yes."

"And did he love you, too?"

"Yes."

"Then that's family. And when family love each other, they stay together, no matter what. If he was alive, he'd come find you." She looked in the rearview mirror at Chemal. "That's how you know he's gone," she said gently. "I'm sorry, love. I'm so sorry."

Chemal stared out the window at the passing trees. *They stay together, no matter what.* Johnny shifted in his seat and tried to adjust his posture to accommodate his sore hip, which he was now realizing he'd twisted during the slide down the creek embankment. It hurt. Oh, God, it hurt.

Johnny thought he'd go mad with the Spanish. Once Chemal reclaimed the wheel, he and Sharon started up with their practice again, and it seemed to lift the kid's spirits. Now the two of them had been at it for more than an hour as they made their way up toward the Highlands and into the steep hills of the Trossachs, with Sharon shouting from the backseat, asking questions from her textbook, while Chemal bellowed his answers from behind the wheel.

> *¿Te gusta el café?*
> *Sí, me gusta el café.*
> *¿De dónde eres?*
> *Soy de Detroit!*

And on and on. For a while Johnny tried napping, but when he leaned his head against the window and closed his eyes, it seemed that Sharon's voice was ricocheting against the glass and hitting his beleaguered eardrums even harder, so he sat up straight, studied the scenery, and tried to simply zone out. It wasn't yet noon, and the growing sunlight behind the mountains was still diffused with mist. He remembered being on this route before for one reason or another, remembered that you could follow the highway until it gave way at the base of the Grampians to the anemic little A82, which would take you all the way to Urquhart Castle if you let it, running as it did along the western edge of Loch Ness. The mountains were always a reference point.

He remembered how lost he had been all those years ago, when he first arrived in Florida, without those immovable peaks to navigate by. He had lived so long in Glasgow with the shadows of the great Grampians to the north—even if you couldn't see them, you could *feel* them, especially on damp days when the wind seemed to ferry toward the concrete city particles of mountain moss and loam. His first weeks in Jacksonville, he remembered asking another worker at the ice plant, "But how do you know which way's north?"

"You don't," the fellow had said. "But north don't matter. East matters." The man closed his eyes and thought, then turned and pointed toward one end of the ice plant. "That's east," he said. "You can always feel the ocean. You always know where it is. And then you figure out the rest." Johnny was dubious. They were twenty miles inland! But sure enough, by the end of his first year in Florida, Johnny had developed the same sort of internal compass so peculiar to those who lived in East Coast America. The ocean exerted a cosmic tug on Johnny's consciousness that he imagined might have something to do with tides and lunar magnetism and what have you. Johnny could be anywhere—inside a mall, deep in the woods, or driving around in a spaghetti-mess of highway overpasses—and he'd still be able to instinctively locate the Atlantic and use its unerring presence to navigate.

But now he was in Scotland. The Atlantic was back on the west. All was confounded.

"*Cordero!*" Chemal shouted. He slowed the car on the approach to Glencoe. "Lamb!"

"We haven't covered that yet," Sharon said, "at least, not in this chapter."

"No, I mean there," Chemal said. He pulled the car over and pointed. "Look at that thing!"

Johnny looked out into the glen, where Chemal was now pointing at a white lamb that was tottering along after its mother. The lamb took a few bouncing steps and then jumped up and kicked its legs behind it like an animated character in a children's movie.

"Sweet," Sharon said. "Late season for that one."

"You see it, Iceman? Look at it jumping! That's the cutest fucking thing I've ever seen," Chemal said.

Johnny saw it. But he was not impressed. The last time he'd been examining a lamb, it had been half mangled under the left front tire of a totaled rental car outside Paisley, and Johnny had been down on the pavement a few feet away, writhing in pain from the shattered hip that had plagued him ever since. They were such skittish damn things! Always leaping around like they had fleas up their asses. The lamb he hit had bolted out from under a wire fence just as Johnny had been turning the corner. It didn't have a chance. The mother had stood just inside the fence, bleating piteously, but Johnny was so stunned with pain that he couldn't even muster a moment's sympathy.

"I'd like to get it," Chemal was saying now about the lamb in the glen before them.

"Get it?" Johnny said.

"Catch it. Just to pet it for a minute." He was unbuckling his seat belt.

"You can't catch it," Johnny said. "They're fast."

"I'm fast."

"I've always wanted to pet one, too," Sharon said mildly.

"I'll just be a sec," Chemal said. "I'm a get that lamb." He turned off the car and got out. He jogged along the wire fencing to a wooden post, where he hoisted himself up and over. He moved toward the lamb, hands outstretched.

"Oh, he's cute," Sharon said. Johnny didn't know whether she was talking about the lamb or Chemal, but he didn't ask. When the sheep and the lamb started to skitter off across the field, Chemal broke into a jog after them. Sharon laughed.

"I wish I had my camera," Sharon said. Indeed, Johnny was finding it hard not to be amused by the scene—a pudgy KISS fanatic running headlong across a field in the middle of Glencoe in hot pursuit of a grotty lamb he could never hope to overtake. They watched the tableau for a little while, then Sharon sighed. "He reminds me of Corran," she said. "Don't you think?"

"Corran?" Johnny said. He looked at Sharon. "No, I don't see it."

Sharon shrugged and didn't answer. Johnny turned back to watch Chemal run after the lamb until, spent, the boy turned and trudged back across the field, grinning and flushed. At least, Johnny thought, he seemed to be in a better mood than he was after the experience with the psychic. He was panting when he arrived back at the car, and as he dropped into the driver's seat, windswept and still flushed, even Johnny was taken, for the moment, with the charm of Chemal's lunatic youth. But only for a moment, because then followed the unmistakable smell of sheep shit.

"Oh, no," he said, pushing at Chemal. "Get back out, you dope. You're tracking dung."

"My heavens," Sharon said. She held her nose. "That's powerful."

"Whoops," Chemal said. He climbed out of the car and looked ruefully at the bottoms of his shoes. "Oh, man, they're covered."

"Shuffle around in that clear patch of grass over there and try to clean it off," Sharon suggested. She rummaged in her purse and came up with a couple of crumpled napkins. "Maybe use these," she said. Chemal did as she suggested and even added the remainder of Johnny's bottle of Germ-X to the procedure, but still the smell persisted when he got back into the car.

"We'll just have to drive with the windows open," Johnny said.

"It's freezing," Sharon said.

"Well, would you rather be frozen or asphyxiated?" Johnny demanded.

Chemal was sitting stock-still in the driver's seat, his hands buried awkwardly in his trouser pockets, staring at Johnny. "I don't think either one of those is going to happen," he said. His voice was oddly quiet.

"Why?"

"Because I don't have the keys," Chemal said.

"What are you talking about?"

"I put them in my pocket when I got out of the car."

Johnny stared at him.

"Oh, my," Sharon said. And then, as a unit, they all turned to stare out at the wide expanse of the valley at Glencoe, where a white lamb and its mother were now two fat drops of cream in the distance.

Chemal cleared his throat.

"If we fan out," he said, "maybe it won't be so bad."

The search for the keys cost them an hour's time and any hope of eradicating the smell of sheep dung, which was now emanating from the bottoms of six shoes instead of just two. But it did, Johnny noted, win them a precious spell of silence, because by the time they found the keys and got back on the road they were all freezing, nettle-ridden, irritable, and, in the case of Chemal and Sharon, blessedly reticent. On the final approach to Port Readie, the weather turned, and a thick wall of what looked like snow clouds gathered in the near distance. The inclines steepened as they drove through the foothills, and Johnny pointed out to Chemal that downshifting might be a good idea.

"I know that," Chemal said.

"Then why haven't you been doing it?"

"Because I made a bet with myself that within five minutes you'd point out that I wasn't."

Up ahead, a man was walking along the upward incline, carrying a bicycle on his back. Or rather, he was staggering. The metal frame was hooked over one shoulder and the bike hung down behind him and bumped the backs of his knees. A plastic baby seat was affixed to the back fender. "Watch out for this guy," Johnny said. "He's drunk."

"I see him," Chemal said. "You don't have to point out every little thing."

"I just don't want you to hit the sot."

"Have I hit anything yet?"

"No, but not for lack of trying."

"Iceman, you are a pain in the ass. Has anyone ever told you that?"

"I have," Sharon said. "Thousands of times. Doesn't do any good."

"Just watch out for this numpty, would you?" Johnny said. "Last thing we need is to run over the town drunk."

They pulled up alongside the man and Chemal gave him a good-natured wave as they passed. The man looked over. He was younger than Johnny had anticipated, and as he stared at the stranger on the roadway he was struck with two realizations. One, that the young man's staggering gait was likely due not to drunkenness, but to the fact that in addition to the bicycle strapped to his back, he also had a corpulent baby strapped to his front. And two, that the man's wide brown eyes, now staring back at him with the look of someone who had long ago ceased to be surprised by what the world was capable of delivering to him, were very familiar.

Sharon laughed from the backseat. "That's no numpty," she said. "That's your son."

"Christ," Johnny said. "What's he doing?"

Chemal stopped the car.

"Looks like he's walking," Chemal said.

They waited at the road's narrow shoulder for Corran to approach, and Johnny watched him in the side mirror. He swallowed a rush of emotion; he'd scarcely admitted this to himself for nearly a year, but the truth was that there were moments, given the state Corran had been in last Christmas, when Johnny wondered if he'd ever see his son alive again. And here he was, trudging up the roadway carrying a baby. Corran was as slightly built as he'd ever been, though he appeared to have lost the rangy angles of his heroin days and had gained a bit more mass. He was still wearing the same type of low-slung pegged jeans, fleece hoodie, and flat skater's shoes he'd adopted as his uniform when he hit about fifteen. Johnny couldn't remember seeing him in anything else since he was a child. Here in the Highlands, the chill certainly warranted more than a sweatshirt. Corran gave no indication that he was cold. He approached Johnny's side of the Polo and bent to look in.

Johnny wasn't sure what, exactly, he had been anticipating as far as the big reunion went, but it wasn't this. He hadn't talked to Corran in so long that it was hard to muster an adequate forecast of how they might react to each other, although he'd certainly entertained a number of dramatic possibilities: an angry rejection, stone-cold silence, a tearful embrace. But what actually happened when Corran drew alongside to look inside the car and saw his father, his mother, and an unknown kid in an overstuffed KISS Army jacket was as unexpected as it was anticlimactic.

"Can you take Lucy?" he said simply.

Sharon opened the back door and extended her arms to the baby, who kicked her feet with excitement when she saw Sharon.

"Wee one!" Sharon said. "Come on, lovey." She took Lucy into her arms and covered the baby's face with kisses. Then she scooted over to make room for Corran.

"Get in, Corry," Sharon said. "It's about to rain, maybe snow."

"No," Corran said. "I've got to carry the bike. We went for biscuits and I had a flat tire down below in the village." He looked at Johnny. "Hiya, Da," he said.

"Hiya, Corran," Johnny said. They gazed at each other for a beat, and Johnny waited for Corran to ask him why he was

suddenly materializing without warning on the A82 to Port
Readie. But Corran just hitched the bicycle onto his shoulder
and pointed up the hill.

"House is right up at the top," he said. "Mum knows where."

"Put the bike in the trunk, or on the roof," Johnny said.

"No need," Corran said. "I'll meet you at the house. It's
not far."

"But it's steep."

Corran looked at him. "I know that. I do it every day." He
reached through the car to shake Chemal's hand. "I'm Corran,"
he said.

Chemal grinned and accepted the handshake. "Dude," he
said. "Chemal." Corran turned and repositioned the bike on
his shoulder, then started walking up the hill. The first drops of
freezing rain hit the windshield.

"Should we just go on?" Chemal said. "And leave him with
that?"

"Just go," Sharon said. "He'll meet us." She was absorbed
in fussing with the baby. Johnny turned around and regarded
them. It was a cute little bairn, he'd say that. Dark hair parted
over on the side and held back with a little blue clip. Bright
brown eyes staring at him mistrustfully, sweet spots of pink
chill in her cheeks.

"Are we supposed to have a baby seat?" Chemal said.

"It's only a half-mile up the hill," Sharon said.

"But isn't it a law?"

"It's fine."

"Safety first," Chemal said stubbornly.

"Did you take an extra asshole pill today?" Johnny said.
"Would you just drive the fucking car?" He was colossally irritated

with this entire situation: sheep shit in the car, Sharon's unyielding efficiency, a yammering teenage dope for a chauffeur, and
most of all, Corran's wordlessly belligerent gaze. *You needn't have
come,* his son's eyes said. *I don't need you.*

"God," Chemal said. He threw an injured look at Johnny,
but then he put the car in drive and started up the hill.

"You needn't be such a crank, Johnny," Sharon said. "And
you might watch your language in front of your granddaughter."

Johnny turned around to look at Lucy again.

"What do you think, Grandda?" Sharon said. She took one
of the baby's hands and waggled it at Johnny. "Say hi to Grandda,"
she trilled. Johnny waved back at the baby, who stared at him,
expressionless.

"How old did you say?" he said.

"Nine months," Sharon said proudly. She licked the corner
of a paper napkin and wiped a smudge of what looked like jam
from around Lucy's mouth and nose. Lucy pointed to her own
nose. "Pah," she said.

"I know, Lucy," Sharon said. "It's sheep dung. It smells
terrible." Chemal was grinning into the rearview mirror.

"She's a cutie, Miss Sharon," he said. "She's just about as
cute as crap."

"*Isn't* she?" Sharon said. *"Bebé bonita!"*

"Sí, muy bonita!" Chemal said.

Johnny looked in the side mirror, where Corran was now
a small figure, receding. He'd be cold and triumphant by the
time he got up the hill. Which was just the way he liked things,
evidently. Up ahead, the road curved toward a tiny croft and wet
winds stirred the trees. Johnny had the feeling, suddenly, that
he was light-years from home.

TWELVE

Pauline was coming to a startling realization: She hadn't been flirted with this overtly since she was in college. Sam Tulley—he was shameless! Comments about her hair, her eyes, her smile. Over-the-top chivalry, close-talking, subtle innuendos: the whole nine yards. "You remind me of Cameron Diaz," he said at one point. "No *really*." She didn't discourage him. So what? She'd admit it. She'd even admit it to Johnny, if he'd been here to admit it *to*. Because it wasn't entirely unpleasant, being on the receiving end of the attentions of a handsome man nearly two decades her junior. No, it wasn't unpleasant at all. "You remind me of Ashton Kutcher," she told him. "No *really*."

But now here was the trouble. Since Sam Tulley had written about the vendor list, dropping a reference to running the Hart Bridge in the process, he seemed to have fallen off the face of the earth. She had held off writing back immediately. It was the weekend, after all. Let him think she was out somewhere, doing something active and sunny and vibrant: maybe kayaking at Salt Run or zip-lining across a pit of crocodilians down at the Alligator Farm, even though what she'd actually done Sunday afternoon was wimp her way through an uninspired half-mile beach jog and then spend the rest of the day on the sofa with General San Jose and *Downton Abbey*.

On Monday morning, she replied to the email and sent along the vendor list, just as he'd asked. She'd kept the body of the email professional and brief (why wouldn't she?) but—in response to the breezy reference he'd made to running the Hart Bridge early in the morning, before traffic built—she included the following remark, which she had considered at the time a stroke of brilliance, but which she was now uncomfortably second-guessing: "Hart in morn sounds great! Where's best parking?" The genius of this particular syntax was in its ambiguity. Was she confirming his assertion that running the Hart Bridge on an early morning—any early morning, in a general sense—was a good thing to do? Or was she interpreting his oblique reference to the Hart as *an invitation to run it together*? Ha. Take that, Sam Tulley. If they were going to tippy-toe around some weird little game that he seemed to be initiating, then she was going to hold him to it and make *him* be the one to nudge his way up to the line.

Not that there *was* any line, not that there was anything inappropriate about two athletes (athletes!) comparing notes on a particularly challenging race route. Or even that there was anything inappropriate about two athletes taking on a little training run together. God. Grow up, Pauline. People did it all the time! Real runners often raced together, taking strength from synced pacing, moral support. All. The. Time. It was just that he wasn't answering. The little shit.

Clean up your language, Pauline, she told herself. She was starting to sound like Packy. Plus, foul language was a reflection of foul thinking. No need to descend to the level of the crew on the factory floor, whom she consistently chastised for their filthy patois. She'd been trying for years to get Johnny to do something about it. "It's disgusting," she told him. "Can't you make a rule?"

"Pauline," he said. "It's a factory, not a quilting bee. Leave 'em alone."

Ah, but it was no wonder she was using bad language. She was in a bad mood. Johnny's insane walkabout had her on pins and needles, for one thing. She kept expecting to hear from Sharon or Corran that he was checked into a Scottish hospital convulsing with seizures. Caroline had sent a peevish text last night, asking Pauline when she next planned to visit Packy.

And then this morning there'd been a hair-related disaster. She had gotten up early to attempt L'Oreal's Buttercream Swirl low-lights hair treatment. She was long overdue for Salon Belleza but hadn't had the time to get over there. The L'Oreal box promised that the product would "cover gray and energize your look with face-framing low-lights in a delectable swirl of creamy color!" In the dim bathroom before dawn, Pauline mixed up the formula and pulled on the plastic gloves that came with the kit. But before she could apply the first blob of mixture to her hair, she knocked the little plastic bowl off the side of the sink and watched in horror as it hit the edge of the commode and sent a spectacular explosion of honey-brown hair dye all over the bathroom. She trashed a good towel trying to remove the stain from her forehead and neck, and then she ran downstairs for paper towels and spray cleaner, but the dye had bonded quickly to the paint, and no amount of scrubbing would remove the brown streaks from the walls. The only solution would be to repaint the entire bathroom.

God! It was always something. She threw the hair color paraphernalia away. Well, fine. She'd paint the bathroom. She'd get it done today, in fact. She'd hit Home Depot at lunchtime for the paint and knock out the job tonight after work. Maybe it would keep her mind off other things. Like brain surgery, for one thing. Like Sam Tulley, for another.

Vendor list, indeed. Pauline wondered whether Sam Tulley really even needed the vendor list, or if he had simply been looking for an excuse to email her. She hadn't bothered copying Johnny and Claire on her reply to Tulley's email request. What would be the point of bothering them with this silly detail? The goal here, she reminded herself, was to manage as much as she possibly could on this end without having to involve her husband, especially as it pertained to the OSHA appeal. He was darned idiotic for taking off to Scotland with a bulging cyst hanging off the side of his brain, there was no doubt about that. But as long as he was over there, she'd make it her business not to add any distractions or concerns to his clearly addled judgment. She was kicking herself for bringing up that ridiculous business about regretting not having a child. What was wrong with her, these days?

Send/Receive. Nothing.

She closed her email program. She left her office and went into the break room, where Claire was pulling Styrofoam containers out of the refrigerator and angrily pitching them into the trash. Claire looked up when Pauline entered, then held out an oil-stained cardboard box with the ancient remnants of someone's pizza.

"Disgusting!" Claire said. "Have you seen this?" She held out another container and flipped up the lid to display a reddish lump of something covered in a wispy fuzz of mold. "And this?" Here came a brown paper bag, dripping grease from its bulging seams. Into the trash it went. "I tell you, Pauline, this is revolting. Do you know how many times I've cleaned out this refrigerator in the last month? I mean *come on*. These people are out of control."

While normally Pauline would have been in wholehearted agreement with Claire on this point—that the communal refrigerator, used by the entire staff, was indeed horrific, a breeding ground for the lowest levels of frigid vermin—this morning she had so many other things on her mind that it was difficult to summon outrage sufficient to mollify Claire. She merely nodded and used her foot to scoot the rubber trash can closer to the refrigerator so that Claire didn't have to throw so far.

"I mean, this gets on my last nerve, Pauline," she said. "Do they think I don't have enough to do? Do they think I'm their mother? I'd like to have this refrigerator *locked up* until they know how to respect other people. That's what I should do. And you get the combination to the lock only if you come through me."

"So do it," Pauline said absently.

"I might," Claire said. She was getting warmed up to the idea. "They have to come see me, and they have to sign an agreement to use the refrigerator. A cleanliness commitment. Like a chastity vow. Something like that. That's what I ought to do."

She slammed the refrigerator closed and stomped to the sink to wash her hands.

"My *last* nerve," she said. "And don't even get me started on the microwave." Pauline glanced at the microwave, which looked passably clean on the outside but which, she suspected, would look like a murder scene if she opened the door. As if in warning, the digital clock on the microwave flashed: *12:00, 12:00, 12:00*. Piece of junk. Every time Pauline looked at that microwave, the clock had shorted itself out. That was the last time she'd put Roy in charge of buying a microwave for the break room.

"See, that's why I don't use this kitchen," Pauline said. "Leave it for the ice crew. It's too dirty and too crappy."

"Well, some of us *have* to use the kitchen," Claire snapped. "Some of us can't afford to eat lunch out every day."

"I don't eat out every day," Pauline said. God, Claire could be testy! "Do what I do," she said. "Keep a little cooler at your desk for your lunch so you don't have to use the refrigerator."

"Well, that's inconvenient," Claire said. "Then I have to fuss with ice packs, all that." She pitched a balled-up paper towel into the trash can.

"Oh, *wah*. Now you're just being ornery," Pauline said.

"I would like to be able to keep my lunch cool," Claire said haughtily.

"Hello? Claire? We work in an ice plant? Just stick it out in the storage room." *Or stick it up your*—now, stop, Pauline, she chastised herself. Foul language. Foul thinking.

"All right, listen," she said instead. "Come to Home Depot with me. I trashed the bathroom this morning with hair color, and now I need to buy paint. And we'll go to lunch. Tidbits. My treat."

Claire dragged the trash can back into place and then turned to look at Pauline. "Well, now I feel bitchy for complaining," she said.

"You are bitchy," Pauline said.

"I *know*, but . . ."

"Just come to lunch."

Claire grinned. My word, this woman's mood could swing on a dime! "Okay," she said. "You're the boss."

In Home Depot, Claire wandered off into hardware and Pauline headed to the paint department, where she picked out a chip of the same paint color she'd been using in the bathroom for two decades, a milky white called "Diaphanous." Then she paused, studied the paint chips for a few moments, and put the white back in favor of a bold ice blue. "Impulse," it was called. Why not? She brought a gallon of semigloss to the mixing counter, and while she waited for the guy to mix the paint, Claire returned with a length of chain and a combination lock.

"Seven dollars," she said. "Fridge problem solved."

"You're asking for a mutiny, Claire."

"They can kiss my freckled white ass."

They paid for the purchases and left the store. Pauline drove to the Southbank, where they stopped at Tidbits to pick up sandwiches.

"Let's eat outside," Claire said. "It won't be too hot if we can find some shade."

They brought the sandwiches to a bench under a cypress near Friendship Fountain and sat looking across the St. Johns. Here at the edge of the river, it was warm, but not unbearable. On the opposite bank, the restaurants and shops of the Jacksonville Landing hunched at the river's edge. A water taxi chugged stubbornly against the current. Pauline checked her phone for a message from Johnny. Finding none, she opened her email. Nothing from Sam Tulley, either.

"You remember when they built that place?" Claire said, nodding toward the Landing.

"Yup," Pauline said. "I was in college. I came back and there it was." She squinted against the sun.

"Mike and I used to bring the kids there when they were little," Claire said. "There was a video arcade. Seems like a long time ago."

"Last time I went was when we took Roy to the Irish pub there for his birthday last year," Pauline said. "Remember that?"

Claire rolled her eyes. It would have been a hard night for anyone to forget, especially Claire. Roy had had too much to drink and ended up singing a sloppy set of karaoke, during which he dedicated "Saving All My Love for You" to Claire, roundly embarrassing himself, Claire, and everyone else within earshot until Johnny had wrestled him down from the karaoke stage and taken him home. Pauline smiled at the memory. Poor Roy, she thought. Poor, sweet Roy.

"Roy's got such a thing for you," she said. Claire pursed her lips and nodded. "Well?" Pauline said. "Is that such a bad thing?"

"Ain't nobody got time for that, Pauline," Claire said.

"It could be fun. You guys could be good together."

"I got three kids standing in line for my attention. I don't need one more." But Claire sounded a bit wistful. Pauline was debating whether to press the point when Claire gasped and grabbed Pauline's arm. "Oh, my God," she said.

"What?"

"Look over there." Claire pointed directly across the river toward the Landing. "It's Rosa and that jackass Owen Vickers," she said.

"Where?" Pauline squinted.

"Right there. In front of Hooters. Standing by the water."

Pauline shielded her eyes and looked harder. There were indeed two people standing by the railing just in front of Hooters. They were pressed close together, and it looked like they might have been kissing. But it was too far, if you asked Pauline, for a positive ID.

"How can you tell that's Rosa?" she said skeptically. "It's too far away."

"It's Rosa," Claire said firmly. "I'd know that little sass anywhere. And I know she was wearing that red shirt when she left home today. Watch," she said. She took her iPhone out of her pocket and snapped a photo of the couple across the river. Then she enlarged the photo on the phone's screen to zoom in on the image. "You see?" she said.

Now it did indeed look like Rosa. Rosa in a passionate clinch with Owen Vickers.

"Oh, I tell you what!" Claire said. "I'm going to wring that girl's neck. I told her to stay away from him. You know how old he is?"

"At least thirty," Pauline guessed.

"He's thirty-*two*. And she's eighteen!" Claire stood up and walked closer to the river. She waved her arms toward the couple across the water. "Rosa!" she shouted. "Get your butt back to the factory!"

"Claire, she can't hear you. It's too far."

Claire scowled. "Well, she can get a text message, can't she?" She angrily thumbed at the phone, then put it back in her pocket. She and Pauline watched as the girl across the way pulled back from the man she was embracing and reached toward her back pocket. She appeared to pull out a phone, examine it, and then look straight across the water toward Claire and Pauline. Claire stood stoically, arms crossed. After a moment, the two figures across the river left the railing and disappeared around the side of the restaurant behind them.

"I'm going to get Roy to fire him," Claire said. "He is prey-ing on my daughter, Pauline. This makes me sick."

"Well, tell Roy to come up with a better reason than dating the receptionist," Pauline said. "The legally adult receptionist. Last I checked that wasn't against the law. I don't need the union crawling all over us. Although I agree with you," she added quickly, seeing Claire's face, "it's not what we want. He *is* too old for her."

Claire sighed and returned to the bench. "Pauline," she said. "This is why I have gray hair. And here I am not even forty."

"Well, I'm sure it's just a little flirtation," Pauline said. "Try not to pay any attention to it." For her part, she tried not to pay any attention to Claire's statement about her age. As if Pauline could forget that Claire was more than ten years younger! For Pete's sake. Claire seemed to take every oppor-tunity to remind her.

"What am I going to do about that girl?" Claire was say-ing. "She has no sense, Pauline. Do you know what she did the other day? She spent her entire paycheck on a pair of sunglasses. Her entire paycheck. Prada sunglasses! She's an eighteen-year-old receptionist! She's supposed to be saving for art school, and she's out buying Prada sunglasses. Oh, I could throttle her. Meanwhile Ethan's failing algebra and the doctor's telling me Chase is ADHD," she continued. "I've been trying to believe he's just a little brat. But it's worse than that. So we're starting medication. It's making me a nervous wreck. Do you know what it feels like to have to medicate an eight-year-old child?" She looked at Pauline sadly. "He misses his dad, he says. Oh, that gets me. Mike was such an asshole to *me*. But he was awfully good to the kids. Of course they miss him."

"You're a good mom," Pauline said gently. "You're doing the best you can." Then, before she could stop herself, she asked the question. "Claire," she said. "Have you ever regretted having children?"

Claire snorted. "Every day," she said.

"No, seriously."

Claire thought about it. "Well, maybe not having *children*," she said. "Having *these* children, though."

"You're terrible."

Claire smiled, then peered at her curiously. "Why do you ask?" she said.

"I don't know. I guess I was just thinking about how we make these decisions when we're so young, you know? Whether to marry a particular man or not, whether to have kids or not. Seems like there's a lot of room for error."

Claire shook her head. "Girl, first of all, you are operating under the mistaken belief that everyone *decides* whether or not to do these things. I didn't decide to have kids. I had one too many Bartles & Jaymes, went skinny-dipping at Jax Beach, and got knocked up. Not a lot of strategy going on there." She paused. "Have you ever regretted *not* having children?" she said.

"No," Pauline said quickly. "Well, possibly. Sometimes. I don't know."

"Well, maybe it's not too late," Claire said.

"I'm fifty!"

"I know. But I've got a couple that I can let go cheap, if you're interested."

"I was thinking—okay, tell me if this is crazy—but I was thinking maybe Johnny and I should offer to keep Corran's baby for a while. Until he gets back on his feet. I mean, after we get Johnny through the surgery, of course. Is that nuts?"

Claire looked at her, surprised. "A baby?" she said. "That's a huge commitment, Pauline."

"Yes, but—"

"I mean, huge! And what do you mean by 'a while'?"

"Few weeks? Months? I don't know. Whatever Corran needs, I guess. Johnny said Sharon's considered having her, but she just can't."

"What about work? What about all the OSHA shit? And your father? Lord. You'd freak out. You'd be overwhelmed. Trust me. Or worse, you'd get attached, Pauline. You won't want to give her back. Or what if Corran can't take her back? What if—God forbid—the drug thing and all, well . . . you know. You'd be, what, raising the poor thing?" Pauline felt foolish. The doubt in Claire's face was eroding the plausibility of the whole idea. And her skepticism was contagious. *She's right,* Pauline thought. *It's insane. It's impossible.*

Pauline shook her head. "Oh, I know. It was just a silly thought. Johnny would probably resist. And anyway, I'm not mom material," she said. "I'm too self-centered."

Claire studied her for a moment. "No you're not," she said finally. "You're self-involved, but that's not the same thing as self-centered."

"Well, thanks a lot."

"You just called yourself self-centered!"

"You were supposed to disagree with me."

"And I did. So you're self-involved. So what? That's only because there are no children in your life demanding your involvement. Anybody would be self-involved if she had the chance."

Self-centered. Self-involved. Pauline didn't really see the difference.

"The difference," Claire said, as if reading her mind, "is that a self-involved person can choose to let someone else in. I don't think a self-centered person can do that."

Oh, for God's sake. Pauline had had enough. The sandwich was dry, her Diet Coke was empty, and she had a wicked mosquito bite rising up on her ankle. Self-involved? What the hell? Claire was on quite the philosophical high horse over there, and Pauline was abruptly hot, bothered, and ready to get back to her office, where the specter of unopened emails beckoned.

"Come on, Socrates," she said. "Let's go make the ice." They gathered the trash and walked to the car. Pauline headed for the bridge, and Claire turned the AC to full blast and leaned forward to meet the rush of air. "Come on," she said. "Come *on!* Will this heat ever let up, Pauline?"

Pauline was too hot to answer, or to speculate, or to care.

*   *   *

Back at the office, Pauline checked her email. There was one from Sam Tulley: *Best place to park is on the downtown side. Near the stadium.*

Lord! Completely noncommittal! Was he asking her to go running with him, or wasn't he? Fine, Sam Tulley. Just forget it. She wasn't going to initiate a meetup, for God's sake. If he wanted to ask her to go for a training run with him, then ask. Go ahead, ask! Because she'd already decided, anyway, that even if he *did* ask, she'd say no. She was a married woman! She couldn't go out running around in the predawn with some overgrown boy. Not to mention that the idea of attempting a training run on the Hart Bridge, of all places, was completely insane. The bridge had no sidewalks! On the day of the actual Gate River Run, the police would close the bridge to car traffic and open up the lanes for runners. But without the benefit of that safety precaution, a run on the Hart Bridge on a foggy, dark weekday morning in a traffic lane, for heaven's sake, was out of the question. Maybe *he* was dumb enough to take it on. But she wasn't.

She was glad, then, to have the distraction of billing and payroll to keep her occupied for the rest of the afternoon, and by the time she started to think about calling it a day, it was well after five. She wondered what Johnny was up to. She texted him—*Send me a pic of Lucy?*—but then realized it might be too late in Scotland for him to see it. She finished up a few more emails and was about to turn off her computer when another message came in. From Sam Tulley. No subject. One line in the body: *Want to run it with me tomorrow?*

Well, well, well. Bingo. Pauline sat back in her chair and looked at the email triumphantly. She turned off the computer and drove home. She took General San Jose for a walk and heated up a Smart Ones meal in the microwave. She decided against painting the bathroom. Maybe tomorrow. She sipped a glass of red wine and ate her dinner in front of the news. Dow improves. Jaguars taking it on the chin. Heat wave continues—no break for Halloween. She poured another glass of wine and took a few sips but then thought about how it might affect her running pace in the morning, so she dumped the rest of the glass down the drain. She took a shower and tried not to look at the hair color stains on the bathroom wall. In bed, she turned on her iPad and pulled up Sam Tulley's email. How many hours since he'd sent it now? Four. That should demonstrate sufficient nonchalance, right?

Sounds good! she wrote. *What time?* Then she pushed Send.

to Dunedin *last* week. She sighed. No use wondering; she knew the answer.

She left the water running and reached under the sink for a roll of paper towels and a can of bathroom cleaner, both of which were exactly where she'd left them last week. She used these to execute a two-minute spot-cleaning around the little bathroom, just enough to more or less sterilize the toilet and vanity and to wipe down the edges of the tub and cabinets. The floor could wait another week. She gave it a cursory wipe with a damp paper towel to sweep up a few scattered hairs and dust bunnies. There. Clean enough. She squirted a burst of bubble bath liquid into the bathwater and then looked around for a clean towel, quickly concluding with annoyance that there were none. Why *this* should surprise her, she had no idea. God, did she have to do *everything* herself?

In the weeks since Anna had been arrested and Corran had found himself on his own with Lucy, Sharon had been driving up to Port Readie from Dunedin every weekend. The idea was that she'd watch the baby and help him with a few things around the house while he picked up extra hours working as a hand on the ferry at Drumscaddle. But "a few things around the house" were turning into "full service housekeeping," and she was spending good money every weekend buying household items for her son and his baby daughter: new towels, crib sheets, clothes for Lucy, even a shower curtain, for heaven's sake. She bought the stroller, which after only two months looked like it had been through heavy combat, and with the way Corran dragged it up and down the hill she was not surprised. She bought the activity quilt, which she noted this evening was balled up in a corner of the living room and no doubt caked in spit-up, or worse. She didn't know how much longer this could go on.

There was a knock on the bathroom door and she opened it. Corran stepped in with a jar of baby food and a box of Weetabix. He wrinkled his nose.

"Close the door," Sharon said. "I'm trying to warm it up in here."

He shut the door behind him and put the food on the edge of the sink. Sharon closed the lid on the toilet and sat down, bending to swish her hand through the warm water and agitate the bubbles. Lucy banged her hands on the side of the tub in anticipation.

"Corry, have ye bathed this child?" Sharon said.

"Of course I have," he said. He glanced quickly at Lucy, as if he thought she might betray him. "We do it different, though. We sponge-bathe."

Sharon raised one eyebrow at him. "The child needs a soak!" she said.

"Pah," Lucy said.

"That's right," Sharon said. "You tell him, love."

"She's clean," Corran said defensively. He licked his thumb and then reached down and rubbed at a sticky-looking patch on Lucy's cheek. Sharon sat Lucy in the warm bathwater and they both watched as the baby let out an elated squeal and set to splashing.

"Look at that," Corran said. "Look at that sweet thing." He stuck his tongue out at Lucy, and she smiled.

"Oh, she's a dolly," Sharon said. She leaned over the tub. "I'm going to eat you up, Lucy!" Lucy threw her arms in the air and doused Sharon's face, then laughed. Again, this was the problem! Sharon couldn't resent Lucy; she loved the little thing so much. She clicked the space heater up to a higher setting and turned to look at Corran.

"It's freezing in this house," she said.

"I'm not cold," he said. She looked at her son. Had he ever been cold? Corran ran hot. His thermostat was different from most people's.

"Well?" Sharon said.

"Well, what?" Corran said.

"Well, aren't you going to fuss at me for bringing your father up here?"

He shrugged.

"Don't make a difference to me," he said.

Well, obviously it didn't, because both her ex-husband and her son seemed to operate on the principle that if you *pretended* you didn't care, then maybe eventually you *wouldn't* care. Fake it till you make it right? Well, wrong. It didn't work that way. Sharon knew what their row was about, of course—Princess Pauline's wedding ring. It was quite awful, Sharon would concede, to have your ring stolen and gone forever. Terrible. No doubt about it. But what kind of cosseted dimwit would leave an expensive piece of jewelry in plain view when she had a heroin addict staying in her house? Corran claimed he couldn't remember taking the ring, but then, what *could* he remember when he was wrecked with heroin?

What Pauline and Johnny never quite seemed to under-stand was that when Corran was using, he wasn't Corran at all. He became somebody else entirely—a person none of them recognized, someone capable of lying and stealing and worse, if he was in need of a hit. Sharon didn't like to admit this about her own son, but it was true. The drugs took her boy away and replaced him with a thief and a liar. But Lucy, it seemed, was bringing Corran back. Watching him clean up over the past year had been miraculous. A rebirth. She gave thanks every day.

And yet still he and Johnny were in a standoff over this damn ring! *He needs to apologize,* Johnny kept saying. *He needs to stop accusing me,* Corran kept saying. For shit's sake. Sharon had seen the ring. Pauline had come over enough times that Sharon was well acquainted with the ring. Yes, it was beautiful. Yes, it was no doubt very expensive. Yes, it was no doubt very meaningful. But for God's sake, Pauline, Sharon sometimes wanted to ask, if it was as irreplaceable as all that, then what did you take it off for? Sharon looked down at her own plain gold band, the line of it gone wavy now in Lucy's shimmering bathwater. She never took *her* ring off. Some of us didn't grow up with money, did we? Some of us know how to *value* our possessions, don't we?

Oh, stop. Take it easy on Pauline, she admonished herself. Really, she was a perfectly nice woman, and she'd certainly done a bang-up job of looking out for the Iceman—of whom Sharon was still exceedingly fond—for all these years. She was just— well—Pauline was just spoiled. That's all there was to it. Sharon remembered something she heard in an election campaign once. One of the two leading candidates had come from a much more privileged background than the other. The less bankrolled of the two went around speechmaking to the working class and underprivileged, trying to capture votes. "It's not that he doesn't *care* about money struggles," he would say of his opponent. "It's that he doesn't *know* about money struggles." That was Johnny's second wife. She just didn't know.

"Can you just make peace with him?" she said to Corran now. "He's come all this way for you."

"He's come all this way for *him*, Mum," he said. "The grand gesture. Whatever. And anyway, I've got no issue with him. He can do whatever he wants."

Sharon edged off the toilet and knelt at the side of the tub. "Hand me that," she said, motioning to the jar of baby food on the sink. "And the spoon." Corran handed them to her, and she popped open the jar and started spooning fat dollops of pureed chicken and rice into Lucy's mouth. This was a trick she'd learned when Corran was a baby. To hell with the high chair and the mess in the kitchen. Feed the baby *in* the bathtub, and kill two birds with one stone. Clean child, full belly. Voilà.

"He's sick, you know," she said to Corran.

"Sick how?"

"Brain cyst. He's having surgery."

"Cancer?"

"Maybe not," she said. "But you never know."

Corran looked at her for a moment, and she watched him arrange something inside himself. He didn't think she could see it when he did that. But she could.

He shrugged and looked away. "I'm sure he'll be fine," he said slowly. "He always is."

Corran had no fear of death. It was remarkable. When she considered the dangers he had put himself through: Oil rigs. HUET training. Heroin! His bullish bravado used to terrify her. She used to interpret it as an actual death wish, used to worry that he was suicidal. But she'd come to understand that it wasn't that he wanted to die. It was just that he wasn't going to limit himself in the normal human ways. By removing fear, Corran removed constraints. It was astounding, if a bit potty. And he was right, actually, not to fear death. After all these years as a hospice nurse, Sharon knew there were plenty of things that were worse than dying. Fear. Pain. Grief. Anger. Those things were worse. Regret was the big one. Regret was so much worse than dying.

Another knock came on the door, and Johnny entered.

"Close the door," Sharon said. "Cold."

He edged farther into the tiny bathroom and closed the door behind him. Sharon scooted her knees to the left to allow him a space to stand. "I was going to ask Corran if we should do something about that bicycle," Johnny said. He seemed to be speaking to Sharon. She looked pointedly at Corran, who was standing no more than an arm's length from his father. Johnny turned to him.

"Is that your only transport? No car?" he said.

"Nope. Just the bike," Corran said.

"Do you want to fix it, then?"

"I can fix it."

"I know you can. I was just wondering if you need help."

"I just need an inner tube."

"Well, we can drive you down to the shops, then," Johnny said. He seemed relieved to have something to offer.

"There are no shops. Nothing but pub and off-license in the village," Corran said. "They don't have tubes."

"Maybe up in Fort William?"

"It's getting late," Corran said. "And it's Sunday."

"Well then, tomorrow," Johnny said, a tinge of exasperation in his voice. He edged backward, but before he could exit the bathroom, Chemal tapped on the door and stuck his head in.

"Why are you all in here?" he said.

"Close the door!" Sharon said. "The baby's in the tub."

Chemal edged into the bathroom and closed the door, effectively barring Johnny's exit. Now they were all five inside a steaming bathroom the size of a toolshed. "I was just wondering if we were going to do anything about food," Chemal said, directing his question to Sharon. "You know. To eat." Sharon looked at each of them: Johnny stiff and rigid by the sink, Corran sulking by the bathtub, Chemal now leaning against the door, waggling his fingers and making faces at Lucy. Really! Didn't a single one of these men have a bit of sense? All coming to her to make all the decisions? She looked at Lucy in the bathtub and shook her head.

"You blokes," she said. "Get out of this bathroom and go do something useful. Run down to the pub for some fish and chips, would you? And get some milk and tea while you're at it. And could one of you please change the bedding in this poor child's crib?" And don't you know they all looked relieved to be told what to do? They opened the bathroom door and shuffled out. And all I want to see, Sharon nearly added, are arseholes and elbows!

"Pah," Lucy said.

"Oh, sister," Sharon said. "You don't know the half."

She finished bathing the baby and pulled her from the tub. She dried her off and fastened a fresh diaper. She curled Lucy's damp hair around a soft-bristled brush and pinned the curl down with the blue plastic barrette. There. Something, at least, was in order.

She'd credit them with this: They could follow directions. Within thirty minutes, Johnny, Corran, and Chemal had managed to procure a few simple groceries, a fish-and-chips dinner, and a clean change of sheets for the crib. Sharon set Lucy up on the activity quilt in the living room. Then she joined them at the kitchen table and sat where she could keep an eye on Lucy. The pleasing aroma of battered cod and ale seemed to have loosened up a bit of conversation, albeit on a rather bizarre topic.

"Hot steak," Chemal was explaining, "that's what they say."

"What?" Sharon said. She pulled a piece of fish onto a paper plate and doused it with lemon and vinegar. She shouldn't be eating this. She'd been back on Weight Watchers online since summer but the scale hadn't budged an ounce, and she knew it was due to all these fried fish dinners here in Port Readie every weekend with Corran. She glanced around the little kitchen. Well, it wasn't as if there was anything else to eat in the house tonight, and it was either eat the fish or go hungry. Circumstances. Always conspiring against her. She dug in.

"Outer space," Chemal said. "I was reading this article. Astronauts have reported that space smells like seared steak."

"That's wild," Corran said. "But how can they smell inside their suits?"

"Like, when they come back aboard the craft," Chemal said. "They smell it *on* their suits and equipment."

"I never thought about what it would *smell* like," Sharon said. She turned to Johnny. "Did you?"

He shrugged. He seemed to have barely touched his food.

"You feeling okay?" she said.

"Yeh," he said.

"I always think about what stuff smells like," Chemal said.

"That's weird," Corran said.

"It's not weird," Sharon said. "It's inquisitive. I think it's smart."

"It's just a habit," Chemal said.

"Like talking too loudly," Johnny said.

"Exactly," Chemal said.

"Like you're doing right now."

"Oh. Right." Chemal lowered his voice and looked sheepish. "Anyway. I have this theory that smell is the most underutilized of our five senses. I think if we paid more attention to smells, we'd be so much more self-aware. You know, as a species." He munched on a chip and then turned to Corran. "So what do oil rigs smell like?" he said.

"Diesel. And sweat. But also salt water. And rain."

"And Miss Sharon? What does your job smell like?"

"Oh, Chemal," she said. "Most of the time you don't want to know. Poop and throw-up. Not pleasant. But then sometimes there's more. Sometimes it smells like peace." They were all quiet, contemplating the smell of peace.

"What does ice smell like?" Sharon said to Johnny.

"Like money," Corran said, before Johnny could answer. "Right, Da?"

Johnny looked at Corran for a beat and then answered slowly. "It doesn't really smell like anything," he said to Chemal. "I think it just smells like work."

Corran chuckled.

"That funny, Corran?" Johnny said.

"Nah," Corran said. He stood up and looked through the doorway to check on Lucy in the next room.

"I can see her," Sharon said. "She's fine." It was reassuring that it occurred to Corran quite frequently to check on Lucy's welfare, that his parental instincts were strong enough to have ignited that sense of constant surveillance peculiar to parents (or, in her case, grandparents) of small children. There were times when Sharon lay awake at night, worrying herself sick about how her son—with the ghost of a heroin needle in his not-too-distant past—could possibly manage the demands of single fatherhood with a baby who hadn't even taken her first steps yet. But clearly he'd mastered the craft of tender hovering. Cooking, cleaning, laundering, and bathing seemed rather beyond his reach, but the devotion, it appeared, was coming naturally.

Corran sat back down and looked at Johnny.

"So, did you get a second opinion?" he said. "On the brain thing?"

"How did you know about that?" Johnny looked at Sharon, and she took a sip of her beer before answering.

"I thought he should know, Johnny," she said. "There's no reason to keep it a secret."

"That's what *I've* been saying," Chemal said.

"So, did you?" Corran said. "Get a second opinion?"

"Don't worry about it," Johnny said.

"Don't you think maybe you should?" Corran said.

"I trust my doctor."

Corran looked at Sharon. "Don't *you* think he should get a second opinion?"

"I think he should do what he thinks is best, Corran."

Corran shook his head. "Seems a little risky to me."

Sharon regarded Johnny, who was gazing at Corran expressionlessly. Good boy, Johnny, she thought. Don't take the bait. She knew exactly what was going through Johnny's mind: *Corran* was going to deliver a lecture on *risk*?

"I got a second opinion," Johnny said. "And a third." He stared at Corran across the table. Corran stared back. For God's sake, these two!

"Well, anyway," Sharon said. "I'm sure it will work out just fine. Let's not worry about it tonight. Your da's on holiday."

"I love that," Chemal said. "How you say 'holiday.' We say 'vacation.' Sounds like a pharmaceutical. 'Holiday' sounds like a party."

Sharon looked around the little cottage, where her son and her ex-husband were squaring off in silent opposition across the table, where her granddaughter was starting to fuss on the activity quilt in the other room, and where a wounded adolescent was inhaling the last of the overfried fish and chips. Yeh, she thought. Some party. She yawned. Well, here's part of the issue, she decided. She was tired. They all were. They'd been out late last night and then on the road half the day today, tromping through sheep shit to boot.

"Let's get settled," she said. "Your father and I can share the pullout," she said to Corran, who looked at her, surprised. "What? It won't be the first time I've slept with him. Just no funny business," she said, waggling a finger at Johnny.

"Don't worry," he grumbled. Really, what a crank he could be!

"And Corran, if you have extra blankets we'll make a spot for Chemal on the floor. We'll use the couch cushions. That all right, love?" she said.

"Fine by me, Miss Sharon. I can sleep anywhere," Chemal said.

Lucy started to cry in earnest. Sharon looked at Corran.

"She needs her bottle," she said.

"I know," he said. "I'm going."

She watched him rise from the table and fetch the bottle from the refrigerator, and she was struck by the slope of her son's shoulders and the abject fatigue she could see in his limbs. Corran. Oh, my sweet boy Corran. Why have you made it all so hard? She got up and took the bottle from him.

"Sit down, Corry," she said. "Finish your dinner."

She took the bottle to Lucy and rocked her in the darkness of Corran's tiny bedroom. It was chilly in here. She'd bring the space heater in for Lucy after the baby fell asleep. From the kitchen came the sounds of dishes and washing up. Chemal was talking loudly, something about the Hubble telescope. What a smart pisser, that kid. She heard Johnny tell him to lower his voice. And after that, silence.

Lucy Locket lost her pocket, she sang to the baby, *and Kitty Fisher found it. Not a penny was there in it, only ribbon round it.*

Later that night, Sharon was roused from a light sleep by the shifting of Johnny's weight on the flimsy pullout mattress. He was awake, she could tell. She eased gently over to her side, turning her back to him, and stared at the wall, listening to the familiar but long-forgotten sounds of Johnny MacKinnon's night breathing, something she hadn't known since the old hard days of Easterhouse. She wondered what Toole would think of this, the two of them sharing a bed. Her phone was on the floor next to her and she considered texting him to tell him about it, have a little laugh, but she decided against it. There was a good chance Toole didn't know where he'd last put down his cell phone, and she didn't want to set him wandering about the house, trying to locate the beeping.

Toole was getting foggy. A terrifying word—dementia—came creeping into her consciousness now and then, but she kicked it out and barred the door as best she could. For now. He wasn't even sixty yet! It couldn't be. Still, she'd heard of these early-onset cases. She pictured Toole at home tonight, propping his throbbing knees up on extra pillows and arranging on his bedside table the doses of pain meds he'd take at intervals to get through the night.

That was another thing. She was getting a little concerned about the pain med situation, to tell the truth. Toole's doctor had warned him that he was on his last prescription refill, and already Toole had intimated to Sharon that maybe she could "hook him up" with something from the hospital when she went to see her patients if his supply ran out before his pain tolerance returned. She'd been astonished he'd asked. They were both career health care professionals; they both knew the inviolate ethics of dispensing regulations. Did he really think she'd risk her job and criminal prosecution to "hook him up" with illegal pain meds? "Forget it," she had snapped at him. "Just get off your ass and increase the PT. You of all people should know."

"You don't understand this pain, Sharon," he'd said, turning to limp into the other room.

Oh, Toole, she'd wanted to say. I understand pain. But then she felt a little guilty for her outburst, so she followed him to the living room and got him settled in the recliner. She brought him a beer and a pair of cold packs to place under his knees. She made a tikka masala and brought it to him on a tray. She even got

down to business with him later in bed, gingerly climbing astride
his hips while giving his tender knees a wide berth, hoping the
sexual release might distract his body's pain receptors and get his
mind off the cursed medications. She did everything she could
do for Toole. For God's sake. She did everything she could do
for *everybody*, she thought, remembering her beleaguered son
in the bedroom. And Lucy. Sweet dolly Lucy.

Here was what they needed to do, Sharon thought, she and
Johnny. They needed to have a serious, sit-down meeting with
Corran and insist that he plot out a real plan for how he was
going to raise his child. This business of working for low wages
on the Drumscaddle ferry and counting on Sharon to haul her
ass up to Port Readie every single weekend for babysitting and
housekeeping was *not* going to work. She'd been doing it for
weeks now; she didn't plan on doing it for much longer.

She'd spent almost her entire life caring for other people—
feeding them, cleaning them, entertaining them, supporting
them, comforting them. Johnny. Corran. Toole. A boatload of
patients, too many to ever count. And now Lucy. Beginning of
the road for that one; think of all that was still to come: teething,
walking, talking, toilet training, ear infections, croup, tantrums,
allergies, nightmares, laundry, school lunches, homework, contact lenses, science projects, acne, boyfriends, driving! Did Corran think that Sharon was supposed to just stand by to be the
point person for all of that, too?

A living assistant. That's what she was. Helping everyone
around her with the basic fuckin' business of *living*. She'd had
enough! Couldn't any of them just do it themselves?

Johnny shifted again on the bed behind her. She thought
about letting him know she was awake, perhaps leaning over and

giving the old boy a pat on the arm, a little squeeze of the hand. He's worried, after all, she thought. About his brain thingy, and his factory, and Corran. About all of it. It even crossed her mind, albeit briefly, to give him a *real* distraction, to climb aboard like she did with Toole and give him something wonderfully basic and corporeal and true to think about, if only for a little while. After all, Chemal was in a dead sleep on the floor and was sure to stay that way until morning. The door to Corran's room was closed tight. What could it hurt? Who would ever know?

Ah, Sharon, she told herself, you've gone 'round the bend, you slutty old thing! She smiled. It was enough to know that she *could* do it. If she wanted to. Which she didn't. She pulled the thin blanket up around her shoulder and kept her back to Johnny. Let him wrestle his own damn worries. She had plenty.

FOURTEEN

Corran had a recurring dream, and it came to him again that night. It went like this: He was standing atop a teetering stepladder in Margaret's kitchen. The stepladder was making him uneasy, and the attic access through which he was about to stick his head and shoulders was yawning blackly, and why he'd agreed to any of this he had no idea. Margaret had called him to come over. The idea was to have Corran investigate a scrabbling noise that had been coming from the crawl space the last several nights. *Rats,* Margaret had said. *I cannae abide rats. Have a look for me, will you, lad?*

The stepladder wobbled. Margaret was standing in the kitchen, Lucy on her hip. From the attic above came a whiff of mildew, and then something else, acrid and rank. From the back of the house, toward the lounge, came television sounds— staccato bursts of music, laughter, a dissociated shriek. Corran looked down at his feet, shifted them slightly to center them on the stepladder's black rubber surface, then looked back up toward the hole above his head. A quick spring would do it. Catch his weight on the perimeter of the access hole and buck up his forearms to make the ascension. Easy. He knew his own weight—spryness came easily. And then what?

What d'ye see, then? Aught? Margaret said.

Nae up there yet, am I?

But do ye?

He had a toothache, too, which certainly wasn't helping matters. Not terribly surprising, because he'd developed a habit lately of sucking on fruit pastilles, one after another, until the candies became little embryos of sugar on his tongue. It was like he was addicted to the damn things. And so now he probably had a cavity. Brilliant.

I smell it, Margaret said. *Oh, my.*

Margaret fluttered her free hand now and then toward the stepladder as if to steady it, but she never actually touched it. Lucy was staring at Corran, and at the gaping hole in the ceiling above his head. She pointed at it.

Pah, she said.

Watch your daddy, Lucy, Margaret said. Corran made the spring. *There he goes!*

Corran fell into a sit at the edge of the hole, legs dangling into the kitchen. The crawl space extended the length of the house, and beyond the scant perimeter of the kitchen access, it clenched into impenetrable darkness. He squinted, willing his eyes to adjust.

What do ye see, then?

Too dark.

Here's the light.

A flashlight flew up into the access. Corran caught it but then dropped it, watched as it clattered past his reach and nearly beyond his sight into the graduated darkness of the crawl space. He cursed. He shimmied into a crouch and moved forward toward it.

Be careful, Corran.

Margaret's voice, a bit muffled now from down in the kitchen below, had a tone of mild reproach, as if Corran were acting the irresponsible fool up here, skylarking about in an attic of his own accord. If she'd really wanted him to be careful, she would have called a proper pest control agency and left Corran well out of it. He crawled farther into darkness. He had a great affection in his heart for Margaret in nearly all things and ways, but this little adventure might have been asking just a bit too much. Never mind.

He retrieved the flashlight and flicked it on at exactly the same time something at the far end of the crawl space exploded. He shone a beam of light toward the commotion. A weasel-like animal was scrambling about the floorboards, looking for escape. It backed into a corner, stood up on its rear legs, and looked at Corran with hatred.

Oh, now.

What d'ye see?

Pine marten.

Give over.

Sure enough.

Rare creatures. Corran had seen a pine marten only a few times in his life. But now here was one, not ten feet away. It was unmistakable: the sleek dark fur, yellow markings around the neck. It looked like it was wearing an ascot. Foxy thing, quite cute, but for the bared teeth. The attic smelled like piss. And now there was a rasping. Corran could actually hear it breathing. He glanced around the attic for a breach, spotted none. The pine marten hissed.

We'll need a trap.

It's always something, isn't it, Corran?

The attic space felt pressurized. Outside, a wind began to buffet the house. The pine marten was staring at Corran. Abruptly, the bared teeth seemed to resolve into a more human expression, something like a salacious grin. Now the animal was watching him intently, smiling wickedly, and Corran found he could not look away. The pine marten got up; it paced in a tight circle three times, then stretched itself supine, its back legs extending straight out toward Corran. Again it looked at him intently. Again he could not look away.

Corran? Come down now. We'll get a trap.

Pah.

The pine marten opened its back legs. It flicked its tongue at Corran and watched him with hooded eyes. The scene was humanly lewd. Corran was aware of the open attic access, now a good six feet behind him. He wanted to inch backward toward the opening. Instead he watched the pine marten. The animal reached its black hands down between its legs and spread apart thick gray fur. It gave a throaty laugh. A woman's voice.

Corran felt a rush of bile ascend in his throat. He tried to shuffle backward but reacted too quickly and hit his head on a beam. He dropped reflexively to his stomach and tried to snake backward toward the opening. The pine marten laughed again. The attic filled with a rush of musky heat. Corran gagged. Margaret's and Lucy's voices had become muffled. He could not make out what Margaret was saying.

Fish mine slipper snow, it sounded like. *Boy drank book feet. Pah.*

The pine marten was still grinning, but it had begun to grunt and buck. A slick darkness was emerging from its slender loins. The darkness took on mass, then shook itself free and writhed wetly on the attic floor. Corran looked behind him. The attic access was gone. There was no egress to the kitchen below.

The dark mass was unfolding itself. It shook like a dog and stood up, and Corran saw that it *was* a dog—an enormous mastiff with a thick mane of matted green hair. It was growing, growing, growing. Its back pressed against the ceiling of the attic; it threw up its head and the beams above it cracked. Then Corran knew what it was: the Cù-Sìth, a green dog big as a bull, known to hunt the Highlands, looking for those who are close to death. The dog swayed from side to side, straining against the walls of the attic. A corner joint gave way. A rush of snow and wind blew into the attic.

The pine marten was dead.

Corran writhed wildly toward where the attic access once was. He ran his hands along the floorboards, looking for a void, but found none. The Cù-Sìth was thrashing like a bull in a chute. In one mighty lunge, it extended itself upward and smashed a gaping hole through the roof, and the wind took over from there, sharking its way across the boards on the roof and whipping them off in quick succession. Corran had the impression of watching a great zipper being opened, then the floor gave way beneath him and Margaret's house crumbled into a pile of kindling, and the kindling became needles, and the needles were carried away on the wind, and then Corran and the Cù-Sìth were alone in the midst of a vast cold moor. The animal looked at him. It appeared to be waiting.

Lucy! Corran tried to scream, but no words came out. Margaret!

Lucy!

Lucy!

It was Johnny who finally jostled Corran awake. He'd entered Corran's bedroom and was now standing over the bed, peering down at his son. He shook Corran's shoulder and let his hand stay there.

"You're dreaming, Corran," he said. "The bairn's right there."

Corran sat up straight and looked over at Lucy in her crib. She was sleeping soundly. He found he was panting. He looked at Johnny blankly for a moment, and then gathered himself. He lay down again and turned his back to his father.

"I'm sorry I woke you," he said.

"You all right, Corran?"

"I'm fine."

Johnny walked softly out of the room. Corran listened while the springs on the pullout sofa creaked as Johnny lowered himself back into it next to Sharon. After a long time, Corran slept.

FIFTEEN

When she found herself in the ridiculous position of trying to run with Sam Tulley across the sidewalkless Hart Bridge, a hundred feet above the St. Johns River in the dark and fog of a late October morning, Pauline had the realization that the terror was actually improving her pace. Maybe it was an evolutionary thing, a holdover from the days when humans served a more elemental role in the basic predator-prey food chain. Or maybe it was simply that the stricture of her heart was revving up blood flow and thus improving muscle contraction. Whatever it was, the fear was feeding her running ability as nothing else ever had. In fact, it was the only thing that could possibly explain how she was keeping up.

Sam Tulley had been talking since they met near the stadium to do a half-mile warm-up loop on flat ground before ascending the ramp to the bridge. He talked through the first quarter-mile and past the point Pauline had come to think of as "the wall"—that two- or three-minute period when every fiber of her being was screaming for her to stop. She had never figured out how to avoid the wall, but she'd figured out how to push through it.

Granted, they hadn't even gotten near the sharpest part of the incline yet, but she was amazed to find that she was keeping pace with Sam Tulley pretty well. It was quite possible that this was not because she was going faster but because he was going slower, a thought which she found both mildly infuriating and strangely gratifying. On the one hand, she hated to be patronized. But on the other hand, there was no way she was going to keep pace—uphill!—with a man nearly two decades her junior and a good six inches taller. Which could mean only one thing. Sam Tulley was trying to make her feel good. How interesting.

She tried to adjust her breathing to her pace. Step-step-step-step-step-*breathe*. Step-step-step-step-step-*breathe*. If she could keep this five-step rhythm going for the first half of the incline, she reasoned, then she could accommodate the inevitable quickening of her breathing once they began to ascend the steepest part of the climb, which, fortunately or unfortunately, depending on how she chose to look at it, was barely visible up ahead through the fog. They were running against traffic. This was a strategic maneuver designed to give them more warning when a car was coming over the bridge. So far only one car had approached, and Sam had held his hands up high overhead as he ran, shining small flashlights to attract the driver's attention.

Lord have mercy, Lord have mercy, Lord have mercy. This was nuts. When she had ACL surgery a few years ago, they'd replaced her torn anterior cruciate ligament with a segment of ligament from a "donor." When the doctor told her he'd be using donor tissue, Pauline hadn't understood at first. Who would donate a ligament? It wasn't like blood, after all, that would replenish itself. Then it dawned on her that the donor was dead. "It's called an allograft," the orthopedist said. "It's from a cadaver harvest."

A cadaver harvest! That one had stayed with Pauline for some time, and after the surgery she often thought about the cadaver from which her new ACL had been harvested. She was running around with a piece of tissue in her knee from a person whom she had never met and would never know a thing about. Sometimes she made up a persona and gave it a backstory, little Walter Mittyish fantasies about the person who might have previously had ownership of the ligament—usually a woman, it was hard to imagine having a man's ligament in her knee, but who knew; maybe it was a small man. This morning, it was not too hard to imagine the ligament's original owner as a tough, foulmouthed battle-ax type, maybe somebody like Claire, who would likely be happy to give Pauline what for when she realized that they were headed for a suicide mission over a wicked-high suspension bridge in the dark. "The fuck you doing?" the ligament was shrieking. "You want to get me killed *again*? I been down this road, sweetheart. It don't end well."

"You ever listen to 'Get Runspired'?" Tulley was saying. Pauline had to recalibrate her breathing before she could answer him. Step-step-step-step-*breathe*. Down to four-step breathing. Hold steady, girl. Three-step breathing was borderline. Two-step was critical, a slow jog at best. One-step meant a dead walk, and that wasn't going to happen. She didn't care what kind of pace she kept, but she was going to keep running over this bridge if it killed her. Failure was not an option.

"Rohan Bergonia? All the time," she said. Talking was difficult. Messed up the four-step. Keep the chatter minimal, Pauline. Save your air.

"He had this thing once where he narrated the story of Pheidippides? Did you hear that one?" Tulley said.

"No."

"It was so good. I mean, so inspiring. I listened to the whole thing. It was like thirty minutes, in the middle of the rest of the podcast. You know Pheidippides, right?"

Pauline shook her head. Step-step-step-step-*breathe*.

"Well, he was this runner in ancient Greece. He ran from Athens to Sparta to warn people about the invading Persians. A long-distance dude. Today he'd be an ultramarathoner. And Ironman and shit. He just kept going, that guy. Then, right after he ran another stretch from Marathon to Athens to announce Greek victory, he dropped dead on the spot."

"I don't think I can talk about it."

"Yeah, it was kind of sad. But it might not even be true. A lot of historians say the death part was a myth."

"I mean," she managed. "I don't think. I can talk. At all."

She was trying not to gasp. Her calves burned, and the plantar fasciitis she thought she'd gotten over last summer seemed to be making an encore. She had no idea how she was continuing to move.

"Okay," Tulley said. "So we'll focus. You got this, Pauline. You can do it. I believe in you."

Oh, God. Was that some bullshit solicitousness? Or honest encouragement? She didn't know which would be worse. She sneaked a glance to her right to see Tulley running up the slope, his stride solid, seemingly untouched by this wicked gradient that was starting to feel nearly vertical. If he was patronizing her with that last remark, she'd like to kick him off the side of this damn bridge, watch him get sucked into the river's current and swept out to sea. Take that, you law school prick! But if he was actually offering her a sincere piece of encouragement, then that implied a dangerous level of camaraderie and concern that—Oh, stop it, Pauline. Just stop it.

Don't stop. If she stopped now, even for just the shortest bit of walking, she'd never be able to restart her legs at running pace to get up over the top of the span.

She ran and ran and ran.

To the west, the black Goliath of Jacksonville's Bank of America building commanded the skyline. It made Pauline think about the World Trade Center attack. She'd been attending a business breakfast in a restaurant on the top floor of the Bank of America building at the time of the catastrophe, and as the morning's boggle of realities came crashing down on the rest of America, as it began to slowly dawn on the most powerful nation in the world that it was under attack, Pauline panicked. Someone pulled a TV into the restaurant and they all crowded around it, watching. People started talking, theorizing. Here they were at the top of the Bank of America Tower—a perfect symbol of American wealth and excess. And in Jacksonville! A perfect target—large enough city to make a horrific impact, small enough city to ensure minimalist security measures. Who would attack Jacksonville? Any smart terrorist, someone said. Think of our Navy bases! Think of our shipping! Think of our vulnerability!

In a rush of terror, she fled the restaurant and took the elevator down forty-two floors to the pavement, where she ran to her car and sped to the factory to pick up Johnny. They went home and watched the replay of the towers collapsing.

But there was the Jacksonville Bank of America Tower, still standing rigid and stubborn, casting its shadow over the snaking St. Johns. It hadn't gone anywhere. And neither had she. She didn't know whether this was a good thing or not. Her calves burned. Her foot throbbed. Step-step-step-step-*breathe.* Step-step-step-step-*breathe.* This wasn't going well. She squinted ahead. The peak of the bridge seemed miles away, a green metal mountain, Florida alpine. Get your mind off it, Pauline. Think about something else. Distraction—that was the ticket. She listened to Tulley's feet hitting the pavement beside her, listened to his ragged breathing. So he was feeling it, too. Good.

"Where were you? When you learned? About 9/11?" she managed. Breathe. Breathe. Step. Step.

"Huh," he said. He chuckled.

"What?"

"It's embarrassing. People have asked me that, and I've usually made up a fib."

"Why?"

"I was in bed with someone I should not have been in bed with."

Lord!

He seemed to be waiting for a response. "Oh," was all she could manage.

"She was one of my professors in law school," he said. "We were at this academic conference in Chicago, and we heard people shouting out in the hallway. It was the cleaning staff. They were watching it on a TV in the room next door. That's how I found out about it. In bed with my married professor. Not my finest hour."

Why, in the name of God, was he telling her this? He could simply have said he was in Chicago. In a hotel room. Leave out that salacious little detail; that would have been the right thing to do. But she knew why. Number one, he knew Pauline would assume his bedfellow was older than him. Do the math: He was in his early twenties on 9/11. Any law school professor would have had a good ten years on him, right? Number two, he was letting her know that sleeping with married women was not on his personal list of no-nos. A picture—unbidden, uncontrollable— came to her just then: Sam Tulley in a hotel bed, morning light at the windows, supporting his weight on tanned arms planted on either side of her body—

"Tenth of a mile!" he shouted. "We've got this!" She nearly stumbled. Then she took a deep breath and pushed on. Her lungs felt ready to collapse. Her thighs trembled. Step, gasp, step, gasp. They peaked at the top of the bridge and Pauline thought her legs might buckle. The sun was crashing over the St. Johns now, and a trio of cars, some of the first commuters of the morning, passed them slowly, friendly. One driver beeped and waved. And now it was all easy, just keep your balance, girl, you got this! The steps were coming steady and strong, down the descent, no problem now. Gotta get back over, sure, but she'd walk it on the way back, no matter, you just do it once, that's all you need, then you know you can do it. They ran down the east side of the bridge, and Pauline had the feeling of descending a slope. Of falling, falling, falling.

They were back at the cars, guzzling water and stretching out the cramps, when it got a little weird.

"Listen," Sam Tulley said. "I want to tell you something, Pauline." She grabbed her right foot and brought it up behind her. She looked at him.

"This is a little hard to say," he said. He took a deep breath. "I really like you, Pauline." Pauline dropped her foot and stood still. What was he saying? He looked at her, waiting for a response. Lord! She chose her words carefully.

"Well, I like you too, Sam," she said evenly. She hesitated. "I think we are working together very well."

"No, I mean, there's more than that," he said. More than that? Pauline felt herself getting flustered. Okay, she'd admit it—she'd been enjoying the flirtation; no doubt. It would have been impossible not to. But what was he doing now? Was he seriously coming on to her? This was ridiculous, of course. It was time to put a stop to it.

"Sam," she said. She put her hands up. "I think we should watch what we are saying."

"No, really, Pauline. Let me say this," he said. He wiped a line of sweat from his brow and stood there, pink-faced and breathing hard. "You don't know. Ever since I left Ann Arbor it's been hard, you know? I miss everybody up there. My friends, my family. The people at the law firm—God, all anybody does there is work. We never talk. So, well, anyway—I don't know. We started talking, you and I, and for the first time, I feel like I'm connected to somebody down here, you know?"

"Sam."

"Wait. I just want to say it. We may not see each other after the appeal is over, and I want you to know that you are very important to me." Pauline's heart was pounding. This was crazy! This lawyer-boy, this Ashton Kutcher look-alike—he'd honestly fallen for her? Unreal! She was both shocked and thrilled. Oh, imagine! And bold, too, wasn't he! Imagine the moxie, making a speech like this to a married woman. Well, my word. Okay, now, let him down easy, she told herself. *It wasn't meant to be,* tell him. *I'm married. No, Sam. In the next lifetime, maybe.*

"I mean, when I'm with you, I feel like I'm with my mom," he was saying.

Wait. What?

"What?" She hadn't realized she said that out loud.

"No, really," he said. "You remind me of her so much. I used to run with my mom all the time at home. I really miss that. *Her*—I guess I really miss *her.* So anyway," he sighed. "I guess I'll just say thanks for hanging out with me, Pauline. *Mom.*" He gave a rueful chuckle.

Pauline teetered on a vast cliff of humiliation.

Mom?

Mom?

Well, shee-ut, as Packy would say. Don't that just beat all. Pauline bit her lip. The tears were right there, up close, but she chewed them back and started babbling. She buried her face in a towel under the pretense of wiping sweat, mouth running the whole time. She really had no idea what she was saying to Sam Tulley—something about *Oh, my pleasure, haha, so great to get to know you, your mom must be very proud of you indeed, blah, blah, blah.*

He gave her an awkward and sweaty half-hug and climbed into his car. She waved benevolently—God, the gesture probably looked *matronly*—and climbed into the Prius. She drove back up the Hart and headed east, moving into the sunrise and feeling a hundred years old.

*   *   *

The aches set in later that morning, after her shower. Fire in her thighs, a stabbing pain in her right hip. Her calves tightened up like cantaloupe rinds. She hobbled to the medicine cabinet and took the last three ibuprofen tablets. She'd need more to make it through the day at the factory, that much she knew. That was the bitch of pain—it always showed up even worse later. She checked her watch. It was still early. She could dash to CVS for ibuprofen and be back in time to have a cup of tea—to try to calm down—before taking on the commute to the factory.

"Come on," she said to General San Jose. "You need an outing."

She let the dog jump into the front seat of the Prius and then drove through Watchers Island to the CVS near the bridge. She parked and left the windows cracked open a few inches. "I'll be right back," she told the General. He looked at her, stricken. "I promise," she said. "Two minutes." Good heavens, she thought, looking at him. He was starting to panic. She might as well have been leaving him at a dachshund abattoir. "You'll be fine!" she said. He started to quake and pant. Oh, for God's sake. She locked him in the car and dashed for the store.

The drugstore was crowded. The drugstore was always crowded! Even on an early morning like this one, when you'd think people would be at work, like she should have been, here they all were at CVS, crowding around the pharmacy counter, poking through the cosmetics, fiddling with the self-serve kiosks at the photo center. She found the ibuprofen and selected the *Valu-Size!* bottle. She stood in line at the register and regarded a rack crowded with Halloween paraphernalia: gigantic bags of candy, gummy-looking makeup kits, cheap witch hats, fat plastic pumpkins. God, when was Halloween? Tomorrow? Good Lord.

"I hate Halloween," she said, to no one in particular.

"Tell me about it," the young woman behind her said. Pauline turned around. The woman was wearing a beach sarong and flip-flops with high wedge heels. She had a baby on one hip and a case of beer on the other. "I got three girls at home who want Kardashian costumes, and I'm running out of time. You think I got money for that? Have you seen what those people wear? Damn."

Pauline smiled politely and turned to face forward again. From where she was standing in line she could see out the store's front windows to where the Prius was parked. General San Jose was standing up in the driver's seat, his paws against the steering wheel, looking toward the store. She knew he was probably about to have a heart attack, being left alone like that. It was the General's worst fear: solitude. She could understand it. He bobbed down from the driver's seat and came up again on the passenger's side. Then down again, up in the backseat. Up, down, up, down. He looked like a jack-in-the-box. What a crazy dog.

She checked Scrabble. It was her turn. Corran had played NOW. Now? What did that mean? No telling. Sometimes the words didn't mean anything at all; sometimes they were just words, just something to come up with for the sake of the move when your turn came up. It all depended on the letters you lucked onto. She looked at her selection of letters and spotted a good opportunity. It almost made her smile, but the morning's humiliation and the aching in her legs canceled out the impulse. Still. BUDDY, she played. It's what she used to call Corran when he was little.

C'mon, buddy! Come gimme a hug, buddy! We missed you, buddy!

Well, now that was depressing. Pauline put the phone in her purse. She looked at the Halloween candy. She'd already stocked up at Publix on Twizzlers and Skittles, the kinds of candies she knew she would dutifully hand out to the evening's trick-or-treaters and not be tempted to eat. Because what was the point? Fruit-flavored candy? Please. If she was going to waste calories on candy, you'd better believe it was going to be chocolate. In fact—she plucked two bags of bite-sized Milky Ways out of the bin and waited her turn at the register.

She made it back to the car before the General succumbed to heart failure. "You need to pull yourself together," she said to him. "I mean, really." He pushed himself into her lap and sat there trembling. At home, she carried him back up the stairs and placed him on the bed. He collapsed on the duvet, exhausted with trauma. She left him there and went down to the kitchen, where she followed her plan and forced herself to sit for ten minutes with a cup of tea to calm down before she went to work, though she found herself jiggling her leg maniacally and staring at the clock the entire time. Eight minutes. Nine. Ten. There. All calmed down. Except she wasn't. She caught a glimpse of herself in the black glass reflecting from the microwave. What was that? She tipped up her chin and regarded herself, then got up and moved toward the oval mirror in the hallway. Jowls. She had jowls, suddenly. She hadn't known you could develop jowls overnight. Well, you don't, dummy. They take fifty years. Duh!

She went back to the kitchen. Her cell phone was vibrating, and she picked it up. A text from Sam Tulley: *Hey Mom. Just got word—appeal hearing scheduled. November 15. We've got our work cut out for us.* Pauline stared at the phone.

Johnny, she thought. Please come home.

Something snapped. Before she even realized what she was doing, her iPhone had hit the ceramic backsplash above the stove and had gone madly skittering—in several different pieces—to the four corners of the kitchen. She watched a piece of the glass screen bounce off the range and settle next to her foot. *Well,* she thought mildly. It occurred to her that this might have been something of an out-of-body experience. *I guess I need a new phone now.*

She had no idea what to do next. So she did the only thing she could think of: She drove to the factory to make ice.

SIXTEEN

It was proving difficult to deal with the issue of Corran's disabled bicycle, and the futility of the effort seemed to Johnny to
mirror the futility of this entire foolhardy, impetuous trip to
Scotland. What had possessed him, anyway, flying over here on
a wild hair like this? The past twenty-four hours had been a study
in frustration—last night spent cooped up in the tiny crofter's
cottage thanks to the cold and rain, then this morning wasted
with trying to find Chemal, who'd gone off with a raincoat and
wellies for a walk to the village, got turned around somehow in
the hedgerows lining the road back to the cottage, and had to be
hunted down and fetched by car with Sharon at the wheel and
Johnny spotting from the passenger seat.

And through it all, Corran putting on a forced, strident
cheerfulness that could be interpreted in only one way—he
wanted to be left the hell alone. At Sharon's urging, Corran had
traded shifts with another bloke from the ferry in order to have

a day free for his father's visit, but the adjustment felt like an awkwardly gallant gesture, in Johnny's opinion. He got the feeling Corran would have rather been on the ferry. They kept walking through the cottage, bumping into each other. It was hard to know what to do.

At one point, during a break in the rain, Corran put on his hoodie and went outside. Johnny waited for a few moments, then followed. He found his son squatting on a patch of concrete outside the cottage's toolshed, hunched over a shallow pan of water. Corran had removed the offending inner tube from the bike tire and now was slowly rotating the tube through the water, looking for the telltale bubbles that would locate the leak. He looked up briefly when Johnny approached, but said nothing and returned his attention to the inner tube.

"Find it?" Johnny said.

Corran shook his head. "Not yet." Johnny upturned an empty bucket and sat down on it. A belt of wind came across the croft and rattled the toolshed.

"My God," Johnny said. "You forget the cold here."

Corran glanced at him. "Do you?" It felt like a challenge. Johnny let it slide. He watched Corran slide the tube through the water. Funny method, this. Johnny had picked it up as a young man and had taught it to Corran himself, many years ago. *Watch for the air,* he remembered telling the boy. Now a bright boiling erupted along the seam of the tube, and Corran sat back on his heels.

"Shit," he said. "Not just one leak. Whole seam's separating."

"You're not going to be able to patch that," Johnny said. Corran didn't answer. Johnny watched his son's hands working over the tube, watched as he slid a rough finger into the broken seam. Corran's hands were rough. Weathered. When had his boy become this man? Johnny took a deep breath. "You look good, Corran. You feeling good?"

"You mean am I shooting up, is what you mean," Corran said immediately. "I thought you'd never ask. And the answer is no." Corran glanced around the croft yard and gestured down the hill. "Unfortunately, skag's in short supply around here. Maybe you could find me some in Florida, send it over."

Was this supposed to be funny? Was Corran attempting a joke? Johnny didn't know how to read his son, but he took a step toward playing along. "I wouldn't know where to look for it," he said.

"Ah, it's closer than you think," Corran said. "Always is." He looked at Johnny for a long, uncomfortable beat.

"What?" Johnny said.

"What are you doing here?"

"Came out to see if I could help you with the tire."

"Not here in this spot. Here in Scotland."

"Ah," Johnny said. "Well." He took a breath. "I thought we should fix it up. Mend the fence, aye?"

Corran stood up. He tossed the wrecked tube into a trash can just inside the toolshed.

"Yep," he said. "Right. Done." He tipped up the rubber pan and let the water run across the concrete. He brushed his hands off and stuffed them into his pockets, then took a step toward the house. "Head in?"

"Wait a minute."

"You said you were cold."

"I mean this, Corran. I'd like to settle up here."

"Yep, brilliant. Done deal. Let's go in."

"I don't think you're taking me seriously. And I can tell you're angry with me. I wish you could let it go."

Corran gave a short laugh. "Look," he said. "I hate to break this to you. But I've had some other shit going on this year. I haven't had a whole lot of time to be mad at *you*." He walked toward the house and stopped midway, then turned back to Johnny. "Sorry you came all this way. You needn't have." Corran disappeared into the cottage. Johnny looked at the rivulets of water, already starting to crystallize on the concrete. He rose and slowly followed his son back inside.

By midday, Sharon said they had to get out of the cottage. "Blooming barmy, we're driving each other," she said. So after lunch they'd all piled into the Polo. They managed, incredibly, to maneuver Lucy's bulky car seat into the middle of the backseat and to still have just enough room for Corran and Sharon to squeeze in on either side. Johnny didn't understand why Lucy had a car seat if Corran didn't even have a car, but when he asked the question Corran was brusque: "Sometimes my sitter takes her places. And then we need a seat." Well, all righty then. Johnny took shotgun, with Chemal at the wheel. "I guess I'll stop asking stupid questions," he muttered. No one answered.

"We're on a quest," Sharon said lightly. "For a tire tube. How lovely."

"We shall be victorious," Chemal intoned. "*Quieres practicar tu español*, Miss Sharon?"

"I don't know what you just said," Johnny said. He held up his hands. "But *no*."

"*Dios mio*," Chemal said. "*Lo siento.*" He raised his eyebrows and exchanged a look in the rearview mirror with Sharon, and then he backed up to turn the car around. They drove in silence down the long road along the loch toward the ferry, only the occasional "Pah!" rising brightly from the backseat.

The mood improved a bit after the bracing ferry crossing and the pleasant distraction of pointing out a trio of bobbing seals to Lucy across the boat's railing, but hours later they were still coming up empty-handed in the tire tube department, and Johnny was getting tired of the search. By late afternoon, they'd been to the bike shop in Fort William, which was out of stock, and then all the way to a five-and-dime near Glencoe, which didn't carry bike parts. Google pointed to an outfitter's shop in Inverlochy that *might* carry tubes, according to the sullen clerk in the five-and-dime, but it was—ridiculously—open only on Saturdays. Which meant once Johnny, Sharon, and Chemal went back to Dunedin with the car on Wednesday, Corran would have no wheels with which to get Lucy to her sitter or himself to his job. He'd be resigned to walking every day with the stroller, which was a pretty tough prospect—a good four-mile hike round-trip, and the forecast was calling for snow. It was a problem. But not one that couldn't be easily solved. And Johnny aimed to solve it, if only to salvage a bit of productivity from a trip that was beginning to reek of failure.

The trouble was that Corran was still acting as if there was no trouble. He was artificially lively, courteous to the point of obsequiousness. Jaunty. Jokey. He had to know that Johnny had come to Port Readie with an olive branch, but he was stubbornly refusing to acknowledge the significance of his father's visit. In fact, he'd evidently scuttled the value of his relationship with his father down to approximately the same level as one he might have with a necessarily proximal but slightly annoying neighbor. Like Jerry, Johnny thought. The realization was as maddening

as it was humiliating. Worse, it neatly undercut Johnny's plan
to launch a discussion that in any way implied reconciliation.
Corran's attitude made it clear: There was nothing to reconcile.
No need to bother.

Now they were sitting in a chippie's just outside Fort William, trying to warm up. The heat in the rented Polo was ham-
strung by a stuck blower motor, and after a day spent running
into and out of shops, they were all feeling the chill, so they'd
headed into the chip shop for a cuppa. They squeezed into a tiny
booth along the front window. Johnny assessed the tableau: Corran was humming and staring at his cell phone across the table;
Chemal was feeding Lucy bits of biscuit from a plastic baggie;
Sharon was rummaging in Lucy's diaper bag. She fished out a
bottle and wiggled from the booth, then asked to use the microwave in the back to warm the bottle. Lucy's cheeks were pink and
her eyes were bright. God, she was a sweet little bairn. Johnny
made a face. She grinned. Johnny caught Corran watching him.

"It's gone Baltic, of a sudden," Sharon said, returning with
the bottle. She rubbed her shoulders. "We should have brought
Lucy another sweater."

"*Sí,*" Chemal said. "*Hace frío.*"

"*Sí, amigo!*" Sharon said, delighted. *"Yo comprendo!"*

Johnny looked at Corran and rolled his eyes, hoping for
commiseration. Corran looked away. In the booth behind Johnny,
two women were chatting.

"My husband can fish a little," one was saying. "But it
doesn't come second nature to him. Not like my first husband,
who died. *He* could fish."

"What's a saveloy?" Chemal said, squinting up at the menu
board behind the counter.

"You hungry again?" Johnny said.

"I could eat," Chemal said defensively. "Don't you ever get hungry?"

In fact, the smell of fried food was making Johnny a bit nauseated, but he decided against mentioning it. It wasn't going to improve anything.

"What's a saveloy?" Chemal said again.

"Sausage," Sharon said.

"Pig brain sausage," Corran said. He grinned.

"No way," Chemal said. He looked horrified. And fascinated.

"Corran, stop it," Sharon said.

"It's true," Corran said. "Pig brains."

"Not anymore, love," Sharon said to Chemal. "That was the old days."

"My God," Chemal said. "That shit would *not* fly in Detroit."

"Just get cod and chips," Sharon said. "You can't go wrong."

"I'll wait," Chemal said. "I've lost my appetite."

"Can you please keep your voice down?" Johnny said.

Chemal sighed. "Yes, Mr. Freeze," he whispered.

"It's a little disappointing," the woman behind Johnny was saying. "There's just something about a man that can fish, am I right?" He pivoted and pretended to scratch his shoulder to get a look at her. She had one of those asymmetrical haircuts he could never understand. You'd think you'd feel off balance. "Your John can fish," the woman said to her companion. "*You* know what I mean. Am I right?"

Johnny checked his phone for messages. Seeing none, he texted Roy. *How ye doon?* he wrote. The waitress came, and they were all absorbed for a time with the liturgy of the tea.

"All right," Johnny said finally. "Now, look. Let's just go back to the bike shop. We'll buy a new bicycle." It certainly seemed a reasonable plan to him. After all, he'd looked at the bike Corran had been using and was astounded it was still operational at all; it was rusted, busted, dented, and battered. The flat tire seemed the least of its failings.

"That's daft," Corran said lightly. "I don't need a new bicycle. I just need a tube." He sipped his tea and grinned at Johnny across the teacup. Johnny grasped for patience. Was his son difficult just for the sake of it, or what?

"Well, you're not going to get a tube today," he said. "And so you're in a pickle. How about a bike?"

Corran shook his head. "No, thanks," he said. "I'll try to patch the tube."

"How would we get a bicycle back to the house?" Sharon said. "Would it fit in the car?"

"We can fit it in the trunk. We'll tie it in," Johnny said.

"I don't need a bicycle," Corran said again. "No worries, Da."

"How are you going to tote a baby four miles a day?" Johnny said.

"I'll figure something out."

"That's fucking potty," Johnny said.

"Watch your language," Sharon said. "This poor baby," she sighed.

"Seriously," Chemal said. He looked sternly at Johnny. Johnny's phone buzzed on the table. He picked it up and looked at Roy's return text.

Another day in paradise. When you back?

Thursday, he typed. *What's going on?*

Beer bottle caps on the ops floor. Pissing me off.

Go get 'em, Roy.

They're going to wish they hadn't done that. How's your head?

Still attached. How's OSHA?

Call Pauline . . . Roy texted. Johnny watched the three dots blinking in the text field. Roy was still typing: *appeal scheduled.*

Shit! The hearing was scheduled? Why hadn't Pauline called him? And why, in the name of God, did this sudden jolt forward in the whole OSHA mess have to happen while Johnny was in Scotland, just as Pauline had feared it would? He wasn't sure what was more upsetting—the knowledge that the appeal hearing was finally on the docket, or the knowledge that Pauline herself was in possession of this information and had yet to call him with it. She was furious, no doubt. And she was right—the trip had been terrible timing. A terrible idea all around, in fact. She was always right.

When? he wrote to Roy.

November 15.

Pauline okay?

I think you better ask her that, Roy wrote.

"Iceman, you are texting like a prom queen over there, dude," Chemal said. Johnny pocketed his phone. "Sorry," he said.

"And you lecture *me* about my manners."

"I don't lecture you about your manners," Johnny said. "I lecture you about wasting your life."

"Chemal, too?" Corran said. "My, you're expanding the effort." This he said with an annoying grin on his face. Johnny held Corran's gaze for a beat. Then he got up and walked outside the chip shop to call Pauline. Still no answer on her cell. He called the factory, and Rosa put him through to Pauline's office.

"November 15?" he said immediately when she picked up the phone.

"Yep," she answered. "Right after your surgery. Nice, huh?" She didn't sound angry. She sounded sad.

"Why didn't you call me?"

"Broke my phone," she said, which hardly seemed an adequate reason. He didn't press it.

"I wonder if we can get a postponement," he said instead.

"No dice. Already asked." There was an off-putting tone of resignation in her voice, something Johnny could not remember hearing before.

"But are we going to be ready?"

She didn't answer right away, and he was afraid he'd lost the connection. "No," she said finally. "We're not."

"Hasn't Tulley gotten anything together yet? Some sort of argument? He shouldn't be sitting around looking at work logs, for God's sake. He should be pressing the police to bust the druggies, get us some documentation of meth-making."

"That's nice," she said.

"What?"

"You got his name right."

"Pauline," he said, frustrated. "You don't seem exactly plugged in here. You sound like you're giving up."

"I am."

"You can't."

"Why can't I?" she demanded. "You're not here to help me fight this. And even when you get here you're down for the count, am I right? Let's be realistic. We don't have it in us right now to fight this thing. Neither one of us. We don't have the evidence. And we don't have the energy to find it. Bottom line: We failed."

"I'll be back in two days," he said.

"I'll be waiting for you," she said. Her voice caught. "And so will the surgeon. And when we get you past this, Johnny, I swear to heaven, we've got to figure out what we're going to *do*. About money. The ice plant is going under. It's over."

She sounded like a different Pauline. He'd never heard her so defeated. He told her to keep the faith. And he told her to get the damn lawyers to put more pressure on the police. He hung up the phone. A tidal wave of panic swept over him. The ice plant. God damn it, OSHA! The *ice plant*! They couldn't lose it. It was their livelihood. With the house remortgaged to pay for Corran's rehabilitation expenses, the only equity they had was in the ice plant. If the federal government wiped them out with fines and foreclosure, where would they be? And if the fingerlike growths were real, and if they continued their wicked march until Johnny was dead and gone—which could happen sooner rather than later, according to what Johnny had read about brain cancer—then where would *Pauline* be? My God. Pauline. She'd be penniless and alone, that's where. Right back where Johnny started.

And whose fault was all of this? Johnny stood on the freezing street in Fort William and looked back through the window of the chip shop, where Corran sat bantering lightly with Chemal. Corran's words from earlier in the day came back to him: *Sorry you came all this way, Da. You needn't have.* Oh, Corran, he thought. You're on the thinnest ice you've ever been on, laddie. Johnny banged back into the chip shop and sat down at the table again.

"How's Pauline?" Sharon said.

"Fine." Sharon's face tightened. He could tell she was reading the fury in his voice, but he didn't care. He stared at

Corran relentlessly until his son finally looked up and caught Johnny's eye.

"Let's go back to the shop and get a bicycle," Johnny said.

"Let's not," Corran said. "And while we're at it, let's back the fuck off." He stirred his tea. Johnny had an impulse to reach across the table and slap him. Sharon lightly kicked Johnny under the table. He looked at her and she shook her head. She was reading his mind. Damn it, Sharon! Do you always know everything? She shook her head again and glared at him. *We got him out of Easterhouse, Sharon,* he wanted to say. *And look at the thanks we get.*

"I think we're finished here," she said pointedly. "And I think it's time to get Lucy back for a nap."

Chemal leaned in and spoke in a conspiratorial whisper to the rest of them: "The ladies back here," he said. "Can't stop talking about fish. It's *weird.*"

They finished their tea in silence and bundled into the Polo for the long ride back to Corran's cottage. On the way, the freezing rain returned. Johnny remembered once having a conversation with Pauline about freezing rain.

"Isn't that the same thing as hail?" she'd said.

"No," he said. "Hail's already frozen. This is in the *process* of freezing. It doesn't crystallize until it makes contact with something. Happens all the time in Scotland."

She looked at him. "So over there you have snow, and hail, and freezing rain."

"Yes."

"And sleet, whatever that is."

"Yep."

She shook her head. "Lord, I don't know how you survived it as long as you did," she said. He clenched his jaw at the memory of that conversation. *Ah, Pauline. Florida girl. The world, for you, has been nothing but warm.* How he wished he could keep it so. Chemal took a turn rather abruptly and Johnny's stomach swiveled. He put his head in his hands. Keep it together, Ice. You ain't dying. Not today, brother. Not today.

Sharon and Chemal worked up an early dinner with a packet of curry and a bag of frozen chicken breasts they'd picked up at the Tesco in Fort William. Johnny found it hard to eat. He was too angry, for one thing. Plus, the nausea from the steroids had yet to abate, and in fact he was wondering if it was getting worse. He was, however, managing to ingest quite a quantity of Tennent's lager. Which might not have been such a great idea.

The problem with alcohol, Johnny had learned, wasn't that it muddled you up. On the contrary—the problem was that it was a *clarifying* agent. At least, that's how it worked with him. There you were, for ten whole months, all mixed up with anger and grief and regret and hope and fear and guilt and love, and what happens after you knock back several cans of Tennent's lager on one rotten evening in the cramped confines of a Highland crofter's cottage? The whole shooting match resolves itself into one pulsing hot beat of . . . well, basically, batshit fury. At Corran. For fuck's sake. Examine the facts, he said to himself. Johnny had tried hard to come to terms with, and even edge toward forgiveness for, the unspeakable theft of Pauline's ring. He had dropped everything, including a massive crisis at the factory, to travel over here, against doctor's orders and against Pauline's wishes, to attempt a reconciliation with Corran, and what did he get for his trouble? A bunch of sarcastic fucking lip from a thirty-year-old man who was behaving like a spoiled adolescent. *That's some chip you got on your shoulder there, Corran,* he wanted to say. *I don't know how you can handle the weight of it.* Never in his life had Johnny seen someone so stubborn. Oh, he got the picture: Corran was as defiant as ever about Pauline's ring. And in his defiance, no matter how badly he needed help, Corran was not going to accept a lick of it from Johnny.

But a bicycle! A fucking bicycle! What was the big deal? It was October. Corran was actually planning to live up here in the Highlands all winter without a car or a bicycle, and with a nine-month-old baby to care for? It was ridiculous. And *inconsiderate,* the way he was putting all this pressure on Sharon every weekend to come up here and help him. Unbelievable.

And. Also. How on *earth* did Corran think he was justified in being so resentful of Johnny? What had Johnny ever done to anger him so? Think of it: Johnny had covered every expense his son had ever incurred growing up and even well into Corran's adulthood, including all that wretchedly expensive rehab! When other people Johnny's age were talking about retirement accounts and investments, Johnny was signing promissory notes against his home to pay for methadone and group therapy. And yes, great, Corran was clean now, but do you think he'd credit any of Johnny's efforts for *that?* Ah, no. Corran was an island unto himself. *I can do it by myself!* Just like when he was a little toddling kid. He'd fly solo, by God. Yes, St. Corran did the whole thing all on his lonesome. Heroin? Not a problem. Cold turkey as soon as he saw his little daughter. A beautiful story. Bye-bye, drugs. What a wonderful young man. And so *independent!*

Johnny told himself not to drink any more beer. He was sitting at the kitchen table. He spent some time on his iPhone trying to figure out if he could get his and Chemal's flight changed to go home earlier, but had no luck. He would have even paid the airline's exorbitant change fees, but there were no seats available on an earlier flight. Well, fine. Today was Monday. They couldn't fly till Thursday. He'd talk to Sharon as soon as he got a moment alone with her, tell her he'd decided to cut his losses here in Port Readie; they could ride back to Dunedin tomorrow. She could get back to work and he and Chemal would just kill some time in Glasgow for a couple of days, maybe ride up and have a look at Stirling Castle. Play tourists. Eat wine gums. Try not to think about brain surgery. He opened one more beer. Last one.

It wasn't even six o'clock yet, but Johnny had the feeling it was the middle of the night. In the living room, where everyone else was sitting, the TV flickered with something or other, a house decorating program, it seemed, but the volume was turned down and it didn't appear that anyone was watching. He picked up his beer, then walked over and turned the television off.

"Play us some music, Corran," he said. He gestured at the keyboard in the corner of the room and then lowered himself a bit unsteadily onto the sofa next to Sharon, who had the baby on her lap. She was teaching Lucy patty-cake. Chemal was on the floor at their feet. Corran was slouched in a chair across the room.

"What?" Corran said.

"The keyboard. Play us something. You still play, right?"

"Oh, Corran plays beautifully," Sharon said to Chemal, who nodded appreciatively.

"Nah," Corran said. He shrugged. "I don't really play."

"Oh, you do!" Sharon said. "Go on, Corry."

Corran didn't move.

"He's being modest," Sharon said to Chemal. "You should hear him play. He used to do recitals, everything. And then he was in bands. He's wonderful."

"I hardly play, Mum," Corran said.

"I got you started on that," Johnny said. He knew he was drunk, but he didn't care. He *did* get Corran started on piano. He knew he did! That day in the Jacksonville Airport. The *Moonlight Sonata*.

"I got you started," he said again.

"You did not," Corran said quietly.

"I did. I saw you loved it, so I told Mum. And I sent the money for lessons. Didn't I, Sharon?"

Sharon had stopped playing patty-cake with Lucy. She was staring at Johnny. "It was a long time ago, Johnny," she said. She was giving him a *look*.

"I'd love to hear you play," Chemal offered.

"Sorry, mate," Corran said. "I'm rusty."

"I got you started," Johnny said. The room was silent.

And then: "You wrote a check, Ice," Corran said. "Anybody can write a check." Johnny had never heard his son call him that before.

"Not anybody," he replied. "Not *you*." Corran looked away.

"Play the *Moonlight Sonata*," Johnny said.

"I don't know it."

"I bet you do."

Corran shrugged. Sharon got up off the sofa. "I wish you two would stop it," she said. She walked Lucy into the kitchen.

"I dare you to play the *Moonlight Sonata*," Johnny said. Corran was silent. "I know you can play it," Johnny said.

"I can't."

"I know you can." The Tennent's was rushing around in Johnny's head. He imagined it marinating the tumor. *(Cyst!)* Go ahead, he said to the cyst. Get yourself pickled. I sure am. "You can do it, Corran. You've had training. We got you out of Easterhouse, and you had the kind of life where you had *piano lessons*. Not everybody gets that, laddie. Did you know that? Not everybody gets out of the schemes."

Corran still didn't reply.

"I'll give you a hundred pounds right now," Johnny said to Corran, "if you'll play the *Moonlight Sonata*."

"No."

"Two hundred."

"No."

"I'll give you a thousand pounds."

"Johnny, stop it," Sharon said. She was standing at the threshold of the kitchen, Lucy on her hip.

"Dude," Chemal said to Corran. "Do it. *I'd* do it."

Johnny stood up. He walked over and stood next to Corran's chair. "I'll give you five thousand pounds," he said, looking down at his son, "if you'll get up off your ass right now and walk across the floor to that keyboard, right there, and play Beethoven's fucking *Moonlight Sonata*."

"Put your superhero cape back into your suitcase, Da," Corran said. "I don't need to be rescued."

"You sure about that, Corran?" Johnny said.

"Johnny," Sharon said. Her face was flushed. "You're being childish."

"Imagine the formula you could buy," Johnny said. "Imagine the diapers."

Corran stared at him.

"Wow, Iceman," Chemal said. "Jeez."

"Stop it," Sharon said. She was starting to cry. "Would you stop it?"

"Play the *Moonlight Sonata*," Johnny said. "And I'll write you a check."

The room fell silent, save the sound of the pattering rain on the rooftop. Oh, why was he doing this? Johnny looked at his son—those round, brown eyes, that broad, open face. *Let me in, Corran,* he thought, *and quick, before I die.*

"Play it," he said. He willed his voice not to crack.

"No," Corran said slowly. "I don't know how to play it." He stood up. He walked over to Sharon and took Lucy from her. He went into his bedroom, closing the door softly behind him. And then Johnny was left with his Tennent's empties, with Chemal's downcast face, and with the sounds of Sharon's crying from somewhere that seemed far, far away.

A reasonable man would probably have called it a night right there. But for Johnny, reason, along with logic and temperance, had left the building somewhere around an hour ago. He looked at his watch: six-ten. He opened the browser on his iPhone and checked Google: The bike shop stayed open until seven. If they hit the ferry just right, they'd make it.

"Driver," he said to Chemal. "Tonight, we ride."

"You're being a bastard, Johnny," Sharon said, sniffling.

"Oh, come on, Sharon," he said. "Let she who is without sin cast—"

"Oh, piss," she snapped. She wiped her eyes with a paper napkin. "I don't know where you're going, and I don't care. But don't you dare wake that wee one when you come back in here." She walked to the couch and started pulling at the cushions. She turned around. "And Chemal, you drive safe. You're evidently the adult tonight."

"Yes, ma'am, Miss Sharon," Chemal said.

Johnny and Chemal left the cottage and drove toward the ferry in silence. A few miles down the road, the rain let up. Johnny opened the sunroof.

"You wasted?" Chemal said finally.

"Not wasted," Johnny said. "But a bit off, I'd say."

He put his head back on the seat and looked up at the sky. Here and there, the clouds parted and presented a glimpse of stars clearer and brighter than any Johnny could recall seeing in Florida. Well, it made sense. They were farther north. Forget that tropical bullshit. Caledonia! Higher up! Closer to the heavens, wasn't that right? He thought of something else then.

"You know about Voyager 1?" he asked Chemal.

"Oh, yeah, I saw a show about that once," Chemal said. "That shit is awesome."

"You know it's gone now?" A few years ago, when the Voyager 1 space probe ended its thirty-five-year jaunt around the solar system and entered interstellar space, NASA overlooked the occurrence for some time and didn't announce it for more than a year. Johnny found the delay emotionally bothersome in a way he could not have anticipated. After all, he had paid attention to Voyager 1, all those years.

How could he not? It had been launched on the day of his father's death. He remembered it vividly. Johnny and his mother sat in metal chairs next to Charlie's hospital bed and watched the BBC news coverage on a color television mounted on the wall. The probe was fitted to an expendable rocket and propelled into the atmosphere against the stunning blue backdrop of a Florida sky. Johnny was riveted, both by the technological wizardry of the process and by the glimpses of exotic terrain around Cape Canaveral. Fat palm trees with heads like pyrotechnics. Spindly pines sprouting from wide swaths of sandy brown earth. And everywhere that blue, blue sky. It was Johnny's first picture of Florida. When the rocket ignited and Voyager lifted off, it seemed to Johnny that the whole place was on fire, that the entire world must have felt the heat. Johnny and his mother watched until the rocket was a distant spark. Then they turned to Charlie, who was gone.

Johnny's adolescent mind had created an unbreakable link between his father's spirit and the wandering of the Voyager 1 probe. When it stopped to observe Jupiter, Johnny felt Charlie was there. When it stopped to collect radiation from Saturn, Charlie was there. And now Voyager 1 had crossed over, had left the solar system for the uncharted mysteries of the interstellar medium beyond. It was the farthest human-made object from Earth, far beyond the reach of our understanding, past the safety and comfort of our known stars. In another decade, the instruments would fail, in another two decades the probe would run out of power. Charlie died at thirty-five years old. He'd barely gotten started. But when Voyager crossed over it was like Charlie died all over again. And now he would float in the Milky Way, untended, forever.

Johnny closed the sunroof. He took out his phone and squinted at the keypad. God, the numbers were so hard to *see*. Pauline's iPhone was broken—he remembered that, somehow. What was their home phone number? He thumbed at the contacts.

"Are you calling Mrs. MacKinnon?" Chemal said.

"I was thinking about it," Johnny said.

"I may make a suggestion here," Chemal said.

"Go, kidda."

"This may not be your finest hour, Iceman."

Johnny looked at him for a long moment. Then he nodded. "You're a mate, Chemal," he said. "A real mate."

Chemal grinned. Johnny put the phone into his pocket.

When they got back to the bike shop in Fort William, Johnny bought a new bicycle—just a basic model, nothing crazy—and a fine new baby seat for Lucy. On a whim, he threw in a pretty little baby's helmet decorated with jumping pink frogs. And a reflective safety plate for the back fender. And a cargo basket. There. Problem solved.

They were too late for the last ferry. They had to drive the north route along the loch, which seemed to take forever. Johnny dozed a bit, and Chemal drove quietly. When they finally got back to the cottage Johnny left the bicycle parked directly outside the front door, where Corran couldn't possibly miss it in the morning. He put the bike accessories in the toolshed. They crept back into the warmth of the cottage. Chemal dropped down onto his makeshift bed. Johnny went into the bathroom and peed on a sugar strip. He swallowed four ibuprofen tablets. The hangover

was going to be a crippler. He crept back to the living room and
crawled into bed next to Sharon, who was still as stone, though
he had a feeling she wasn't sleeping.

"Dude.

"Dude.

"Dude."

Johnny opened his eyes. Chemal was standing over him.

"It's, like, almost nine o'clock, dude. You gonna get up?"
The last Johnny looked at his watch it had been three-thirty a.m.,
and he'd been in such despair over being unable to fall asleep
that he had been considering taking the Polo for a drive along
the loch. He talked himself out of it on the grounds that he was,
one, still drunk; and two, still a seizure risk. Well, at least he
had some sense. And then evidently he'd fallen asleep, because
here it was mid-morning, with a dull misty light pushing into
the cottage's front window and the faint smell of toast in the air.
He sat up. The headache hit him like a brick, and he groaned.

"Shouldn'ta drank so much," Chemal said. He was shaking
his head. "I mean, *seriously*."

"Where is everyone?" Johnny said.

"Miss Sharon took Lucy for a walk. Corran went to work."

Johnny dragged himself out of the sofa-bed and stumbled
to the bathroom. More ibuprofen. Fistfuls of tap water. Deep
breath. He looked at himself in the mirror. Get some tea in you.
You'll make it. He plunged himself into an icy cold shower and
waited for the water to warm just a little, then he dressed and
returned to the living room. He walked to the cottage's front
window and peered out to the walkway.

The bicycle was sitting just where he'd left it last night. *Nicely done, Corran,* Johnny thought. *Game, set, match.* Johnny sat down at the table. He managed some tea and toast and sat still until he started to feel slightly more human.

"We ought to go back to Dunedin today," he said to Chemal.

Chemal shook his head. He had a mouthful of toast. "We can't. Miss Sharon told Corran to cancel his babysitter today. We're watching Lucy. Since we were all gonna be here anyway. You missed the whole conversation this morning."

Johnny looked over at the rumpled sofa-bed and imagined himself lying there in a dead sleep while Sharon and Corran held a powwow over schedules and child care. He could only imagine what else they might have had to say this morning. About *him,* for example. He took another sip of tea. Well, it didn't matter. Yes, he was hungover, and yes, he was more than a little rueful about the bullishness of his behavior last night. But did it set the scales back to even? Not by a long shot. And if he'd had any doubt, the sight of the bicycle on the walkway this morning eliminated it. The battle wasn't resolved. But it was over. Johnny was *done.*

"Then tomorrow," he said to Chemal. "First thing. We'll go back to Sharon's, aye? Flight home on Thursday."

"Hey, Iceman," Chemal said. "You know we're flying home on Halloween? That's not a bad omen or anything, is it?"

Johnny didn't answer. He closed the sofa-bed and washed the breakfast dishes. Chemal bundled up and wandered off through the misty morning to explore the hills behind the house. Johnny thought about calling Pauline, but it was still too early in Florida. Pauline would be asleep. After a half hour, Sharon still hadn't returned with the baby, and Johnny thought he might text her, but then he saw that she'd left her cell phone on the

334 Laura Lee Smith

kitchen counter. He picked it up and looked at it. A text from Toole: *I'm lost,* it said. Johnny put the phone down. Did Toole mean figuratively? Or literally? It was a little disconcerting. But none of his business.

He put on his jacket and borrowed a pair of Corran's gloves from a basket by the front door. He went outside and got on the new bicycle, then rode it down the hill, along the narrow winding road fronting Loch Linnhe. By the time he reached the village, his eyes were watering and his lungs aching from the cold. He felt like he was in the ice factory. At a curve in the road about a quarter-mile from the ferry ramp, he pulled the bicycle down to a rocky beach and stood looking across the loch. The ferry was headed for the opposite bank. Johnny squinted his eyes and watched the three yellow jackets of the ferry crew pacing around the deck. After a moment, he identified Corran. Last night's fury stumbled a bit. His son looked so small. And so distant.

In a year's time, Johnny wondered, where would they all be? If he was honest, he knew that statistics painted a fairly predictable picture: There was a good chance Corran would relapse into heroin use. He couldn't keep up this bizarre hermitlike exile forever, not with a child to raise. At some point he'd end up back in the city, with ready access to all his old skag friends. And if Corran relapsed, there was a good chance that Sharon's heart would finally break, and that she'd throw in the towel, and that little Lucy would go to foster care. And there was more: There was a good chance Toole would lose his mind. There was a good chance Pauline would be in the poorhouse. There was a good chance Johnny would be dead. *You have the potential to have cancer. Don't we all have that, Dr. Tosh? Yes. You just have more of it, friend.*

The ferry horn sounded as it approached the opposite landing. Corran walked to the front of the ferry and stood with a rope.
A song, unbidden, presented itself to Johnny.

Oh, Danny boy, the pipes, the pipes are calling.
From glen to glen, and down the mountainside.
The summer's gone, and all the roses falling.
It's you, it's you must go, and I must bide.

The boat's bow bumped against a row of pilings. Corran
lassoed a stanchion. He steadied himself on the ferry deck for
the impact. Then he disappeared behind a lorry on the ferry
deck, and Johnny looked down. The loch was a deep, deep black.
Here at the edge, though, the water clarified and danced over
fist-sized stones worn smooth and round. Johnny bent down. He
took off the gloves and dipped his hands into the water, holding
them there until his bones started to ache. He fingered a stone
and imagined it had originated on the beach in Watchers Island,
imagined that he himself had launched it eastward, years ago, for
Corran to find. Could the boy not have just admitted to stealing
the ring? It would have been a start, wouldn't it? They could have
begun to build something again. They could have been honest
with each other. *I'm sorry I took the ring,* Corran could have said.
I'm sorry I wasn't a better da, Johnny could have said. *I got you
out of Easterhouse. But I could have done so much more.* Well, we
were almost there, Corran, he thought. But almost counts only
in horseshoes.

But when ye come, and all the flowers are dying,
If I am dead, as dead I well may be,

Ye'll come and find the place where I am lying,
And kneel and say an Ave there for me.

All right now, enough of that! Get it together, Ice. He stood up and wiped his hands on his pants. He put the gloves back on. Nothing good at the end of that road. Maudlin old ditty, let it go. It was like he told the boys on the ice floor when they started kvetching about the work and the cold: Buck up, grow a pair, show some fortitude! And for God's sake, he told himself now, change the channel. You can't save him.

The floaters appeared out of nowhere, and for a split second Johnny worried that he was about to have another seizure, but when he recognized the feeling as his own long-familiar anger returning, he was both relieved and galvanized. He'd tried to fix all of this. And he'd failed. To hell with everything. He stood next to the new bicycle; he put one hand on the seat and the other between the handlebars. He picked up the bike and executed a half-turn to build up momentum, and then he pitched the bicycle through a long slow arc into the dark swirling waters of Loch Linnhe. In seconds, it was gone.

Time to go, pal. Time to go. Back to the cottage, and keep your head down, fella. Game over. Two more days. Call it a draw, and give Corran a wide berth, wide as you can in that saltbox cottage. That's the way he wants it. You got this, Ice. You know what to do. Just wait it out until tomorrow, then load up the Polo and move 'em out. Tomorrow they'd go back to Dunedin. Thursday, on to Jacksonville. He'd be home with Pauline in time to pass out Halloween candy to the trick-or-treaters on Watchers Island. No tricks, kids, please. No tricks. Next stop: craniotomy.

The heavy mist was turning to snow right before Johnny's eyes. He watched the crystals settling on his jacket. Then he looked back at the ferry across the loch, and at the bright yellow spot that was Corran's jacket. And here it was, he realized: water again. Corran was on one side, burning and distant and irritated. Johnny was on the other, damp and cold and lost. Which meant they were in exactly the same position they'd been in three days ago, two men standing on opposite shores, and neither one knowing how to swim.

Oh Danny boy, oh Danny boy, I love you so.

Johnny turned and started up the hill. It looked like a long walk.

It wasn't Chemal's fault, they would tell him afterward. Not *at all.* You did the best you could, mate. It was unavoidable. It was these tourists from the Continent, God's sake, these Europeans! They come over and they're not used to the left-hand drive, not paying a whit of attention. They drift over and there we are— happens all the time, mate. We're left to be the ones on our toes. My God, how many Scots have to *die* in these head-on muck-ups on country lanes? You did the best you could, mate.

It was Wednesday morning. The Polo was packed with luggage and with Lucy's collapsed stroller. They'd been coming down from the croft, along the tiny lane hugging the loch: Chemal at the wheel, Corran riding surly shotgun, Johnny and Sharon flanking Lucy's baby seat in the back. They'd gotten Lucy's seat buckled in but then couldn't fit their hands into the small space that was left to buckle their own. But no matter. They weren't going far. Sharon had orchestrated the details: They'd drop Lucy at Margaret's and leave Corran at the ferry on their way back to Dunedin. That way he'd only have to walk with the stroller *one* way today, not *both* ways. Johnny would have liked to suggest that perhaps Corran could do with a bicycle. But he held his tongue.

At any rate, the collision happened fast. The driver of the oncoming car was on the right side of the road. Which was the *wrong* side of the road, no doubt a just momentary lapse of reason but nonetheless a damnable offense, considering the consequences. It was a Range Rover; Johnny caught the familiar logo veering close—oh, God, too close! Had the two cars not met on such a tight curve, Chemal might have had time to correct. But with visibility obscured by the rising hillside, and with the damned other driver *on the wrong side,* the impact was inevitable.

Chemal swerved, but too late. The Range Rover caught the Polo's back fender and gave it a mighty wallop, enough to scuttle it down the steep embankment and launch it into a sideways roll toward the icy waters of Loch Linnhe. Johnny had the sensation that they were flying, and indeed they might have been, but then the shock of cold water rushed across his face and he turned his head to see a chaos of limbs, shoulders, he couldn't tell who was who—there was Chemal and there was Sharon and there was Corran. There was a baby's blanket. There were air bags erupting. There was a galaxy of glass shards and the sickening noise of metal on rock. Johnny was thrown toward the front seat.

The car came to a stop in the loch's pebbly shallows, pointing nose-first toward the road whence it came. A gasping cluster of bodies climbing; Johnny cleared the car and stood up in waist-high water. He staggered a few steps, then looked back. Though the front of the car was jutting up and the front seat was mostly clearing the water, the back of the car was becoming submerged. He counted: Corran, Sharon, Chemal.

Lucy.

Sharon was screaming about the car seat, about straps and buckles. Johnny struggled back toward the Polo through the frigid water, stumbling once and going down, then fighting his way back up. The car was losing purchase against the shifting rocks. Johnny reached one side just as Corran reached the other. Their eyes met across the car's roofline, and the thin line of panic that bound them then was like an electric jolt.

The Polo's rear end was filling with water, and Lucy, strapped in her car seat, was kicking her legs in abject panic. Her eyes were wide, her mouth pursed into a small pink button. On Johnny's side of the car, the back window was open a few inches. He pulled on the pane of glass, trying to snap it, but it wouldn't give. He moved back and kicked at it until it caved in. But now the car slid backward a few feet, then a few more, and then the backseat was fully underwater. Johnny dived. He pushed his shoulders through the car's open window, seeing the white of Lucy's skin ghostlike through the brown water. He reached for the buckle on the car seat's T-strap but couldn't find the plastic button to depress the release. His fingers were tangling in Lucy's sweater. *Don't inhale, baby, don't!* Where was the button? Corran was now on the opposite side of the baby seat. He knelt over Lucy, his shoulders banging the car's ceiling as he fought his own buoyancy. He gestured to Johnny—pull the straps, pull the straps!

They both worked, panicking, knuckles knocking against each other as they fought the wretched straps, fumbled for the button. Corran tried to go for the seat belt securing the whole contraption to the car's back seat; he couldn't reach it. The seat belt buckle was on Johnny's side. But Johnny was wedged in the narrow window space; he couldn't maneuver his arms to get to the buckle. He couldn't do it, he couldn't do it. Get up, get up, get air, get air! A pressure was building in his head, beating like a drum.

Lucy's eyes darting.

The little blue barrette pinning soft hair that swayed like wheat in the roiled water.

From far away, Sharon screaming, screaming.

Johnny pulled himself completely into the car's backseat and kicked around until he could reposition his arms. He found the seat belt buckle. He released it. Corran ripped the whole car seat through his open door and thrust it upward, toward the light. Lucy's arms were twitching. Johnny watched her from the prison of the Polo's submerged backseat as he tried to move himself backward and out, but now his ankle was threaded through the flopping seat belt and his knee was in the wrong position, he couldn't get this figured out *at all*. Out! Out! Out!

A curtain of floaters fell across Johnny's vision. He convulsed backward. His head made contact with the gearshift. The surface of the water, far above, still shimmered. "Kaleidoscopic" was the word, it occurred to him. He felt strangely calm now, watching the movement. White diamonds flashing, shards of blue pulsing, crescents of refracted orange moshing on the rented Polo's windshield. And then it all stopped, and the world turned a cold, dark brown.

SEVENTEEN

Corran's first recollection of the moments immediately following the car accident were blurry, but they included these: Sharon on her knees on the pebbled beach, deftly extricating Lucy from the car seat; a babbling Dutch tourist on a cell phone, pacing nervously along the edge of the water after having caused the accident; and, blessedly, Lucy crying in frightened, full-throated shrieks. "Sweet dolly," Sharon was saying. "All right, sweet dolly." And there was one more: himself and Chemal dragging Johnny out of the water and onto a muddy patch of seaweed, where Johnny hunched up on his hands and knees and started vomiting water. A thick rivulet of blood traced down the side of Johnny's face.

"Iceman," Chemal said. He started to cry. "Iceman."

Johnny waved a hand dismissively.

"I'm fine," he was saying. "I'm fine."

"You're bleeding," Corran said. "Your head."

Johnny reached up and touched the side of his head. He pulled his hand back and looked at the blood on his fingers. "It's naught," he said. He was pale. He was starting to tremble. Corran felt unsteady on his feet, and he looked at his hands to find that Johnny wasn't the only one shaking. Sharon stood up with Lucy and starting telling people what to do, thank Jesus. She started with the Range Rover numpty, who followed her barked orders, dashed to the boot of his battered car, opened a suitcase, and procured two thick sweaters to bundle around the baby.

Johnny looked at Chemal. "Stop bawling, kidda," he said. Chemal dragged a wet sleeve across his face and looked away. Sharon handed Lucy to Corran and crouched next to Johnny. She wriggled out of her wet jacket and wrapped it into a turban around Johnny's head, then guided him prone. "Breathe, Johnny," she said. "Just breathe."

The police and ambulance arrived impressively quickly, given the remote location of the accident and the fact that the person who made the emergency call—the driver of the wayward Range Rover—was a blubbering mess with fear-hampered English. The paramedics wrapped up the whole lot of them in thick gray blankets and gave a good looking-over to Lucy, who responded to their attentions with lusty, indignant wails. Chemal, God love him, was clever enough to splash out to the doomed Polo and retrieve from the front seat whatever he could find that hadn't been submerged, which thankfully included Corran's cell phone and the two American passports. Then Johnny irritated everyone by refusing to go to the hospital, but eventually Sharon and even the paramedics conceded that the head wound was superficial enough—"Just bleeding like a *fucker*," as one of the paramedics inelegantly concluded.

For his part, Corran watched all the proceedings like a man half-asleep. He didn't know if it was simply the astonishment of being not only alive but also cold and wet that was getting to him, or if he was perhaps suffering from a mild case of actual shock, but either way, he was dazed, that was for sure. He wanted to get warm. They all did, but walking up the hill to the cottage seemed like an impossibly Herculean feat, given the circumstances. So after the paramedics proclaimed everyone to be more or less in one piece, after the tow trucks arrived to deal with the wrecks, and after the police departed with the Range Rover driver, who had evidently failed his Breathalyzer, Corran did the only thing he could think of to do: He called Margaret to come get them.

Now they were all seated in Margaret's tiny living room, possessed of steaming cups of tea and knocking knees around a snapping fire, trying to get warm. Had he not been so shaken up, and had he not been longing so desperately for a hit of skag to settle his raging nerves, Corran might even have found the tableau rather amusing. He looked around the room: He, Sharon, and Johnny were each wearing one of Margaret's velour tracksuits—Sharon's a shimmering coral, Johnny's a jewel-toned teal, and Corran's, thank God, a sensible black. Margaret herself was wearing her favorite suit—autumnal brown with yellow piping. All the available pantsuits were thus spoken for, so Chemal, who likely wouldn't have fit in one anyway, was instead outfitted in a voluminous blue fleece robe, which might have been androgynously passable enough had the fleece not been accessorized with tiny appliqués representing climbing roses. Lucy, warm and enjoying the familiarity of a bottle and Margaret's ample lap, was freshly diapered and bundled in a thick afghan. They all, including Lucy, wore matching socks of the fuzzy house-slipper variety, each a different pastel shade. Corran felt they might have all been in an ad for fabric softener. From where he sat on a flouncy slipcovered sofa, he could see everyone's clothing draped on drying racks in Margaret's bright, warm kitchen.

The discussion was on what to do. All the cell phones except Corran's were a loss, and they'd been passing his around for the last two hours, making calls and lining up remedies. The car rental company would track down the police report and call the wreckers about the sunken Polo. Sharon called her supervisor at hospice and told her she'd not make the afternoon's rounds. Corran canceled his ferry shift. Toole was on his way up from Dunedin to fetch Sharon, Johnny, and Chemal. Now there was little to do but drink tea, eat digestive biscuits, and wait for the clothes to dry.

"It's a miracle nobody was hurt, innit?" Margaret said for what must have been the hundredth time. "I tell you, they ought to put the other driver in prison. What was he even doing over this side of the loch, anyway? There's naught this side for the tourists. But he couldn't stay where he ought to have, now could he?"

Johnny didn't look good. Corran regarded him: His father's hands shook and his face was pale. Now and then he reached up to touch his head—once where the gash from the accident was now knitting itself back together under an oversized Band-Aid, but more frequently to the side of his left temple. He's thinking about his brain, Corran realized. The tumor.

"You hitting your head," Corran said. "Is that affecting your brain thing?"

Johnny shrugged. Sharon looked at him closely. "You should go to a doctor," she said. "In Glasgow. Let's get you in somewhere."

Johnny shook his head. "I just need to get home," he said. "The flight's tomorrow. I'm fine."

Margaret was still on the wayward tourist. "Thing is, there's all kinds of nonsense spreading over from that side to this. Tourists are just the beginning of it. Used to be you could go weeks, months up here and never see a face you didn't know. Everyone who was in Port Readie was here because we *lived* in Port Readie, aye? But now," she sighed. "All kinds of mess spreading this way. In fact," and here she pushed her eyeglasses up on top of her head emphatically, "do you know that yesterday I looked up the road toward the beach there and saw some old sot fly-tipping an entire bicycle into the loch?"

"What's fly-tipping?" Chemal said.

"Littering!" Margaret said. "Dumping! And an entire bicycle? What kind of idjit puts rubbish like that in Loch Linnhe? What does he think it is, a landfill? I'd have liked to get him cited for that. Thought about it, too, was going to march out there and get a good look at him, try to get his name, but by the time I got my plimsolls on he was gone."

The room fell silent. Sharon looked over at Corran and raised her eyebrows. They both looked at Johnny, who lowered his head into his hands. Okay, now *this* was actually funny, Corran thought.

"That's just awful," Chemal said. "Who would do that?" He seemed to be trying not to laugh. Margaret looked at him and tipped her head.

"You needn't shout at me lad," she said. "I'm sitting right here."

"I'm sorry, Miss Margaret," Chemal said. He cleared his throat and made an attempt to lower his voice. "It's just, I have a thing."

"Poor prosody," Margaret said.

"Yes!" Chemal said. "How did you know?"

"My youngest had that. He couldn't calculate pitch, is what it was. I cured him of it."

"How did you do that?" Sharon said.

"Got him an app. He uses it on his phone. It's a voice meter. When he's talking too loud, it vibrates in his pocket. Works like a charm."

"Seriously?" Chemal said. "Oh, man. Miss Margaret, dude, that is awesome."

"Well, that's just what you need, Chemal!" Sharon said. Chemal nodded. He turned to Johnny. "You think I can get Jerry to buy me an iPhone?" he said.

Johnny didn't answer right away.

"Iceman?"

Johnny looked at Chemal, but it seemed like it took him a moment to focus. "What?"

"Do you think I can get Jerry to buy me an iPhone?"

"Oh. Well," Johnny said. "He might. But you might want to stop calling him an ass-wipe before you ask him."

Chemal nodded thoughtfully. "You speak the truth, brother," he said.

Johnny was clearly trembling. "You cold?" Sharon said.

"Nah," Johnny said. "Maybe just some air." He got up and walked through Margaret's kitchen and out the back door into the garden. After a moment, Corran followed. He found his father sitting on a stone bench under a rose arbor. Most of the rose vines had been pruned down to nearly nothing, but a few stubborn blooms remained. Tough little nuts, Corran thought, with it late autumn and cold as holy shite. Johnny looked very small under the arbor. Corran sat down next to him.

"You don't look good, Da," he said.

"Thank you."

"I'm serious."

"I'm all right, Corry," Johnny said. "You got a smoke?"

Corran shook his head. "I don't smoke."

Johnny turned and looked at him. "No?"

"Never have. I guess you never noticed."

"I guess I didn't," Johnny said.

"It's not good for you, you know."

"I know that."

"I like to take care of myself, you know," Corran said.

Johnny stared at him. Corran attempted a smile. "A joke, Da," he said.

They were silent for a moment. A magpie lighted on the arbor, looked at them, and took off again. From nearby, the ferry horn sounded.

"I've heard about the factory thing," Corran said. "I'm sorry about that."

Johnny nodded.

"You might get shut down?"

Johnny shrugged. "It's not looking good. We can't prove our theory about what caused the accident. We're going to have to take the fall."

"What's your theory?"

"Meth-head across the way steals ammonia. Messes up the pressure in the tank. Boom." Johnny ran down the details. An unexplained rupture. No clues left behind. No video surveillance. But that didn't mean anything, Corran knew. Johnny's theory was probably dead-on. In Corran's experience, dealers and manufacturers were always smarter than you'd expect. Brilliant, really: evasive, strategic, and creative criminal geniuses. He had no doubt Johnny's explanation was plausible. Guy wants ammonia to cook meth and it's right across the street at the ice factory? Yep, he'll get it. He'll put out feelers. He'll find a way.

"Somebody helped him," he told Johnny. "Somebody on the inside."

Johnny looked at him. He shook his head. "Nah," he said. "Our guys are drug-tested all the time. Zero tolerance."

"I didn't say the person had to be a user. But my guess is somebody's getting paid to provide access. You're not going to catch your guy scaling the gates because I'll bet you a quid he's walking in the front door." Johnny had stopped shaking his head and was peering at him intently. And this was almost funny, it occurred to Corran, to be sitting here in Margaret's back garden, schooling his father in the methodologies of drug crime. Good to know all that experience was good for something.

"Here it is, Da," he said. "Remember this: They're never working alone. And they're always closer than you think."

Johnny reached up to his head again.

"When's your surgery?" Corran said.

"Next week." Corran tried to imagine his father submitting to the indignity of any sort of medical procedure. It was hard to reckon. Would he wear his work boots with his hospital gown? Would he criticize the quality of the gurney, maybe offer to retool a set of casters in his garage-cum-machine-shop on Watchers Island? Would he do what the nurses told him—pee on command and eat applesauce and shuffle around in post-op physical therapy like one of Toole's pitiful seniors?

"Well, I hope it goes well," Corran said, realizing as the words left his mouth how utterly lame they sounded. "I mean, I hope you're up and running again quick."

"Thank you, Corran."

Corran heard a car pulling up in Margaret's driveway in front of the house. Toole, most likely, come to take Sharon, Johnny, and Chemal back to Dunedin. This was it, then. Real soon. The big goodbye. Johnny was headed back to Florida tomorrow for a date with a scalpel. And he was headed back empty-handed. The one thing he wanted when he came over here was Corran's apology. *Do it,* Corran said to himself. It doesn't matter that you didn't take the ring. Because maybe you did. *Just say it. Get it over with. Do it.* He took a deep breath.

"Da," he began. "About Pauline's ring—"

Johnny held up a hand. "Don't say it, Corran," he said. "It doesn't matter. Christ. Listen to me. I don't care about the ring. Pauline doesn't care about the ring. The only thing we've ever cared about is you, lad." He reached over and took Corran's hand. His voice was rough. "I don't want an apology. I just want you to be all right. Do you hear me?"

Maybe it was the relief of Lucy being safe. Maybe it was the twitching agony of the longing for skag that had been war-dancing around in his head all morning. Or maybe it was the warmth of his father's hand against his own. Whatever it was, Corran realized he was crying. Crying! He hadn't cried since he was a boy. He dipped his head quickly, hoping Johnny hadn't seen. Too late. Johnny put an arm around Corran's shoulders.

"Ah, lad," he said quietly.

"It's hard, Da," Corran managed.

"I know."

"I'm trying, Da."

"I know you are. And you know what you do now?" Johnny said.

Corran looked at him.

"You let me help you," Johnny said.

Corran nodded. They sat for a little while longer, hands clasped. It was a little awkward, Corran thought, but then again it wasn't. The kitchen door opened and Toole walked out. He stared at them silently, and Corran took a moment to register what Toole must have been seeing: two grown men in fuzzy socks and women's tracksuits, leaning together and holding hands under a half-frozen rose arbor.

Toole shook his head.

"And Sharon says *I'm* going potty," he said.

Corran was standing atop a teetering stepladder in Margaret's kitchen. The stepladder was making him uneasy, and the attic access through which he was about to stick his head and shoulders was yawning blackly, and why he'd agreed to any of this he had no idea. Margaret had called him to come over—

The thrashing of his arms woke Corran from the dream, and for this he was grateful. He looked across the room and saw the pajama-clad mound of Lucy's backside motionless in her crib. She gave a soft sigh in her sleep. He shook himself fully awake and walked into the kitchen. He looked out the window. Down the hill from the croft, the shimmer of Loch Linnhe wavered in the moonlight. The Drumscaddle ferry light was off. Corran's phone buzzed with a text from Jintzy: *Call me.*

Corran dialed the number and kept his voice low so he wouldn't wake Lucy.

"Jintz?" he said. December, Jintzy said. He'd gotten the report from the company. Corran could come back to the rigs in December. Class Two engineer. Full benefits. Ten days out, four in with an option for overtime. Jintzy talked them into waiving Corran's HUET training for another year, since he'd completed a session within the last twenty-four months.

"I did it, mate," Jintzy said, laughing. "Got you back. All you need to do is show up December first. You're back aboard."

"Brilliant," Corran said softly.

"They'll be sending the forms."

"Thanks, Jintzy."

Corran went to the kitchen. He checked the time: nearly midnight. In six hours, his father would be on a plane back to Florida. He wondered if Johnny was getting any sleep. He pictured him in the little room in Sharon's house on Boscombe Road, dozing in the twin bed under the eaves like he used to do when Corran was a little kid. It was comforting, then, to listen to his father snoring. He would try to memorize the sound of it for the months and months when he didn't hear it. But now he could scarcely remember it at all. Last night he'd cracked open the bedroom door to see if he'd catch it. But there was nothing.

In the shadows of the living room the activity quilt was balled up on the sofa. It looked like a living thing, something warm and resting. He walked over and picked it up, then sat down on the sofa and held the quilt to his face, inhaling Lucy's sweet scent. An image of her frightened face, trapped underwater, appeared to him, and he tried to push it back. Great—another horror to add to his mental photo album. Fabulous. But no, he reminded himself, this one was different. Lucy was alive.

It was funny, because during the seconds he was struggling underwater with Lucy's straps, a quiet, dispassionate voice was speaking in Corran's ear. If Lucy dies, it was saying, you'll simply follow her, that's all. Get a gun, take a leap, tie a noose: Do whatever you have to do. You'll figure it out. You've held off this long, for her, but now you can get it done. Maybe shoot up a liter of skag, needles in every vein, go out in a sweet, hot blaze of glory. Just get it over with, at long last, whatever it takes, because there's no *way* you can survive this one, kidda. Forget it.

But Lucy was alive.

And wasn't it fucking ironic? All that HUET training, all those underwater simulations—strapping and unstrapping yourself, fighting for egress. What good had it done him when his own daughter was trapped in that situation? If Johnny hadn't been there on the other side of the car seat, Corran's daughter would have drowned. Corran wouldn't have been able to get her out in time. And God knows Johnny was in no shape to be thrashing about underwater and bashing his head in the process. He knew the risk. He went underwater anyway. So, the lesson here, folks? Corran wanted to email the HUET trainers, tell them to add a little something to their curriculum. You can get pretty damn good at saving yourself. But saving somebody else? That takes something more. Courage? Yeah, courage. Sacrifice, perhaps. No—*love*. It took love.

And Lucy was alive.

Let me help you, Johnny said.

Okay, Da. Okay.

Imagine, Corran thought, just for a moment: Lucy growing up in the warm breezes on Watchers Island. Running down to meet the surf, retreating back when the foamy waters approached. Soft towels. Cry of gulls. Sunscreen and bathing suits. Her own bedroom. And Pauline, sweet Pauline, leaning over the crib in the night, telling Lucy stories of valiant, good, hardworking Scotsmen who lived cleanly and braved the raging North Sea and loved their little girls more than anything else in the world. And Johnny—Johnny even!—making little pots of treacle-sweetened porridge and spooning it into Lucy's mouth, hungry little bird she'd be. Imagine it. She'd never be cold again, his Lucy.

He could ask them. He could.

Can you help me, Da?

Can you help me, Pauline?

Corran went to the keyboard in the living room and set the volume down to zero. He played the *Moonlight Sonata*. No sound—he didn't want to wake Lucy. Just touch. Just sense. Just memory.

EIGHTEEN

Inversion, Johnny thought. Inversion might do it. He was somewhere over the rocky coastline of Newfoundland, trying to tough out a headache and turbulence-induced nausea, when the thought occurred to him. He closed his eyes and pictured the frozen piston in the engine block of the VW back on Watchers Island. He was willing to bet that when he got home this evening, he'd find the damn thing still immobilized and, if Pauline's assessment was correct, still dripping Marvel Mystery Oil like a leaky faucet. There was no reason to assume that the frozen piston would have done as he'd hoped and self-corrected while he was off negotiating a truce with Corran and nearly drowning in Loch Linnhe in the process. That would have been just too easy.

Fine. So, next tactic. Think inversion—turning the whole thing upside down. Not easy to do, sure, given the structure of the piston housing. But still. If he invested the time to take out the entire mount and then used a lift to turn the contraption upside down, then he could clobber it from the bottom and try to break it loose. It was worth a try. Not a bad idea at all, in fact. He was pretty proud of himself for noodling this one through, and with a tumor lodged in his brain, no less. If it worked, that was.

Admittedly, studying the problem of the piston was a smoke screen for the problem Johnny was trying to avoid thinking about, which was Corran and Lucy and the cold, bleak remove of the little cottage at the top of the hill. But with the way his head had begun to throb since the plane reached cruising altitude, Johnny had determined that little good was going to come from continuing to fixate on *that* particular problem, especially here at thirty thousand feet, with Chemal dozing next to him, with the shores of Northeastern America growing closer, and with the reality of all that was awaiting him at home looming larger by the minute. For now, there was only this: Corran was alive. And Lucy was alive, and if they all put their heads together, maybe they could find a way to keep them that way.

All right, so! What's to worry about next? *Shit.* Johnny opened his eyes. A wave of nausea broke. He took a deep breath. The conk on the noggin he'd suffered yesterday while bumping about in the sunken Polo in Loch Linnhe had triggered something in the tumor/cyst situation, no doubt about it. Sharon had pestered him nearly blind over it when they got back to Dunedin last night, taking his vitals every twenty minutes, then wanting to take him to the ER and get it checked. But he'd refused. Twenty-four hours, he reasoned. In twenty-four hours, he'd be home and could stagger into Dr. Tosh's office if his condition hadn't improved. Tosh would know what to do.

Starting the whole business over again in Scotland was out of the question. Johnny could picture it: repeat MRIs, blood tests, medical history—the whole nine yards. And then what? If tumor trouble was indeed found, it would only delay the trip home—he could picture it already: Hospital admittance and a missed flight would be sure bets. No thank you. Johnny had paid for two seats on the morning's Virgin Atlantic departure from Glasgow to Jacksonville, connect in Charlotte. And come takeoff, he intended for his and Chemal's asses to be planted in them.

"You're being stubborn," Sharon told him last night. They were in her kitchen in Dunedin, sorting through waterlogged luggage. The suitcases were a loss, but the clothing, at least, was salvageable. Sharon had been running loads through the little clothes dryer under the counter for the last hour, and now they were trying to reassign Johnny's and Chemal's belongings into a pair of worn duffel bags Toole had produced from somewhere.

"I just want to get home, Sharon," Johnny replied.

"You're gambling with your health."

"I'll be fine," he said. Sharon and Toole exchanged a look.

"Don't do that," Johnny said.

"Do what?"

"Look at each other like I'm some sort of disobedient child."

"Well, if the shoe fits, Johnny," Sharon said.

Johnny held up his hands. "I've got a wicked headache, Sharon," he said. "Let's try not to make it worse." He left the rest of the soggy packing job to Chemal and made his way to the little room at the top of the stairs, where he spent a fitful night tossing in the twin bed, choking back nausea, and listening to the wind batter a loose piece of flashing under the eaves.

Don't die, he told himself over and over through what seemed an interminable night. Not yet. We've come this far.

Let me help you, he'd said to Corran.

Okay, Corran had said.

And what did that mean, exactly? An idea had begun to form in the back of Johnny's beleaguered mind: They could bring Lucy to Watchers Island. But in order for this idea to even *begin* to be given any serious consideration at all, three things had to happen. One, Johnny needed to survive brain surgery; two, he needed *not* to have cancer; and three, Pauline needed to be on board. The third point seemed easy; but in the darkness of Corran's old bedroom last night, neither point one nor point two seemed a foregone conclusion. At some point, Johnny dozed. All afternoon and evening he'd been worried about what kinds of dreams would visit after the nightmare of the car crash and the vision of little Lucy's wide, terrified eyes, but as it happened, once he finally fell asleep, there was only blackness, for better or for worse.

In the morning, Sharon and Chemal took care of everything. Toole had already departed for work, leaving a jolly enough note on the kitchen counter for Johnny: *A's weel that ends weel, Johnny. Safe journey.* Chemal loaded the replacement rental car they'd picked up in Dunedin, a robust Mercedes that—for the love of Pete—they would enjoy no farther than the rental return corral at Glasgow Airport. Sharon printed out the boarding passes and made a bit of porridge. "Try, love," she said to Johnny. "It may help." It did. The nausea had abated for most of the flight, in fact, not returning until just a little while ago, when the plane hit a patch of turbulence. Deep breath, Johnny told himself now. He caught a glimpse of the motion-sickness bag in the seat pocket in front of him, and he spent a panicked moment wondering if he needed to go for it, but then he averted his eyes from the bag and the sickness seemed to recede. Power of suggestion, Ice, he told himself. Don't look at it again.

Think positive.

Easier said than done.

Then just think of something *else*.

Sex. That ought to do it. The deep curve of Pauline's back when he came up behind her. The roll of her hips. The way she laughed when she climaxed. Laughed! Little joyous barks. Every time. It was the most wondrous thing, though now he found himself fretting a bit over what he'd seen in recent years as a disturbing wind-down in Pauline's libido, even though *his* never seemed to so much as hiccup. Most nights when they got into bed she fiddled with her iPad for an hour or so, then pecked his cheek, drew her knees up pertly, and rolled away. She had told him many times that her waning enthusiasm for sex was not about him, that he shouldn't take it so personally. "It's natural," she would say. "I'm just getting older, that's all. Paul Newman himself could walk in here right now and get down on his knees and I'd still feel the same way."

"Paul Newman's been dead for years," Johnny would say.

"Still."

"So you're saying I've the same odds as a dead man?"

"I'm saying you have no worse."

Sometimes she took another tack: "It's biologic checks and balances, you know," she'd begin. "One gender has to want it more than the other. If nobody ever wanted it, the species would die out. On the other hand, if *everybody* wanted to have sex constantly," and here she'd look at him a bit reprovingly, "then we'd be in a huge overpopulation mess, wouldn't we?"

"There's such a thing as birth control," Johnny said.

"You're messing with the human genome, Johnny. I'd watch it if I were you."

And so it went.

He finally dozed for a few moments, but he was jolted awake by a bump of turbulence and realized he'd been dreaming of orphan babies haunting the rafters of the ice plant. One of the babies looked like Lucy. He rubbed his eyes and tried to push away the image.

Death! He kept coming back to it. Johnny had once heard a story about a famous starlet—Marilyn?—being asked about death. "What does it feel like?" she was asked. "Well," she replied. "I suppose you feel the same as you did before you were conceived." Which was brilliant, really, and which ought to have been quite reassuring, this promise of oblivion, of unawareness, of a sleep so deep it wasn't even sleep. Should have been. But wasn't, really.

Johnny looked out at the clouds over Newfoundland and wondered.

Chemal nudged him from the next seat. "Want some M&M's?" he said. Johnny declined. Chemal yawned loudly. "Yo. I'm tired, Mr. Freeze," he said.

"Me too," Johnny said.

"I don't usually get tired."

"I've noticed."

Chemal peered at him carefully.

"You all right?"

Johnny shrugged.

"Dang," Chemal said. "I'll be glad when we get your ass home. You think it's getting worse?"

"I don't want to talk about it, Chemal."

Chemal looked a little hurt. Oh, shit. Now this. Johnny shifted in his seat and leaned against the window. Pass the time, he told himself. Talk to the kid, why don't you.

"I'm thinking about the piston on that VW," he said. "About turning it upside down and trying to break it loose that way." Chemal narrowed his eyes and seemed to study the seat back in front of him. After a moment, he nodded.

"Might work," he said. "But that's a big job, Iceman. You'll have to take the whole housing apart." He drummed his fingers on the tray table. "Isn't there another way? Something more, like, direct?"

"Been trying to figure it," Johnny said. "Let me know if you come up with an idea."

Chemal snapped his fingers. "Delighted, dude. I'll study on this. Hey, I can even help you with it when we get home!" He grinned. "We'll get that muther out of there one way or another," he said. He plugged his earbuds back in and commenced bobbing. Johnny tapped him on the shoulder. Chemal took the earbuds out.

"What *are* you going to do when we get home?" Johnny said.

Chemal looked at him blankly. "Work on the piston? Didn't we just cover that?"

"I mean in a bigger sense. With your days. Your future. What are you going to do with your life?"

Chemal grimaced. "Please," he said. "Don't pull a Jerry on me here."

"I'm serious," Johnny said.

Chemal closed his eyes and leaned back against the seat.

Johnny put the tray table in front of Chemal up so that the kid could have more room. He nudged Chemal and handed him an airline pillow flat as a potholder. Chemal still hadn't opened his eyes, but he took the pillow and wordlessly shifted into a sideways scrunch around it. After a few moments, his breathing evened out. Johnny watched him. It was hard to tell whether he was sleeping or not. The captain announced another hour of flight time. Johnny turned back to the window and rubbed a bit at the condensation to clear a view, but there was nothing to see but grayness, and now and then a stream of slipping cold vapor. He leaned his head against the glass and wished for home.

Nineteen

On Halloween morning, Roy Grassi woke with the conviction that he wasn't going to rush today. He just wasn't. And he didn't care who got mad about it. Roy had been pulling twelve-hour shifts since Johnny conked out in the men's room last week, and he was quite frankly sick and tired of being the only one on the payroll who appeared to be paying a lick of attention to what was going on at Bold City Ice. Claire was overwrought about Rosa. Johnny had run off to Scotland. Pauline was—well, Pauline was *distracted*, put it that way. For his own part, Roy was exhausted. He'd get to the factory when he got there. Maybe mid-morning. Maybe lunchtime. Maybe.

He got up in the dark and shuffled to the kitchen, where he made a pot of strong coffee. He showered and dressed, then spent a distressing hour on BankofAmerica.com trying to play the monthly chess game of online bill payment. The data usage on Nathan's cell phone—and the accompanying charges—had

skyrocketed this month; what was Nathan doing, anyway, down-
loading feature films while sitting on the beach? Broadcasting
porn? Roy sent Nathan an email. *What's up bro? Hope you're good.
AT&T, man, they suck! Check the bill, they're killing us!* Then he
labored over an email to the UF Study Abroad committee to plead
a case for letting him submit half of the fee for Ally's Florence
trip *this* month, and half *next* month, but after twenty minutes
he deleted the email before sending it. Who was he kidding?
Why should they cut Ally Grassi any financial slack, when all
the other students were probably lining up with fistfuls of cash
supplied by white-collar dads who could send their daughters to
study fashion design in Florence as easily as if they were sending them to discount surf camp in Jax Beach? Ah, forget it. He
logged off the computer.

He got up reluctantly and went to the kitchen. *Extermina-
tors. Termites. Get moving, Roy.* On top of everything else, the
house was being tented today. The timing! Two weeks ago, he'd
discovered a termite infestation in one corner of the ceiling in
Ally's old bedroom. He might not have noticed had he not gone
in there to sit on her bed one evening, feeling lonesome for the
mess and noise of his daughter. That's when he found the layer
of silvery wings spread across her pillow like phosphorus. The
sight startled him at first; it seemed supernatural and significant, and for a few seconds he worried that it was some macabre
portent of harm to his daughter. He texted her immediately and
held his breath until she replied. Then he settled himself down
and called the exterminator.

He was relieved to find that his house was still covered
under the bond he'd purchased along with the mortgage. He
was *not* relieved to find that the only solution to the current

infestation would be to tent the house. It was a common enough practice. You could scarcely ride through an older Florida neighborhood these days without seeing a house or two disguised as a circus tent under heavy sheets of industrial vinyl. So he wasn't worried about the procedure itself; he was only irritated with himself for having forgotten it was scheduled until he arrived home last night to find the reminder card hanging from his front door. Well, damn! So now he had only this morning to prepare, which meant not only bagging up all the food in the house, but also figuring out a place to stay for the night. Because unless he wanted to join the ranks of all the other living things in the house that would soon be belly-up in sulfuryl fluoride, he had to get out.

He opened all the cabinet doors and utensil drawers, per the exterminator's instructions. Then he went to work bagging the food. The tenting crew had said they'd be over by noon to begin work, and every morsel of food that Roy planned to be able to eat after the fumigation procedure, plus medicines, had to be collected and stored in special nonpermeable bags that would keep out the pesticides. He opened the pantry. A box of stale cranberry Great Grains, left over from Ally's last visit: into the trash. Two packets of Zatarain's jambalaya that would make two perfectly good dinners later in the week: into the fumigant-proof bags. Two bags of Halloween candy that he'd been planning to hand out to trick-or-treaters tonight: These he tossed into his work bag. Maybe he'd give them to the packing crew. Or, if he ended up sleeping at Claire's tonight, maybe he'd bring them with him. He pictured himself showing up at the door, all Jolly Uncle Roy with bags of candy for the kids.

Well, let's think about this, now. Did he really have the nerve to ask Claire if he could sleep there tonight? The busy little jury inside his head was still out on this one. The idea of crashing at her house had occurred to him last evening when he realized he needed to vacate his own place for the fumigation and when he realized that there was no way, given his current financial situation, that he could spend money on a hotel. Just no way. It wasn't *such* an outlandish idea, Roy told himself. After all, he'd slept at Claire's house before—had crashed on the couch twice after a few too many when she'd had some of the ice folks over on a Friday night—but both times were years ago, when her husband Mike was still alive. Still, he'd known Claire for twenty years now; they were old friends. What was the big scandal in asking his old buddy if he could bunk on her couch for eight hours, just catch a few z's before heading back in to the Ice Capades for another marathon shift?

The only problem was that he hadn't asked her yet. Something was slowing him down. He should have texted her last night when the idea first occurred to him. Instead he'd let it simmer in his uneasy brain all night, so now the entire proposition had taken on a weight that was making him anxious in a vaguely hopeful way. All right, get a grip, he said to himself, shaking his head as he tossed a jar of peanut butter into a fumigation bag. Stop making such a big deal of it. Just call her up:

"Claire?" he'd say. "Can I crash tonight? My house is getting tented."

"Sure," she'd say. "We'll watch *Modern Family*."

And that would be it. No big deal! Don't overthink it, Grassi. He'd head over there after work, maybe bring some subs. Ethan liked Firehouse Subs. And he'd have the bags of Halloween candy with him, would toss one to Chase and one to Rosa and watch them fall on them like predators. And he'd maybe have a bottle of wine, too, for Claire. She liked Shiraz. There! It would be perfectly fine. All casual and warm and nothing out of the ordinary at all. Just Uncle Roy camping out, he was like one of the family, after all, what fun!

He could help Ethan with his algebra, maybe play a round or two of Guitar Hero with Chase. Do something useful—maybe change the cat litter? Tote the recycling bin out to the road? The boys would go trick-or-treating. But not Rosa; she'd say she was too old for such stuff. She'd stay home and hand out candy at the door, and she'd be *home*, by God, not out with that son of a bitch Vickers; Roy would give her a coded nod (*'Atsa girl, Rosa, he's not good enough for you*), and she'd smile, agreeing. They'd all pile on to the big brown sectional and watch TV and eat subs and candy. Claire and Rosa would fuss at each other about something or other and Ethan and Chase would kick around for a bit like boys do until they all settled down and fell quiet with the hypnosis of the blue screen. Rosa would lean her head on her mother's shoulder and Claire would play with her hair, just like Roy used to do with Ally. Chase would ask Roy for another piece of candy. There'd be a basket of laundry at Claire's feet, waiting for folding, but she'd nudge it aside and tuck her feet up under her backside. Roy would refill Claire's wineglass. Then Claire would look over at Roy and smile, and it would finally occur to her, just as it had occurred to him so many times: Wouldn't this be nice, if they could do this all the time? Wouldn't this just be *super*?

Roy finished packing the food and took a walk through the house, looking around to see if anything else needed to be removed before the tenting. There wasn't much to be concerned with, he decided: a stained microfiber living room set from Rooms to Go, a few cheap art prints on the walls, a stack of unread *National Geographics*. It looked like a waiting room in a health clinic. He took Ally's baby pictures off the bookshelf and put those in his work bag. There was a neglected African violet in the kitchen that someone gave Ally after her dance recital last spring. Roy put it on the back porch to spare it from the fumigants, though he was willing to bet it was on its last legs anyway. He returned to the kitchen to find his cell phone buzzing on the counter. It was Claire.

"Roy, are you planning to come to work today?" she snapped.

"Good morning to you, too," he said.

"No, it's not a good morning, Roy. Do you know why?"

"Claire—" he began.

"Because this place is going to shit and Johnny's not here and Pauline's not here and *you're* not here and I'm about ready to lose it, Roy. Lose it." Her voice had taken on an ire he knew quite well, though he was dismayed to hear it directed at him personally, particularly on a morning when there was so much, already, bringing him down.

"Where's Pauline?" he said.

"I don't *know*," she replied. "She's not answering her cell. But do you know that Ed from Sales is out there thinking he knows how to fix Dumbo?" she continued. "He's kicking at the damn thing and I don't know which one of them is going to win, but I do know that I don't feel like having to fill out an injury report on that dimwit when he throws out his back beating up an ice machine. Oh, and the bag threader is off track. And there's water in the catch bin again. And are you going to *get here*?"

"Yes," he replied, his voice a bit more defensive than he'd planned. "I will. Give me a bit. My house is getting tented today. And I've got to get it ready."

"I mean, I don't have the nerves today for Ed, Roy."

"I'll be there soon," he said. He swallowed a bulb of fear and was opening his mouth to say it—*Oh, and by the way, can I crash at your place tonight, Claire?*—when she cut him off at the pass:

"I thought I could count on *you*, Roy."

He closed his mouth. All right, now that was just too much, right there. What was that supposed to mean? Just because he took a couple of hours off from work *one* morning, she was going to turn on him like this, turn one day's tardiness into some sort of huge assessment of his character? Like it wasn't even about work at all, like she was *personally* disappointed in him? His anger flared up before he could contain it.

"Look, Claire," he said. "There's more to my life than Bold City Ice, okay? I got a lot to do. I got other people counting on me for stuff."

"Oh, *please*," she said, and he realized too late that he'd just pushed a particularly testy button with Claire, who liked to think she had the market cornered on martyrdom. "We've all got a lot to do," she said. "Don't even start with me on that. And if you're referring to that Nathan situation? You can dump that load anytime you want to. I've been telling you for years that you should."

"I know. You've been telling me for years to do all sorts of things," he said. "But guess what, Claire? Today you're not telling me to do shit."

He hung up. And it took a couple of minutes, but when the regret came, it was titanic.

TWENTY

The plane descended sharply on its approach to Charlotte. Chemal woke up and yawned. Johnny shifted position to pull his bag out from under the seat in front of him. And when the pain showed up this time, it owned him. It sliced through his eyes, pulsed against his eardrums. It was worse than any pain he'd felt yet. He sat back against his seat while the plane landed and was vaguely aware of the tumult of passengers beginning the dance of the overhead baggage retrieval. He dry-swallowed three ibuprofen tablets and started to pray. Finally, they disembarked, and he made it to the chairs outside the gate, then sat down again.

"You okay, Iceman?" Chemal said. He took Johnny's bag from him and slung it over his shoulder.

"Not great," Johnny managed. "Can you get me some water?"

Chemal dashed off to a shop and returned with a bottle of water. Johnny took a few deep swallows and put his head back. After a minute, he opened his eyes and looked at Chemal. "Wicked headache," he said. "Holy shit."

"Is it your tumor?" Chemal said. He looked worried.

"I don't know," Johnny said.

"Dude," said Chemal. "Don't, like, die or anything."

"I'll try not to, Chemal."

He stood up and waited for the airport to stop spinning. "Let's go get the connection," he said. Chemal carried both bags. Johnny put his sunglasses on and kept his eyes trained on the carpet a few feet in front of him. They walked from one concourse to another to find that the connecting flight was not only three hours late, it was also overbooked. The airline was offering vouchers to passengers willing to be bumped. The waiting game had already started, but nobody was stepping up to accept the bump. The voucher was up to $150 each plus a night's stay at the airport Days Inn. Then $200. Then $250. Johnny found a vinyl seat in a dim corner of the waiting area and closed his eyes.

"We should just do the voucher dealio," Chemal said after thirty minutes, when an additional hour's flight delay was announced. He was looking at Johnny with some concern, and Johnny was surprised that Chemal's voice had taken on an unexpected maturity.

"I don't want to spend the night in Charlotte," Johnny said.

"I know, but dude, you look rough. Maybe we should find a doctor."

"No. I just want to get home."

"Well, okay, but we don't even know when our plane is going to leave. At the rate we're going, we'll be sitting here forever waiting for the flight, and we won't get back till practically morning anyway. Maybe you need to just sleep it off before you go up in the air again, you know? Get some rest."

The kid was right. And what was more, Johnny didn't have the energy to argue. They stepped up to take the voucher, and Chemal led the way to a shuttle bus that carted them to the Days Inn. On arrival, they found the women working the check-in desk dressed in Halloween costumes. One was a witch. The other was wearing a red shirt and red pants and had a box of laundry detergent affixed to her hat.

"I don't get it," Chemal said.

"Red," the woman said, pointing to her clothing, "and TIDE. Get it? Red Tide!"

Chemal laughed politely but looked at Johnny when the woman turned away and rolled his eyes. Then Chemal's gaze fell on a sign near the hotel's lounge, and Johnny was suddenly worried that Chemal was the one who might have a seizure.

"Get. Out. Of. Town," Chemal said. "Oh, dude. Oh, *dude*!!"

"What?" Johnny said. He took his sunglasses off and squinted toward the lounge.

"Love Gun!" Chemal said. He started to jump up and down. "LOVE FREAKING GUN!"

"We're having a KISS tribute band here tonight," one of the clerks said. She pointed at the sign. "Love Gun," it said. "Halloween Only!"

"I can't believe this is happening," Chemal said. Neither could Johnny. He gave the clerk the reservation voucher and they made their way up to the room, where he tried to call Pauline's cell from the room phone but got no answer. He called the house phone on Watchers Island: again, no answer. He left a brief message on the home voicemail about the flight delay, but he couldn't bring himself to attempt a sound-bite summary of the *other* headline events of the past couple of days: the car crash, developments with Corran, his own deteriorating condition. He called the factory and caught Rosa, who told him Pauline had just left to go home. How, Johnny wondered, did anybody ever communicate before cell phones? Two iPhones down, and he and his wife were incommunicado.

"Roy there?" Johnny said. "Or your mom?"

"Everyone just went home," Rosa said. "I was just about to switch the phones over to the answering service when you called."

"Do me a favor while you're driving home?" Johnny said. "Keep trying our house till you get Pauline. Tell her we talked, okay? And that I'm spending the night in Charlotte. Back tomorrow."

"You okay, Johnny?" Rosa said.

"I'm okay, Rosa. You'll talk to Pauline for me?" She assured him she would.

Chemal was waving around a room-service brochure. They ordered hamburgers, but Johnny managed only a bite before he fell back onto the bed, exhausted and nauseated. Chemal finished both burgers, then took a shower and paced the room, vacillating between euphoria and concern.

"I'm, like, worried your brain is blowing up or something," Chemal said.

"It's not," Johnny said. "Go see Love Gun. If I need you I'll call the front desk and have them go get you."

Chemal gave Johnny one last searching look. "You sure, dude?"

"I'm sure," Johnny said. "I just want to get some sleep."

Chemal pulled on his KISS Army jacket and bumped out of the room. Johnny stared at the ceiling and listened to the start of the Love Gun concert in the lounge just below the room. He realized that he actually *liked* KISS. He recognized a few of the songs: "Lick it Up." "Strutter." "Detroit Rock City." After a few moments, the music was making the whole room shake, but Johnny found that if he kept his head perfectly still on the pillow, the pain receded and the vibrations became gentler, almost soothing. He'd just begun to doze when a thought came to him out of nowhere, and it was so startling that he sat straight up in bed. A wave of pain swept upward through his neck and into his head, but he steeled himself against it and tried to think. What was it Corran had said? *Here it is, Da. They're never working alone. And they're always closer than you think.*

My God! *Closer than you think.*

Johnny closed his eyes and tried to dispassionately review the facts: There were four sets of keys to the Bold City Ice Plant. The only people who had access to those keys were himself, Pauline, Roy, and Claire. He pictured Claire's fringed leather purse, the one always hanging sloppily over her chair back with half the contents ready to spill out. Claire had often complained, when she opened her wallet and found herself possessed of five or ten dollars less than she thought she'd had, that her kids seemed to consider it open season on the contents of her purse once she went to bed. Bits of money, chewing gum, Germ-X, pens: Everything was at risk. Even, presumably, keys.

Johnny slid carefully out of the bed and went to the bathroom to splash cold water on his face. He went down to the lobby. At the reception desk, the witch was still fully in character, but Red Tide had given up the laundry detergent hat and now just looked like a woman in a red T-shirt and stretch pants. Johnny asked her if the Days Inn had a business center. "I need a computer," he said, "with Internet."

"Ah, honey," she said. "I keep telling them we need a little business center. You know, to compete? People want that. One less waffle station, I say. How many waffle stations do you need? We could put a little area over there with a computer and a phone and such, you know what I'm saying? I tell the manager and the owner all the time. Do they listen to me? Of course not. But here." She got out of her seat and motioned to Johnny to come around the counter. "Come sit and use my computer, honey. I'ma take a break anyway." He thanked her. Red Tide left the reception desk and Johnny sat down at her computer. The witch waved at him, friendly. She was busy taking a phone reservation.

Johnny opened a browser. The ice factory's surveillance videos were managed with cloud-based software that enabled "Anywhere, anytime access!" as the salesman had proclaimed. When they'd first subscribed to the program Johnny was annoyed by the expense, but now he was glad they'd done it. He remembered the password. It was the same password he used for everything: Boniface15. As he waited for the log-in to verify, he mentally catalogued a disturbing set of details: The blown security bulbs. The constantly resetting router. The flashing microwave clock. The bottle caps on the ops floor.

He accessed the directory of surveillance films and scanned his options. There were eight surveillance cameras posted around the exterior perimeter of the factory. Four of them were trained on the tank yard. Two were trained on the loading dock, one on the fleet parking area, and one on the factory front door. Johnny clicked back through the storage files and found the folder containing films from all eight cameras from the night before the accident. He pulled up the films from the four cameras that were focused on the ammonia tank yard. They'd all looked at these films a dozen times. He, Roy, and the lawyers had watched them again and again, hoping to catch a glimpse of an intruder in the tank yard that would bolster their OSHA appeal. And the OSHA investigators themselves had looked at the films, muttering as they did about "path of failure" and lapsed maintenance. But nobody had seen anything notable in the films.

Johnny put the films on a quick-scan setting. He kept his eye trained on the lower left corner of the screen, where the time and date stamps were rapid-cycling like a stopwatch. He watched the clock move through hours and minutes in a smooth, even progression, the numbers spinning higher and higher as the clock moved through the night. And then he saw it. He stopped the film, backed up a bit, played it again. There it was: a jump in the time stamp. The clock flicked from 9:37 p.m. to 10:19 p.m. Which meant what? Which meant this: On the night before the accident, the surveillance video covering the tank yard was interrupted. For forty-two minutes, there was no record of what might have occurred on or near the doomed ammonia tank.

Johnny thought for a moment, and then went to the files containing films captured from the camera trained on the factory's front door. Nobody had accessed these films during the accident investigation. Why would anyone? All focus had been on the *tank yard*, on finding the physical cause for the tank's rupture. Obviously, the factory itself had not been broken into. There was no reason to examine footage covering the main employee entry. Johnny clicked on the film now. He sat back in his chair and let the footage run, and as it did, he went down a very unpleasant but increasingly convincing chain of events that could have occurred to account for the gap in the surveillance video: Someone had entered the factory and accessed the main breaker panel on the wall just outside Roy's office. That same someone had thrown the switch to cut off electrical power to the tank yard, which was on the same circuit as the admin wing. The surveillance system had been disabled for forty-two minutes. When the breaker was thrown back on, not only were clocks and routers resetting, but the rush of resumed electricity was overwhelming the circuit and wreaking havoc with some of the more sensitive receptors throughout the building. Security lightbulbs were blowing. Dumbo was shorting.

On the computer monitor, the front door surveillance video flickered with movement. Johnny backed it up and replayed it in slow motion. At 9:32 on the night before the accident, Rosa Kaplan and Owen Vickers walked up to the front door of the Bold City Ice Plant. Vickers was carrying a six-pack of beer. Rosa was laughing. She stumbled a bit, and Vickers grabbed her arm to right her. She unlocked the door, and they walked inside. Johnny held his breath and waited. At 9:37, the time stamp jumped forward to 10:19. Johnny stopped the film and closed the file. He tried to think of another possible alternative to what the evidence was suggesting, but there simply was none.

Owen Vickers was tapping Bold City Ice ammonia. And Rosa Kaplan—dumb, gullible Rosa—was letting him in to do it.

Shit. Just shit.

Red Tide was back. "You got what you need, honey?" she said. "You good?"

"Yes, thank you," Johnny said. He stood up and had to grab the back of the chair to steady himself. Red Tide looked at him, concerned. "You all right, baby?" she said.

"Head congestion," he said. "I get a little dizzy. Sorry. Thanks for the computer." He made his way back up to the hotel room and lay on the bed. He wanted to call Pauline, wanted to call Roy, wanted to *think* about this new information—what was it going to mean?—but he was finding it was taking most of his energy simply to focus on breathing. Eventually, the music in the club downstairs stopped. Chemal tiptoed into the room and fell onto the other bed in the dark. Johnny could sense himself being observed. Finally, he opened his eyes, and though the room was nearly dark he could tell Chemal was staring at him. "You okay, dude?" he said.

"Yeah."

"Is your brain thing getting worse?"

"I think so," Johnny said. "But you needn't worry. I just need to get home." The air conditioner chugged. A kid ran down the hallway just outside their door, yelling.

"Iceman," Chemal said. He propped himself up on one elbow, his silhouette barely visible, his voice unusually hushed. "I wish you felt better. And I want you to know: This is the best Halloween I've ever had."

Johnny was glad that someone, at least, was enjoying it.

TWENTY-ONE

It was just that he didn't want to answer any *questions*. That's what Roy was thinking as he staged the pretense of preparing to exit the factory when the whistle blew to end the shift on Halloween evening. He turned off the ringer on his phone, powered down his computer, and closed the blinds in his office. He waved goodbye to the packing crew, who would be hustling their own way out within minutes, damn straight. He put his parka back on one of the hooks just inside the door to the admin wing and walked toward Pauline's office to tell her good night, just like he always did. He'd gone out of his way today to stay out of the admin wing. Not that it was Pauline he was avoiding. *Good night, Pauline, you heading out? Yep, right behind you, good night, Roy. See you tomorrow. Uh-huh.*

He wasn't actually going home. He just needed to kill a couple of hours, let the factory clear out, and then he'd be back. To avoid the termite tenting at his house, he'd decided to crash for the night on the plaid sofa in his office, a course of action which was his *own business*, thank you very much, and not something he wanted to have to explain to every nosy Bold City Ice employee who would want to know why he wasn't hitting the road with everyone else come quitting time. (*What do you mean, you're sleeping here, Roy? That's crazy, Roy! Get a hotel, Roy! Don't you have someone you can stay with?*) And by every nosy Bold City Ice employee, of course, he meant Claire.

So he left. And now it was headed toward dusk on a sweltering weekday evening in Jacksonville and—surprise!—he'd hit eastbound rush hour right on the button. Traffic was a snarl. Normally, his homeward route led him due west from the factory, which was an easier nut to crack, trafficwise, and easily navigable for a Westsider like Roy who'd grown up sharking his way through the gridded network of cut-through streets in maneuvers that, over the course of his driving life, had probably saved him hours—shit, *days*—of sitting-in-traffic time.

But tonight, something had come over him, and he'd headed out toward the beach with a thought to order up a plate of coconut shrimp at Ragtime, maybe treat himself to a Red Brick Ale. He was beginning to see now, with a clear view of the nearly immobilized eastbound lanes of Atlantic Boulevard, that this was a terrible plan. Plus, the longer he sat in traffic, the longer he had to gnaw on the fact that the shrimp and beer would run him a cool $20 that he simply didn't have, especially in light of his good friends Nathan and AT&T. He rode along the current for a little while, aimless, and then he bagged the whole shebang and pulled in to the parking lot at the Regency Mall. Food court. Something simple. Then back to the factory, maybe get some shipping reports caught up, and then bed down. Call this day a draw.

He parked outside Penney's and walked through the store into the mall, where the atmosphere was claustrophobically cavernous, if there could be such a thing. Big as it was, the place was crowded, surprisingly for a weekday, and Roy had the feeling of walking in a small retail city. He walked past surf stores and dress boutiques, shoe outlets and one entire store that sold nothing but candles, another that sold nothing but tea. Nothing but tea! He didn't know how such a business could exist. He passed the Dial-N-Style cell phone kiosk. The Piercing Pagoda. Hair Cuttery. Puppy Avenue. He tried to think of the last time he'd been in a shopping mall. It had been quite a while. Years, probably.

He realized he was walking much faster than the average shopper, and he had to keep adjusting his stride after finding himself tailgating one slow-moving band after another: first a broad-bottomed trio of women in stretch pants and platform sandals, then a pair of seniors in Velcro shoes, next a sprawling family pushing a rented mall stroller shaped like a small car.

From somewhere, faintly, he could hear piped-in music. Who was that—Elvis? Cher? Had those two always sounded so similar? A pair of women walked past, clear plastic handbags dangling on their arms. Roy had heard once that department store workers were told to use clear handbags to protect against internal theft—the jewelry girl walking off with the wares and such. How demeaning, he thought, to be assumed a wrongdoer when all you're trying to do is pay the bills. Malls. Why do they make these places? Like giant human Habitrails, everyone running, aimless, exhausted.

He bought a sandwich at Miami Subs in the food court and sat down at a table next to a young woman feeding french fries to a baby in a high chair. The baby wore striped leggings, green socks, and a red T-shirt. Roy couldn't tell if it was a boy or a girl. It looked like an elf. He checked his phone for a text from Ally, and finding none, he opened his email app to see if Nathan had responded about the AT&T charges. Negative. When he looked up, the young woman was gone. The baby was sitting there alone.

Roy stood up and turned in a slow circle, looking at the people waiting in the various lines at restaurants around the food court: Sbarro and Mandarin Express, Reggae Island Grille and French Fry Heaven. Nowhere did he see the young woman, or anyone, for that matter, looking back attentively toward the baby. What was wrong with the world? Sometimes he honestly did not know if he could keep up. He sat down at his table again, and he and the baby regarded each other. The baby had brown curls and bright dark eyes. Roy decided it was a boy. There was just something about the little guy's face.

"Well, damn," Roy said. "Where's your mama?" The baby stared at him solemnly, still chewing potato. Roy hoped this wasn't going to be one of those child abandonment stories. He looked at his watch. One more minute, maybe two, tops. Then he was calling the police. The overhead music had clarified now. "Who Let the Dogs Out?" My God. The noise and chaos of the mall were starting to feel overwhelming. He worked his way through his sandwich, which was terrible, truly. He told the little elf about it.

The young woman finally returned to take ownership of the elf baby, who raised his arms to her absently, almost wearily.

"Well, well," Roy said. The woman looked at him defensively. "You shouldn't leave your baby," he said.

"Well, you shouldn't be up in my *business*," she said. "I didn't leave him with *you*."

She gathered the baby and walked away. Roy finished his sandwich. He stopped at a kiosk and bought a cardboard cone filled with chocolate chip cookies. He made his way out to the parking lot and drove toward the city. The traffic going *toward* the Bold City's center, he noted, was nearly naught. Everyone, it seemed, was bound for the perimeter.

The factory was quiet. There were no cars left in the lot. Roy parked and fetched the sleeping bag he'd stashed in the trunk of his car. He unlocked the front door, entered, and locked the door again behind him, and then he made his way through the dark admin wing, out to the ice floor, and back to his office. He turned on his space heater and waited for the room to warm. He pulled out his phone and turned it back on. There was a missed call and a voicemail from a number he didn't recognize, but he ignored it. Bill collector. Nooooooo thank you. He texted Ally.

Boo, he typed. *Happy Halloween.*

Boo, you, she wrote back.

What are you doing tonight?

Pizza thing at the student union, she wrote. *And then Megan's having a party. I made a costume. Hang on.*

He waited. He knew she was taking a selfie. Sure enough, after a few seconds a headshot came through: Ally with her face painted up like a cat's, cheeks sucked in and her head tilted to the side—a little flirtatiously, if you asked Roy. He was glad he couldn't see the rest of the costume, which he suspected involved something stretchy and black. They called them catsuits for a reason, didn't they? He sighed. Last he checked, Ally was nine years old, making pom-poms and singing Disney songs on summer days in the factory with Rosa. And now here she was mugging sexy-kitty in a college dorm and headed for a party.

Very cute, he wrote back.

Thanks, Daddy. Miss you. Mwah.

Miss you too, Ally. Be safe tonight. Mwah.

He spread the sleeping bag on the sofa. Well, cat-suit or not, at least she was possessed of a focus, he thought. She had a real future ahead of her, that kid. UF was a tough school to get into, but Ally had done it. He was so proud of her sometimes it hurt. It made him feel a little sad, though, for Rosa. He wondered if the two girls still kept in touch. He really had no idea, though it was certainly likely that they were connected on Facebook and probably clicked around in cyberspace from time to time, each to see what the other was up to: Ally taking college life by the horns and Rosa letting her artistic dreams slowly fade and letting herself grow doughy and wan as she sat out her days holding down the receptionist's chair in an ice factory.

Rosa's one of us, he thought. *Me and Claire and all the other working-class cogs in the Bold City Ice machine.* But Ally was different. Ally was on her way out. Go Gators! She was headed into Johnny's world, Pauline's world, even Ed from Sales's world, which was a place where people didn't put groceries on a credit card or ride around in a car with no air-conditioning or sleep in their offices because they couldn't afford a hotel room. You go, girl, he thought. Catch a star, sweet baby, and ride it up and out. Ride it to Florence and back, and all the way into a great job and a nice house and a good marriage and sweet little kids, all of it. We'll make it happen, somehow. But just don't forget *me,* Ally. Just don't forget I'm still here.

Someone had left a pair of sunglasses on the small table next to the sofa. He picked them up to move them to the desk. One of the ops guys, he thought. Someone will come looking tomorrow. But wait. He looked at them again. They were *women's* sunglasses, enormous Jackie-O circles. He squinted at them; his eyesight was getting worse, by God. A line of type was etched along one arm. Prada, it said. Well, that was odd. He tossed the glasses onto his desk. He fell back onto the couch and listened to the buzzing rush of the space heater in the corner. It wasn't bad company. After a while, the heat in the room built, and the unit's thermostat tripped a sensor and shut it down. Then the silence was unbearable. Roy pulled out his phone and watched a few Jimmy Fallon clips on YouTube, waiting for sleep to come. No dice. He watched a few more. There was one where Jimmy was being visited by the animal expert guy who brings critters to the show and talks about them. By coincidence this clip was featuring animals from the St. Augustine Alligator Farm.

What do you know? Just down the road. Roy had taken Ally lots of times when she was little. Quite a lovely place it was, too: alligators and crocodiles to look at, sure, but also a bird rookery that attracted roseate spoonbills to nest in the spring. That was Ally's favorite part, all those pink birds sitting in the trees. She said it looked like Dr. Seuss. Roy hadn't been to the Alligator Farm in a long while. He'd had no idea it was now on the national radar. People knew about the Alligator Farm? People knew about St. Augustine? *The Tonight Show*! Roy was impressed.

On the video, the animal expert guy dragged a huge albino alligator onto the stage and Jimmy Fallon feigned terror and the whole thing was quite entertaining. *An albino alligator!* Jimmy said. *That's crazy!* Roy had seen that very same albino alligator at the park many times, he was sure of it. The sign near the enclosure said that if you gazed into the eyes of an albino alligator, you'd experience great good fortune. Once when she was around twelve, he and Ally had stood there for the longest time, hands clasped, gazing at the gator's milky pink eyes. Roy wished he could do it again now. I don't need *great* good fortune, he'd say to the alligator. Just a *little* good fortune. Just enough to send Ally to Italy. Come on, pal, whaddya say?

Roy jumped when the video was interrupted by the buzzing of an incoming text. It was Ally. A selfie she'd taken at the Halloween pizza party. She was holding a slice of pizza up to her face and grinning. *Mamma mia, delizioso,* the text read. And then one more: *Ti amo papà!* Roy stared at the ceiling for the longest time, listening to the silence. Then he got up and sat down at his computer to start composing an email.

Dear Nathan, it began. *Guess what? Party's over, dude. Times are tough, as they say. I'm sorry you're paralyzed. But I'm even sorrier that I've spent so much money on you. I got better things to spend money on, Nathan, like my daughter.* He stopped for a second and grinned. Claire would love this, he thought. Oh, Claire would just love it.

TWENTY-TWO

Pauline didn't want to be home. She'd left the factory earlier and driven all the way out to Watchers Island, where she entered the kitchen to the sound of the ringing phone and found out from Rosa that Johnny was delayed in Charlotte. She checked the house phone's voicemail and found Johnny himself leaving the same message. His voice sounded okay, but she sensed something underneath his words. She couldn't put her finger on what it was. He said he was calling from the hotel phone and that he'd lost his cell phone the day before. Lost his phone? Well, that was irresponsible. Then she remembered that she herself had earlier thrown a tantrum and smashed a $600 iPhone against the kitchen wall, breaking a backsplash tile in the process. Yep.

She fed and walked the General. Lord, this dog was slower than molasses. "Pee," she said to him, grumpily. "Will you freaking *pee*?" They finally got the business completed. She moved through the house restlessly for a little while, tidying up. Then she sat down on the sofa with a glass of wine and the iPad and a thought to play Scrabble with Corran, but when she pulled up the game she saw they were still stalled on the last word she'd played: WONDER, which hadn't really meant anything at all. She didn't know how he'd interpret that one. Although come to think of it, the word was rather fitting. As in "I wonder what went on over there with you and your father, Corran? I wonder if you two made peace?" She thought about simply calling Corran to find out. She still had a house phone, after all. Johnny might be unreachable, but Corran wasn't. But then she decided against it. She'd given her word to her husband. Maybe she should just finish painting the bathroom.

Pauline felt like the walls were closing in on her. She dumped the wine down the sink and got back into the Prius to take a ride along the ocean road. She drove across the Intracoastal and watched an osprey circle for prey, then dive. For a few moments, her mind felt blessedly vacant, but as she followed the receding sun westward, the light turning soft and pink, the nagging mantra returned: *We can't beat OSHA. The factory is going to close.* How would she and Johnny make a living? she wondered. In time, of course, Packy Knight would die, and he would leave a substantial nest egg to her and Caroline. But the nest egg was certainly not what it used to be, she'd wager, given the years of private home health care and the hefty tax bill on the big house on the river. It would *maybe* be enough for her and Johnny to get out from under part of the weight of the refinance on the Watchers Island house. Maybe. But then what? They had to work, didn't they? They were too young to retire. And what, exactly, was she suited to do, after running her own ice factory for all these years: coming and going as she pleased, counting on the staff to fill in the gaps left when she herself was out running, or getting her hair done, or farting around Publix looking for wine gums in the middle of the day? Maybe she could get a job at Salon Belleza answering the phones. Or maybe she could be a Starbucks barista. The baristas always looked relatively content.

She crossed the river into downtown Jacksonville. She'd been driving a long time. She pulled over at EverBank Field, the Jacksonville Jaguars' home stadium. It was fully dark now. Across the parking lot, a group of boys were doing something under a cluster of streetlamps. What was that called? Parquet? Parkour? Parkour. That was it. Jumping. Flying. Falling. They were practicing moves against the oversized jaguar statue near the front entrance of the stadium.

She remembered that sculpture; it was quite an imposing replica. When the designers commissioned it from a local marble artist, they were careless with the measurements of the big cat's gaping mouth. It was just big enough for someone to get into trouble, and someone did. A nine-year-old boy, horsing around, put his head into the jaguar's jaws and got stuck. Then came the police. Then the fire department. Then the evening news. The kid ended up fine, but by the time the whole kerfuffle was resolved, the statue was down a marble tooth. When they fixed the sculpture, they rigged it with wires behind the teeth to prevent others from putting their heads into the jaguar's mouth. Human beings, Pauline thought. We're our own worst enemies. Always needing to be protected from ourselves.

Well, she was this close to the factory, it occurred to her. Here it was Halloween, the last day of the month, and she hadn't finished processing overtime payroll. She might as well stop in and pick up time sheets so she could finish the work at home. It wasn't like she was going to be sleeping much tonight, anyway. She watched the parkour boys for another minute. They were beautiful. They could run straight toward a wall, sneaker their way up the concrete, and then flip over backward. Amazing!

She reached the factory and parked. She entered through the back door, disabled the alarm, and made her way through the admin wing, past workstations and equipment blinking blue on desks. Funny, she'd been coming to this factory since she was a little girl, but she could hardly remember a time when she had been here in the dark of night, alone. She went straight to her office and found that someone had left a hand truck just outside her door. Why did they do things like this? Too lazy to wheel it back out to the loading area where it belonged. She rolled the hand truck back toward the factory to put it away.

Before she entered the ops floor, she picked up Johnny's parka from the peg beside the door and slipped it on. The faint scent of his sweat muddled her, and she stood still in the hallway, trying to steady herself. Then she opened the door to the factory floor and steeled herself against the cold rush. The icemakers hummed. They were on auto-ops for the night, maintaining temperatures but pausing production until the first morning crew came in tomorrow. She put the hand truck back where it belonged, then went over to Dumbo and found that the old ice machine was still. She kicked it. Nothing. She didn't know how to kick it like Johnny did.

Something scuttled under a catch bin, and a twinge of fear pinched at her spine. She pulled Johnny's parka tighter and turned to head back toward the admin wing. A movement appeared at the corner of her eye. She looked toward the storage room and stopped in terror. The silhouette of a man was bobbing toward her in the dark. She screamed.

"Pauline!" the man said. "It's me!"

Roy! Pauline felt her knees literally weaken. He stepped forward and peered at her.

"Oh, Lord have mercy, Roy. You scared the living daylights out of me," she said.

"What are you doing here?" he said.

"Picking up payroll," she said. She looked at him closely. "But what are *you* doing here?" she said. "I didn't see your car."

"Pulled it into the loading yard. I'm having my house tented. I needed a place to sleep. Gonna crash on my little sofa there," he said, gesturing toward his office.

"You could have come to our house, Roy."

He shrugged. "I didn't want to bother anyone. Isn't Johnny coming home tonight?"

"He got bumped in Charlotte. Home tomorrow. I'm not sure what time. He lost his phone. And I *broke* my phone. It's ridiculous." She was annoyed with herself to find her eyes filling with tears.

"Aw, Pauline," Roy said. "It's just a phone." He looked alarmed. He patted her shoulder awkwardly.

"It's not the phone, Roy," she said. She sniffled. "It's everything. I'm so worried about Johnny."

"I know, I know," he said. "But Pauline, now come on. That man is tougher than cowhide. He could probably drill his *own* head open and be back up and running within a day."

"And then the hearing, Roy," she said. "We don't have a case."

Roy didn't answer right away. He nodded and gazed off, a little vacantly, it seemed to Pauline, toward the old icemakers.

"Might be the end of the road, is what you're saying, I'm guessing," he finally said.

"Might be."

Roy leaned in to give her an awkward hug, his hand patting her back like he was burping a baby. "Come on now, Pauline," he said. "We can't give up yet. We gotta keep trying. We still got two weeks, right?"

She pulled back and wiped her eyes with the hem of her shirt. "Yes, we've got two weeks," she said. "And my husband is about to undergo brain surgery. Something tells me I'm not going to be particularly focused on a fucking OSHA appeal."

Roy's eyes grew wide. He gave a low whistle.

"What?" she said.

"I don't think I've ever heard you drop an F-bomb, Pauline," Roy said. "That was most impressive."

"Desperate times, Roy," she said. She found a tissue in her pocket and blew her nose. "Desperate measures."

The back door banged. Somebody was entering the factory.

"Did you leave the door open?" Roy said.

"Oh, my God," she said. "I must have."

"Stay here," he said. He moved toward the door to the admin wing. She ignored his command and followed. When they got to the door, Roy jerked it open quickly and called into the darkness. "Who's there?" he said. "Somebody there?"

"Happy Halloween," came a deep voice. Pauline's heart stopped. Who was that? She couldn't see anyone. She squinted. A dark figure loomed in the hallway. Two smaller figures bobbed behind it.

"Who is it?" Roy said again. "We can't see you." Pauline could hear the beginnings of panic in his voice.

"It's Ford," the voice said. Ford! Pauline started to breathe again. She felt Roy relax next to her. Sure enough, now old Ford stepped forward into the light. He was wearing a Lone Ranger mask and carrying a bright plastic pumpkin filled with candy. Two little girls trailed behind him: One was outfitted in a blue princess gown and an elaborate blond wig, and the other was wearing some sort of faux-leather dress and was carrying a fake microphone. "These my grandbabies," Ford said. "We trick-or-treating." The little girls gazed up at Pauline with wide eyes. The one in the princess dress had two fingers in her mouth. "But I come to tell you that you left your car window open," Ford said, looking at Pauline. "You better shut it—you won't have no radio left, you don't."

Outside, Little Silver was coming alive with trick-or-treaters. Pauline was surprised. Even in the few minutes since she'd arrived at the factory, activity had increased significantly. As a rule, she and Johnny stayed home on Watchers Island to hand out candy on Halloween nights. She'd never observed the holiday in this neighborhood before. It was like something out of a movie. She looked up and down the street. With the exception of Leonard's house across the way, which was thankfully dark and quiet, the porches as far as Pauline could see were filled with people. Some had strung orange lights along decaying railings and banisters. Some had hung tissue-paper ghosts in trees. One ambitious crew halfway down the block had rigged a smoke machine and a Halloween sound track, and the result was a raucous haunted house—spooky enough to entice the older kids. But the sounds of laughter and the sweet calls of older women on the porch—*"Come on up here, baby, come get you a candy, it's all right, honey"*—were keeping the younger kids approaching the house as well, even the tiny ones, fat toddlers dressed as pumpkins, wobbling up the battered sidewalk to dip their sticky hands into a huge bowl overflowing with packets of candy.

Up and down King Street, a parade of costumed children undulated through the dusk. The evening had grown blessedly cooler, and though it was still warm enough to raise an immediate dampness under the back of Pauline's T-shirt when she stepped out of the factory, there was also an insistent breeze to keep the trees stirring and the mosquitoes at bay. From the top of a live oak, a barred owl chanted, his dirge interrupted periodically by a pair of cranky mockingbirds. It was a beautiful night in poor old Little Silver, Pauline thought. Beautiful.

She closed the windows in the Prius but then pulled the car to the front edge of the parking lot and opened the hatch. She and Roy and Ford sat in the Prius's cargo area like it was a park bench. The bags of candy she bought earlier at CVS were still in the car. She opened them up and dumped one whole bag of Milky Way packets into Ford's granddaughters' plastic pumpkin. The candies looked a little melted, but Pauline didn't think the girls would care. Then Roy went back into the factory and emerged with two more bags of candy.

"That's a lot of candy!" the girl in the leather dress exclaimed, delighted. "Milky Way!" shouted the princess.

"Come tell me what you are for Halloween," Pauline said to them. The girls stood before her, very serious. "I'm Beyoncé," said the leather-clad girl. She pointed to her sister. "And this is Elsa."

The girl in the blue princess dress smiled. "From *Frozen*," she clarified. "You know *Frozen*?"

"I've heard of it," Pauline said. "But I haven't seen it."

"You should see it," the blue princess said. "You would love it." Beyoncé nodded. "It's not, like, *my* style," she said. "But it's a good movie."

"How old are you?" Pauline said.

"I'm four," Elsa said. "And she's five." She looked at her sister proudly.

Beyoncé rolled her eyes. "I'm six," she said. "She forgets."

"Why don't you give out the rest of this candy?" Pauline said. She opened the two remaining bags and handed them to Beyoncé and Elsa, who left their pumpkin with Ford and darted to the edge of the parking lot to greet an approaching group of costumed kids.

"Trick or treat!" the kids were bellowing. Three young mothers were trailing behind the kids. They smiled tiredly and waved at Pauline. Pauline waved back. *You don't know what you have there,* she wanted to say to them. *Or maybe you do.*

Roy and Ford were talking about Leonard's house. "You ever see anything go down there?" Roy was saying. "Drugwise?"

"Hell, yes," Ford said. "Day after day. Ever since Leonard moved in."

"Like what?"

"Like selling," Ford said. "Clear as day. Other day car pulls up, guy runs up to porch. Hands Leonard a wad of cash, leaves with a baggie. They don't give a shit."

"We sure wish they'd get busted," Roy said. "It would strengthen the OSHA appeal we're dealing with."

"Oh, yeah," Ford said. "I done heard about that."

Pauline looked at Ford. "Maybe you could help us," she said. "Maybe you could testify that you've seen stuff, too. That way we'd have a neutral witness. All the accusations wouldn't be coming straight from the ice plant." Her mind started to race. Or better yet, she thought, Ford's testimony could help bolster probable cause for a search warrant on Leonard's house. Couldn't it? This could be important. This could help! She looked at Ford hopefully.

Ford shook his head. "I like it here *above*ground, baby. You know, you talk too much about someone like Leonard, you get your head blown off. You know that?"

"What if we kept it confidential? Would you be willing to sign a statement about this?"

Ford snorted and gave her a hard look. "I don't think I owe the ice plant too many favors, baby," he said. He took a piece of chocolate out of the Halloween pumpkin and unwrapped it slowly. He was quiet for so long that Pauline wasn't sure if he was going to continue.

"You Packy Knight's girl, aren't you?" he said finally. She hesitated, then nodded. Girl? It had been a long time since anybody called her a girl. She appreciated it, though her gratitude was counterweighted by the dawning knowledge that Ford knew full well who she was, and he most likely always had. It's not something you can hide, Pauline, she chided herself. You're Packy Knight's daughter. You're the Ice Princess. Congratulations. I should be wearing a *Frozen* costume myself.

"Did you know I used to work over here?" Ford gestured across the parking lot to the factory. "Years ago. Even before Packy Knight bought the place. I was a loader. And then I was a bagger. I was learning all about ice, you know what I'm saying? I could have been a foreman eventually. But I got hurt. So I couldn't do that work no more. I been on and off disability my whole life. Odd jobs. Parking cars at EverBank. That's it. That's the only kind of work I've been able to do. You know why? You know how I got hurt?"

Roy and Pauline were silent. Ford popped the chocolate into his mouth and leaned back. He pulled up his right pants leg to reveal a sickeningly atrophied shin. "That's me and Packy Knight, right there," he said, pointing to his leg. "Me and Packy Knight's ax handle. Shattered my tibia, nerves never healed right. So there I am. Ford the Cripple. Ford No Work. Ford the Drunk." He looked at Pauline for such a long time that she fought the urge to actually squirm. "Why should I help you?" he said.

"You helped me once before," she said. And she was suddenly sure of it. A wide-faced man with gray hair at the temples. Skin gnarled as oak bark. That day on the roller skates. The men on bicycles. Ford was the one who told Billy to leave her alone. He was the one who stopped his bike and reached out his hand. *Come now, Jesus, where you at?*

"Yes, I did," he said quietly. "And where did that get me?"

Pauline had no answer. The barred owl seemed to be getting tired. His call was fading through the trees. Pauline was remembering something silly now, and why this piece of information should now present itself in her addled mind she wasn't sure, but she understood the portent of it. Years ago, there was a craze going around—stereogram 3-D artwork. Images of mountains or spaceships or whatnot, and when you stared at the image long enough a secondary image presented itself. An ascending rocket, say. Or a howling wolf. The secondary information was there all along, you just had to cross your eyes a little bit to see it. Like now. Pauline had spent her whole life glibly sidestepping the fact that her father was a bigoted sociopath. *His problem, not mine,* she'd always told herself. After all, *she'd* never gone after anyone with an ax handle, for God's sake. *She'd* never called anyone a slur. *She'd* never discriminated against a job candidate.

Yes, but what *had* she done? Enjoyed the money, that's what. Reveled all her life in the spoils of ice, the empire built on Packy's cronyism. Money! Comfort! Security! She'd never been without it, had she? Her complicity dissolved forward, an image uncomfortably envisioned through the tight pixels of innocence she'd crafted all her life. She drew her eyes back to Ford's injured leg and resisted the impulse to look away. The limb was long and misshapen; a web of scar tissue snaked from shin to calf, shiny and taut against the old man's brown skin. The sins of the father. Roy sat wordlessly next to Pauline in the back of the Prius. Behind them, the security lights on the ice plant flicked erratically alight. Pauline kept her eyes on Ford's shin until he rolled down the pants leg, and when she looked back at the old man's face she saw something there she hadn't expected and was sure she didn't deserve: forgiveness.

"I'm sorry," she said quietly.

"Well, that's a start," he said.

"And I don't blame you," she said. "If I were you, I wouldn't help me, either."

Ford nodded. "I'm glad you see my point," he said.

The girls came back to the Prius, the bags of candy now empty.

"Hey, you eating our candy!" Elsa said to her grandfather.

"Aw, you got plenty," he said. He helped himself to another chocolate, and then stood up. He turned to Pauline and Roy. "I am eighty-four years old," Ford said. "And I been out trick-or-treating. And I am tired. Thank you for the candy. You all stay away from that Leonard. Don't go trying to push a bust. We don't need no dead people, hear?" Pauline and Roy watched him limp up King Street, Elsa and Beyoncé trailing behind him. The breeze had let them down now; the mosquitoes were reasserting dominance. Pauline slapped at her forearm. She and Roy retreated back into the factory, where now she could hear the clatter of catbirds in the rafters. This again. She'd have to get Johnny to look into it.

Pauline pitched the empty candy bags into the trash can in the break room. "I'm going home, Roy," she said. "And I think you should come with me." He didn't argue. He fetched his car keys and overnight bag from his office, and they locked up the ice plant. They headed east out of downtown and started the long drive back to the island, Pauline leading and Roy following closely behind. Pauline had a thought to try phoning Johnny again, and she rummaged one-handed in her purse for a moment before remembering she no longer *had* a phone. These stupid habits we create, she thought. And now I can't live without a cell phone? It was ludicrous.

Her eye fell on Bob Logan's brown napkin clipped on the passenger-side visor. The turnoff on Southside Boulevard was just ahead; she yielded to an impulse and hung a left. It was only five minutes up the road to Packy's house. She might as well get it over with. She tried to wave a chaotic hand signal out the window of the Prius to tell Roy to go ahead out to the house, but of course he had no idea what she was trying to communicate. He followed, placid and loyal. Oh, well, fine. Let him follow. It would give her a reason to keep things brief.

* * *

The wide streets of Laudonnière were quiet save for a few stray groups of late-night teenage Halloweeners, gangly kids in thrown-together costumes: zombies, clowns, witches. Pauline remembered those days. Too cool to trick-or-treat until the evening wore on and you started thinking about how nice it would be to run around the streets in the dark like a kid again, free candy for the taking. She cut her speed and waited for Roy, who'd been lagging, to catch up behind her.

Again she twitched futilely for her phone; she would have liked to call Roy, narrate a tour of her childhood neighborhood, even though she was a bit abashed by its affluence. There was the Mosleys' house—ah, legendary! When Pauline was a kid, old Mrs. Mosley used to give out full-sized Nestlé Crunch bars on Halloween. Kids were widely known to have their parents drive them into Laudonnière from other neighborhoods just to hit the Mosleys' house. And there was the Andersons' house—they stubbornly distributed boxes of Sun-Maid Raisins. Famously disappointing; usually avoided. Pauline felt a hungerlike longing for her mother. Twenty years was an awfully long time.

She turned onto Packy's street. Here the wide lawns looked like lush blankets in the moonlight, and though the windows of each house flicked LCD-blue, the front porches were hushed and empty. White people sat on *back* porches. Decks, rather. Screened-in patios. What the hell. She reached her father's house—a sweeping ranch guarded by the sentry of a half dozen oaks, twin picture windows flanking the double front doors, chalk-white columns supporting the overhang. A damned *plantation*, Pauline thought. Fucking *Tara*. This newfound penchant for dropping the F-bomb was proving both useful and satisfying. Fuck, fuck, fuck, fuck, fuck. *Fuck*.

Normally she'd have pulled her car around to the rear of the house and entered through the back door. But with Roy still trailing perplexedly behind her, she parked at the curb in front of Packy's house, pulled the Starbucks napkin off the visor, and ran back to Roy's car.

"Sorry," she told him through his rolled-down window. "I've just got to drop this off for my dad and check in on him real quick. I was trying to tell you to go on to my house."

"No biggie," he said. "I'll just wait." He adjusted his glasses and settled himself. There was something quite gallant about Roy, she decided. A prince, really.

"You want to say hi to him?" she said, seeing an opportunity. With Roy in tow, she could steer the conversation with Packy safely to matters of ice manufacture, a topic Packy never seemed to tire of and the details of which he never seemed to forget. *Compressor ratings,* they'd prattle about. *Screw conveyors.* It would save her from the usual go-round with Packy:

You feeling okay, Daddy?

Hello, Pauline.

You need anything?

No, Pauline.

Johnny says hi, you remember Johnny?

Hello, Pauline.

But Roy shook his head. "You go ahead," he said. "I don't want to interfere."

She left Roy sitting in his car and walked up the curving brick path to the front door. The landscaping was impeccable: African iris and crotons and head-high hibiscus. Well, it should be. She herself took care of making the payments to the lawn maintenance company out of Packy's checking account—and to the caregivers, the housekeepers, the nutritionists, the exercise therapists, and the pool guy. The care and keeping of Packy Knight was quite the mighty effort. When he finally passed on, he'd be putting a small army out of work, she sometimes thought. Well, maybe she could refer them all over to Bob Logan's family. He'd be in need of services soon enough.

She stood on the front porch and, feeling a little odd, rang the doorbell. Backdoor visits warranted a straight walk-on-in, a knock-knock on the door frame to announce her arrival. But this was the front door. This was different. After a moment, a stooped shadow appeared through the crescent-shaped window at the top of the door, and then the door swung slowly open to reveal her father standing unsteadily in the foyer, his arm curled around an orange bucket of Halloween candy. Packy wore an ice-blue guayabera shirt tucked hectically into loose-fitting Dickies. His white hair was in chaos on one side of his head, combed into impeccable lines on the other. He looked very thin, Pauline thought. Thinner than the last time she'd seen him, which was . . . when? Two weeks ago, she decided. Maybe three.

Packy looked at her blankly.

"Hi, Daddy," she said. He blinked. He reached into the bucket of candy and clawed around for a moment before coming up with a handful of bite-sized Snickers bars, which he extended toward Pauline. She'd been working herself into a thick anger on the drive over. After Ford's revelation at the ice plant, she'd considered forcing a come-to-Jesus with her father. *I know all about you,* she'd say. *I know what you did. I've always known! But I never confronted you. And now I'm so ashamed. Of the two of us.* Only now she didn't know if she could say the words. Packy's chin trembled. He took a half-step shuffle toward her, offering the candy.

There was a movement behind him in the hallway—it was Janine, the night nurse. She maneuvered around Packy and gave Pauline a brief hug.

"He's giving out candy to the kids," she said. "He seems to be enjoying it. You coming in?"

Pauline hesitated. She looked at her father, who was still standing in the threshold extending the handful of candy to her. Those gnarled knuckles, so familiar, skin taut across bone.

"Hi, Daddy," she said again.

"Boo. What are you?" he said finally.

"What?"

"A ghost, a witch, what?"

Pauline looked down at her clothes—jeans and a simple blue T-shirt.

"Boo. Boo. Boo," Packy said. "Trick or treat. Here, honey. Trick or treat. Where's your friends?" He was pushing the candy toward Pauline's stomach, craning to see behind her. She took the candy finally, then looked at Janine, who was now gazing at Packy.

"Oh, my," Janine said softly to Pauline. "I thought he'd hold on to you and your sister a bit longer."

A trio of teenagers in zombie face-paint appeared on the walkway. "Trick or treat," they intoned. Pauline took a step sideways and the kids jostled onto the porch and thrust their opened pillowcases out toward Packy, who dropped candy in obligingly.

"Boo. Boo. Boo," he said to them. "Shee-ut. What are you?"

Pauline felt a pulsing current begin in her feet and rush quickly up through her chest. It was warm and cold at the same time.

Free.

Daddy.

Free.

Fuck.

"I'm not going to stay," she said quietly to Janine. She gestured out toward Roy's car at the curb. "One of my coworkers is waiting for me." Janine nodded. Pauline handed her Bob Logan's phone number. "That's some old friend of his," Pauline said. "I guess you could have him call the guy, if he's up to it at some point. He seems to remember the past more than the present."

The teenagers were mumbling thanks and retreating from the front porch. Packy turned from the door and shuffled through the living room toward the back of the house. Pauline stood at the threshold, watching him. He made it to an enormous leather recliner and dropped into it, parking the bucket of candy on a low table next to the chair. *Judge Judy* was on the television.

"You never know," Janine said. She patted Pauline's arm. "He might remember you tomorrow. Or next week. Or never again. I'm sorry, sweetie. It's always hard, the first time it happens."

"I guess I didn't expect it," Pauline said. "Even though I knew it was coming. Does that make sense?"

Janine nodded. "We'll see what happens with Caroline," she said. "She said she's coming tomorrow." She glanced over her shoulder toward Packy, then back at Pauline. "You sure you don't want to come in? I just made a lemon cake. You know how he likes those. Tell your friend out there to come in."

A lemon cake. Served on the Portmeirion stoneware, no doubt. Brought to Packy in his recliner. Cup of fresh decaf at his elbow.

"What did he eat for dinner?" Pauline said.

"Chicken and a baked potato. He wanted steak but I told him no—he just had that last night. He always wants steak!" Janine chuckled. "Man's got champagne taste, doesn't he?"

Pauline's hands were shaking, suddenly, with some combination of emancipation and grief and rage that she intuited would take years to parse. Fine. She had years. She pushed her hands into her pockets. Packy turned back toward the front door and gazed at her tranquilly from the recliner. Ten miles away, in the shadows of Little Silver, there was a good bet Ford was eating lemons for dinner.

I hate what you did, Pauline thought, staring at her father. *I hate who you are. I hate that you left me to fix it.*

She turned abruptly from the doorway. She called a goodbye to Janine from the brick pathway on the way back toward the Prius and gave Roy the thumbs-up to resume their caravan to Watchers Island. He started his car. Her hands were still shaking. She gripped the steering wheel tightly to steady herself and looked up at the house again as the blue flicker of Packy's television pulsed against the draperies.

I also love you, she thought. *Though I don't know if I ever told you that, or if I ever will.*

She glanced back to make sure Roy was still with her. Then she motored slowly out of Laudonnière, seared and seduced by a bitter new freedom.

At home, she set Roy up in the spare room and told him good night. She took a shower and climbed into bed, listening for a while to the sounds of Roy bumping around down the hall. She wondered if the Meehans across the street were getting a good view of Roy's car parked in the driveway. *Husband goes out of town and right away she's got somebody over there!* she imagined them saying. But she was too tired to give a single shit. She pulled General San Jose onto her lap and stroked his ears for a long time, but when the dog stood and started to retch, she sat up straight.

"What is *wrong* with you?" she said. She tried to scramble him off the bed and onto the floor, but it was too late. He vomited across Johnny's pillow and she watched with dismay as the mess trickled down the headboard and into the dark crevice between the mattress and the bed frame. The General looked at her, chagrined. "Oh, for God's sake," Pauline said. She thought about just going to sleep in the guest room, but then she remembered Roy was in there. "For the love of Moses," she muttered. She pulled the duvet cover and the pillowcases off the bed and went down to the kitchen, where she deposited them outside the laundry room door. She went back upstairs with a roll of paper towels and a can of Scrubbing Bubbles. The mattress was too tightly wedged against the bed frame to let her adequately eliminate the trail of vomit. She glared at the General, who was now tucked comfortably on a fuzzy throw draped over the ottoman across the room. She pulled the bed away from the wall and wrestled with the mattress to create a gap wide enough to flick a paper towel around.

Her eye fell on an object embedded in the tight gap between the edge of the carpet and the wall. The tiniest glitter of something metallic was sparking upward from a tumbleweed of dust and dog hair. She reached down, and when her hand closed around it, she felt something like an electric shock.

Her wedding ring.

She pulled it up and looked at it. She took it to the bathroom and rinsed it off. She slid it onto her finger and climbed back into bed. She clenched her hand into a tight fist and felt the familiar but long-absent push of the ring on her fingers.

Pauline had never thought of herself as a big crier. But recent events had proved her wrong. She hoped Roy couldn't hear.

TWENTY-THREE

November. Normally the happiest and most hopeful of months in Jacksonville, when the long-reigning heat of the summer began to stumble, when people rolled their car windows down, pulled out their long-sleeved shirts, started to use their ovens again. Crock-Pots were dug out, porches swept, and browser home pages reset from the National Hurricane Center back to CNN or Fox News, depending. Latte sales skyrocketed. Leftover pumpkins moldered in churchyards and bank parking lots, where young mothers plopped their overalled toddlers into a sea of orange and tried desperately to capture a jaunty autumnal photograph, even as the smell of the rotted pumpkins that had been left too long in the sun in the weeks prior soured the air and stained the blacktop. But no matter—the lots would be cleared in less than a month to make way for Scotch pines and blue spruce, because what else was Thanksgiving weekend for but to put up the Christmas tree?

But something was wrong this year, Pauline thought. Something was different. It was the first of November and the heat was showing no sign of surrender. Ennui had settled in like a fog, and in fact she'd noticed lately that nobody was even talking about the weather anymore. But then, why should anyone talk about it? Resignation was in the air. Discomfort was the new normal.

The morning after Halloween she found herself in front of the house, swatting mosquitoes with one hand and dragging the garbage can out to curb with the other. Normally this was Johnny's job. She'd been peevishly proud of herself for remembering to do it. *See? I'm not helpless,* she mentally told her husband. My heavens, fifteen steps to the street and she'd already broken a sweat. This heat. It was revolting. She was halfway back to the house when she heard the phone ringing in the kitchen. Johnny! She broke into a jog, but in her haste to get to the kitchen she stumbled on the back step and twisted her ankle something fierce. She yelped in pain but kept moving, hopping on one foot to get to the phone.

"Hello?" she gasped.

"Pauline?"

"Yes, sorry. I twisted my ankle, running to the phone." She realized she was panting. She tried to steady her breathing. She sat down at the kitchen table and put her foot up on a chair. Lord! It hurt like a bugger!

"Are you all right?"

"Johnny, are *you* all right? I haven't heard from you."

"Yes, I know. Lost my phone, big long story."

"But are you okay?" She didn't like the timbre of his voice. He still didn't sound like himself.

"I think so," he said.

"You think so?"

Roy walked into the kitchen.

"And how did it go with Corran? And the baby? I've been on pins and needles over here."

"Good. Okay. I don't know. Listen, Pauline, let me tell you some stuff pretty quick here. I'm on the hotel phone, but I've got to get going to catch the flight. I found out something really important about the accident."

"Hang on," she said. "There's coffee made," she said to Roy. "And cups in the cabinet there." God, her ankle was throbbing. She looked at it. A purplish swelling had begun to emerge.

"Who's there?" Johnny said.

"Roy."

"Roy's there? It's seven-thirty in the morning."

"Sugar in the canister there," she said to Roy. "Now what?" she said to Johnny. "The accident? How can you be finding out anything about that all the way from Charlotte?"

"Listen! I need to get this out quick, and it's important, okay? Put me on speaker, as long as Roy's there."

"But how is your *head*? Are you feeling okay?"

"Pauline, please! I'm in a mad rush."

She put him on speakerphone. "All right, here we are," she said.

"Hiya, Johnny," Roy said. He leaned against the counter and stirred his coffee, looking a bit sheepish. "I'm getting my house tented. And I needed a place to—"

"Listen, now, both of you," Johnny said. "Here's the deal. I accessed the security films online and looked at some areas we'd never examined before. Owen Vickers has been entering the factory after hours." Pauline looked at Roy. His eyes widened.

"Vickers?" he said.

"Yes," Johnny said. "And it gets worse." He told them, then, about his discoveries: Rosa letting Vickers into the plant, the shutdown of the electricity to throw off the surveillance system. "All the shorts we've been having? The fucked-up electric? The beer caps on the ops floor? Now we know."

"The sunglasses in my office," Roy said. He'd gone a bit pale.

"He's been providing access to someone—and I'm betting it's Leonard—to tap the ammonia. Quite a nifty scheme," Johnny said bitterly. "And Rosa gave him the opportunity. She's right there on the films, letting him in."

Rosa? Pauline was staggered. *Rosa?* How could she?

"She's being used, Pauline," Johnny said, as if reading her mind. "Vickers is behind the whole thing, I know it. Rosa's too naïve to know what the hell she's doing. She barely knows how to tie her shoelaces, for God's sake."

There was a moment's silence in the kitchen. Pauline stared at Roy, knowing he was doing the same thing she was—trying to make sense of it all.

"Are you there?" Johnny said.

"We're screwed," Pauline said, finally. It had taken only a moment to whittle the implications of Johnny's revelation down to the obvious terminus, which was that Bold City Ice was stuck between the proverbial rock and a hard place. If they gave the surveillance films to the lawyers to bolster the argument that the tank had been tampered with before the accident, they were exposing Rosa to certain prosecution. On the other hand, if they *didn't* hand over the films as evidence, they were leaving Knowles & Frusciante with zero evidence of outside tampering and, therefore, little choice other than to bail on the appeal and accept the OSHA fines. Path of failure, after all.

"Screwed we are," Roy said. He'd come to the same conclusions, Pauline could tell. He looked like he might be sick.

"Lord, I need ice," she said.

"I'm *trying* to get back, Pauline." Johnny sounded impatient.

"No. I mean I need ice for my ankle. It's all swelling up and looks horrible. Roy, can you get me some ice? There's plastic bags in that drawer there." Roy walked over to the freezer.

"All right, I gotta go," Johnny said. "We're getting a shuttle to the airport. Chemal's waiting for me. I'll be home quick as I can, aye? And meantime, maybe you two can figure out what the hell we should do."

"But what about Corran?" Pauline said.

"I gotta go."

"What about your cyst?"

"Back by noon, Pauline." Johnny hung up.

"Oh, for the love of Moses!" Pauline said. Roy brought her a bag of ice and she held it against her swelling ankle. "He makes me crazy, Roy!"

Roy slumped in the chair opposite her.

"This is bad, Pauline," he said. "Really bad."

"What should we do?" Pauline said. Roy shook his head.

"Should we call the police?" she said.

Roy now looked at her as if she was crazy. "The police? Are you kidding? We're talking about Rosa here. Claire's firstborn.

We can't call the police. And anyway, what would we tell them? Two ice plant employees came into the factory after hours? I'm not sure there's anything illegal about that."

"Well, then, I guess we just tell the lawyers? Maybe we can cut a deal of some sort, get them to go easy on Rosa?"

Roy was getting agitated. He stood up and paced the kitchen, then sat down again.

"No," he said. "Nope."

"Roy," she said quietly. "If we don't present new evidence, we're looking at three-quarters of a million dollars in fines. The factory will shut down. We'll all lose our jobs."

"We can't implicate Rosa, Pauline. We can't."

"What would *you* do, Roy? I mean, for work? You've been with us for so long. Where would you go? You need your job! What about Ally?"

Roy took off his glasses and laid them on the table. His eyes looked smaller now, and frightened. Pauline didn't like it. His jaw was clenched.

"This might be our only way out, Roy," she said.

Roy put his glasses back on and looked at her intently. "We gotta find another way, Pauline," he said. "We can't do this to Claire. If she thought Rosa had anything to do with the accident . . ." His voice trailed off.

Pauline felt herself panicking. What did he think she was, heartless? She didn't want to implicate Rosa either. But what else were they going to do? "Roy, everything's at stake here!" she said. She threw her hands up in emphasis, and the shift in her body made the ice pack slide off her ankle and onto the floor.

"Yes, it is!" he said. "Including Claire's heart." His face was flushed. He put his coffee cup down on the counter, and Pauline could see that his hand was shaking. And then she understood: To Roy, Claire's heart was the most important thing of all.

"I gotta go make ice," he muttered. "Thanks for letting me stay." He walked out of the kitchen, but returned a moment later. He approached Pauline and picked up the ice pack from under her chair. He laid it on her swollen ankle.

"You can drive all right?" he said.

"Yes," she said. She waved her hand at him. "I'm fine. Go. I'll be in shortly." She heard the front door open and close. She heard Roy's truck start up and then listened to the whine of its engine as it moved down Beacon Street and out toward the Watchers Island bridge. She repositioned the ice pack and sat in the kitchen a little longer, watching the General. He was asleep on a dog bed near the laundry room. He must have been having a bad dream; he was twitching and moaning, his fat little legs pumping like he was running. Pauline banged her hand on the table to wake him up and he jolted up and stared at her, disoriented and vacant. She watched him focus on her, catalogue the situation, and lay his head back down. Within a minute, he was asleep again.

Let's make a deal! Pauline thought.

Behind curtain number one? A perfectly *thriving* ice trade, and your best friend's daughter in jail!

And behind curtain number two? Off to the poorhouse with the lot of us, but at least our *hearts* are intact! Wheeee!

Then another thought occurred to her. She was the CEO of the Bold City Ice Plant. Which meant that it didn't matter what Roy thought they should do. In fact, if it came right down to it, it didn't even matter what Johnny thought they should do. Johnny? Johnny who? Oh, the Johnny who flew off to Scotland

and left her here alone to deal with this mess? The COO? *That* Johnny? You're on deck, Pauline, she told herself. You da boss, baby. You call da shots.

So call 'em.

She tossed the melting ice pack into the kitchen sink and limped up the stairs to take a shower.

When she reached the factory, she went straight to the ice floor. The machines were in full swing, production was hopping, and the noise was nearly deafening. Even Dumbo seemed to be cooperating. Roy was fastening a padlock on the storage room door.

"What's that about?" she said.

"I got something in there I don't want the crew messing with," he said. His eyebrows were knitted; his jaw was still set as it had been earlier this morning after they'd talked to Johnny. "Don't worry about it," he said. "Your ankle okay?"

"No," she said. "But I wrapped it. I'm just going to ignore it. Mind over matter. Now listen—the lawyers are coming shortly, to discuss the appeal. I think you should be in on that meeting."

"Did you call the meeting?"

She shook her head. "They did. It was set up yesterday. I think they're going to tell us they're giving up on the appeal, to be honest."

He gave her a hard look. "Are you going to tell them about the films?" he said.

She pretended he hadn't asked the question. "I want Claire at the meeting too," she said. "We need to all be on the same page here."

"Are you going to tell them?" he said again.

"Roy," she said. "You're asking me to let the business be ruined."

"I'm not asking you anything of the sort," he said. "I'm asking you if you're going to tell them about the films."

She turned away, exasperated. She started walking back to the admin wing. God, her ankle was throbbing.

"Pauline!" he shouted.

She turned around.

"I don't know, Roy!" she shouted back. "I don't fucking know!" Four guys on the conveyor line stopped what they were doing and turned to stare at her. "What?" she said to them. "Your virgin ears?" They returned to their work.

She turned to look back at Roy, but he had already started walking away.

Thirty minutes later Pauline was seated at the head of the table in the Bold City Ice conference room. There'd been no word from Johnny yet, though she consoled herself with the thought that he'd probably be calling her from the house on Watchers Island before long. He said he'd be home by noon. She glanced at her watch. It was only eleven-thirty. Roy and Claire were seated to her right. Sam Tulley and—in a rare cameo—Thomas Knowles, Esquire, were seated to her left.

Pauline was wishing she could park her beleaguered ankle on the chair next to her to elevate it, but said chair was occupied by Sam Tulley, and she had no desire to demonstrate to *him* that she'd been injured. And, no, not while running a marathon, she'd have to tell him; on the kitchen step, as a matter of fact. He'd probably offer to go buy her a walker, maybe the type outfitted with tennis ball glides on the back legs. God! All right, focus. Important meeting here, Pauline. Pay attention.

The topic, as she'd expected, was abandoning the OSHA appeal, given the fact that they'd developed zero effective tactics that would change the ruling or diminish the fines. "Damage control, at this point," Knowles was saying. "I guess what I'm saying is exit strategy, you understand? Liquidating equipment. Eliminating staff. I suppose the goal now is to plan a way to shut down the business with the least possible stressors."

Least possible stressors? Pauline wanted to laugh. Oh, too late for that, Mr. Knowles! Give me a break. You're telling me to jump out of a burning building, but don't be stressed about it! No big deal! *We're here for you.* She looked around the table. Sam Tulley wouldn't meet her eye. Claire and Roy both looked like they were at a funeral. Which, of course, they were.

Exit strategy. Pauline tried to think about what such a process would even look like. Firing the staff would probably come first. But no—wait—they'd have to retain at least enough of the crew to help dismantle the equipment and power down the ops processes. And then what? Sell stuff, that's what. The fleet vehicles. The conveyors. The entire cooling system in the storage room. An auction? Yes, maybe an auction. That's how these things were done, wasn't it? Open the doors, let 'em in. Bidders and buyers and the busybodies who'd be *posing* as buyers, all come to gawk and judge, to pore over and pick through what was left of the entire history of the working life Pauline and Johnny had shared for all these years. Wouldn't the opinion editors at the *Times-Union* love it!

But let's not get too excited about the prospect of said auction bringing in any liquid cash, Pauline told herself. If the

OSHA people were so expert at levying fines, they were no doubt equally talented in orchestrating liens and forfeitures. Pauline could picture it now: the old ice plant yawning cavernous and silent, empty as a bucket, staff gone, lights dim, doors thrown open wide, and the creeping hot humidity of Little Silver making its way in to melt any stubborn remnants of ice that might still be clinging to the innards of Dumbo. Because *Dumbo* would still be there, of course. Nobody would want to buy an old shitter like Dumbo.

"I don't think I'm ready to completely throw in the towel," Pauline said to Knowles. "We have two weeks. I feel that we should still be working toward an appeal, not planning a shutdown."

Knowles leaned forward and spread his paws out on the conference table. "Mrs. MacKinnon," he said. "Part of my job is to share with you my vast experience in working with the United States Occupational Safety and Health Administration. I'd be remiss if I didn't counsel you to act in preparation for the inevitable. We've had our staff working on the discovery phase for a significant time"—Knowles made a sweeping gesture toward Sam Tulley, who smiled wanly but did not look up—"and we have not unearthed any additional evidence to bolster an appeal. If anything, we've found even *more* gaps in your maintenance logs, which certainly does not work in your favor. Our firm's role has to evolve at this point, Mrs. Mac-Kinnon. You need to think of us now as not so much fighting to save the business as helping you shut it down in the most painless way possible."

He sat back in his chair. "No compelling evidence of tank tampering, do you see?" he said. He shook his head. "I'm sorry, Mrs. MacKinnon. We've got nothing."

We've got something! a voice inside her head was screaming, but Pauline didn't know whether to listen to it or not. She
couldn't think. She couldn't think! Roy was staring darkly at the
table. Claire was looking at her, questioning. Claire! My sweet
friend, Pauline thought. My sweet, bitchy Claire. Pauline looked
away. *I'm sorry, Claire.* Because here it was: It would be ludicrous to intentionally let the appeal crumble just to spare Claire's
daughter the consequences of her mistake. Rosa did something
stupid, and it was something *wrong,* and it led to catastrophe.
And if Pauline didn't speak up now, the entire staff would soon
be unemployed. Failure is not an option.

Oh, *shut* it, Rohan Bergonia! She was suddenly filled with
loathing for that smarmy podcaster. What did he know, anyway,
about failure? It *is* an option, you idiot. Case in point: She could
choose to fail at business, or she could choose to fail at friendship. See? Failure is *always* an option. Roy raised his eyes from
the table and looked at her, and the sorrow on his wide, furry
face nearly broke her heart. *Say it,* she told herself. *We have new
evidence. You have to say it, Pauline.*

There were footsteps outside the door. Ed from Sales stuck
his head into the conference room. "I think y'all better come
outside," he said. "You're going to want to see this."

"This isn't a good time, Ed," Pauline said.

"No, seriously, Pauline," Ed said. "This is big."

Everyone in the room was silent.

"People? Hello?" Ed said. "Breaking news here, folks. They
got Leonard."

They all turned to look at Ed.

"Yep," he said. "Bing, bang, bam. Dude is *busted.*"

* * *

The cop was in the street sweeper.

Pauline stood in the parking lot of the ice factory, shaking her head, trying to process the enviable brilliance behind the orchestration of the bust now taking place in Leonard's front yard.

The cop was in the street sweeper!

Word was spreading fast. A tight throng of neighbors had gathered in the ice plant parking lot to watch events unfold, and from them Pauline had gotten most of the story: JSO's narcotics division had come up with the idea of putting a surveillance officer in the sweeper several weeks ago, and said officer had been circling the neighborhood at odd intervals, watching the activity at Leonard's house, shooting cell phone video, and compiling enough probable cause to obtain a search warrant. Then, rather than make a hasty bust, they'd been waiting for the ideal time to strike—a moment that would present evidence damning not just Leonard and his Little Silver operation, but also the large-scale drug ring that was *supplying* Leonard, a notorious Orlando outfit that had been the subject of a five-county investigation for years.

This morning the police got a tip from an informer that a delivery was imminent. The street sweeper circled, waiting for the Orlando supplier to appear. A black Nissan pickup truck pulled up to Leonard's house just a little while ago, and the supplier got out with a suitcase and disappeared into the house. That's when the cop in the sweeper called in the cavalry, and law enforcement pounced. *Bing, bang,* in Ed's words. *Bam.* Now the entire operation was being laid bare on a cordoned-off area in front of the house. Four police cars manned the perimeter, lights flashing. A mobile crime lab was setting up shop in the driveway. Leonard, two of his cronies, and the Orlando perp were handcuffed, sitting on the curb.

"I can't believe it," Pauline said. *"Finally."* She, Roy, Claire, and Ed from Sales were clustered in the shade of a live oak, watching the proceedings. Knowles and Sam Tulley were taking it all in as well.

"Well, hot damn," Knowles was saying. "Just hot damn." Tulley nodded, grinning.

A group of men were huddled around the police car closest to the factory. One—an ancient guy—peeled off and walked over, and Pauline did a double take when she realized who it was: the old city attorney Sid Hoying, who lived out near the beach on Watchers Island. He was beaming.

"What are you doing here, Sid?" Pauline said.

"Are you kidding?" Sid said proudly. He patted her on the back, nodded to Claire and Ed, and shook hands with Roy and the two attorneys. "This is my baby, right here. My little project. I can't stay out of City of Jax business, you know. So I've been paying attention to this one. I knew we'd bust it open eventually. I've been riding JSO like a bicycle. *Get a move on!* I've been telling them. I think they finally got going just to shut me up." He cackled and rocked back on his heels. "I can still get a few things done in this cow town, you know," he said.

"And guess what?" he continued. "Leonard's already been spilling his guts. They told him if he started talking, they might go a bit easier on him." Sid lowered his voice conspiratorially. "But just between you, me, and the lamppost? That's bullshit. Leonard's going down hard; he just doesn't know it yet. Anyway— he's singing like a bird, as they say. And guess what one of his songs is about? It's about tapping ammonia from the Bold City

Ice Plant. I love it!" Sid said. "I swear to God, I don't need to watch *CSI*. I live it."

He looked at Knowles and Tulley. "You guys are the attorneys," he said. "I can spot 'em a mile away." Knowles nodded wryly. "Well, listen. We got path of failure out the wazoo," Sid said to them. "Reasonable cause for the tank rupture. Y'all can thank me later for winning your case for you."

Knowles looked like he wasn't sure whether to be irritated or relieved, but he seemed to opt for the latter. "Mr. Hoying," he said. "With all these strings you pull, how 'bout pulling one to get JSO to fast-track the police report? We got an appeal to write and not a hell of a lot of time to write it."

"Bingo," Sid said. "As good as done." The old man was positively gleeful, Pauline thought. We all need to be needed, she decided. We all do. She gave Sid a hug.

"Thank you, Sid," she said. "This is tremendous." He seemed to be enjoying the hug an awful lot. Pauline wriggled free.

"Where's Johnny, anyway?" Sid said. The old man looked around the parking lot. "I wanted to throw it in his face that I saved his butt."

"Traveling," Pauline said simply. She couldn't bear to get into it. "He's coming back today." Something caught her eye across the parking lot. It was Ford, sitting on his bicycle and leaning against a tree. He was watching the drug bust activity with great interest. He seemed almost proud.

"Sid," Pauline said. She kept her eyes on Ford. "Who was the informer?"

"Well, now, Pauline," Sid said. "I can't tell you that. That's dangerous stuff, you know? People get shot over stuff like that."

Pauline waved to Ford. He waved back, and after a moment, he smiled. Then he pushed off the tree and rode away. A little wobbly, but more or less in a straight line.

It was wickedly hot out in the parking lot. People were starting to flap their hands in front of their faces, trying to stir the air. Pauline noted with satisfaction that the handcuffed drug suspects were sweating like livestock on the curb and that the police were making no effort to move them out of the direct sun. Good.

By the time they'd finished up business with Knowles and Sam Tulley ("Now we're cooking with gas!" Knowles kept saying), it was nearly lunchtime. Roy and Claire went back to work. Pauline still hadn't heard from Johnny. She crooked her left thumb and pressed it against her wedding band, then closed her eyes and tried telepathy with her husband: I found the ring. Corran's not a thief. They busted Leonard. Where are you? After a moment, receiving no reply, she gathered her files and limped out of the conference room into the lobby. She stopped at the reception desk on the way back to her office.

"Has Johnny called?" she said to Rosa. Rosa shook her head.

"And has Owen Vickers come in yet?" Pauline said. Rosa's eyes widened.

"I don't think so," she said. "I haven't seen him."

"Well, when he does, have him come directly to my office," Pauline said. She leaned over the reception desk and lowered her voice. "And later on, Rosa, you and I are going to have a little chat."

Rosa swallowed hard. "Why?" she said.

"Because you've been sleeping with somebody you shouldn't have, and you almost found yourself in a world of hurt," Pauline said. It was hard to keep the anger out of her voice, though she was trying. "Say goodbye to your boyfriend. His days at the Bold City Ice Plant are over."

Rosa looked almost relieved, Pauline thought. But in the next moment her eyes filled. "He's not my boyfriend, Pauline," she said. "He hasn't even texted me in, like, three days." The girl looked so abject that Pauline found herself softening.

"Does my mother know?" Rosa said.

"A bit," Pauline said. "But not all." She walked around the reception desk and drew Rosa's head toward her in a hug. "He doesn't deserve you, Rosa. All right?" Rosa sniffled into Pauline's shirt for a few moments, and then straightened up and cleared her throat. "Don't worry, Pauline," she said. "It's over. That asshole."

"Watch your mouth, Rosa," Pauline said. "That ain't how a lady talks."

Pauline headed back to her office. She needed to elevate her throbbing ankle. And she had a thought to check Delta.com and see if any of the flights from Charlotte had been delayed, but before she could reach the office she was waylaid by Roy, who gestured to her from the doorway to the ops floor.

"Can you come here a sec, Pauline?" he said. "I need to show you something. Bring a parka." She donned Johnny's parka and followed Roy through the manufacturing wing until they reached the storage room. Roy opened the padlock and stepped inside, motioning for Pauline to follow him. He closed the door.

"What are we doing, Roy?" she said. "It's freezing in here." She wedged her hands into the pockets of Johnny's parka. Indeed, the storage room was by far the coldest place in the entire factory—it had to be, in order to keep the bagged ice loose and crisp before shipment. An enormous compressor maintained round-the-clock subfreezing temps. Today the room was nearly filled with towering pallets of bagged ice; one of the biggest shipments of the week was scheduled to go out tomorrow. It was difficult to maneuver in the storage room, Pauline noted. You had to turn sideways and slide between ice pallets to get anywhere.

"C'mere," Roy said. He edged through towers of ice. Pauline followed. When they reached the back of the room, she gasped and felt her stomach flip. Owen Vickers was curled in a fetal position behind the last ice pallet. His face was battered. A trickle of blood was frozen under his nose. His wrists and ankles were bound together with electrician's tape. He wasn't moving.

"Oh, my God!" Pauline said.

"Don't scream," Roy said.

"Is he dead?"

"Nah." Roy approached Vickers and nudged him roughly with one steel-toed boot. "But he sure is cold. I guess that's because he's been in here a while. Get up, jackass," he said. Vickers stirred and moaned. "Get *up*," Roy said. He leaned over and pulled out a pocketknife.

"Roy!" Pauline said.

"Don't worry," Roy said. He cut the tape on Vickers' wrists and ankles and pulled him roughly to his feet. Vickers' lips were blue. His eyes were unfocused. Pauline now noticed that he was wearing only work pants and a T-shirt. The bare skin on his arms and neck had a papery look to it. He swayed.

"Can you hear me, Owen?" Roy said. He pushed Vickers against the back wall to prop him up. "Can you hear me?" Vickers nodded weakly.

"Good. Because I want to tell you some things, and they're important, m'kay? We know what you did. We know what you did to Rosa, and we know what you did to the factory. You let Leonard in to tap the ammonia." Vickers looked at him. Being made to stand upright seemed to be improving his cognition a bit. He still looked pretty foggy, but now there was something besides vacuity in his eyes. Now there was fear as well. "So here's the deal," Roy said. "If I ever get wind that you've set foot any-where inside Duval County again—and I mean, I don't care if you're on the beach or picking out panties at Wal-Mart or sitting in your mama's house taking a dump—I will find you myself. And I will kill you."

Pauline was half terrified. But she was also impressed. Roy!

"And do you know how I'll do it, Owen?" Roy continued. "Easy. We'll come right on back here to the storage room, where we'll send you on a permanent vacation. All I need is a ten-dollar padlock from Home Depot. And you know, if I position you just so behind the pallets, like you are right now, and if I do it on a Friday afternoon, nobody will find you until Monday at the earli-est. You know what I've read? When you freeze to death, after a while—say after the first thirty hours or so—it starts to feel not so much like cold. It starts to feel like heat. It starts to feel like you're being burned alive. That goes on for a while, evidently."

Vickers stared at him. For the briefest moment, Pauline thought she might have seen a bit of swagger, but there must have been something in the milky-white blur of Roy's damaged left eye that got to Vickers, because after a moment, Pauline saw the defiance flicker and die. Vickers blinked. He looked away.

"So bye-bye, Owen," Roy said. "We understand each other?"

Vickers nodded.

"What did you say?" Roy said. He shoved Vickers roughly against the wall again.

"Yes," Vickers whispered.

"Where are you never going to come again?"

"Jacksonville."

"Wrong."

"Duval County."

"Bingo! You got a wide world out there to take your sorry ass to," Roy said. "But Duval County is no longer a part of it. And you know, me and Pauline here, we've lived in this area a long, long time. Haven't we, Pauline?"

"Yes, we have," she said.

"We know almost everybody, don't we, Pauline?"

"Yes, we do," she said.

"And if the stench of Owen Vickers were to turn up inside county lines, we'd know it pretty quick, wouldn't we, Pauline?"

"Yes," Pauline said. "We would."

Roy gave Vickers a final shove, and this time he fell to his knees. "Oh, no, no, no, Owen," Roy said. "Don't get comfortable. You're on your way out." He dragged Vickers to his feet and kept dragging until they were all the way out of the Bold City Ice Plant. Then he pushed him, staggering and frozen, onto the burning blacktop in the loading yard. Pauline followed, limping. Roy threw Vickers' car keys onto the pavement in front of him, and he and Pauline watched as Vickers hobbled, crouched and trembling, into his truck and drove haltingly away from the Bold City Ice Plant.

"My word, Roy," she said. He was breathing hard. He looked at her; she could see he was almost as astonished at his behavior as she was.

"Well," he said. "Had ta be done." They reentered the factory to the sight of Rosa hurrying across the ice floor toward them.

"Pauline," she said. "Get line one, quick." Pauline stepped into Roy's office and picked up the phone.

"Pauline, this is Russell."

"Russell?" Pauline was drawing a blank.

"Russell Tosh," he said. "Sorry. Dr. Tosh. A young kid just showed up in the ER with Johnny. They paged me down here. We've got some serious seizure action happening. You're going to want to get over here."

He hung up. Pauline turned to Roy and found she couldn't speak.

"St. Vincent's?" Roy said. Pauline nodded. He picked up his keys. "Let's go," he said. They left through the loading bay. On the way out, Pauline could hear the sounds of the crew shouting, and of ice splitting, and of Dumbo, off her bushings, thrashing and thrashing and thrashing.

Twenty-Four

Vogel. And Tosh. Cold. Lights. Gimme Shelter. Street Fighting Man. I Can't Get No Satisfaction.

We're going to get you into this robe, stand up for me, sir. Stand up. Stand up.

Pauline, there's someone knocking. It's Donald Stone, Pauline, but don't be afraid. He's in the floorboards; he's waking up. He's doing fine, doing fine, pirates in the lighthouse, what can you do? I love you, Pauline, do you know that? And the General. I love the General, too. And James and Fayette. They're taking their grandbabies to the Blue Men. I want to go home, Pauline.

This is the anesthesiologist, Dr. Olusola. We just call him Dr. O. Right, Dr. O.?

It's cold in here, Pauline. I'm freezing. I slept with Sharon in Port Readie, but don't worry, it's not what you think. We touched for a moment, then she sank like a bicycle into the black waters of Loch Linnhe and I was afraid but I was not sorry. Corran has a Lucy and the Lucy is a bird. Silly, silly bird. The bird chased the lamb. The lamb ran away.

The piston, Pauline. Did you see it melt? Did you see, how beautiful?

Right here in this bed, Mr. MacKinnon, and we're going to get you all hooked up, okay? I know it hurts. I know. I need you to be strong, Mr. MacKinnon. It will be over before you know it. Yes sir. Yes sir. Emergency resection, that's how Vogel wants it. Here we go now!

Screw you, Ed. The pallet heights are fine. Hit and run, you say?

I changed the channel on Corran, Pauline. I couldn't watch it anymore. There was blood and there was pain and there was fear and it was hurting, hurting, hurting. Like now. Hurting. Like always. Hurting. These needles! They're putting skag in me, Pauline, skag! I don't do it. I don't want it. It's death. And once you do it you cannot stop. Only the brave. Only the bravest. The moonlight solana. The moonlight sostana. The moonlight setenta. What? Out of Easterhouse. We got him out of Easterhouse. There's a bird in the icehouse. Up in the rafters.

It hurts, Pauline. My head. My eye. Paint it black. If he would just let me help him. If I would just let him help me. Too late now, daftie, the train has left the station. Tell 'em on the flip side, jive? Those ice boys—the things they say. Word.

Charlie! Good to see you. My old da. Tide's coming in now, watch your feet, Charlie. Sandpipers and seaweed, water's got a chill this year. Sailing, sailing, over the bounding main. Fuck that, Charlie. No. I'm not ready.

You're going to feel something very cold in your arm, Mr. Mac-Kinnon. And then you're going to fall asleep. All right, sir? All right?

All right.

Pauline.

Pauline.

Pauline.

TWENTY-FIVE

The local NPR station had a scientist on. He was talking about sinkholes in the Florida aquifer. Johnny turned it up. It was hard to hear these days, but Tosh said that was to be expected. All your senses may be a little wonky, he said. Don't let it worry you. The garage was stuffy. Johnny pushed the button and the door clanked open. In the three weeks since the surgery, the air had cooled slightly and the light had clarified thanks to the long-awaited reduction in humidity. Now, the day before Thanksgiving, life felt warm, still, but drier, crisper. A little clearer.

The thing about sinkholes, and geology, and science in general, the guy on the radio was saying, is that they are initiated by chaos. Much is predictable, he said. Science thrives on rules and laws and conclusions, after all. But without the influence of chance, of accident, the odds of discovery are reduced. Think of penicillin, for example. If Alexander Fleming had not taken a closer look at the mold that had accidentally contaminated one of his petri dishes, he'd never have begun the line of research that led to the development of one of the most important drugs in the world. The point, the scientist was saying, is to be open to the unknown.

So, he said. Back to sinkholes. There are two types, he explained. There are those that are formed by the slow, gradual erosion of soil and sand, which creates a depression. Then there are those which form quickly, the inevitable conclusion of a chance void in the aquifer. These are the dramatic cases, the scientist said, the ones where the holes appear suddenly and can sometimes cause damage to structures.

"But," said the radio host, "doesn't that mean we're all vulnerable? Walking around with potential sinkholes beneath our feet? I saw one on the news last week. It collapsed under a house in a suburban neighborhood. That makes me nervous."

"I think most of us," the scientist said, "take for granted that the foundations of our life are solid."

Nicely stated, Johnny thought. Put that one on a bumper sticker. Make yourself a mint. His head itched where the staples were removed last week. He ran his fingers over the scar and scratched around the perimeter. Ignore it, he told himself. Nothing you can do.

It was a benign cyst. Meningioma. No malignancy. Russell Tosh was downright jolly when he delivered the news. Johnny was just waking up from the anesthesia. "Didn't I tell you to trust us, Johnny? Didn't I?" Tosh said. He was bumping his wheelchair from side to side in glee.

"You did." Johnny had been groggy and uncomfortable and scarcely focused, but the sight of the relief on Pauline's face had been all he needed.

"Nice job, Tosh," he said. "Schedule the golf game."

"Oh, hell yes," Tosh said. "Giddyup!"

That was three weeks ago. The road back—so far—was proving easier than Johnny had anticipated. The itching at the incision site was one of the biggest annoyances, which, all things considered, was not too terrible at all. Could have been worse, he reminded himself. Much worse. And if he did tend to forget this, Pauline was quick to remind him.

He opened the hood on the VW and regarded the frozen piston. Today was the first day he'd felt up to facing it, and as he examined the engine mount and the impossibly snug layout of the entire engine area, he realized that his genius idea of taking the housing out and beating on the piston from underneath would require many, many hours of work. It was prohibitive, in fact. Not worth the time, definitely not worth the effort. Which put him back where he started—trying to beat the piston out from the top down. He was still leaning into the engine compartment, regarding the situation, when the sound of Chemal's voice startled him.

"Dude, you get it out yet?" he said.

Johnny straightened up and shook his head. Since Johnny had been discharged from the hospital, Chemal had begun a habit of daily visits, and Johnny couldn't say he disliked the new routine. The kid was rather handy to have around. Johnny still couldn't drive, and Pauline had returned to work a week after the craniotomy, so having Chemal pop in each day meant an extra set of hands to take the General out when Johnny wasn't feeling up to it, to fire up the leaf blower after a nor'easter stripped the buttonwood tree and deposited the spoils on the back deck, to run up to CVS for prescriptions.

"No," Johnny said to Chemal now. "I think it's hopeless."

Chemal came over and examined the frozen piston. He tapped it with a mallet. "You've got to expand the housing," he said. "Heat."

"There's no way," Johnny said. "If you heat the housing, you heat the piston, too. They'll both expand. It'll get tighter."

Chemal studied it.

"Mind if I try an idea?" he said.

Johnny shrugged. "Try whatever you like," he said. "I've given up."

"You got fabric?" Chemal said. "And something flammable?"

They wandered through the house and found some quilt batting in a sewing basket Pauline had shoved up on a shelf in the laundry room. Back in the garage, Johnny fetched a bottle of brake fluid from under the workbench. Chemal put a piece of batting soaked with brake fluid on top of the piston. He ignited it like a wick and kept a stream of fluid directed onto the fabric. After a few moments, the heated fluid began to run down the sides of the cylinder walls, seeping into the tiny voids between the piston and the housing.

"See that?" Chemal said, grinning. "It's a-gonna heat up them walls, you'll see."

Johnny watched, astonished. Chemal kept up the process— a stream of brake fluid would hit the burning batting, get hot, and dribble into the cylinder. After about ten minutes, Chemal doused the flame and grabbed the mallet.

"Ready?" he said.

"Ready," Johnny said.

Chemal reared back and bashed the top of the piston with the mallet. The piston broke free of its housing and clanged to the garage floor underneath the VW. Johnny took a step back and looked at Chemal, who was swinging the mallet and grinning from ear to ear. "How do you like me *now*, Mr. Freeze?" he said. "How do you like me *now?*"

They fetched the piston from under the car and cleaned up the puddles of Marvel Mystery Oil which had accumulated over the past month.

"Heat, Iceman," Chemal said. "When something's frozen, you need heat."

"When's your birthday, Chemal?" Johnny said.

"Next month."

"Eighteen?"

"Indeed."

"Clear your schedule," Johnny said. "I've got plans for you."

He went inside and texted Roy with his new phone.

I got us a new driver, he wrote. *Hell, give him a couple of years. Maybe a foreman.*

Roy had come over to see Johnny last week and told him and Pauline about his idea for reusing some of the leftover boner ice that didn't make it into the shipping bags. Melt it, Roy explained, and refreeze the water in oversized cubes. Sure, it's not sterile anymore, he said, but it's clean enough for a new novelty product line: ice sculptures. All the rage at parties and events, he said, and hardly anybody in Jacksonville was competing. Only new equipment needed was the cube molds.

And Bold City Ice had all the talent right there in-house with Rosa Kaplan, whose artistic sensibilities were about to come in handy. They could get Rosa to do some sculptures in the repurposed ice, get Ed to add it to the marketing mix, and whammo! A new profit center, a recycling triumph, and a hell of a focus for a girl who clearly needed one. Claire and Rosa loved the idea, Roy said. They'd all put their heads together, in fact, and developed this business plan. Roy had dug into a bag and produced a neatly formatted document to demonstrate how the new add-on could increase profits and expand the brand.

"You and Claire did this?" Johnny said.

"Yep," Roy said. He flushed a bit. "And Rosa. We've been spending some time on it," he said.

"I see," Johnny said. "Well, I think it's bully."

"Seriously?"

"Why not?" Johnny said. "That shit is just going down the drain. We might as well try to make it profitable."

Roy had tucked the plan back into his bag and grinned. "I always told you ice can have more than one life," he said. "You just didn't believe me."

The OSHA fines were steep. But not devastating. Bold City Ice had been held liable for inadequate security in the tank yard, but no mention was made in the report of negligent maintenance on the tank itself. Now that Johnny and Pauline knew the bottom line—about eighty grand—the ground was feeling a bit firmer beneath their feet. Already Pauline was talking with the bank about an equity line on the factory that would enable them to knock out the fines in one bash and even award a few good-sized bonuses to the key staffers—namely Claire, Roy, and (with Johnny's grudging approval) Ed from Sales—who had pitched in more than their fair share to help keep the factory humming during the turmoil of recent months. Pauline also pitched a plan to hire a new night watchman: Ford from the neighborhood. ("You sure?" Johnny had asked, surprised. "I'm sure," she said.) Pauline was even talking about scaling back her own commitment by promoting Claire to VP of Administration.

"I'm tired," she told Johnny, "of living and breathing ice. I'd like to think there's a bit more to life." She was sitting at the kitchen table, drinking a glass of cabernet and folding a warm load of baby laundry: onesies, bibs, tiny dresses, and polka-dotted crib sheets. As she moved her hands, the familiar glimmer of her diamond ring cast a tiny prism on the ceiling.

"She's not even here yet," Johnny said. "How is it we have laundry?"

"You have to wash it all before they wear it," Pauline said. "They have sensitive skin. I bought special baby detergent." She folded a pink blanket and looked at him. "We only have a week, Johnny," she said. "There's a lot to *do.*"

Sharon and Toole were arriving next Wednesday with Lucy. They would return to Scotland the following Wednesday without her. Corran was headed back out to the North Sea rigs at the beginning of December, and the plan had been arranged—Johnny and Pauline would take care of Lucy for a few months. Through the spring, perhaps, maybe even into the summer, until Corran got himself a bit steadier on his feet. He'd make some real money out on the rigs, he told Johnny on the phone.

Sharon had later emailed Johnny with a bit more insight, confirming what Johnny had already intuited: Corran felt the rig work helped him stay off heroin, she said, and a few more good, solid months of sobriety could only help in the long run, couldn't it? Fine then. Lucy for the spring. And then . . . and then? And then we'll just have to see, Johnny decided. One day at a time. He was trying hard not to think about the moment when Corran would have to say goodbye to his daughter. It hurt, saying goodbye to a child. Johnny knew all about it.

The guest room upstairs was now outfitted with a suite of furniture from Babies-Я-Us, and it seemed that every day a new mail-order package arrived, each one bearing baby clothes, baby toys, baby books. Pauline was beside herself. The General was looking more suspicious by the minute, and Pauline had been preemptively scolding him. "Open your *heart*, General," she kept saying. "The house is plenty big enough for one more." On a whim, Johnny had gotten online and dropped a small fortune arranging a long weekend for his ex-wife and her husband at Disney's Grand Floridian Resort. Tickets to the theme parks, a luau at the Polynesian, even a "Keys to the Kingdom" tour that would bring them into the fabled tunnels beneath the parks. *Tell Toole to bring his autograph book,* he texted Sharon. *He can get Cinderella to sign it.* Let him live it up, Johnny was thinking. He shook his head against the specter of Toole's progressing fog and watched Pauline matching baby socks.

Pauline. In the three weeks since she'd quit running, her face had already taken on a slight softness Johnny found appealing, comforting. The resignation had come abruptly—he realized after he'd been home from the hospital for a couple of days that he hadn't seen her lacing up her Nikes and heading out.

"You must be craving a run," he said to her. "You haven't gone in a while, have you?"

"My ankle still hurts," she told him. "I'm not running."

"What about your training schedule?" he said. "For the Gate River Run?"

She waved her hand. "I'm not doing it," she said. "It hurts, and it's hard, and I hate it. I quit." She told him she'd find other ways to exercise. And then she crawled into bed with him and they practiced one.

Now she stopped folding laundry. "Oh, my God," she said. She looked at him, dismayed.

"What?"

"I forgot to get a Diaper Genie."

"A what?"

"I was at the store and I meant to pick it up, and then I got tied up in the strollers and I completely forgot. Now I've got to go back."

"What in bloody hell is a Diaper Genie?" Johnny said.

"You see! Now there you go again. I told you that you *have* to clean up your language before Lucy arrives." Pauline stacked the folded laundry into a basket and stood. She was still dealing with a bit of a limp, Johnny noted, but she made it to the refrigerator and turned to ask him if he wanted a beer. Well, yes. She opened him a beer and refilled her wineglass, and together they made their way up into the old lighthouse cupola, where they sat for a while, watching the evening sun push through the branches of the buttonwood tree and create long shadows against the walls.

"Pauline," Johnny said, after a while.

"Yes?"

"I don't think it's going to be temporary," Johnny said. "Lucy being here. I think she'll be staying."

Pauline didn't answer for a moment. She took a sip from her wineglass and then placed it carefully on the floor next to her chair. "I know," she said quietly.

"I don't think Corran's able. Or that he will be."

"I know."

They said nothing for a long time. As the dusk advanced, Pauline must have sensed him staring at her. She turned to him.

"You're sure about this now, kidda?" he said. "It's a lot of work, you know. And they don't always turn out just like you hope."

She nodded. There was a light in her eyes Johnny didn't think he'd ever seen before. She took his hand, and he felt her trembling. "Do you really think we can do it?" she said, "I mean, do you think *I* can do it? I'm not too old?"

"You can do anything, Pauline," he said. "And this you'll do best of all."

That night the rains blew inland. Johnny dreamed the waters flooded Beacon Street and swept them all into the ocean—he and Pauline and Corran and Lucy—but as they bobbed in the black current and dipped under the waves, the instinct to swim came easy, and he was not afraid. He reached out and gathered them all to him. They sank down, then ascended again toward the light. Silence. Surface. Catch a wave and ride it in.

TWENTY-SIX

"Get the bore, worm," Andy was saying to Corran. Andy was the lead roughneck. He had six years on the team. They were painting a stair banister on the deck of the rig. It was cold as death, the wind whipping off the North Sea in great wide coils. Six *years*, Andy liked to remind him. Big shit. Corran had one. So Corran was the worm. Fine.

He left off painting and went to wrestle the bore into place. It needed to be aligned over the borehole to begin its descent into the drill pipe. The bore was taller than Corran, slick with mud and fat as a utility pole. It was suspended from the bore housing, dangling like a filthy cold pendulum. Corran hugged it with his arms and knees and pulled it into place. Get it, sucker, Corran thought. Do your thing. The bore went plunging into darkness. The whole rig was like a giant hypodermic needle, sucking up oil, drawing blood from the bottom of the sea.

He went back to the stair banister and dipped the brush into the bucket of paint. He and Andy painted, not talking. The deck rolled. Corran rolled with it. His knuckles were bleeding. They were always bleeding. The wind hurt the skin under his eyes. Everything hurt. But that was okay. It had taken him a while to figure this out, but he understood it now: Pain is the only way we know we're alive. Numbness means death. He was hurting, which meant he was alive. For now.

Once, when he was in a stint of rehab—the one in Jacksonville, maybe, couldn't remember, didn't matter—Corran overheard Johnny and Sharon talking in his room. They thought he was asleep.

I don't think he's going to make it, Sharon, Johnny was saying.

Stop it. Yes he will. He'll pull though.

Not just this one time. Not just now. I mean forever. I don't think he will.

Well, nobody does, Johnny, Sharon said. *Nobody lives forever, do they?* She was angry.

We have to be prepared, Johnny said.

For what?

For the fact that he can't beat this. It's going to get him in the long run.

Fuck you, Johnny, Sharon said.

Corran wanted to smile at the memory. His mother. What a mouth on her. Who had a mother who talked like that? He did. But he didn't smile. It wasn't funny. Johnny was right. Corran was clean now. Would he be clean in a year? In five years? In ten?

Roll of the dice, chief. The skag would be there when he got back to the mainland. It was never going away. In some dreams Corran's hand hovered over a latch on a cage. *No, Da.*

Don't let it out, Lucy would say in these dreams, and Corran was so surprised to hear her talking—Already! Clever girl!—that he would pull his hand away from the latch. In other dreams Lucy was gone, and his hand hovered over the latch again, shaking so hard, until one quaking thumb hit the cage door—No, an accident!—and the latch clicked and the Cù-Sìth was out, snarling and heaving, smelling like bile and planting great wide, wet paws on Corran's chest. He was as likely to have one dream as the other. Going to sleep was as big a crapshoot as waking up. It would be nice, he thought, if the dreams would simply stop.

Corran left the painting and walked to the rig railing. He looked out over the sea and watched as the clouds rearranged themselves. Lucy is warm now, he thought. In Florida the sun shines and warm breezes stir the trees. Pauline had been sending photos: Lucy on the beach under a broad flopping hat. Lucy in a high chair, eating chunked banana. Lucy in a plastic wading pool, water beading on her fat shoulders.

Lucy.

Corran looked down into the black water, roiling mountains that rose and fell and rose again. *I don't think he's going to make it.* Try. Fail. Try. Fail. It is all I have, Corran thought. It is all I know.

He stood a long time in the cold, until the sound of Andy's voice cut through the wind. The paint. Ah, yes. The paint. The banister. Corran pulled his gaze up from the darkness and caught a hunch of white on the distant horizon, which might have been clouds dying. Or maybe ice, quietly forming.

ACKNOWLEDGMENTS

Enthusiastic thanks are due once again to my agent, Judith Weber; and my editor, Amy Hundley. These women can see a diamond in the rough and push me to make it shine. Without their vision, integrity, and patient faith, this book would not exist. Thank you, also, to the many wonderful people I've come to know at both Sobel Weber and Grove Press. I'm lucky to partner with these gifted professionals. Thank you to Todd Sanders, Anthony Gilroy, Elizabeth Olsen, and the entire team at Steinway & Sons, for letting me write about pianos for a living. My job is the beautiful sound track to my writing life. Thank you to the readers, booksellers, book groups, librarians, bloggers, and reviewers who received my first novel so kindly and who gave me the courage to write another. Thank you to Liz Robbins, Ian Mairs, and Michael Carroll. Thank you to my friends and neighbors in St. Augustine, especially Dawn Langton and Dale DiLeo, who gave me a room to write in when I needed it; and Kim Bradley, fiction comrade forever. Thank you to my mother, Judy Cook, who read every draft of this book with patience and wisdom. Thank you to Chris, Iain, and Gemma—my loves. Thank you to all my family near and far, especially the late Johnny Readie, who found his way from Scotland to America all those years ago, and who taught us that if you can say *it's a braw bricht moonlicht nicht*, then you're all right.

GROVE PRESS

Reading Group Guide

by Jacqueline Sather

THE ICE HOUSE

Laura Lee Smith

ABOUT THIS GUIDE

We hope that these discussion questions will enhance your reading group's exploration of Laura Lee Smith's *The Ice House*. They are meant to stimulate discussion, offer new viewpoints, and enrich your enjoyment of the book.

More reading group guides and additional information, including summaries, author tours, and author sites for other fine Grove Atlantic titles may be found on our website, groveatlantic.com.

QUESTIONS FOR DISCUSSION

The novel begins with a T.S. Eliot epigraph: *"Between melting and freezing / The soul's sap quivers."* Explore the dichotomy between heat and ice. What does each symbolize in the context of the novel, and how do their meanings transform?

Consider the ice factory: "a cavernous rectangle, somber as a basilica, three stories high with column-like fenestration that lent the place the look of an art deco Parthenon [...] looming silhouette of barrels against the tall windows was like a Gotham City skyline" (pg. 19). In what ways do the descriptions of the ice factory mirror the characters, particularly Johnny and Pauline?

Continue this discussion by thinking about Jacksonville, home to the ice factory. "She skated into the neighborhood, past crumbling wooden cottages, broken curbing, a dilapidated concrete-block house collapsing upon itself. An overturned grocery cart rusted on an empty lot" (pg. 53). What does the local community think of the ice factory's looming presence, and what does the ice factory symbolize for the residents of Jacksonville?

Fear of death haunts nearly every character in this novel. "One of the few passions that incline men to peace is fear of death. Thomas Hobbes said that; Johnny had read it somewhere. It's a pity, he realized now, that we don't think of it sooner" (pg. 51). Expand upon how each character fears death and how this fear holds them in time.

Illness and pain are recurring themes throughout the novel, influencing the characters and their actions as well as binding them together. Susan Sontag wrote: "Compassion is an unstable emotion. It needs to be translated into action, or it withers." How do you think this statement applies to the ways in which the characters deal with not only their own pain and illness, but that of those close to them?

Think about Corran's heroin addiction in relation to the opioid epidemic. Do Johnny's initial reactions to Corran's addiction struggles reveal a deeper societal ignorance regarding addiction? At what point in the novel does Johnny begin to understand Corran's addiction more deeply? When does he stop blaming Corran?

Money and the American dream serve as a temptation to many characters in the novel, namely, Johnny, Roy, and Pauline. Why does Corran resent Johnny for his love of money? Discuss Roy's disillusion and dissatisfaction with his social milieu. How do these depictions imitate the lives of many Americans?

What anxieties and deeper feelings do Johnny's and Corran's dreams reveal? Why do you think Smith decided to make dreams a commonality between them?

Filled with regret and uncertainty, Pauline frequently muses on whether or not she should have had a baby. What pressures do women face to bear children? What do you think Pauline is truly seeking?

Did you expect Rosa to be part of the scheme to tap the factory's ammonia tanks? Who were you led to believe was responsible? When Roy became more desperate financially, (pg. 362) and hostile towards his job, did you think he may have been the one? How well do you think the mystery element unfolded?

Discuss how Jacksonville and Scotland are characters in themselves. "He remembered how lost he had been all those years ago, when he first arrived in Florida, without those immovable peaks to navigate by" (pg. 251). How do these places inform Johnny's perspective? Discuss each place as it pertains to the immigrant experience and displacement.

Given Johnny's relationship with his son Corran, what do you think draws Johnny to Chemal? How does Chemal serve as Johnny's foil? Does Chemal's character allow Johnny and Corran to reconcile their differences? Why does Johnny deny the resemblance between Chemal and Corran when Sharon mentions it on pg. 253?

"No man is an island. So said John Donne" (pg. 187). Do you think Corran and Johnny see themselves as islands? How does their behavior cut them off emotionally and physically from their family and the world?

Discuss the significance of the car accident. How did this event alter the course of Johnny and Corran's relationship? Do you think this event was the only hope to reunite them? Discuss how their relationship evolves in the aftermath.

What are the different ways Smith explores the strength of family bonds despite the characters' troubled relationships with their family members? How does Pauline grapple with her father's violent and hateful behavior? What does this say about the resilience of love?

What significance does the Voyager 1 launch hold for Johnny and his deceased father, and how does this relate to Johnny's relationship with his son? Discuss how the wandering Voyager speaks to the connection between the living and the dead.

Do you think Johnny's assessment that he and Pauline will have Lucy for a long time is fair? After Pauline's numerous musings on not having a child, how do you think she feels about caring for Lucy?

"Pain is the only way we know we're alive. Numbness means death." Discuss the consequences of Corran's sentiment. What does this mean at the end of the book with regards to Corran's life back on the rigs?

The novel's commitment to realism is carried through to the final paragraphs. Discuss what you think the future holds for Corran and the possible meanings of the mounds of white forming on the distant horizon.

SUGGESTIONS FOR FURTHER READING:

State of Grace by Joy Williams

History of Wolves by Emily Fridlund

Revolutionary Road by Richard Yates

Empire Falls by Richard Russo

Regarding the Pain of Others by Susan Sontag

A Little Life by Hanya Yanagihara

Florida by Lauren Groff

Brooklyn by Colm Tóibín

The Sea by John Banville

Gilead by Marilynne Robinson